AN EYE FOR AN EYE

CAROLINE FARDIG

SEVERN RIVER
PUBLISHING

AN EYE FOR AN EYE

Copyright © 2018 Caroline Fardig.

Severn River Publishing
www.SevernRiverBooks.com

This is a work of fiction. Names, characters, businesses, places, events and incidents are either the products of the author's imagination or used in a fictitious manner. Any resemblance to actual persons, living or dead, or actual events is purely coincidental.

ISBN: 978-1-64875-470-8 (Paperback)

ALSO BY CAROLINE FARDIG

Ellie Matthews Novels

Bitter Past

An Eye for an Eye

Dead Sprint

Parted by Death

Relative Harm

To find out more about Caroline Fardig and her books, visit

severnriverbooks.com/authors/caroline-fardig

To Joan Fardig, one of my biggest cheerleaders.

PROLOGUE

Late one December evening, the first snow of the season began to fall, blanketing the quiet neighborhood in white. Christmas lights adorning the homes gave off a warm, festive glow. As the snow piled up, children watched excitedly out their bedroom windows, hoping enough would fall so school would be cancelled the next day and their winter fun could begin.

In the house at the end of the street, a woman stood alone, eating Chinese takeout over the kitchen sink and wishing for the snow to stop. She dreaded wintertime and the slick roads it caused. She had to show up for work regardless of the weather, and her car's tires were bald and in need of replacement. She'd be lucky to make it through the season without ending up in a ditch somewhere.

She heard a noise coming from the backyard, so she set her container of food on the kitchen counter and shuffled over to the back door. That cat of hers had better not be walking around on her potting bench again, knocking tools and empty pots onto the ground. She'd had to pick up the shards of a busted terra-cotta pot only last week.

Opening the door, she called out, "Whiskers, is that you? Come inside before you freeze to death."

It was silent within the walls of her privacy fence; she heard not so much as a meow from Whiskers in reply. She closed the door and returned to her dinner, figuring he would soon change his mind and come crying to be let inside. A crash outside got her attention. This time, she donned a coat and boots, determined to find that stubborn cat and bring him in from the cold whether he liked it or not.

On her way out the door, she flipped the switch for the outside carriage light on the back patio, but nothing happened. She sighed to herself, making a mental note to put "change light bulb" on her endless to-do list. Stepping down onto the patio, she let her eyes adjust to the darkness. Visibility outside had grown worse since a couple of minutes ago. The snow was now falling fast in huge clumps.

"Whiskers, kitty-kitty. Here, kitty-kitty." Hearing a rustling to her left, she turned and peered into the bushes near the fence. "Come on, Whiskers," she complained, walking toward the source of the sound. "It's freezing out—"

Before she could finish her sentence, a blinding pain exploded at the back of her head. She stumbled forward, disoriented and dizzy. Unable to keep her feet under her, she collapsed to the ground. She managed to roll onto her back and wrench open her eyes, searching for what had hit her. Black spots, bright stars, and double vision clouding her sight, she could barely make out a dark figure swooping down on her. She raised her arms to push the person away, but her movements were slow, as if she were stuck in mud.

The figure clamped two gloved hands around her neck and squeezed. She gasped for air and tried to struggle free, but her body was sluggish and her energy sapped. She cried out, but could voice nothing more than a whimper with the pressure crushing her throat. As she wheezed out her last breath, she could have sworn she heard Whiskers let out a forlorn meow from the nearby bushes.

1

"Auntie Ellie, will you pull me around the yard on the sled again? Please, please, please?" my nephew Nate cried, tugging on the wet leg of my jeans.

I wasn't properly dressed for a Saturday afternoon full of outdoor fun. The snow had hung around for days, but it was melting fast. The unreliable December weather in Central Indiana had gone from frigid to downright balmy within a twenty-four-hour period, which meant the eight inches of snow lingering on the ground was fast transforming into one giant mess. I'd expected Nate to lose interest once the snow began degrading into slush, and therefore didn't bother with changing either of us into weather-resistant clothing before coming outside. I'd been wrong. Muddy slop seemed to be equally fun to a three-year-old—mainly, I believed, because he could splash in the puddles and get us both soaking wet.

"Okay, one more time. And then you are getting in the tub, sir," I said, picking up the sled's rope to pull the excited boy across the soupy mix of snow and grass.

Once we were finished, I made him strip off his wet clothes in the kitchen. He ran to the bathroom, stopping to squeal, "Hey, I'm naked!" as he darted past his mom and her friends, who were congregated in our living room. Our faithful golden retriever, Trixie, was hot on his heels. At least I'd had the good sense to keep the long-haired dog inside during this play session.

I rolled up my muddy pant legs and tiptoed through as my sister Rachel and her friends giggled over their study session crasher. "Hey, ladies. Sorry about the interruption. And the male nudity."

Rachel's friend Chelsea said, "No worries, Professor Matthews. We've got the hard stuff knocked out."

Eyeing my clothes, Rachel said, "I would have told the kid that outside time was a no-go this afternoon."

I wrinkled my nose at her. "That's because you're the mean mom and I'm the fun aunt."

She smiled. "Well, then the fun aunt gets to clean up the mess."

After cleaning up said mess and getting Nate settled into his bath, I couldn't help but eavesdrop on my younger half-sister and her friends. They were all students at Ashmore College, where I taught forensic science classes, and they always seemed to have some kind of drama going on. Rachel didn't participate, for the most part. Being a young single mom and a full-time student, she had more than enough on her plate. But like me, she enjoyed listening to their nonsense. From my post at the bathroom door, I could keep one eye on Nate in the tub and still see down the hallway into the living room.

Jenna Walsh, a friend of Rachel's since their childhood, stood and gathered her things. "Sorry, but I'm going to have to duck out early."

Her snippy roommate Miranda said, "Get a better offer?"

Jenna grinned. "Yes, actually. I'm spending the rest of the weekend downtown."

Never one to pass up a juicy story, Chelsea asked, "Ooh, a romantic getaway with your new man?"

Jenna blushed and nodded.

Rachel's eyebrows shot up. "You've known the guy a week, Jen. Aren't you rushing things a bit?"

Jenna was rushing things, all right. She had a tendency to fall hard and fast for guys who were all wrong for her, but this had to be a new record. I couldn't imagine Jenna's aunt Jayne, a close friend of mine who was the no-nonsense county sheriff, would approve.

"Who cares? I like him. Why not live while we're young? See you guys Monday." Jenna waved goodbye and disappeared out the door.

After she was out of earshot, her friends were quick to start gossiping about her love life.

Miranda said, "I can't believe she still won't tell us who this mystery guy is. I say it's someone we know and wouldn't approve of, and that's why she won't tell us his name."

Chelsea nodded. "It could be one of those sketchy theater majors she's always hanging out with."

Miranda tossed her hair. "No, none of them would be able to afford to take her on a romantic weekend in downtown Indy. I bet he's a professor."

Chelsea's eyes widened. "Yeah, and maybe it's a secret relationship. What if he's married?"

Turning up her nose, Miranda said, "Or worse, what if he's old?"

As Miranda and Chelsea giggled over Jenna's "old" boyfriend, Rachel didn't contribute anything to the conversation. I wondered if it was because her own boyfriend was both old (my age) and sketchy, not to mention an Ashmore College employee. Although not a professor, he was a dorm director, which in my opinion made him an equally if not more inappropriate choice for her. She and I had already had it out over her current dating situation, and I was doing my best not to tell her how to live her life. I kept my mouth shut, although some days my contempt for that douche Tony Dante was difficult to bottle up.

"Auntie Ellie, watch this!" Nate crashed the toy boat he was playing with into his bathwater, sloshing a wave over the side of the tub, which the dog decided to dance around in. Lovely. Another mess for the fun aunt to clean up.

"Have things quieted down for you yet?" Jayne Walsh asked me over dinner later that evening.

"For the most part," I replied.

Jayne, the Hamilton County Sheriff, was who had inspired me to become a criminalist, and I even worked for her department for a few years before taking my teaching job. A few months ago, Jayne had asked me to consult on a murder investigation, and the expedited trial for the accused had wrapped up last week. For my involvement in the case, I'd been bothered incessantly by reporters. I'd had to change my phone number and my email address to get some peace. When I was beginning to think I couldn't take it anymore, they'd finally lost interest and moved on to the next big news story. I'd only begun to get my privacy back in the last few days.

"Good. You know, if you like the attention, there's always a place for you in the department. Just say the word."

I rolled my eyes at her. "You know I hate the attention. Always have."

Grinning, she said, "Nevertheless, we miss you. Detective Baxter asked about you the other day."

"Mmm," was all I replied.

Nick Baxter and I had worked closely on the case, but had had a falling out over my refusal to even consider consulting again and his refusal to stay out of my personal business. I'd been through too much when I worked for the department to come back for more than a one-time favor to Jayne. My days in the field were done.

I changed the subject. "Do you have any idea who Jenna's new mystery man is?"

"No. All I've heard is that my niece is head over heels for him, and way too soon if you want my opinion."

"You're not the only one who thinks that. Rachel's not exactly thrilled about their romantic getaway this weekend. Granted, they're barely going out of town, but still."

Jayne raised one eyebrow. "Given that Jenna's taste in men is about as good as yours, it's cause for me to worry."

"Ha, ha. Very funny."

Before we could continue our conversation, Jayne's phone rang. "Sorry. The sheriff is never off duty." She hurried away from our table to take the call.

After a few minutes, she returned. I could tell by the look on her face that it hadn't been a social call. She waved the waiter over and asked for a to-go box and the check.

Sitting back down to gather her things, she said, "I take it you wouldn't be up for another homicide."

My jaw dropped. "Another one so soon? And no, I wouldn't be."

"I didn't expect so." She lowered her voice. "This isn't for public knowledge yet, but I know you can keep your mouth shut. Amy Donovan was found dead in the backyard of her home."

Amy's father, Frank Donovan, had been Jayne's partner years ago when she'd first been promoted to detective. He'd since retired, but the two of them remained close friends, which was how I knew Frank and his family.

My dinner churned in my stomach at the thought of it. "Oh, Jayne. I'm so sorry. That's terrible. Poor Amy. Poor Frank."

I could tell Jayne was struggling to find a way to shut down her emotions in order to be clear-headed enough to do her job. "The worst part is that it must've happened days ago, because her body was buried under the snow. A neighbor happened to peek over the fence tonight and saw her lying there."

I shuddered. Amy was a single thirty-something lady living alone, evidently with no one to miss her too much if she fell of the radar for a few days. "Do you have an idea on cause of death? Any possibility it could have been an accident or bad health or something?"

"No chance of that. She'd been hit in the head and strangled from the looks of it."

Letting out a long sigh, I said, "I don't envy the night ahead of you." And I certainly didn't envy the task of the crime scene investigators or the detectives. With Amy's body being buried for days under the snow and the resulting mess of slush, most of the physical evidence at the scene would be either gone or degraded beyond use.

Jayne packed up her half-eaten dinner and put on her coat. "Right. Well, if you get bored, come on out. We could use an extra set of hands."

I smiled. "I appreciate the standing job offer, but I don't think I'll ever be that bored. Be careful out there, Sheriff."

After I'd finished teaching on Monday afternoon, I found a scruffy young man bundled in a puffy coat and a knit Ashmore College beanie waiting for me at my office in the science building. I almost turned and ran the other way. But, my purse and car keys were in my office, and I wanted nothing more than to go home and relax. After the recent student murders and my subsequent involvement in the cases, it seemed that every student at Ashmore suddenly wanted to take a criminalistics class. From me. For the upcoming semester, my classes were already full and had lengthy wait lists. That didn't keep students from approaching me personally to try to go around the system and get me to agree to admit them to the class. I was tired of being harassed.

The young man brightened when I got to the door. "Professor Matthews?"

"Yes?" I replied, pasting on a smile.

Sticking out his hand, he said, "Hi, I'm Hunter Parsons."

I shook his hand. "Hi, Hunter. My classes are full for next semester, but—"

"Oh, I'm not here about that. I'd like to interview you for the *Ashmore Voice*."

I bit back a groan. That was even worse.

The *Voice* was Ashmore's campus newspaper, but they were at best a college version of *TMZ*. Sure, they cranked out a physical newspaper, but their main fare was their video blog, or "vlog," as it was called. The *Voice* had a street team that ran around campus taking videos, trying to catch students and faculty saying and doing things they shouldn't. Not only had I managed to land myself on the vlog for cussing out a local news reporter who'd snuck into the science building to ambush me for an exclusive, but I'd also been the subject of countless front-page articles in the *Voice's* newspaper. Since the homicide investigation I'd been part of had involved several Ashmore College students and staff, it was big news around here, and I was still being hounded about it.

"Hunter, I—"

"Please, Professor? I'm...not on the *Voice* staff just yet." He smoothed his scraggly brown beard self-consciously and peered at me pleadingly through his thick dark-framed glasses. "This article is like my audition. Al

Nishimura said if I can come up with a great story, I'm in. He said you'd be cool about talking with me."

Al Nishimura was the new idiot-in-chief of the *Voice*. Even after countless explanations, he could not get it through his thick head that I was *not* in fact "cool" with all the interviews. However, this nerdy kid seemed nice enough (especially for an aspiring reporter), and I hated to be the one to dash his dreams of working for the campus news organization, such as it was.

I opened my office door and gestured inside. "Okay, Hunter. Go easy on me, okay?"

He broke into a smile. "You bet. Thanks, Professor."

All in all, it wasn't such a bad interview. Instead of asking about the recent investigation, Hunter wanted to do a piece about what it was like for me being a criminalist working for Hamilton County. I didn't mind talking about my time there, unless the subject of my resignation came up. Which of course it did.

Hunter said, "It sounds like you were doing great work with the sheriff's department." He picked up a glass award from my desk. It was one I'd received from the mayor of Noblesville for being part of the team that caught a serial child molester. "Why did you make the change to teaching? Don't you miss being out in the field?"

As I was about to give my noncommittal stock answer to that question, Rachel burst into my office without knocking.

Wide eyes fixed on me, she said, "I need you. Now."

My heart did a flip-flop. "Is it Nate?"

"No, Nate's fine. It's Jenna. She's gone."

2

I hopped up and rushed over to put an arm around Rachel's shoulders. I steered her over to my chair, where she collapsed and put her head in her hands, letting her long blond hair fall like a curtain in front of her face.

I glanced at Hunter. "We're going to have to cut this short. Family emergency."

He had read the room and was already packing up and heading for the door. "Family first. I totally understand. Thanks for talking with me."

Once he was gone, I kneeled down in front of Rachel's chair, worried by her demeanor. My levelheaded little sister wasn't one to jump to conclusions and think the worst. If she was worried about Jenna, it was well warranted.

"Okay, Rach. Talk to me."

She raised her head, her eyes red-rimmed. "Jenna didn't come back to campus last night like she'd said she would. She missed all of her classes today, and she won't answer her phone."

"Are you worried something's happened to her?"

Shrugging helplessly, she said, "It's not like she hasn't cut class before. We all do it. But today was the presentation we'd been working on in our study group. She would *never* miss this—it's fifty percent of our final grade. Even if she'd been sick with her head in the toilet, she would have called.

Miranda said she hasn't been back to their dorm yet. We haven't heard a word from her since Saturday afternoon. Something's wrong. I can feel it."

I felt it, too. Jenna was too responsible—at least when it came to her schoolwork—to not show up for a major presentation. I began to worry she was lying in a hospital somewhere, unable to get word to her friends.

"Let's call Jayne. She may know where Jenna is."

I dialed Jayne's cell, and her tired voice answered, "Hello, Ellie."

"Hi, Jayne. Case going okay?"

"No, not at all."

Rachel made a "hurry up" gesture at me.

I said, "Sorry to hear that. Um, do you know where Jenna is?"

"I assume at school. Why?"

"No one's been able to get in touch with her since her weekend trip. I'm going to put you on speaker with Rachel." I did so and placed my phone on my desk.

Trying her best to keep her voice even, Rachel said, "Hey, Jayne. Um... Jenna missed our big presentation today, and she hasn't come back to campus yet. She hasn't been picking up her phone, either. Have you or her parents spoken to her lately?"

There was a pause. Jayne's voice sounded tight. "Not lately. I'll make some calls. Thanks for letting me know." The call ended.

Rachel's face crumpled. "That's it?"

I squeezed her shoulder. "Jayne is in sheriff mode, which means she's turned off her emotions. I'm sure she's having Jenna's cell signal located as we speak. She'll find her."

"What do we do in the meantime? I can't just sit here and do nothing."

I looked my sister straight in the eye. "Jayne will find her. I'm sure of it. It won't be long before we know something. Why don't we pick up Nate and go home?"

She wiped her eyes. "I don't want him to see me like this."

"Well, where's Miranda? Could you wait for Jenna in their dorm room?"

Hauling herself out of the chair, she nodded. "Yeah, that would probably be best."

I pulled her into a tight hug. "She's fine, Rach. I'm sure this is only a misunderstanding."

After she left, I straightened up my desk and got ready to leave for the day. On my way out of my office, I got a call from Jayne.

"Did you find her?" I asked.

Sounding confused and slightly put out, Jayne replied, "She's on campus. Or at least her phone is."

I put on my coat and headed out of the science building. "Where? I'm here. I'll go find her."

"Her phone's GPS location is showing she's in the courtyard between the library and Fenton Hall."

I took off at a jog, as fast as I dared in my high-heeled boots. After going the distance of about one city block, I slowed as I reached the courtyard. I didn't see Jenna anywhere. "Can you narrow it down any for me?"

"She should be just east of the library. Closer to the library than to Fenton."

I walked in that direction, still not seeing Jenna. I looked at each student carefully, thinking she may have been wearing a hat or a hood and I'd missed her. She wasn't here.

I said to Jayne, "Can you call her cell? I'm not seeing her."

After a pause, she replied, "It's ringing."

I heard a faint ringtone, but I saw none of the girls in the area reach for their phones. Heading toward the noise, I noticed a tiny glow of light by the east wall of the library, under some leafless bushes. I hurried toward it and crouched down. There was a new Android phone lying there ringing, and the caller on the screen was named "Aunt Jayne."

My breath caught in my throat. "Jayne..."

"What is it?" she asked, her tone sharp.

"I...found the phone. It's been thrown in the bushes. Jayne, I—"

"Don't. I'm sending a deputy out there now. Do what you can to secure the area. I'll be there soon."

"Okay," I replied, hoping my voice wasn't shaking as much as the rest of me.

I hadn't ever secured an area before, but since it was later in the afternoon and chilly, there weren't many students milling around the courtyard. I created my own imaginary bubble around Jenna's cellphone, and luckily for me no one tried to enter it. Within minutes, I spotted two Hamilton County sheriff's deputies striding toward me.

One of them said, "I'm Deputy Chris Lester. Are you Ellie Matthews?"

"Yes," I replied. I pointed to the phone. "Jenna Walsh's phone is right there."

"Thank you, ma'am. Come with me, please." While the other deputy took over my post securing the area around the phone, Lester pulled me aside. "You found the phone after the Sheriff gave you the location of it?"

"Yes. I'd called Sheriff Walsh when I found out her niece Jenna hadn't returned from a weekend trip. Jenna's friends were worried about her, so the Sheriff located her cellphone. Since I was already on campus, she had me run over here to find Jenna. When I got here, I didn't see Jenna, so I had the Sheriff call her phone so it would ring. I found the phone over in the bushes."

"And you're positive you didn't see Jenna Walsh anywhere in the area?"

"No. I haven't seen her since Saturday afternoon."

Lester nodded. "Thank you, ma'am. Sheriff should be here shortly. You're to wait for her."

"No problem."

I wandered over to a nearby bench and sat down, turning my back against the blustering wind. My mind was racing, knowing from experience that it was never a good sign to find someone's cellphone tossed aside, especially in a location where it had little chance of being found by passersby. It wasn't like the phone had been forgotten on a table in the library. It clearly hadn't been stolen to be used or sold. I knew I needed to tell Rachel about this at some point, but made the decision to protect her until I knew more.

After a long fifteen minutes, Jayne came hurrying across the courtyard, Detective Nick Baxter in tow. I was surprised (and not entirely happy) she'd brought him with her. According to the news, Baxter was busy working on Amy Donovan's unsolved homicide, so I wouldn't have thought she would have pulled him from that to work a missing persons case. On a personal note, I hadn't spoken to him since the argument we'd had a few months ago.

Jayne and Baxter conferred with Lester and the other deputy. They took turns studying the area around the phone, careful to stay a few feet away to preserve what part—if any—of the scene hadn't already been ruined by students and staff walking by. There was no way to pinpoint how long that phone had been there.

I stood as Jayne and Baxter approached me. Based on our earlier conversation and the set of her jaw, I knew better than to try to offer Jayne a hug or any words of consolation over her missing niece.

"You're sure you didn't see Jenna out here anywhere?" Jayne asked me, her voice strained.

"No, Jayne. I was careful to take a look at every girl in the courtyard. I'm sor—"

She cut me off. "I want you and Detective Baxter on this scene. Scour it and find me something."

My eyes flicked to Baxter's grim face and then back to Jayne's. "You want...what?"

"You heard me. Detective, get her set up." She turned on her heel and marched back toward the area around the cellphone, now cordoned off by yellow crime scene tape.

I stared after her, blinking and slack-jawed, still unsure of what had just happened here.

"Well, that's one way to hire somebody for a job," Baxter said. "Let's get you suited up."

I followed him across the courtyard to the adjacent parking lot, still dumbfounded.

"How've you been, Ellie?" he finally asked.

"Fine," I replied, not feeling ready to be chummy with him after the way we'd left things.

My phone rang, so I didn't have to say more. I stopped walking to answer it. My heart sank when I saw the caller ID.

"Hey, Rach," I said, trying not to give anything away with my tone of voice.

"Have you heard anything?"

"Um..." Omission was one thing. Lying was another. "Sort of. Jenna's phone has been found in the library courtyard."

"Her phone? Is she there?" she cried.

"No."

"Are you there?"

"Yes."

After a pause, she said, "I'm coming over."

"No," I said louder than I intended, causing Baxter turn around. He watched me as I added, "There's no need. Jayne is here along with some of the department. There's nothing for you to do."

She let out a sob. "I can't just sit here. Jenna is one of my best friends."

"I know. Look, can you get Nate at daycare and find someone to watch him tonight? You're in no shape to do it, and I'm going to be...tied up for a while."

"What do you mean?"

"I have to go. I'll call you soon." I ended the call before she could ask me any more questions, then I approached Baxter.

"I hear Jenna is one of your sister's friends."

I nodded. "We've all known each other for years."

"Right. Which is why we need to make sure our heads are in the game. Are you okay to do this?"

Who was he to ask me that question? "I'm fine."

"Yes, you've mentioned that."

Trying to control the anger bubbling up, I clenched my jaw and walked with him to the back of his SUV. We put on jumpsuits over our clothing, along with hats, gloves, and booties. He shouldered a field kit and led the way back to the scene. Deputy Lester held the crime scene tape up for us so we could approach the phone. Baxter laid the field kit down and got out a camera. I backed away so he could take a few wide-angle shots.

As he walked around the area where the phone was, shooting mid-range and close-up photos, I began thinking how unlikely it was that we would find any evidence of value. The phone lay in a flowerbed next to the library under some bushes. The flowerbed was five or six feet deep. Its back edge was the library itself, and its front edge butted up against a sidewalk. A sidewalk used day in and day out by hundreds of people. Even if we found a shoeprint or a personal item during our search, what were the odds it belonged to whoever disposed of Jenna's phone? Unless there were fingerprints on the phone, I felt like this was an exercise in futility.

Baxter handed me a stack of evidence markers and a ruler. "See anything besides the phone?"

I could tell he'd drawn the same conclusion I had. "No, but maybe we will when we get up close and personal."

I pulled a magnifying glass and a flashlight out of the field kit and went over to the flowerbed. Down on my hands and knees, I shined the light around, but there was nothing to see. I sifted through the mulch, only finding fallen leaves from the bare bushes and a few bugs. I set an evidence marker next to the phone and stepped back to let Baxter take a couple pictures of it, then put the scale next to the phone and had him shoot a few more.

When he straightened up, he came close to me and murmured, "I think this was a case of someone simply walking down the sidewalk and tossing the phone. We're not going to find anything here to tell us who did it."

"I agree. I say we bag and tag the phone and get it to the lab ASAP. It's our best and only shot at getting some prints."

"And our best shot at finding out where Jenna could be. That is, if we can get into the phone."

I handed him a paper bag and a new pair of gloves. He changed his gloves and headed over to the bushes, reaching in and carefully picking up the phone. He tapped the screen and frowned, then placed the phone in the bag and folded the top. He handed the bag to me to seal with evidence tape while he filled out a stick-on evidence tag. I retrieved the evidence marker and scale.

Noticing that we were packing up, Jayne marched over to us. "Well? What did you find?"

Baxter said, "Only the phone, Sheriff. Passcode or fingerprint protected, so I can't get into it here."

She stared us down. "That's it?"

I cleared my throat. "There was nothing else. We're hoping there are fingerprints we can lift from the phone."

"Get to the lab and find them. And get into that phone." Over her shoulder she yelled, "Deputy Lester, drive Ms. Matthews to the station." To Baxter, she said, "We need to meet with campus security now."

We'd gotten our orders, so Baxter and I hurried back to the SUV to strip off our protective coverings.

"Good to see you again, Ellie." He sounded like he meant it.

"Yeah, you too." I sounded like I didn't.

He sighed. "Look, I'm sorry about—"

"Nick...while I appreciate your apology, we don't have the time to get into it right now. I have to go." I picked up the evidence bag with the phone and headed over to Deputy Lester's cruiser, leaving Baxter frowning as we drove away.

3

The drive from Ashmore College in Carmel to the sheriff's station in Noblesville was long and aggravating in near rush hour traffic, even with Deputy Lester using his siren and lights. It had been a long time since I'd ridden along in a cruiser, but I hadn't forgotten how much I hated it. People around here couldn't be bothered get out of the way of an emergency vehicle, and I lost count of how many times we had to stop for traffic and bumbling drivers.

While we drove, I texted my sister. *Did you find someone to watch Nate?*

She replied, *David,* our stepdad. *I'm going back to campus. We're going to search for Jenna. You should be here to help. Where the hell are you?*

I didn't feel right lying to her, especially with how upset she was. *Jayne sent me to the station to examine the phone we found. Sorry I was cryptic earlier. I didn't know how much I was allowed to tell you.*

After a pause, she replied, *Exactly how worried should I be right now?*

I rubbed my forehead, not knowing what to say. I didn't want to assume the worst, and I didn't want my baby sister to, either. *Please don't worry yet. Jayne and Baxter are working on finding her. Start your search, and I'll join you when I'm done.*

Lester dropped me at the station, my nerves worse for wear. I'd tried not to dwell on what Jenna's missing phone meant for her situation, but dark thoughts kept swirling in my mind. I'd tried to convince myself that she and her guy had done something selfish and stupid. Maybe they'd run away together and gotten married, or decided to extend their romantic weekend without bothering to tell anyone. But in the back of my mind, I didn't believe any of that.

I checked the phone in with the evidence clerk and then took it to the lab, hesitating for a moment before pushing open the door. If I was on bad terms with Baxter, I was on worse terms with Beck Durant, the head criminalist. I used to be his boss, but now he was the boss. When I had come back to consult, he was less than gracious about me being in *his* lab.

When I entered the room, Beck popped his head up and sneered at me, right on cue. "What are you doing here?"

I held up my bag. "I have evidence Sheriff Walsh asked me to process."

"Nobody told me."

That was no surprise. Beck didn't get much respect around here. Mostly because he did nothing to earn it.

"You can call Baxter and ask him."

Amanda Carmack, Beck's assistant and a new friend of mine, heard us and came out of the adjacent office smiling. "Hey, Ellie. Are you consulting again?"

"Hi, Amanda. It happened kind of fast...but I guess I am." I shrugged into a lab coat and twisted my long, dark hair into a messy bun.

"Great. What can we do to help?"

Beck threw me a glare and stalked away, likely going to take one of his infamous "smoke breaks," even though I didn't think he did any actual smoking during them. It was my opinion that he exploited a legitimate addiction to get out of as much work as he could.

"I need to pull some fingerprints off this phone and find a way into it. It belongs to Jenna Walsh."

Amanda's face fell. "Oh, I heard about her disappearance." She beckoned me over to a workstation and helped me get out some fingerprint powder and brushes. "I'm sure you want to get this done quickly. As you lift the prints, I'll input them into AFIS. Speed things up a bit. If we can get a good print of Jenna's, I can run it through our 3D printer and get her phone unlocked. If she's got the fingerprint sensor set up, that is. It's worth a shot."

"Thanks," I replied, impressed that the lab had gotten some new equipment since I'd been gone. I put on some gloves and took the phone out of the evidence bag. As I examined the phone under the bench magnifier, I said, "Am I taking you away from Amy Donovan's homicide investigation, though? I assume you guys are knee deep in it."

"We are, but..." She trailed off uncertainly.

I got out a camera and snapped a few photos of the phone under the bright light. "But what?"

"This case has the priority right now."

I put the phone back down again and set out the black fingerprint dust, a brush, and some DNA swabs. "I get it. Sheriff's niece."

First, I swabbed a few smudged prints I could see, hoping to get some touch DNA from them. After I was finished with the DNA collection, I dusted the phone's screen, then studied it again through the magnifier. I saw a few prints I thought were viable to lift, but most of them were unfortunately partials. I got out some fingerprint lifts and collected the first print, which I passed to Amanda. She disappeared into the next room to begin examining it.

I continued lifting prints, stopping for a moment to run a few over to Amanda, who was concentrating on a blown-up version of the first print on an enormous computer screen. The first print I'd given her hadn't been terribly clear, so it was taking a while for her to plot the individual characteristics, which was the information she needed to run it through AFIS, the Automated Fingerprint Identification System. I returned to my station and turned the phone over, brushing powder over the decorative case. Its colorful pattern made prints difficult to see, but the smooth surface made it easy to get good lifts. I pulled several prints from this side, some of them full. Once I'd finished, I relieved Amanda at the computer and let her do an independent second examination of the phone.

The first three fingerprints she'd entered had come back with a list of possible matches in AFIS, with Jenna's name at the top of every list. I called to Amanda, "Do we know why Jenna is in AFIS? She's a goody two-shoes."

Amanda yelled back, "The Sheriff said she'd been fingerprinted as a kid for safety reasons."

I nodded, thinking I probably should have known that. Jayne insisted

Rachel and I be fingerprinted when we were minors as well for the same reason. Nate, too. She'd seen too much not to be cautious about the people she loved. I tried to put that out of my mind as I took the next print and scanned it into the computer.

After several minutes, Amanda came into the office. "I finished my examination of the phone and didn't find anything further. I'd help you with the prints, but we only have the one machine to work with."

"No problem, and thanks," I said, not taking my eyes off the screen. Seven out of the thirteen prints we'd run had been Jenna's. I was beginning to lose hope.

Amanda said hesitantly, "You should probably know that...we think Amy Donovan's death and Jenna Walsh's disappearance may be connected."

I stopped what I was doing to stare at her. "Connected? How? Why?"

She walked over to another table and picked up a file. Flipping through it, she found a photo and handed it to me. "Because of this."

It was a large photo of a crumpled up note. My stomach plummeted when I read what was scrawled on it in black ink:

My life was ruined by your mistakes,
  And now you understand how my heart aches.
  For your incompetence I will show no pity
  As I strike terror across the city.
  Your only child is now dearly departed.
  An eye for an eye? I'm just getting started.

"Where was this found?" I asked, afraid of the answer.

"In Amy Donovan's mouth."

My jaw dropped. "That's straight up serial killer stuff."

Her expression was grim. "It is, especially considering one of her eyes had been removed."

"What?" I breathed. They hadn't divulged that on the news.

"I know. It's beyond disturbing, and they don't have any leads on who did it. What they do know is that someone killed Amy to get back at Frank. The department secured the rest of Frank's family thinking that the '*I'm just getting started*' line meant the killer intends to go after them." She blew out a breath. "But now that Jenna Walsh is missing…it puts a different spin on things. They're worried now that the retaliation is also against the Sheriff since she and Frank were partners. Her niece ended up being the target since Sheriff Walsh has no children of her own."

As the gravity of this hit me, I felt like I was going to be sick. I choked out, "So whoever killed Amy may now have Jenna."

"Yes." She put her hand on my shoulder. "You go get some air. I'll take over while you wrap your mind around this."

I did as she suggested, slinking out the back door of the station and collapsing on the concrete steps. As I sat there with my head in my hands, trying not to cry or vomit, my phone rang. It was Baxter.

"Yes," I said around the lump in my throat.

"It's Nick. Do you have anything for us on those fingerprints yet?"

"So far they've all come back as Jenna's." I frowned. "When exactly were you going to tell me that Jenna's disappearance is connected to Amy Donovan's murder?"

He sighed into the phone. "After you did the job we needed you for."

A hot tear ran down my cheek. "I see."

I hung up on him. Damn Baxter. We'd worked side by side for a good thirty minutes, and he hadn't said a word about the cases being connected. Again he decided that he knew what was best for me and did whatever the hell he wanted to get the outcome he needed. I stood, clenching my jaw until I gained control of myself, then stomped back to the lab. I wanted to get my task over and done. My sister needed me, and I needed to get out of this soul-sucking place.

Beck was back in the lab processing some evidence. He ignored me as I passed him on my way to the adjacent office. Amanda was still hard at work at the computer station when I went in and pulled up a chair next to her.

She gave me a sympathetic smile. "More of the same on the AFIS hits, I'm afraid. But the 3D model of Jenna's fingerprint is ready if you want to try to unlock her phone. I waited for you before I tried it. I didn't know if you'd ever used one before."

I nodded. "Thanks. I've used one in a classroom setting, but never in an actual case."

She hopped up. "Let's do it, then."

She had laid out everything we'd need on a workstation, but stepped aside for me to do the task. Amanda loved tech. Since I'd met her, she was always emailing me articles she'd read on advances in forensics and attending scientific conferences when she could. It was too bad she was stuck in this lab with its outdated equipment.

Hoping Jenna preferred biometrics over a passcode to unlock her phone, I picked up the 3D image of her fingerprint and placed it against the fingerprint scanner on the screen. Nothing happened. Amanda and I grimaced at each other, and I repositioned the print and tried again. This time, the phone came to life. We heaved a sigh of relief and gave each other a high five.

She said, "I'll leave you to have a look through that, and I'll get back to work on the rest of the prints."

I sat down on a nearby stool and began scrolling through her text messages. Her last outgoing text message was sent about an hour after she'd left my house on Saturday. That was forty-eight hours ago, but I tried not to let that fact cloud my focus. The text was to a girlfriend of hers, declining an invite to meet for dinner Saturday night because she had a date. There were dozens of unanswered incoming texts from her friends, most of them similar messages asking where she was, with newer ones becoming more frantic and begging for her to reply. I recognized many of the names on the list, and there didn't seem to be any conversations between Jenna and any males that would indicate that they were dating. The texts I read were all platonically friendly. No mention of planning for a weekend getaway or any sweet talk of any kind. All young people texted each other, so why was there no messaging between Jenna and her mystery man? Were we dealing with a much older man like Miranda had wondered?

Her Snapchat and Instagram private messages were much the same as her text messages—all platonic. I opened her email folder, not that I thought college kids used email as a primary communication tool these days. Her emails were mainly spam, Internet order confirmations, and a few to and from her professors, mostly to turn in electronic assignments and discuss class topics. There were no personal conversations in any of her email folders, either.

I checked the phone call log and found one number that showed up over and over in the last week. The contact's name was "Derek" with no last name and no photo. I hit the message button, but it brought up a blank text message screen. "Derek" was someone she'd spent a lot of time talking to on the phone but had never texted. I hurried into the office and ran the phone number, but it came back as a prepaid cell.

I let out a groan.

"What's up?" Amanda asked.

"The one contact I can find on this phone that could be Jenna's new mystery man is someone she only calls and never texts, has no last name or photo in his contact info, and whose number is to a burner phone."

Amanda's face grew concerned. "That's not good."

"No, it's not."

I pulled up Jenna's photos and scrolled through them. Her photos were mostly either selfies or photos with her girlfriends. Any photos with guys in them were shots of larger groups. There were no photos she'd taken in the last month that would indicate she was in a relationship. Rachel had said Jenna had only known this guy for a week.

I got my phone out and took a photo of the database showing that the number I'd found for "Derek" was to a burner phone, then sent a quick text to Jayne outlining the lack of information I'd found on Jenna's phone about where she might have gone.

Amanda said, "If you'd input the last fingerprint, I'll take the phone over to our cyber guys and see if they can delve any deeper."

"Sure," I said flatly, handing the phone over to her. I was fast beginning to lose hope that we were going to find Jenna happily holed up in a love nest somewhere.

I scanned the last fingerprint I'd collected and plotted the individual characteristics of it, having to stop a couple of times to rub my tired eyes as they clouded over. The AFIS results were again the same—Jenna Walsh was at the top of the list of several potential matches. Whoever had thrown her phone in the bushes hadn't touched it with bare hands, so this was all for nothing. I shot Jayne another text to let her know that we'd struck out with the fingerprints. Her response was that I was to come back to Ashmore to participate in a campus-wide search for Jenna.

I sighed to myself. As much as I wanted to find Jenna, I thought it was a waste to do a physical search. Jenna would never deliberately hide on campus, and if someone had abducted her, it would be stupid to try to hold her somewhere against her will on a busy campus full of people. But, like Rachel, I couldn't just sit and do nothing.

I said my goodbyes to Amanda and had a deputy drive me home to get some warm clothes and more sensible shoes. On the way back to Ashmore, I contacted Rachel to ask if she had ever heard Jenna speak of anyone named Derek. She hadn't, which was the answer I'd expected. For all I knew, Derek wasn't even the guy's real name. I had the deputy drop me at the science building. Once inside, I headed for the sanctuary of my office. After all that had happened in the past few hours, I could think of only one thing that could help me get through this night. I took two shots of vodka from the bottle I kept locked in my desk, then rinsed with minty mouthwash and popped a cough drop into my mouth to mask any telltale odor.

4

Jayne had set up a makeshift command center in the main dining hall of the Ashmore Student Center, a building which also housed the student life offices, bookstore, campus radio station, and the *Ashmore Voice* office. Baxter and several deputies were busy passing out flyers with Jenna's picture on them to groups of students eager to help with the search.

When I approached her, Jayne looked up from the campus map she'd been studying. "Thanks for coming back over, Ellie."

"No problem. Sorry I couldn't get much off the phone."

She shook her head wearily. "It's fine. Without you, I wouldn't have even known..." Shaking off that thought, she continued, "Anyway, I want you and Detective Baxter to go through Jenna's dorm room. Her roommate said that to her knowledge, the boy she planned to go away with had never been to the room. But maybe you can find some clue as to where they were headed."

I didn't want to spend a minute more with Baxter than was absolutely necessary, but it wasn't like I had a choice in the matter. You didn't say no to Jayne when she was in a mood like this—but more importantly, I would do anything to help her find Jenna.

"Okay."

She pointed to a silver case at the end of the table. "There's the kit.

Report to me when you know something. Detective Baxter has the search warrant."

I nodded and picked up the case. Baxter saw me and held up one finger to signal me to wait for him. He finished up his conversation and came over to me.

"I hear we have a dorm room to process," he said, his expression wary.

"Yep."

We walked over to Harris Hall in an uncomfortable silence. Baxter showed the dorm director our warrant, and she escorted us upstairs and unlocked Jenna and Miranda's room for us.

Baxter said, "There's no need for jumpsuits and all that. There have been students in and out of here all evening, so the scene is contaminated. We're only looking for some clue as to where Jenna went. Or at least where she thought she was going."

Nodding, I set the field kit on the floor. I then peeled off my coat and set it outside in the hallway. We both put on gloves, then I started looking through Jenna's closet as Baxter went for her desk.

Nothing seemed amiss. There were no clothes strewn around or hangers askew like she'd packed in a hurry. Her toiletries were nowhere to be found, but that made sense given the fact that she planned to be away overnight. I took a step back and glanced around the room. Both beds were made, and the entire room was neat, clean, and organized. Nothing was out of place.

"No luck?" Baxter asked.

"No."

"I can't find anything, either."

"Mmm."

"Ellie?"

I groaned inwardly. I was not in the mood to talk about our earlier disagreement, but Baxter could never leave anything unsaid. "What?" I replied, pretending to be interested in a music box on Jenna's dresser.

He put his hand on my arm and turned me to face him. "I can't work like this."

"Me either, Nick. It's hard for me to do a job when I don't have all the information I need."

He frowned. "I'm sorry about earlier. Look, it wasn't my idea to keep you in the dark. The Sheriff asked me not to burden you with information about the other case."

"Oh." It hurt equally that Jayne didn't think I could handle myself, but then again, she'd always mothered me—especially since my own mother hadn't. "Well, in that case I apologize for hanging up on you."

As I tried to end the conversation by getting back to our task, he said, "But you're still pissed at me for looking into your mother's case."

"Wow. It's like you're a detective or something," I snipped.

"Ellie, I was only trying to help. I told you that."

I turned around to face him again. "Right. Because of your hero complex. Well, guess what? I don't need a hero. And I don't need my mother's murder case reopened."

His jaw had clenched at my hero comment. "Her killer could be running free right now. Wouldn't you feel better with him behind bars?"

"I'd feel better if you'd stay the hell out of my business like I asked you to."

Baxter held up his hands. "Fine. Consider me officially out of your business."

"Fine."

In a terse silence, we traded search areas and went over the room a second time. He got out his phone and called Jayne to let her know we'd struck out while I put on my coat and closed up the field kit.

After he ended the call, he said, "I know neither of us is in the mood to talk, but I have to get an official statement from you since you were one of the last people to see Jenna before she disappeared."

I leaned up against Jenna's closet, working to put my personal feelings aside so I could be helpful. "Okay."

"I talked to your sister and her friends. They said Jenna Walsh was at a study group at your house for three hours on Saturday afternoon. What time did she leave?"

"A little before five."

"How did she seem? Nervous, excited? Was she behaving normally?"

I shrugged. "She seemed like normal Jenna to me. She told the girls she needed to leave early to go get ready to 'spend the rest of the weekend downtown,' as she put it. Chelsea asked her if it was a romantic getaway with her new man, and Jenna said yes. Rachel gave her some crap about it. She seemed bothered by the fact that Jenna had only known this guy for a week and was moving too fast. Jenna brushed it off and said she was going to live while she was young. Now she, um..." I swallowed the lump that had formed in my throat. "She may not..." I trailed off, afraid to finish the sentence.

Baxter's face softened. "Hey, come on. We're going to find her."

I shook my head, willing myself to hold it together. "Not on campus. She's not here."

He sighed. "I agree with you there. Someone's not just going to stumble over her during the search. However, I think the search is useful to get her picture in front of as many people as possible and find out who was last to see her on Saturday night. That way we can get an idea of a timeline. We know she left your house a little before five and then came here to pack. The girls across the hall saw her leave this room with a bag around six, which was roughly when she sent her last text message. If I were to guess, I would assume Jenna went missing shortly after that—probably right around the time she was supposed to meet this mystery guy. You're sure she never mentioned his name, even in passing?"

"No. Her friends had a fit over it after she left my house. She refused to tell any of them his name, even her roommate. They think he's an old married professor or something like that. I can't say I disagree too much, because from what I saw on her phone, she did zero texting with the guy. So he's either too old to want to communicate via text, or he doesn't want a paper trail, so to speak. Plenty of calls to a contact named Derek with a burner phone, though. And burner phones scream infidelity."

Nodding, he said, "Right. Sheriff and I thought the same thing. But there are no staff members named Derek at this school. We checked."

"But I'm sure there are plenty of Dereks in the greater Indianapolis area, if that is his real name."

"I'm betting it isn't, but we're still going to pursue that angle. Anyway, the cyber investigators should be able to find out where the phone was when she sent the last text, which might give us another clue. And although she made no more texts or calls after six, if she opened an app that used any data, they should be able to at least determine what area she was in based on which cell tower her signal went through."

I let out a sigh. "At least that's something."

As we trudged back to the Ashmore Student Center, I could feel the tension wasn't gone between us. I hated it. Baxter was a good guy, but I hadn't found it in me to forgive him yet.

My estranged mother's murder case was the reason I quit the department and took up teaching. She was a Jane Doe case, her body parts scattered around the county and found over the course of a month, too degraded to be identified until I (the head criminalist at the time) noticed her one-of-a-kind earrings. Only Jayne knew that the victim we'd been examining the pieces of was my mother, and she'd kept it a secret from the rest of the department at my request.

I'd finally broken down and trusted Baxter with the information, only to have him delve into the case behind my back when I had expressly asked him to leave it alone. Rachel's crazy father had killed our mother, I was certain, and I didn't want him to think someone was tracking him for fear he might assume it was Rachel and come after her. She'd even changed her name to make sure he never found her. More than that, neither of us wanted to open up that old wound again.

Once we got to the dining hall, Baxter and I went our separate ways. He went to confer with a couple of deputies while I approached Jayne.

She gave me a weary smile. "No luck, huh?"

"No. I wish I didn't have to keep reporting to you that I failed."

"I didn't expect you to find anything."

"What can I do now to help?"

"Take a stack of flyers and start canvassing an area. I think that's our best bet."

I nodded. "You got it." After grabbing a handful of flyers, I headed outside and called Rachel.

"Hey, do you have any new information?" she asked.

"Sorry, but no. Baxter and I went through Jenna's room, but found nothing."

"I've been asking everyone about her mentioning a guy named Derek, but no one's ever heard of him."

I stifled a sigh. "Where are you?"

"Going door to door in Schroeder Hall."

"Care if I join you?"

Her voice hitched. "That would be great. Sis?"

"Yes?"

"Will you bring some hot chocolate when you come?"

"You got it," I replied, my heart breaking a little. From when she was Nate's age, if anything upset her, hot chocolate could fix it. It wasn't going to fix her current problem, but I was willing to get her anything that would give her a measure of comfort.

After making a pit stop at the campus Starbucks, I arrived at Schroeder Hall and met Rachel in the lobby. The poor thing was haggard and drawn, nothing like her usual vivacious self. I enveloped her in a hug, but (like I often did) she pulled away before too much empathy caused her strong façade to crack. We might have had two different fathers, but in many ways we were exactly alike.

She took a sip from her hot chocolate and sighed heavily. "Miranda and Chelsea are working on the top two floors here, and I'm ready to move on. Want to tackle the music building with me? Should be plenty of band geeks in the practice rooms right about now."

I smiled. "Sure."

As we walked toward the music building, she said, "Tell me straight— what are the odds that we're going to find out anything useful about where Jenna disappeared to?"

"Pretty good, actually. If we can find someone who saw her leave campus, then we can start piecing together who she was with and where they went."

"Do you find it suspicious that this guy she was seeing made a big deal about keeping their relationship a secret? I mean, was he planning to abduct her all along?"

This was dangerous territory. I couldn't tell Rachel the department's theory on the connection between Jenna's disappearance and Amy Donovan's murder.

"Yes, I think it could be a possibility. He could have spun the secrecy thing as being romantic and exciting."

A tear ran down her cheek. "And he turned out to be a monster."

I stopped her and gripped her shoulders. "We don't know that anything bad has happened to her."

She sobbed, "I can tell from the look on Jayne's face that she thinks the worst."

I held Rachel close to me, stroking her back in an attempt to soothe her. I had recognized that look, too. Jayne had seen too much to hold out hope that situations like this ever ended any way but badly. After a few minutes, Rachel pulled away and wiped her tears with her jacket sleeve.

"This isn't helping Jenna," she said, her voice trembling. "Let's go."

Rachel and I scoured every inch of the music building, asking every person we found if they'd seen Jenna on Saturday night. We got the same answer from everyone: no. Dejected, we headed back to the Ashmore Student Center to get more flyers.

Jayne was looking even worse for wear, so I had Rachel pair back up with Miranda and Chelsea while I tried to talk Jayne into taking a break.

"Can I buy you a coffee?" I asked.

She didn't look up from her phone. "You can buy a coffee and bring it to me."

I put my hand on hers. "Jayne. You need a break. For your sanity. Have you eaten?"

"I can't eat."

"Bathroom break?"

"I don't need to."

"It's after eleven-thirty. Are you planning to stay all night?"

Jayne finally flicked angry eyes up at me. "As long as it takes to find my niece."

"Then you'll need caffeine. Come with me. Ten minutes max."

Her shoulders slumped. "Okay."

The Starbucks in the lower level of the building had stayed open later than usual to provide drinks for people helping with the search. They were getting ready to close, but we managed to get our coffees before they stopped serving. I talked Jayne into sitting at a table in the adjacent food court instead of going straight back to her post.

She collapsed into a chair and rubbed her eyes. "This is all my fault."

I placed my hand on her shoulder. "No, it's not. You can't think like that."

"There's something you don't know."

"I saw the note that was found in Amy's mouth."

Blowing out a breath, she said, "So you do know. This is bad."

We sat there in silence, sipping our coffees, until Jayne got a call.

"Sheriff Walsh." She listened for a moment, then her face drained of color. "You found... No... Are you positive?" Her hand fluttered to her mouth, and tears began pouring from her eyes. She managed to croak out, "Call Baxter and Sterling. I'm on my way."

"Jayne, what is it?" I breathed.

"My niece is dead."

5

As Jayne got up, I caught her in a crushing hug. She allowed herself to sob for only a moment before pulling herself together and taking a step back from me. I tried to hold back my tears for her sake, but watching this strong woman break down was more than I could bear. We both wiped our eyes, unable to look at each other.

"Jayne, I'm so sorry. What can I do for you? Name it."

She swallowed. "I want you to work the scene with Amanda Carmack. Can you handle it?"

Work the death scene of a girl who was like family to me? I didn't know how I was going to do it, but I couldn't bring myself to turn Jayne down after what had just happened. I would have to disconnect and wait until later to break down. I believed I could manage that, but I was certain it would wreak havoc on my mind and my heart.

"Yes, I can," I replied, my voice sounding more confident than I felt.

I followed her up to the main dining area. Baxter was on his phone, his face ashen. He locked eyes with me and began walking my way. Jayne hurried ahead and began conferring with two of her deputies.

Baxter ended his call and stopped in front of me. "You okay?"

I nodded. "Jayne asked me to work the scene with Amanda."

"I'm headed there. Ride over with me, and I'll bring you up to speed on the Amy Donovan case."

"Okay, thanks." We exited the building and hurried toward his vehicle. As I had a thought, I stopped dead in my tracks. "Wait...Rachel...and Jenna's other friends. I don't want them hearing about this on the news or through campus gossip..." I ran my hands through my hair, my heart breaking for those girls.

He stopped and said patiently, "The college is assigning counselors to speak with the students. There's protocol in place to take particular care with deceased students' roommates and close friends."

Still not feeling right about this, I said, "But shouldn't I be there for my sister?"

"I think the Sheriff needs you more. There's not a lot you can do for Rachel right now, but we can start making headway on getting justice for Jenna."

I swallowed hard and nodded.

"Come on."

He put his hand on my shoulder and steered me toward the parking lot. Once we got to his SUV, he opened the passenger door for me and then went and got in the driver's seat. I knew I had to lock down my emotions. I was way too close to the situation, and I had to find a way to detach. I'd always been fairly good at setting aside my feelings in order to do my job, but I was out of practice.

To keep my mind off it, I said, "Okay, tell me what I need to know about Amy Donovan."

Baxter said, "As you've heard, a neighbor found her in her backyard Saturday night. But she was killed days before, most likely on Wednesday. They're basing that on a receipt for a half-eaten container of take-out on her kitchen counter and the coroner's best estimation. Her body was partially frozen, so it was difficult to pinpoint an exact time of death."

I shook my head. "It's sad that no one went looking for her before that."

He shrugged. "She lived alone. She was scheduled off work from Thursday until Sunday. No one missed her."

I shivered at the thought. "Jayne said she sustained blunt force trauma to the head and was strangled. That sounds like a crime of passion. How do the cryptic note and the...eye thing fit with that? Leaving a calling card—especially a creepy-ass poem that someone clearly spent time writing—implies premeditation."

Giving me a nod, he said, "Excellent observation. I thought the same thing." His face clouded over. "And with this second death, I have a feeling we're going to get another piece of the puzzle."

Another shiver ran through me.

He continued, "We found no real evidence at the Donovan scene. No footprints because of the snow. There was a broken light bulb in her patio light and a mangled latch on her fence gate, but neither of them yielded any prints. We have nothing to go on aside from the note, which isn't much."

He pulled into Richards Park, a new park that had been constructed between Carmel and Fishers in honor of the retired judge Walter Richards. Judge Richards had been a well-respected Hamilton County superior court judge for over thirty years, and the county recognized him last year by building this park.

There were already several emergency vehicles here, including the coroner's van and the criminalists' SUV. Baxter and I got out, and I put on a clean jumpsuit and one of Baxter's ever-present baseball caps I found in the back of his SUV. On the way into the park, we met Amanda, who was struggling to carry two kits toward the scene.

"Thanks," she breathed as Baxter relieved her of the cases and went ahead of us. To me she said, "I can't even imagine what you're feeling right now. I'm gutted, and I barely knew Jenna."

Having successfully gotten hold of my emotions on the way over here, I was finally able to discuss Jenna's death without breaking down. "Yes, this won't be easy. But the Sheriff asked me to do this for her, and I want to nail whoever killed Jenna to the wall."

"Agreed."

My phone rang, and I had to fumble in my pocket to get it. It was Rachel. I said to Amanda, "I need to take this," and hung back to talk to my sister in private. "Hey, Rach."

She was sobbing into the phone. "Jenna's dead. She's dead."

I clenched my jaw hard, hating the fact that I wasn't able to console my sister in person. "I know. I'm so sorry I can't be there for you."

"Why did this happen?" she wailed.

"I have no idea, but I'm going to help find out who did it. Look, Rachel, I won't be home tonight. Jayne asked me to process the scene, and I agreed. I feel awful that I'm not there for you, but—"

"No, don't worry about me." Her tone got an edge to it. "You do your job and find the bastard who took Jenna from us. Promise me you'll find him."

"I'll do everything I can. Do you have somewhere to go so you won't be alone?"

"I'm staying with Miranda. She needs me."

I breathed a sigh of relief. "Yes, she does. I'll see you in the morning, okay?"

"I love you, Ellie."

I was doing fine until then. I choked out, "I love you, too."

I stashed my phone back in my pocket and shook off the emotion I was feeling. I had a job to do, and nothing could get in the way of that.

I signed the crime scene entry log at the entrance to the park. The outer perimeter had been set up at the fence across the front of the small park, and the surrounding trees made a natural perimeter around the sides and back. It was a fairly secluded location, so it made sense that the killer had chosen it.

An inner perimeter was set up around a wrought iron gazebo that was the centerpiece of the park. Portable floodlights had been brought in to illuminate the darkness. When I got closer, I saw a person sitting on a bench inside the gazebo and wondered momentarily why anyone was allowing that to happen. Then I noticed the person wasn't moving. My stomach lurched as I realized it was Jenna.

Seated on a bench like she was enjoying an evening in the park, Jenna held a bouquet of daisies and a piece of paper in her hands. She looked peaceful. Her legs were crossed and her head was up, although her eyes were closed. When I got closer, I could see the glint of a web of fishing line holding her body in place, tied to the intricate wrought iron work of the gazebo.

Before I let myself think too much about that, I went and found Amanda, who was standing with Baxter and his arrogant partner, Detective Jason Sterling. Sterling was the second worse thing I'd have to contend with tonight, aside from death itself. We didn't get along well at all.

"Hey, Matthews," he said as I joined their group. I steeled myself for a nasty comment, but instead he said, "Sorry about your friend. Looks like we have a long night ahead of us."

I stared at him, not knowing how to respond to him being nice to me. "Um, yeah. Thanks, Sterling."

This had to be Amanda's doing. The two of them had been dating on and off for the past few months. Maybe she'd been able to beat some manners into him.

The coroner, Dr. Everett Berg, and his assistant, Kenny Strange, were examining the body. They were no doubt wondering how in the hell they were going to get her cut away from the endless tangle of fishing line holding her lifeless body in an upright position. Dr. Berg beckoned us over. The four of us stopped to put on booties and gloves before entering the inner perimeter of the scene.

"Good evening, all," Dr. Berg said. His eyes registered pain. As a friend of Jayne's, he'd watched Jenna grow up. "As you can see, the victim has been posed. She's been dead for approximately six hours, maybe more. And considering I believe she died from exsanguination and there's no sign of blood around here..."

Baxter finished his thought. "This is not our primary crime scene."

Sterling swore under his breath. I felt the same way. We wouldn't find a murder weapon or much else here to point us toward the killer.

Dr. Berg gestured toward a deep cut on Jenna's neck. "I believe this laceration severed a jugular vein, but I'll of course know the complete extent of her injuries once the autopsy is completed. Now if you'd like to take photos and study the scene, we'll leave you for a few moments while we gather our equipment."

On his way past me, Dr. Berg gave me a pat on the shoulder. Kenny gave me an encouraging but sad smile.

Sterling said to Baxter, "You need to read the note."

Baxter walked closer to the body and crouched down, taking care not to touch anything. He read aloud:

An innocent man went to jail that night
   Because you decided what was wrong and right.
   You thought you knew. You were so sure.
   She died; he died. How much must a child have to endure?
   A tooth for a tooth. Are you catching on?
   It won't be long before the next one's gone.

After taking a picture of the note with his phone, he stood and turned to us. "This poem is as bad as the first one. '*It won't be long before the next one's gone.*' Is he saying he's going after more Walsh and Donovan family members or does he have more law enforcement vendettas to settle?"

"Hell if I know, but I do know we're dealing with one sick son of a bitch here," Sterling replied. He chin-nodded at us. "Get to it, girls."

The two detectives left the gazebo to go confer privately.

Amanda got a camera out of her kit and handed it to me. "Well, boss. Sounds like it's go time."

I took the camera from her. "I'll get shots of the whole scene and of the body, then Dr. Berg and Kenny can cut her down."

Starting at the entrance to the gazebo, I began taking pictures. Wide shots at first, showing the entire gazebo area, then some mid-range shots of the victim's body, then finally close-ups of each aspect of the staging. I worked to focus my thoughts on the science of the situation rather than allowing the reality to sink in. My state of mind was precarious at best, but I had a lock on it at the moment.

Amanda said, "Check out her cowboy boots."

I glanced down. Those clunky boots were not quite in keeping with Jenna's chic style. "Jenna Walsh would never have put those on her feet." I took in the rest of her outfit—a peasant top, a flowered bohemian skirt, a wide belt embellished with coins, and several mismatched necklaces. "And she most certainly didn't do boho."

Amanda's brow furrowed. "Maybe she was going to a costume party."

"I don't think so." I zoomed my camera in on the victim's neck and took a photo. Her throat had been slit, but the wound had been wiped clean, and there was no blood on her shirt. "The killer redressed her."

"That's creepy."

"So is going to all this trouble to pose the body. It took some time and a lot of thought." I snapped several close-ups of how the fishing line was tied to the gazebo.

At that time, Dr. Berg and Kenny came back to collect the body. Dr. Berg removed the flowers from the victim's hands, placing them into a large bag Amanda had waiting. He pulled the note from her fingers and handed it to me. I placed it into a plastic sleeve, then slid that into a manila envelope and sealed it. After that, Amanda and I left the gazebo to give Dr. Berg and Kenny some space. We walked around back so we could watch what they were doing from the other side. Baxter and Sterling joined us.

Amanda gestured at the body and said to the detectives, "We noticed that the victim has been redressed."

"No shit, Sherlocks. There's no blood on her clothes," Sterling jeered, earning a glare from both Amanda and me. Sterling couldn't be nice for too long.

Amanda replied, "It's not just that she's been redressed; it's *how* she's been redressed. Those clothes are not from this decade."

I said, "Right. They're probably..." I did some quick math in my head. "I'd say around fifteen years old."

"How do you know that?" he asked.

"Because it's exactly what I would have worn in high school, down to the belt."

Sterling looked at Amanda and me like we were crazy. "We're trying to catch a possible serial killer, and you two are fixated on the fact that our vic's clothing is outdated? We're the real police, not the fashion police."

Baxter rolled his eyes at his partner. "They make a good point. The killer dressed the victim a certain way either to send a specific message or to satisfy a sick fantasy." He took out his phone and pulled up the picture he'd taken of the note. "Maybe the clothes, like the poem, are another piece of his sadistic puzzle. We figure out the connection, and it might give us an idea as to who this lunatic is."

As we watched Dr. Berg and Kenny begin cutting the fishing line holding the body upright, Sterling said, "Okay, I'll bite. Let's say the killer is trying to make a point about something that happened a while ago or recreate something or someone. Maybe this vic represents a woman in his life—a wife, girlfriend, mom, or other family member. The killer went to a lot of trouble to stage this body. It's got to mean something. Read that stupid poem again."

Baxter read from his phone, " '*An innocent man went to jail that night because you decided what was wrong and right.*' "

Amanda said, "Wait. Do you have a photo of the first poem, too? If we put both of them together it might help."

Baxter scrolled back through his photos. "Here we go. The first one says: *My life was ruined by your mistakes, and now you understand how my heart aches. For your incompetence I will show no pity as I strike terror across the city.*"

I cut in, "It sounds like the killer thinks Jayne and Frank sent the wrong guy to jail. It could be the killer himself or someone close to him. Keep going."

Baxter continued, " '*Your only child is now dearly departed. An eye for an eye? I'm just getting started.*' " He scrolled to the photo of tonight's poem. " '*An innocent man went to jail that night because you decided what was wrong and right. You thought you knew. You were so sure. She died; he died. How much must a child have to endure?*' "

Sterling kicked at the ground. "Two people died, an innocent man went to jail, and a child suffered. When there are kids involved in any way in a crime, they always suffer. And every asshole in the joint will tell you he's innocent. This could literally be any case."

"How about the two people who died?" I asked.

Shrugging, he replied, "It doesn't say when or how or what relation they are to the killer. Not enough specifics to base anything on."

Baxter kept reading. "*A tooth for a tooth. Are you catching on? It won't be long before the next one's gone.*" He winced. "Anyone hear if the Doc looked in the victim's mouth yet? What do you want to bet she's missing a tooth?"

I closed my eyes, hoping that wasn't true.

Of course Sterling had to add, "And the psycho kept it for a trophy like Amy Donovan's right eye."

My stomach lurched at the mental image of the killer's "trophies."

Baxter brought the conversation back to something I could handle. "The killer seems to be pointing to a certain incident that both the Sheriff and Detective Donovan were involved in. What was it, about ten, fifteen years ago that they became partners?"

"Fourteen," I said. "She made detective when I was seventeen, and they were partners for about four years after that."

"That roughly coincides with your wardrobe timeframe." He typed something into his phone. "I'm sending this second poem to the crypto guys at the FBI field office. I hope they can glean more from this one than they did from the first one. Since the first poem referenced Detective Donovan, we've been looking into threats made on him over the years. But now that we have another piece of the puzzle, I'm going to have some deputies start combing through old case files the Sheriff and Donovan worked together, looking for any kind of similarities to these two victims or situations surrounding their deaths."

"That's going to be dozens upon dozens of cases. Maybe hundreds," Amanda said.

Sterling had grown quiet, staring off toward the front of the park. "I think I have a way to narrow it down. Have them cross-reference the cases with any that Judge Richards presided over."

"Why Judge Rich—" My jaw dropped. "Oh..."

Sterling nodded. "If this whack job is so caught up in symbolism, it makes sense he might try to get back at Judge Richards by making his fancy new park a crime scene."

Baxter's expression darkened. "Or he's sending yet another message. We'd better get someone to secure Judge Richards and his family ASAP."

6

Baxter and Sterling ran off to investigate their growing suspicions, leaving Amanda and me to worry over unanswered questions.

She frowned. "If all this symbolism stuff is for real, then we have a really crafty psycho on our hands."

"I agree," I replied, watching as Dr. Berg and Kenny wheeled Jenna's body, now zipped into a bag, out of the gazebo and toward their waiting van.

Amanda and I walked over to the entrance of the gazebo to get back to work. It was going to be a long night. Not only would I have to spend hours here at the scene collecting evidence, I'd then also have meetings to attend and lab work to do. Sleep would have to wait until tomorrow; not that I had a chance of falling asleep after everything that had happened in the past several hours.

Amanda and I put on respirator masks and new gloves, then went back into the gazebo. Our first focus was the concrete floor and anything the killer might have dropped. There was only one path of entry and exit, and out of necessity it had been used by several of us, so it was unlikely that we'd find anything that hadn't been noticed already. Dividing the small space into imaginary quadrants, we each took a section and scoured it. We both looked over each section, so the floor was examined twice. For an outdoor area, it was fairly clean. Neither of us collected anything as evidence.

Realizing I'd forgotten a key part of my usual investigative process, I hurried over to the field kit and got out a voice recorder, which I switched on and started recording. I rattled off my name and the case information I knew, then I said, "The body of the victim, Jenna Walsh, was suspended inside the gazebo of Richards Park by a clear, thin material that looks to be fishing line. The body was found in a seated position on a bench, holding a bouquet of white daisies and a note. The note and flowers have been taken as evidence. The victim was found wearing clothing and shoes I believe not to be part of her normal wardrobe, and appears to have been redressed after death. No evidence found upon examination of the floor of the gazebo."

Amanda, who had been scribbling in a notebook, pulled her mask down and gave me a smile. "Audio notes?"

"Yeah, I'm lazy. I'd rather talk to myself now and type my scene notes out later."

"I tried that, but I remember things better if I write them down." She shrugged. "To each her own."

We both stood staring at the bench where the victim had been sitting, hoping for something to jump out at us. Aside from the fishing line still hanging from the wrought iron of the gazebo and the slats of the wooden bench, there seemed to be nothing for us to collect.

Amanda set out evidence markers by the places the fishing line was tied to the bench. I took photos and continued to mumble out my case notes. We collected the fishing line and placed it into evidence bags. We then photographed, cut down, bagged, and tagged the fishing line tied to the wrought iron supports.

I got out a flashlight and a magnifying glass and kneeled down in front of the bench. Shining the light on the bench's seat, I looked for any kind of trace that could have been left behind by the killer, but found nothing. I examined the rest of the bench, again coming up empty-handed. I stood and pulled down my mask, frowning.

"Nothing?" Amanda asked.

"Nothing."

"Well, now what? Do we dust the whole bench?"

I groaned. "A public bench? I don't even want to know how many fingerprints are on this thing."

She was studying the bench with a thoughtful expression. "Well, maybe we focus on dusting the areas around where the fishing line was tied rather than, say, on the arms of the bench where people might rest their hands. That should narrow it down."

"Great idea." I gestured to the ironwork supports holding up the gazebo's roof. "You want to do that while I dust up there where the rest of the fishing line was tied?"

"Sure."

The gazebo was gorgeous and had to have cost thousands of dollars to construct. It had a copper roof, and the supports weren't simple posts. They were made of intricate, scrolled metalwork—perfect for wrapping yards and yards of fishing line around to hold up a dead body. I brushed gray fingerprint powder on the dark metal and used the magnifying glass and flashlight to search for prints. I saw nothing. I brushed on some more powder, this time fanning out to a larger area, but still got nothing from it.

I sighed. "I'm calling it—the killer wore gloves. It's freezing out here, so maybe instead of being paranoid, he was just cold and had his hands covered up. Either way, I've got nothing."

Amanda stood and placed the fingerprint paraphernalia back in the kit. "Same here. Since this isn't the primary crime scene, we're not going to find much. We'd do a lot more good by getting started examining the victim's clothes and the flowers and note. We could stay all night and look for stuff that isn't here, or we could go work on actual evidence. Jason said he'd have a couple of deputies take care of searching the parking lot and paths leading to the gazebo, so I think we're good to go."

"Let's complete a rough sketch. Then we can pack it up."

After we measured the dimensions of the gazebo and made a sketch of the scene, notating where the body and our evidence had been found, Amanda drove us to Noblesville to the sheriff's station. We checked in our evidence with the evidence clerk and then took it down the hall to the lab.

As she shrugged on her lab coat, Amanda said, "Well, at least we're in from the cold. And I'm glad I'm not the one who has to inform Jason and Nick at the pre-autopsy meeting that there's pretty much no evidence. Good luck with that."

I smiled. "Oh, come on, now. We have three whole items to process. No, wait—make that two. I forgot we're sending the fishing line to the state lab for DNA processing. Do you want the flowers or the note?"

"I'll take the pretty flowers. You take the weird note."

Chuckling, I grabbed the envelope containing the note and took it to a workstation. I donned gloves and a mask and pulled the document out of the manila envelope and the plastic sleeve. Positioning the bench magnifier over it, I gave the note a good once-over. It was handwritten in black ink, the penmanship messy but nondescript. I studied its eerie message.

An innocent man went to jail that night
    Because you decided what was wrong and right.
    You thought you knew. You were so sure.
    She died; he died. How much must a child have to endure?
    A tooth for a tooth. Are you catching on?
    It won't be long before the next one's gone.

I was glad Baxter had sent the poem over to the FBI for their crypto people to take a crack at deciphering it. I certainly didn't want to have to delve into it to figure out any hidden meanings it held.

Since we knew the message was from the killer, there was no reason for the item to be sent to the Questioned Documents examiner. It wouldn't help us to know what brand of paper it was written on or what kind of ink was used, or if there had been any alterations made to the written message. Satisfied that the only thing left to do would be to process the paper for fingerprints, I took several photos of the note. I then went to the cabinet where the chemicals were kept and got out a spray bottle of DFO, a solution that was used to develop fingerprints on paper. I sprayed the front and back of the paper, then took it to the fume hood in the corner of the lab to dry.

As I waited, I wandered over to Amanda's station. She said, "I'm loving this plastic sleeve the flowers came in. I've already swabbed some smudged prints for DNA and pulled two partials."

"Good for you. I've—"

We turned when the door opened and Baxter walked in, carrying my purse. "Ellie, Dr. Berg is ready for us at the morgue, and then we have to hurry back and meet with the team here."

"Okay," I replied, removing my lab coat. "You know, that purse does not go with your outfit."

He chuckled. "Right. You left this in my vehicle."

I took the purse from him and said over my shoulder, "Amanda, can you take over processing the note for me? I've made one application of DFO, and it's drying now."

"Consider it done," she said, grinning. "Don't have too much fun, now."

As Baxter and I walked down the hall, he asked, "Why did she tell you not to have too much fun?"

I wrinkled my nose. "Because I get the task of informing you and Sterling and the Sheriff that we found little to no evidence at the park. We have the poem, the flowers, and the fishing line. That's it. No fingerprints, no trace, no nothing."

Shrugging, he said, "That's how it goes sometimes. Maybe Dr. Berg will have something for us. Oh, and by the way, there have been new developments."

"Good or bad?"

He held the front door open for me. "One of each. After we left Ashmore, one of the search groups came back with news that two students they spoke to had seen Jenna Walsh get in a silver Toyota Corolla that pulled up near her dorm around six on Saturday night."

"Did they see who was driving or get a plate number?"

"No."

"Then how is that a good development? Silver Corollas are a dime a dozen in the US. It'll take days to go through the BMV records for Hamilton County alone." I was referring to Indiana's Bureau of Motor Vehicles.

He smiled. "Even mediocre developments are good when you have nothing. Ready for the bad one?"

"Maybe not, since you don't seem to know the difference between good and mediocre."

Baxter's boyish face grew serious. "Judge Richards's twenty-four-year-old granddaughter is missing."

I sucked in a breath. "What?"

"She went to a late movie with her coworkers, but never made it home. Her cell goes directly to voicemail, and worse, we can't find the signal to track the phone. She was last seen at eleven-thirty at the movie theater in Castleton Square Mall. Right around the time we got the call from a "concerned neighbor" about there being a dead girl in Richards Park."

That poor woman. Shaking my head, I got into his SUV. Then I had a thought. "Wait. There are no houses around the park. It faces the back side of a golf course. How could there be a 'concerned neighbor'?"

"Exactly. When we ran the phone number, it was to a pay phone—"

"Please don't say at the mall."

"At the mall."

"I told you not to say at the mall," I complained.

He gave me a rueful smile as he started his vehicle. "We're dealing with a grade-A sociopath, here. I'm afraid it could get worse before it gets better. But to tackle the situation at hand, we've got two missing persons detectives working on Michaela Richards's case and a civilian search underway, plus every law enforcement official in the county is on alert. And of course the media has caught wind of this, so it won't be long before they're comparing the victims and developing conspiracy theories of their own."

Another young woman's disappearance was a lot to process. I rubbed my temples. "I'm not sure I wanted to know all that."

"I'm only trying to keep you in the loop like you asked."

"Right. Well, at least you're treating me like a member of the team this time instead of some stupid civilian."

"You *are* a civilian, though."

I rolled my eyes. "You know what I mean."

When we arrived at the morgue, Baxter and I went inside to suit up in surgical gowns, masks, and gloves.

He asked me, "Are you ready for this?"

I tied my gown at my waist. "Considering how much the DA likes to yell when you guys have no leads on a case, not really."

Hesitating, he said, "I meant for seeing Jenna again."

By this point, I'd been around Jenna's body enough that I'd been able to disconnect the lifeless shell from the vibrant girl I'd known. That didn't mean I'd worked through my feelings about it, though. Or that I wanted to talk about it—especially with Baxter. "I'm good," I replied, and pushed past him to open the double doors to the room where the autopsy would be conducted. Sterling and District Attorney Wade McAlister were already there with Dr. Berg.

The morgue had a considerably more somber atmosphere than the last time I'd been here, which I was sure Dr. Berg preferred. He thought of the morgue as a sacred place, but during the last investigation everyone had been at each other's throats. This time, everyone seemed shell-shocked and sad. With a young woman we all knew lying there on the slab, the morgue felt especially bleak and oppressive.

Dr. Berg said, "We'll begin. The autopsy for Jenna Walsh will be at ten o'clock this morning. Detectives, as usual, one of you will need to be in attendance. As we discussed at the scene, I believe the preliminary cause of death to be exsanguination." He pointed to the three-inch gash on the left side of Jenna's neck. "Notice the laceration on the victim's neck, which did indeed sever a jugular vein. It's the only major wound on the body." He pulled back her top lip to reveal a gaping hole where her right front tooth should have been. "Her upper right central incisor was removed post-mortem." He raised one of her arms to show us the underside of her wrist, which had a band of reddish discoloration. "But note that there are a few defensive wounds on the victim's hands and arms, plus some ligature marks on her wrists and ankles. She was held against her will for a time before she was killed."

His voice grave, Baxter said, "Jenna went missing Saturday night. It's possible that she was bound and held for nearly two days before she was killed."

At the thought of Jenna being tied up by a crazy person, tears welled in my eyes before I could stop them. It was sickening to imagine what she might have had to endure in those two days. She would have been terrified and defenseless, hoping for someone to rescue her. But help never came. Based on the horror evident in their eyes, everyone in the room was thinking the same thing I was.

DA McAlister pulled down his mask and wiped a hand over his face. "This sick bastard has to be stopped. And soon. If we don't find this guy and lock him up, there's no telling who he's going to target next." I wondered if the DA was beginning to fear for his own family's safety.

Dr. Berg said, "I agree. Moving on, I've just sent the victim's clothes to the lab, so they should be there momentarily. As I believe I overheard some of you discussing at the scene, the victim was indeed cleaned and redressed after death. Ellie, you'll see this when you examine the clothing, but I wanted to point out that I found pieces of straw in the victim's boots when I removed them from her feet. That could help us pinpoint where the killer may have taken her before her death."

I nodded, afraid that if I spoke my voice would waver.

Sterling said, "If you found straw, it sounds like she may have been in a barn or on a farm. Unfortunately there's no shortage of those in the northern half of this county."

The DA grunted and turned to the detectives. "You know if you don't get a handle on this now, *before* another body turns up, the Feds will step in. And that will be a nightmare for all of us."

He was right. Three related deaths (especially with ritualistic elements) would bump our killer into the territory of serial killer. The FBI tended to take notice at that. It was possible they already had, considering that family members of local law enforcement were being targeted specifically.

"We're well aware of that, and we're doing everything we can," Sterling replied, his tone tight.

Dr. Berg cleared his throat, bringing our attention back to his report. "We've established that the park wasn't the primary crime scene. To further support that, I've noticed some lividity on the victim's back, which means she was lying flat for some time after her death. I'm assuming it was when the killer was cleaning and redressing the body. There was also some blood pooling in the feet and legs, which means she was moved to the park and posed in a sitting position within six hours of her death, when livor mortis would become fixed. Based on what I've found so far, I'm putting the time of death window between four and six PM."

Sterling had begun pacing the room as Dr. Berg was speaking. "We can't know whether the killer will keep the same timeframe from abduction to time of death that he did with Jenna Walsh, but it's safe to assume that if we don't find Michaela Richards within at least forty-eight hours, it could be too late for her."

DA McAlister spat, "Well, then why are you standing around here like an asshole? Get to work!"

Ripping off his mask, Sterling stopped pacing and faced the DA, stone-faced.

Dr. Berg cut in, "Wade, that's enough. If no one has any other questions, we can reconvene in the morning."

Sterling stalked out of the room. Grumbling, the DA followed him out.

Dr. Berg sighed and turned to Baxter and me. "You two be safe out there."

Baxter nodded. "Of course we will. See you soon."

"Goodnight, Doc," I said, feeling his troubled eyes on me as I exited the morgue.

As we removed our protective coverings and disposed of them, I noticed the same concerned look in Baxter's eyes. He said, "You okay?"

"I will be."

We exited the cold, dreary morgue, only to be hit with a biting wind as we hurried across the parking lot to Baxter's SUV. From the look of consternation on his face, I could tell he was struggling to come up with a way to insert some kind of normalcy into our situation.

"Do you feel like eating?" he finally asked.

I had a strong stomach around death, but the situation had me somewhat nauseous. However, knowing that I'd be stuck at the station the rest of the night, I figured I'd better get some food while I could. It was helpful for energy and focus to eat every few hours when pulling all-nighters.

"I guess."

He smiled. "Good. Because I lost my dinner out at the park."

I nodded knowingly. "Still got that nasty gag reflex at death scenes, huh?" Baxter vomited at first sight of a dead body. As soon as he lost the contents of his stomach, he was fine, and you'd never know he'd had a problem.

"You know me well."

7

The only dining establishment open at this ungodly hour was a twenty-four-hour fast food taco joint, so we grabbed some drive-thru on the way back to the station. After choking down part of a limp taco on the way from Baxter's SUV to the conference room, I decided eating was a bad decision in my current state of agitation and trashed the rest. What I really needed was a drink and a good night's sleep, but that wasn't going to happen tonight.

Baxter and I entered the conference room to find Sterling and Amanda with Chief Deputy Sheriff Rick Esparza. My heart sank, realizing Jayne had either been removed from this case or had excused herself. This was always *her* meeting.

I sat down next to Amanda, who gave me a pat on the arm. I returned a half-hearted smile. From Esparza, I got a head nod, which was more than I'd expected from the always-focused Chief Deputy.

Esparza said, "Okay, guys, let's do this and get back to work. We can't waste a moment on this one. Sterling, go."

Frowning, Sterling closed the file he'd been perusing. "I hate to say it, Chief, but I don't have jack shit to tell you. Without the primary crime scene, we're flying blind. And as meticulous as this guy was about staging

Jenna Walsh's body, he's going to be damn near impossible to find unless he decides he *wants* to be found."

Sterling was gruff and grumbly as a rule, but I'd never seen him with the wind out of his sails like this. The man had enough confidence for several people, plus he'd had the best case closure rate in the county for years.

Esparza stared him down. "That doesn't mean we give up, Detective."

Sterling clenched his jaw. "I'm simply saying we don't have a lot to go on."

After flicking her eyes toward Sterling for a moment, Amanda slid photos of two fingerprints and two printouts of possible AFIS fingerprint matches toward Esparza. "It isn't much, but I found the same fingerprints on the poem and on the plastic wrapping around the flowers. Unfortunately, there was no positive match to any prints in AFIS."

"Another dead end," Sterling muttered.

She went on, "For now, yes. But the good news is that these prints have to belong to the killer. They don't match Jenna Walsh's. And they couldn't be from the store clerk who sold the flowers, for example, because the only people who could possibly have come into contact with both the flowers *and* the note were the killer and Jenna."

Sterling griped, "Which again proves my earlier point. This asshole is taunting us, leaving prints he knows we can't use."

Baxter sat up straighter in his chair. "But when we finally do nail this psycho, we can tie him definitively to the crime. That's a big deal."

Nodding, Esparza said, "There you go. What else?"

Amanda said, "The killer changed the victim's clothes after he killed her. There was no visible blood on what she was wearing when she was found. And Ellie felt like the clothes didn't belong to her." Amanda passed Esparza a full-length photo of Jenna sitting on the bench at Richards Park.

"Right," I said. "The whole outfit is dated—probably about fifteen years old by my guess. It's also something Jenna would never have worn."

Baxter added, "We think the killer dressed the victim a certain way to satisfy a fantasy or to make her look like someone he knew."

"Also, Dr. Berg told us he found straw inside her boots, so there's a good possibility she'd been in a barn or at a farm at some point," I said. "Amanda, have you received the clothes from him?"

"Yes, right before this meeting. I haven't begun processing them yet," she replied.

"We also learned from Dr. Berg that the victim is missing a tooth... which had been removed after her death. And he found ligature marks on her wrists and ankles." I cleared my throat, trying to rid it of the lump that was yet again trying to form there. "It seemed to him that she'd been restrained for a while."

Amanda threw me a sympathetic glance. She knew how much this case was getting to me.

Fidgety and nervous, Sterling was not his usual cocksure self, either. "Anything pop yet from the old case files?"

Baxter frowned. "Not yet, but we've got several people on it. We have the incident reports stored electronically, but to go into the kind of detail we need, the physical case files have to be pulled. It's a lot of paperwork to wade through—it'll take some time."

Esparza had been listening quietly as we spoke, writing notes on a legal pad he'd brought with him. He put his pen down. "I think we've got more going for us than we might realize. I sat down with the Sheriff and Frank Donovan this evening. They're both distraught, obviously, but they were able to put their heads together and come up with a few cases from their time as partners that might fit with what the killer alluded to in his poems. I had your guys going through the files prioritize those cases."

Baxter nodded. "Good. Thanks, Chief. We're also compiling a list of people who own silver Toyota Corollas, which is the type of vehicle Jenna Walsh got into at six PM on Saturday night, the last time she was seen. We can cross-reference those names with the old case files we pull. And we're searching property records for anyone who owns a barn, which we can also use to narrow down a list of suspects. While we're at it, we're pulling addresses for abandoned and foreclosed properties with barns. If we get desperate, we can physically search those. I've also got an FBI cryptanalyst working on the two poems we found at the two death scenes."

After scribbling more onto his notepad, Esparza said, "Excellent work. I know it doesn't seem like we have much to go on at the moment, but it sounds like with one stroke of good luck we could get what we need to start tracking this maniac down. Where are we with surveillance footage from the mall showing the pay phone where the tip call was placed?"

Sterling shook his head, still seeming unconvinced that a clue was going to suddenly drop into our laps. "We've got someone scrubbing through it. The angle of the camera near the pay phone didn't give us a shot of the guy's face, so we're having to look through the rest of the tapes, trying to track him to a place where there's a better shot of him. Again, it's going to take time we don't have."

I said, "Speaking of phones, did the cyber guys find anything more on Jenna's cell? Based on her call log, this new boyfriend of hers called himself 'Derek.' But his number was to a burner phone."

"We called it," replied Sterling. "All we got was a preprogrammed voice-mail. No signal to be tracked. He probably tossed it already. They haven't found anything on her phone we can use."

Esparza nodded. "Okay. Well, I know you all are working your asses off on this, which the Sheriff and I appreciate. With how this whole thing is playing out, it sounds like we're going to have to stay on this for a while. Make sure to take breaks, and don't run yourselves into the ground. We need to stay sharp. If no one has anything else, then I'll let you get back to work."

We all got up quietly and exited the room. I headed straight for the restroom to splash some water on my face. I'd been close to the case I'd worked a few months ago, but it had been nothing like this. In fact, this case was dredging up unwanted memories of my mother's murder case for some reason. Even though I hadn't known the pieces of victim we'd been finding one by one had been my mother, I'd had this sick, squirmy feeling throughout the case that was eerily similar to the unease bubbling inside me at the moment. I tried to bottle it all up and push it out of my mind. But knowing I had to go to the lab and study the clothes Jenna had been wearing, I couldn't seem to completely shake it off.

Thinking some chocolate might help, I headed out of the restroom to find a vending machine. I nearly ran into Baxter, who was leaning against the wall just outside the door.

"Why are you loitering outside the ladies' room?" I asked, only half-joking.

"To give you this." He handed me a Twix, my favorite chocolate bar. "I thought you looked like you could use it."

"Since you just gave me candy, I'm not going to bring up the fact that I think it's super freaky that you can sometimes read my mind like a book. I was literally on my way to the break room just now to get a Twix."

Baxter grinned. "I'm a man of many talents. Unfortunately, one of them is not wading through old case files, which is what I'm going to be doing for the next few hours. When I get to the point where I want to eat my service pistol, would you want to go somewhere and get some breakfast? I assume the task of processing the victim's clothing is going to have a similar effect on you."

Again with the mind reading. Like the candy bar, an invitation to breakfast in the morning was a nice gesture, but I wasn't sure about sharing a meal with Baxter. I still harbored some resentment toward him. Although I could easily keep it at bay while we were working, I didn't know if I could handle being around him once I relaxed and let my guard down.

He correctly interpreted my silence. The man was three for three. Sighing, he said, "I get it that I might not be your first choice for a breakfast companion. But if I have to go with Sterling, *he* is going to be the one on the wrong end of my service pistol. The guy is driving me nuts. Do me a solid and go to breakfast with me. He won't try to come along if he knows you'll be there."

I laughed for the first time all night. "Well, since you put it that way, I guess I have to say yes, if only to save Sterling's miserable life."

When I got back to the lab, Beck was gone. I said to a bleary-eyed Amanda, who was staring at the AFIS computer in the office, "Did Beck ditch us in the middle of two active murder investigations?"

"No, although I wouldn't put it past him. Since we didn't get a ton of evidence on either case, we're trying to spread out our time and pull as few double shifts as possible. The department is convinced this is long from over, so like the Chief said, we need to save our energy while we can. Beck pulled a double on the Donovan case, so I took this one."

"Got it." I tore into my Twix and took a big bite, feeling marginally better.

Her eyebrows shot up. "Hitting the hard stuff already?"

"Had to," I mumbled. "Are the clothes still in evidence?"

"They are. I have two more fingerprints to analyze and run through AFIS, but I know they're more of the killer's prints. He has an interesting tented arch pattern. Pretty uncommon."

"Well, that should make your life easier, in the unfortunate event you have another scene to process. I hope that's not the case."

"Me, too." She stared at me for a moment before continuing. "If there are more incidences tied to these cases...will you come back and work them with us?"

I hadn't thought that far ahead. My normal answer to the "will you come back" question had always been an automatic no. But if the killer struck again and I worked the scene, it would give me another crack at finding the bastard who killed Jenna, which I wanted to do more than anything.

"Uh...maybe. Probably."

Relief washed over her face. "That would be great. I feel like I'm up for it, but I'd really like to have you by my side instead of Beck. Every time he and I go out to a scene, I get this horrible feeling he's going to miss something, which inevitably will become my problem. So I run around like a lunatic, doing my job plus looking over his shoulder. And worse, *he's* making the big bucks for being the head criminalist!"

I chuckled. "Trust me, he's not making big bucks. But I get where you're coming from. I'll see this thing through. But after that, I'm going back to being only a mild-mannered college professor."

"I'll take what I can get."

I headed over to see the evidence clerk and checked out the clothes Jenna had been wearing when she'd been found. After I brought them back to the lab, Amanda and I divided them up and began our examinations.

I took the white peasant top out of the paper bag and laid it out on my workstation. In the bright lighting of the lab, the top wasn't as white as it seemed. It certainly wasn't a new garment. The fabric was yellowed around the inside of the neckline and at the armpits. The multicolored embroidery pattern across the front of the shirt was picked and unraveling from wear. I didn't find any hairs or fibers on it—not that I'd expected to. Dr. Berg would have found and removed any trace during his initial examination. Like we'd noticed at the scene, there was no visible sign of blood on the garment. That didn't mean there hadn't been blood on it at one time. It could have been bleached away, but the shirt smelled musty and like it hadn't been washed in a long time. There could have been other bodily fluids on it, though, like saliva or semen or sweat, any of which could have belonged to the killer.

I went to one of the cabinets along the wall and found a UV light. I turned out the light over my worktable as well as the overhead lights in my end of the lab. After changing into a new pair of gloves, I shined the UV light on the shirt. A couple of smudges illuminated slightly, which I thought could have been swipes of sweat or saliva. After examining the front and back of the shirt, I circled the area of the stains with a Sharpie, cut out pieces of them, and placed the sample pieces in separate small manila envelopes. I filled out an evidence tag for each as well as a lab request form for the DNA analysts at the Indiana State Police lab in Indianapolis.

Our lab didn't begin to have the equipment necessary to process DNA or anything much beyond fingerprints, so we sent out most of our evidence to the state lab. With the ever-present backlog of every law enforcement lab in the country, it would take close to a month to get the results back. This evidence wouldn't necessarily point us toward a suspect, assuming our killer was even in CODIS, the Combined DNA Index System, which I doubted, since his fingerprints weren't in AFIS. However, it could turn out to be the concrete evidence we'd need at trial to tie the killer to the victim.

I repackaged the garment and sealed the evidence bag again. After stripping off my gloves, I turned the lights back on and began examining the boots. I noticed that Amanda was now working on the underwear. We would both have to process each piece of clothing to check each other's work, and although I hated to ask, I needed to know what I was getting into so I had time to mentally prepare before I began my examination of the underwear. Sexual assault had been a worry in the back of my mind, which would probably continue to nag at me until I learned the results of the autopsy examination.

I cleared my throat. "Um...did you find any evidence of..."

Amanda looked up from what she was doing. "I know what you're thinking, and you can relax. I did an acid phosphatase test, and there's no semen here. Unless he used a condom, I don't think Jenna was raped."

I smiled. "That's at least some good news."

"However, I'll warn you the underwear is pretty bad otherwise. I'm thinking she may have had them on for a while during the time he was holding her prisoner, and also probably when she died. There are stains on top of stains. It's an awful thought, but not as bad as sexual assault."

"Right."

My spirits lifted somewhat, I set the leather boots out on my workstation and examined them the exact same way I did the shirt. As Dr. Berg had mentioned, there was straw inside the boots, which I removed with tweezers, placed in a plastic pillbox, and labeled. On the outside of the boots, I saw a few visible stains, which were likely from normal wear. (Not Jenna's normal wear, as I assumed the killer got these boots secondhand, like the peasant top.) Nothing illuminated when I used the UV light on the boots. But there could be fingerprints.

Lifting viable fingerprints off the soft leather would be a challenge, but it was one I was more than willing to take on. In the areas where the leather was smooth and devoid of decorative stitching, I dusted with black fingerprint powder. Then I put the boots under the bench magnifier to take a look.

I let out a little yelp as I found what seemed to be a decent print.

Amanda popped her head up from what she was doing. "Was that a good noise or a bad noise?"

"You said our killer's prints are tented arches, right?

"Right."

I sucked in a breath. "Then it's a fantastic noise. I've got a tented arch on this boot, if I can get it off."

Her eyes lit up. "Ooh! Do we get to use Mikrosil?"

"That was my next move."

She abandoned her workstation and watched as I squeezed some gooey white Mikrosil silicon base out of a tube and then added the hardener out of a smaller tube.

"Don't you just love playing with the Mikrosil? It's so much more fun than straight tape lifting," she said.

"I agree."

Mikrosil is a silicone casting material used to make casts of small tool mark impressions and also for pulling latent fingerprints from curved surfaces where tape lifts don't work well. In this case, the fingerprint was on the toe of the boot, which I could never get a piece of flat tape to smooth out over. Plus leather was already a difficult surface to pull fingerprints from, so Mikrosil was a better choice, anyway.

I mixed the base and hardener together with a clean wooden stick and applied the resulting material over the fingerprint I'd found. The Mikrosil would harden in about twenty minutes into a putty-like consistency, and when I peeled it off, it would bring the fingerprint dust with it.

Rather than literally watching something dry, I set the boots aside and went for the bra Jenna had been wearing. It was a beautiful, lacy thing from Victoria's Secret, and seemed to match the underwear Amanda had already processed. I wondered if Jenna had bought the set purposely for what was supposed to be a romantic weekend getaway. I couldn't even imagine how she must have felt when she realized her fantasy weekend was turning into a nightmare.

The left shoulder strap of the bra was stained dark brown from what I assumed was blood. It made sense, considering the wound on Jenna's neck was on the left side. I knew it was more than likely Jenna's blood, but it still had to be processed, so I moistened the tip of a swab with distilled water and rubbed it over the strap. The swab came back tinged with blood, and I placed it out of sight in a cardboard swab box to dry. I didn't plan on sending the sample to the lab for DNA analysis, but at least the evidence was there if needed.

The idea of sexual assault still weighing heavily on my mind, I turned the bra inside out and shut the lights out over my workstation. With a UV light, I searched the surface of the inside of the bra cup carefully. Saliva stains would fluoresce under UV rays, and while the presence of saliva wouldn't prove sexual assault, it could prove that some kind of sexual activity had gone on, and it could prove who had done it. When I found no signs of any stains, I breathed a sigh of relief. It bothered me enough that Jenna had been held against her will and killed, but adding additional assault to that, especially sexual, made me feel ill, and worse—vengeful. I had to keep a cool head through this, or I could miss key evidence.

I repackaged the bra and went back to take a look at the Mikrosil on the boots. "Hey, Amanda. It's time to peel off the Mikrosil. You want the honors?"

She grinned. "You know I do." After changing her gloves, she came over to my workstation and picked up the boot, gently peeling back the silicon cast. She held it out to me. "It's perfect. And I know from looking it's that bastard's print. Want me to go run it through AFIS and make it official?"

I glanced at the door, which had just opened. A weary-looking Baxter ambled through, giving me a tired wave. To Amanda, I said, "Yes, if you don't mind. You're going off shift at seven, right?"

She nodded. "Yes. Finally home to sleep. Beck should be getting here around then."

"Looks like I'm going to breakfast now, then I'll come back. I can't say I'm looking forward to alone time in the lab with Beck."

Amanda snorted. "No, I can't imagine so. Enjoy your breakfast."

As she headed to the office to run the print, I said to Baxter, "Give me two minutes."

He leaned against the doorframe. "Take your time."

I repackaged the boots and bra and resealed the bags they'd come in. After ditching my gloves, lab coat, and mask, I hurried to grab my purse and met Baxter at the door.

"Have any good news for me?" he asked as we walked down the hall.

"Sort of. We know that the same person handled the poem, the flowers, and the boots Jenna was wearing."

"And I assume the bad news is that you still don't know who that person is."

"Correct. But when you catch the guy, we can at least tie him to the crime."

Baxter stopped before we reached the front door of the station and turned to me. "Would you rather talk here about the case or discuss it over breakfast? If you're needing breakfast to be a total break from everything, I can certainly respect that."

It would be nice to have a break from thinking about the case, but it was also one topic I knew I could handle talking about with him. If we didn't talk about the case, I felt like our conversation could easily veer into some personal territory I wasn't up to hashing out with him just yet. I did want to put our previous argument behind us for good, but this morning was not the proper time to get into it for either of us.

I shook my head. "It's fine to discuss the case. I think we need to focus on it as much as humanly possible right now." We began walking again, out into the cold morning air. It was six AM and the sun wasn't even thinking about rising yet. "Any news on Judge Richards's granddaughter?"

His face fell. "No." We got into his vehicle, and after a moment, he admitted quietly, "And it's really starting to get to me."

My heart wrenched. This was what made Baxter such an excellent detective—his empathy for the victim and his all-consuming drive to see justice served. The problem was that sometimes he beat himself up when progress was not being made to his liking.

I reached out and laid a hand on his arm. "I can see that, and I get it. I want to nail this sick son of a bitch as much as anyone, and all the dead ends are frustrating. We'll get him, though. I'm sure of it."

He pulled his arm away and started the car. "Right. I just hope we find him before it's too late for another young woman."

8

We rode in silence to Mabel's Coffeeshop, where we'd gone one early morning after our last all-night investigation. Mabel's was old and dingy, in a rundown building in downtown Noblesville. But you couldn't beat the omelets or the coffee, or the fact that it was always open early.

They'd made a sad attempt at Christmas decorations. There were colored twinkle lights haphazardly nailed up around every window. Limp strands of red tinsel garland were strung around from one stained ceiling tile to another so unevenly that it had to have been done by a drunken person. The ancient wood paneled walls were dotted with yellowed cardboard cutouts of Santas, angels, and snowmen like the ones that had adorned my elementary school classrooms.

Baxter glanced around, clearly underwhelmed by the décor as well. "Merry effing Christmas," he muttered under his breath as we slid into the cracked pleather booth.

I had to admit, the place mirrored both our moods. The holiday season, which should have been joyous and filled with fun and excitement, was always covered with a shroud when there was any kind of death investigation to contend with. I'd forgotten about that part of the job since I'd made the move to teaching.

After we'd placed our order, Baxter said, "Sterling and I have spent the night wading through the case files the Sheriff and Frank suggested we should look over." He ran his hands through his dark blond hair. "We've come up with a lot of nothing. There are no similarities between these deaths and the old cases. The causes of death are different than the ones our victims suffered. The situations are different. Not all the victims are even women. There were only a couple of cases where children were involved, and the kids weren't harmed in any way and didn't have to 'endure' anything like the second poem said, aside maybe from a parent being put in jail." He shook his head. "I don't get it."

I thought for a moment. "How about the vehicle or the barn? Did you find any BMV or property records tying anyone involved in those cases to a silver Corolla or a farm in the area?"

"No. And most of the people don't even live around here anymore. A few of them are locked up, so that leaves even fewer possibilities. I feel like I've wasted my night."

Our waitress brought our food—two steaming stuffed omelets with a greasy side of hash browns.

As we dug into our breakfasts, I said, "I understand. While we did get some fingerprints, they're useless until you have a suspect to compare them to. We can collect all the evidence we want, but if it doesn't point us in the right direction, we might as well have nothing."

Around a mouthful of eggs, Baxter said, "The guys watching the surveillance tape from the mall assure me they'll have some kind of better footage of the guy soon so we can try to ID him." He swallowed. "They have a pretty far away clip of a guy talking to a woman in the parking lot. She collapses against him, and he helps her into his car and drives off. It took him only seconds to abduct her."

I sucked in a breath. "Is the car a silver Corolla?"

"Yes."

"So you have footage of the killer kidnapping Michaela Richards? That's fantastic. Did it show a license plate?"

"It did. That plate was reported stolen last week."

My shoulders slumped. "Ugh. Smart. Masking a stolen car with a different stolen plate."

"Exactly. I'm telling you—this guy has thought of everything."

"He clearly knows he's not in AFIS or CODIS, because he's leaving fingerprints for us to find. That's arrogance at its best. He's assuming we'll never catch him." I was beginning to have the sinking feeling that I wasn't smart enough to outwit this guy. I hoped someone was.

"I agree. He took a big risk by holding Jenna Walsh for so long before he killed her. Maybe wherever he's holed up is so remote that there's no chance he'll be stumbled on."

"True. You know, he'd promised her a romantic weekend vacation. I wonder at what point it turned. I mean, did he immediately kidnap her at six PM on Saturday night, or did he keep up the charade for a while?"

Baxter regarded me for a moment. "You're worried about what she had to endure in those forty-eight hours, aren't you?"

I sighed. "Yes. Amanda didn't find any signs of sexual assault on the underwear Jenna was wearing." I wrinkled my forehead and added, "Not that you could tell a whole lot from it. For as much detail as the guy went into to pose her and redress her, he steered clear of cleaning up the inevitable bowel mess."

Baxter had just shoveled a forkful of hash browns into his mouth. He groaned and swallowed hard. "Come on. No shit talk at breakfast, Ellie."

"Sorry. Nate is nearly four and hasn't quite mastered the art of potty training. Human waste no longer fazes me."

"Well, it fazes me, so can we talk about something else until I'm done with my food?"

I shrugged and took a big bite of my omelet. "Whatever," I mumbled.

His phone beeped, and he put his fork down to scroll the screen. "Hallelujah. We have a photo of that bastard's face. Finally. Now all we need to do is find someone who can ID him."

He turned his phone toward me, and when I saw the grainy image of the young man on the screen, I dropped my fork.

"Uh..." I breathed. "I think you've found her." My heart hammered in my chest, and suddenly I felt light-headed.

Baxter leaned across the table. "Are you saying you know this guy? Who is it?"

"I... His name is Hunter Parsons. He's an Ashmore student... Seemed to be a nice enough kid..." I trailed off, totally in shock.

"You're sure."

"Um...yeah. He's wearing the same coat, hat, and glasses he had on when I met him, and that's definitely his scruffy beard and hair."

While I was talking, Baxter had slid out of the booth, tossed some bills onto the table, and had his phone out, speaking to someone. Grabbing me by the arm, he dragged me out of the booth and out of the coffeeshop. Before I could get my bearings, he had me in his SUV, lights and siren on, and we were speeding toward Carmel.

I finally got a grip on myself enough to register what he was saying into the phone. He was speaking to Sterling, ordering him to mobilize the entire county and meet at Ashmore to apprehend Hunter.

Once he'd hung up, he turned to me, his face ashen. "You've met this guy? How do you know him? Is he a student in one of your classes?"

"No, he's not one of my students. He interviewed me for the *Ashmore Voice*. He said it was an audition of sorts to get a position. That he wasn't part of the staff yet but if he did a good job, he was in."

Baxter's knuckles were white on the steering wheel. "When was this?"

"Monday afternoon. Right before... Oh, no. No, no—" My breath caught, and I covered my face with my hands.

"Right before you found Jenna's phone."

I looked over at him, dread filling me. "Yes."

Baxter started rapid-firing questions at me. "What did he ask you about? Did he say anything about Jenna Walsh or Amy Donovan? What did he want to know?"

"He, um...he didn't want to talk about the last case we worked on, which is what I've been interviewed about *ad nauseam* for months. He wanted to know what it was like when I worked as a criminalist for the county. He wanted to know why I made the switch to teaching and whether or not I missed fieldwork. He made no mention of any specific cases. There was no actual story. It was almost more of a biographical puff piece on me."

He said quietly, "He was profiling you."

I closed my eyes. I was clearly not smart enough to take this guy on. "Damn it."

"There was no way you could have known."

"Why me, though? I was in high school and college while Jayne and

Frank were partners. I had no possible way of being involved in any of their cases."

He thought for a moment. "But did you talk about the Sheriff being like a second mom to you and all the mentoring she's done for you?"

I nodded slowly. "I did. Do you think he was planning to use me to be another way to get to Jayne?"

"I'd say it's a good possibility. Think about it—you've been surrounded by law enforcement ever since you spoke to him. What if he was planning to nab you instead of Michaela Richards, but he couldn't get to you so he had to go with his plan B?"

Ice washed through my veins. "I don't think I want to think about that."

He clenched his jaw. "Me either. Until we catch this guy, you're not leaving my sight. Got it?"

I nodded. I wasn't going to give him any lip about that.

"Are your sister and nephew at home?"

"No. Rachel is staying on campus with Jenna's roommate, and Nate is with my stepdad."

"Good. Let's keep it that way. For the time being, I think that setup will be safer for both of them."

With shaking fingers, I texted Rachel and David and relayed Baxter's orders as well as I could. There was no way I could speak to either of them without breaking down, so I took the easy way out. By the time I was finished, we were screeching into the parking lot near the Ashmore Student Center, where there were already several other law enforcement vehicles waiting.

Baxter hopped out of his vehicle and went to confer with a group of deputies standing on the sidewalk. I felt sick. I had sat and chatted with a murderer, completely oblivious to the fact that he was in my office trying to glean information about me. I'd been out of the game too long, and my radar for danger was rusty.

I got a text from Baxter: *We need you over here.*

Willing myself to keep it together and focus on the case rather than the pity party I was throwing for myself, I got out of the SUV and joined Baxter and the deputies.

Baxter had taken charge and had already given out assigned tasks. He asked me, "How do we find out where Hunter Parsons lives?"

"The Residence Life office should have that information. They're located in the administration building on the third floor."

"What about his class schedule?"

"Registrar. Administration building, first floor."

Baxter turned to address the deputies. "You heard her. Fan out across campus and find this son of a bitch. I want updates every fifteen minutes."

The deputies scattered, leaving the two of us alone.

"What do we do?" I asked.

A slight smirk played at the corner of his mouth. "I figured we'd talk to the *Voice* staff since we know them so well. See what they know about Hunter Parsons."

I couldn't help but smile a little. During our last investigation, Baxter and I had had an interesting afternoon interviewing the quirky staff members of the campus newspaper.

"Since Hunter wasn't on staff yet, I doubt many of them know him too well. I take it he talked to Al Nishimura, though. We could start with him. Any idea where he lives?"

"Unfortunately, yes. In addition to his duties at the *Voice*, he's the president of the Betas, so he lives at the Beta house."

"Al's a frat boy? How did I not sense that last time, brah?" When I didn't react to his joke, Baxter threw his arm around my shoulder and steered me north toward Fraternity Row. "Come on, old Al's always good for a laugh. You and I could both use one."

"What the hell? Zane, that better not be your dumb ass pounding on my freakin' door this early!"

Baxter and I exchanged an amused glance as we waited outside Al Nishimura's room in the Beta house. The hallway reeked of a blend of beer, puke, weed, sweat, and cheap cologne, the signature stench of frat houses everywhere. I preferred the scent of a death scene to this one.

Finally, the door opened, and a shirtless Al Nishimura blinked at us through bleary eyes. Once recognition dawned on him, he exclaimed, "Hey! If it isn't my favorite detective and the lovely Professor Matthews." He held out his hand to Baxter. "Long time no see. How's it hangin', brah?"

Baxter's mouth twitched as he shook Al's hand. "I'm good, thanks. We have a few questions for you."

Al crossed his arms over his scrawny chest and leaned against the doorframe. "Shoot."

I said, "Yesterday I was interviewed—*again*—for the *Voice*. This time it was by a student named Hunter Parsons. He said you'd told him that if his story was good, you'd give him a staff position."

Al stared at me. "Who?"

"Hunter Parsons. He said specifically that 'Al Nishimura said' I'd be cool with him interviewing me."

He still seemed flummoxed. "You made it super clear that you were done with interviews when you came into the *Voice* office last week and yelled at me. I'm not stupid enough to send any more of my crew to bother you of all people."

Baxter covered up a snort as he got out his phone. He showed the screen to Al. "This is the guy she's talking about."

Al squinted at the photo of Hunter and shook his head. "I'm really sorry, brah. I don't think I've ever seen this guy before. And I definitely don't know any dudes named Hunter Parsons. Honest."

I glanced up at Baxter, whose face had suddenly grown dark. Finding Hunter may have just gotten complicated.

Baxter said to Al, "I know the photo's not the best, but you're sure you've never seen this guy around campus? Not once?"

I chimed in, "Maybe using the name Derek?"

Al looked at the screen again. "No, I'm sorry. He doesn't look familiar to me. And I know practically everyone."

Baxter nodded, his jaw set. "Okay. Thanks for your time, Al."

"No probs. Hey, why are you looking for this Hunter Parsons kid anyway?" His face grew serious. "Does it have to do with Jenna Walsh's death?"

Baxter regarded him for a moment. "I tell you what—I'll give you an exclusive interview with me tomorrow if you do me a favor today."

Al's eyes bulged out. "Shit, yeah. Anything."

"I want this photo and Hunter Parsons's name and description plastered over every *Voice* news vehicle you have at your discretion. Someone has to know him."

Al nodded. "Text me the deets. I'll make it happen."

Baxter and Al exchanged contact information, and then we were on our way. Once we got outside the frat house, Baxter pulled me aside.

"We are dealing with a slippery sociopath here."

"I know. Nick, I don't like this."

He frowned. "I don't either. I think we've been fooled. Again. What do you want to bet Hunter Parsons doesn't even exist?" He shook his head and got out his phone. Walking a few steps away from me, he made a call.

I didn't know what to feel about this new turn of events besides despair. "Hunter" had done his homework. He knew all the right things to say and dropped the right name to get me to talk with him, and then he'd vanished like a ghost. For all we knew, he'd never even been on campus except to pick up Jenna on Saturday night and on Monday afternoon to interview me, which would have given him ample opportunity to discard Jenna's phone near the library. With all the activity going on at any given time on campus, he could have slipped around virtually unnoticed.

I heard Baxter let out a string of expletives before he turned back around with a hard expression on his face.

I winced. "More bad news?"

He stomped over to me. "Yeah, you could say that. The damn Feds have sent in an agent to oversee our investigation. That ought to guarantee Michaela Richards will never be heard from again." He gave a swift kick to the nearest object, a metal trash can, knocking it over and sending the contents spilling out onto the ground. It wasn't often that laid-back Nick Baxter lost his cool.

I understood and agreed completely, though. The FBI had a way of taking over and bringing an investigation to a screeching halt. Not only was it an ego thing between the two departments (the lowly Sheriff's department was seen as not "good" enough to solve the case), but it was also a red tape thing. With more people and agencies in the mix, the paperwork and meetings increased, which wasted precious time. If Baxter was this angry, Sterling was going to have an aneurism.

"Let's go back," Baxter muttered, heading toward the center of campus. "Neither Residence Life nor the registrar has a record of Hunter Parsons. We're wasting time here. Except... When 'Hunter' came to your office, did he touch anything?"

Yesterday afternoon seemed like an age ago, but when I thought back, I remembered him picking up an award on my desk. "Yes..." I blew out a disgusted breath. "And now that I know what I know, I think he did it on purpose to leave his prints."

9

I unlocked my office, thinking that when I'd done this only yesterday morning, I hadn't had a care in the world. I hadn't yet heard that Jenna was missing. I hadn't seen Baxter and dredged up all those uncomfortable memories. I hadn't seen sweet young Jenna dead at the hands of a mad man, and Jayne crumple in front of my eyes. When I walked in, my thoughts zeroed in on the fact that comfort was only feet away, hidden inside my desk. It might as well have been miles away with Baxter watching my every move.

Baxter had retrieved a crime scene kit from one of the deputies and brought it along. His eyes fell on the award sitting on my desk. "That the one?"

"Yes, that's it. He purposely picked it up to look at it."

Baxter set the case down on the floor and stepped back. "I'll let you do your thing. Restroom is which way?"

Well, that was a stroke of luck in my otherwise shitty day. "Left and then another left."

"Lock the door behind me."

Gladly. I locked the door, and the first thing I did was to go for the vodka and take a long swig straight from the bottle. The burn in my throat was like a welcome friend, and I felt instant calm as it warmed my stomach.

Now I could deal with anything. I swished and swallowed strong mouth-wash and stuffed a handful of red-hot cinnamon candies in my mouth from an open bag in my desk.

Sufficiently relaxed, I opened the kit and donned a pair of gloves, then got out the magnetic fingerprint powder and applicator. Regular fingerprint powder was best, but in this case, it would make a giant mess all over my desk, and I would have to be the one to clean it. I picked up my engraved award and set a piece of clean paper under it to catch any errant powder, then got out a magnifying glass and a flashlight to look for fingerprints. Luckily, the clear glass this thing was made of showed even the slightest smudge, and because of that, I was forever having to wipe it down when anyone happened to pick it up. Hunter was the last person to have touched it.

I spotted a perfect latent thumbprint on the front of the award, almost as if he'd intended to put it there, which he probably had. It was again one of those unusual tented arches like the ones I'd found on the evidence from last night's crime scene. He was our guy.

My stomach suddenly plummeted, and I broke out in a sweat. I'd had the killer in this office and hadn't had a damn clue. How could I have sat and chatted with him and had no inkling he had a murderous dark side? I didn't think I was going to be able to forgive myself for missing something like that.

Wiping my brow with my forearm, I managed to stop berating myself long enough to focus my energy on the task at hand. After brushing on some fingerprint powder, I was about ready to do a tape lift when a knock on my door startled me. I carefully set down the award and let Baxter in.

He took one look at me and asked, "What's wrong?"

"Hunter Parsons is our killer. I'm sure of it. I found his fingerprint on my award."

"Don't you have to do a little more than eyeball it to make that kind of blanket statement?"

I frowned. "Damn it, Baxter. I've stared at his prints all night long. This is it."

He held up his hands. "Okay, I believe you."

Turning my back on him, I returned to my task, smoothing the lift tape over the fingerprint. After making sure there were no air bubbles, I slowly pulled the tape off and secured it to the card. It was a good print.

I handed it to Baxter. "There you go. I hope you've got a brilliant idea up your sleeve as to how to find this guy. I feel officially outsmarted."

"I think our next step is to go to the media. I've already set the *Voice* in motion, so if we can get the local media to run the photo, we might be able to find someone who knows him. Someone has to. By the way, I want you to sit down with a sketch artist this morning. That photo is all we have, and I'm afraid it's too grainy to be of much use on TV. I want a composite sketch, too."

I looked at my watch. "When? I have class in thirty minutes."

He stared at me. "Seriously? We're going to do this again? Get a sub or cancel."

Frowning, I replied, "I'm sorry my career is getting in your way, Detective. Finals are next week, and I can't be cancelling classes."

Baxter wiped a hand down his face. "What's your schedule like this morning?"

"I have an hour break at ten."

"Okay, I'll see if the sketch artist can come to you. You're a real pain in the ass sometimes, you know that?"

"Back at ya."

He rolled his eyes. "Anyway, I meant what I said before about keeping an eye on you until we catch our killer. But I have things to do, so if you insist on staying here, I'm going to have to assign a deputy to you."

I hated to have an officer of the law waste time babysitting me when there was a young woman in real danger. "I don't think it's necessary if I'm only going to be here on campus. Hunter isn't going to show his face at Ashmore once the *Voice* starts running his photo. It's too risky."

"I'm not putting anything past this guy. But more importantly, your safety is non-negotiable to me."

I didn't quite know how to respond to that, so I busied myself with bagging up the award and scribbling information on the evidence tag. "Oh," was my noncommittal response. I handed him the bag. "I guess if you're going back now, you should take this to evidence."

"Sure. Now stay put and lock the door. A deputy will be here shortly."

I nodded. "Okay."

"When you're done with your classes, you'll need to come back to the station." He frowned. "We all have to meet individually with the Fed today."

I let out a disgusted snort. "Talk about a pain in the ass."

With a wry grin, Baxter said, "I'll see you soon. Stay safe, please."

⸺

The class I had fought so hard to teach didn't turn out as well as I'd hoped. It was supposed to be the first part of the final review for my Intro to Criminalistics class. I had everything I was going to go over on a PowerPoint presentation, but for some reason I couldn't keep my mind on the material.

I wasn't the only one. My students were not much better off than I was. Some looked haggard, I assumed from participating in the late-night search. Some were downright distraught—pale and sickly-looking. Jenna Walsh's death had hit campus hard, especially on the heels of the last string of student deaths these poor kids had had to deal with. It was all too much, and it was dredging up old fears. It also didn't help that there was a Hamilton County sheriff's deputy sitting in the back of my classroom.

About halfway through the review, I couldn't take it anymore. "Guys, I feel your pain. Jenna Walsh was a close friend of mine and of my sister's. She was like family to us. I know this is hard, especially since it's probably also bringing up bad memories from earlier in the semester. I understand that your heads are somewhere else." I sighed. "Unfortunately for you, this couldn't have occurred at a worse time. Finals are going to happen, whether we're ready for them or not. And I don't want you to ruin the grades you've worked so hard for all semester with one test. Please, if you're grieving, scared, or upset in any way, get help now. Go to your RAs, and they'll point you in the right direction. Work through it as well as you can. Get your mind healthy so you can get through next week. Most of you are freshman, and you're probably already overwhelmed at the thought of your first round of finals. It's going to be a difficult week. But it'll be much more difficult if you don't make the effort to pull yourselves together so you're clear-headed enough to study. Like I always say, emotional control is one of the most important skills you can have as a criminalist. This is one of those times when it's essential."

I heard some murmurs and groans, and one student raised her hand. After I called on her, she asked, "How do you develop emotional control? Don't you have to be born with it, at least a little?"

I shrugged. "I suppose it helps to have some natural tendencies to keep your emotions in check. Not everyone has the self-control to stay calm in difficult situations. I would say that you should first find a thought that centers you. Focus on something that makes you happy or comforted and try not to let the negative thoughts take hold."

She replied, "But isn't that basically pushing your real feelings aside? Isn't that unhealthy?"

My young students never seemed to shy away from showing how they really felt about a situation, which I often found grating.

"Yes and no. Part of being a functioning adult is not letting every little problem derail your walk through life. At the same time, you shouldn't always bottle up your feelings. Emotional control is about picking and choosing the times to be strong and the times it's okay to let go. When you're on the job, you do what you have to do to stay strong, even at your own psychological expense. Otherwise, you're doing a disservice to the victims, their families, your fellow law enforcement officers, and the law itself."

Another student raised his hand. "Did you work Jenna's...the murder scene last night?"

"Yes."

"If she was so close to you, how are you even functioning this morning after doing that?"

I hated to ever speak about personal matters with my classes, but this was one that pertained to their future professions, and they needed a dose of real-life experience. "I know you're going to have mixed feelings about this, but I'm going to tell you the truth. The Sheriff, Jenna's aunt, is one of my closest friends. She asked me to work the scene because she trusts me. I couldn't let her down, and I couldn't let Jenna down." I blew out a breath. "So, I detached myself from my relationship to Jenna. I tried to only refer to her and think of her as 'the victim' while I was on the scene. I focused on the science of the case, not the emotional side. I did the job—that's it. My co-workers knew better than to give me too much in the way of condolences. They went on like it was business as usual, which helped me to stay focused. When my job is done, I will allow myself to grieve. But until then, I owe it to Jenna and her family to put my feelings aside so I can do my part to catch her killer."

One of the students in the front row raised his hand. "Isn't this way of thinking what turns so many law enforcement workers to substance abuse? And doesn't it also cause astronomically high statistics of depression in the field?"

"Yes, absolutely."

"Then why has no one come up with a better way of managing the psychological impact of violence?"

"I'd love it if someone would, but I don't know if it's possible given the millions of different ways human beings deal with stressors. In the meantime, when we are tasked with processing a brutal, gruesome death scene, we get through it any way we can. If you're going to work in law enforcement, you have to make a commitment to put the safety and welfare of others before your own—physical *and* emotional. If you're more worried about yourself than about others and the greater good, this profession isn't for you. Honestly, if you can't manage to put aside your personal feelings in order to get through your finals—which is your 'job' as a student—maybe it's time to start thinking about a new major."

That comment got me a lot of grumbling. They always hated it when I said it, but why waste four years and a couple hundred thousand dollars only to find out that you can't stomach the only thing you're qualified to do? I knew from experience that it was heart-breaking to give up the career you'd built your life around. If I'd known at eighteen what I knew now, I might have chosen a different path.

I glanced at the clock. "We only have a few minutes left, so let's try to get through the review of the chapter on trace evidence."

The sketch artist was waiting at my office when I finished class. Called in from the Indianapolis Metropolitan Police Department, Officer Charlotte Mains was an older woman about Jayne's age. She reminded me of Jayne quite a lot in her rigid stature and determined expression. But once we got inside my office (with my assigned deputy staying outside to guard the door), she was as kind and soft as she could be, taking time to introduce herself and get to know me.

After asking me a few general questions about Hunter's appearance, she began sketching a generic face. It was amazing to watch her hand as it moved quickly across the paper. I'd never had any dealings with a sketch artist before, but she made it a painless experience.

"What was the one facial feature that stood out about him?"

I thought for a moment. "I guess his eyes. They seemed big and...soulful, for lack of a better word. He was wearing glasses, though, so maybe they were magnified or something."

"Was the iris part of his eye large or was it his entire eyeball that you thought was large?" Charlotte asked.

"The iris. His eyes are dark brown, and the iris seemed to take up most of his eyeball. Eyes you could get lost in...if he weren't a deranged sociopath."

"That's a good description," she replied, her hand again zipping across the page, making seemingly random strokes that suddenly came together as a set of deep, bewitching eyes.

I stared at her drawing. "No, *you're* good. That's really close."

"What do I need to tweak?"

"His eyes are a little farther apart. The bridge of his nose is kind of wide in between."

She made that change. "Better?"

"Yes."

"Okay, then. Let's move out from there. Glasses, eyebrows, and nose are next."

I kept describing Hunter's features, and Charlotte kept drawing. She never seemed to mind when I'd make a mistake and had to have her erase and redraw.

Once she had the facial features pretty well finished, she asked, "How about his hair?"

"Dark brown, curly. Kind of longish, I think. It stuck out a good couple of inches all around the beanie hat he was wearing."

She nodded and kept sketching. After a few minutes she said, "You said something about a beard. Short or long?"

"Probably about an inch long. Not too well groomed."

Charlotte made a few more strokes, then began shading in areas of the face. Suddenly Hunter Parsons came to life on the page.

"Oh, shit," I breathed.

She smiled sympathetically. "I take it I got him?"

I nodded. "Spot on." It was creepy to see our killer staring back at me, looking like the seemingly sweet kid he'd pretended to be when I met him.

She put her pencil down. "If you're happy with this, I'll get it to Detective Baxter. Then we can only hope that between this sketch and the photo that someone will recognize who he really is." Standing, she held out her hand. "It was nice to meet you, Ellie. I hope your investigation goes well."

"Thank you, and thanks for your help." She left me alone with my thoughts, haunted by the big soulful eyes of Hunter Parsons, murderer.

10

In the few minutes I had before my next class, I checked in on Rachel and on Nate, who seemed to be doing as well as could be expected, given the circumstances. We hadn't told Nate about Jenna and didn't have a clue how to begin. But he could sense that something was off from the fact that his mom had suddenly shipped him off to David's house. Even though David had only been married to our mother for a short time many years ago, he made it a point to be a father figure to us throughout our lives. He regularly did things with Nate, and the two were as close as any grandfather and grandson. However, Rachel did not make it a habit to go this long without seeing her son. The boy might have only been three, but he could pick up on the wrong kind of vibes coming from his mommy.

I had wondered when I would hit a wall of exhaustion after being awake for over twenty-four hours, and I'd just found it. After I hung up with David, I had to all but drag myself to the staff lounge for a cup of coffee. On the way, I ran into my friend, Dr. Samantha Jordan, who was an anthropology professor at Ashmore.

"Ellie!" she exclaimed. "I was coming to check on you." She swept me into a hug. "I'm so sorry about Jenna. I just heard."

"Thanks, Sam."

She let me go and held me at arm's length to search my face. "Tell me you didn't work the scene."

"I did."

"Oh, sweetie," she said, pulling me in for another hug. "That had to have been awful. How are you holding up?"

"I would be better if I could get some coffee," I said pointedly.

She released me and put on an apologetic face. "Sorry. I forget you're a no-sympathy gal."

As we walked, I said, "Rachel is not doing well. They were very close."

Sam's face crumpled. "Poor thing. I didn't even think about that. I'd be happy to watch Nate if you're spending your free time at the station and she needs some time to herself."

I smiled. "Thank you. We might take you up on that."

She glanced behind us, where my faithful deputy was following along about twenty steps back. "What's with the beefy tagalong?"

I hated this part. Samantha was my closest girlfriend, but I couldn't tell her a damn thing about the case. "Long story."

Her eyes widened. "Are you in danger?"

"No..." I walked ahead of her into the lounge and started pouring my coffee.

Sam didn't buy my noncommittal response. Her normally light complexion turned white against her red hair. "Oh, Ellie. Please tell me you'll be safe."

"I'll be fine. Baxter's just being overly cautious. He's keeping an eye on me, so don't worry."

She blew out a sigh of relief. "I hope that's all it is. And not for nothing, but I wouldn't mind at all if Detective Baxter kept his eye on me. I know you've had your differences, but he's hot, and he's into you."

I poured another cup of coffee and handed it to her. "He's not into me. We work together, and he has an unholy obsession with keeping people safe."

"Still, you could do worse." She wrinkled her nose. "In fact, you *always* do worse."

After two more botched classes (at least minus the sermon on emotional control), I was more than ready to get back to the sheriff's station to finish up my work. I had the deputy drive me home to shower and change, and then we headed to the station. I'd received a text from Baxter that my scheduled time to meet with the Fed was three PM, but that would have meant no shower for me. The Fed could wait. A shower after over twenty-four hours and time spent at a crime scene couldn't.

As I walked into the conference room, a low voice barked, "You're late."

I stopped short when I laid eyes on the man sitting alone at the conference table surrounded by files and crime scene photos. The Fed was not some stodgy old pencil pusher like I'd expected. This guy was more GQ than G-man. He had the requisite dark suit, but instead of a starched shirt and cinched-up tie, he wore a silky blue button-down, open at the collar. Muscular, dark-haired, forty-ish, and with intense blue eyes, the Fed was one gorgeous man. But his presence here was still unwanted. It was an unwritten rule that you didn't get chummy with the Fed who took over your case.

When I didn't respond fast enough, he glared at me and added, "This is the part where you say you're sorry and give me some lame excuse."

Even his good looks were not able to make up for the condescending asshole vibe radiating from him.

I took a seat across the table. "I'm *so* sorry. I had to wash my hair."

He stared me down from across the table for a moment, sizing me up. Then he gave me a cocky smirk and stuck out his hand toward me. "I'm Special Agent Vic Manetti from the FBI field office in Indianapolis. I've been sent in to oversee the investigation of the Eye for an Eye Killer."

Resisting the urge to roll my eyes at the fact that the Feds felt the need to give a cheeky moniker to every high-profile suspect, I shook his hand. "Ellie Matthews."

"Just Ellie Matthews? What, no fancy title or list of accomplishments to try to one-up me? I've been hearing all afternoon how great these guys around here think they are."

I shrugged. "Girls generally don't feel the need to compare dicks at a first meeting." When his only response was a dazed expression, I added,

"Plus you have a file marked 'Personnel' sitting in front of you. I figure you've already read my history and formed an opinion about me, so why waste my breath?"

A slow smile spread across his face. I had to admit the view wasn't altogether unpleasant, but he was essentially the enemy until he proved otherwise. "I see it holds true that the criminalist always reads the room and catches the small stuff. Well, Ellie Matthews, bring me up to speed on what you've done so far."

I wearily launched into a narrative starting with the conversation Jenna had with her friends Saturday night at my house and ending with finding the killer's fingerprints in my office. His demeanor now serious, Agent Manetti nodded a few times during my story and wrote down several bullet points on the legal pad in front of him.

When I was finished, he asked, "What do you have left to do for your part of the investigation?"

"Since all of the evidence has been processed at least once, I'm heading to the lab to assist in the second independent examinations. At some point I'll complete a finished sketch of the scene, but it's not a real priority until and unless the case goes to trial. I should be finished with my part by tonight."

Manetti nodded. "So after the day's over, we won't be seeing each other anymore."

"That's the plan."

"Too bad. Having a firecracker like you on the task force would certainly keep things interesting."

I wasn't sure if that was a compliment or not. "If we're done here, I'd like to get to work so I can go home."

The agent's face slipped into a frown. "Oh, yes, by all means. You hurry up so you can go on home. Meanwhile there's a girl out there whose life is at stake."

"There's also a girl out there who's lost one of her best friends, whose big sister—her primary support system—has had to ignore her in order to do this job. Don't go getting preachy on me, Agent. We all have our own battles to fight."

His eyes bored into me again, this time with significantly less contempt. After a moment, he said, "You're free to go, Ms. Matthews."

I left the conference room without another word. Halfway down the hall, Sterling fell into step with me.

"I see you've had your meeting with our new HBIC. Did being alone with the pretty G-man get your panties all wet, Matthews?"

"Oh, *you* think he's pretty? Got a bit of a man crush going on, Sterling?"

My quick comeback had Sterling stopped dead in his tracks, sputtering curses at me all the way down the hall. I was sure I'd pay for it later, but for now I took the small victory in our ongoing battle of putdowns.

On my way to the lab, I noticed a light on in Jayne's office, which I didn't expect to see. She was off the case for personal reasons, plus with Special Agent Manetti here, her job as overseer would have been stripped regardless. I knocked on her door.

Her voice called quietly, "Come in."

I wasn't prepared for seeing her this way. She never wore athletic wear to work, but today she had on a rumpled tracksuit and sneakers. Her usually sleek bob was disheveled as well, almost as if she'd rolled out of bed this way. Her eyes were rimmed with red, and there were dark circles underneath. She was staring at the photo of Jenna that she kept on her desk, looking like her heart was breaking all over again. Jayne was always in control and professional, no matter what. But this situation was more than she could handle, and rightfully so.

"I saw your light on and came to check on you," I said, coming over to stand near her.

She blew her nose on a crumpled tissue. "Thank you. I'm...fine."

I knew from experience that she wouldn't want to talk about her feelings and burden me with her problems, but she needed someone. Her brother Mark and his wife Carol, Jenna's parents, were all the family Jayne had left, and I couldn't imagine either of them being in a place to offer a shoulder for her to cry on right now.

I reached out and put my hand on her shoulder. "Jayne, you don't need to go through this alone. I'm here for you. Whatever you need."

She looked up at me angrily. "What I need is not to have failed my only *niece!*" she bellowed, only to dissolve into racking sobs.

I knelt down beside her and put my arms around her, my own heart breaking. She cried against me for a time, longer than I ever would have expected. When she quieted down, she continued to cling to me, almost like a child. It took all I had not to break down along with her.

When she finally composed herself and pulled away, she murmured, "This is all my fault."

I took her by the shoulders and made her look at me. "Jayne Walsh, it is absolutely *not* your fault. You know this. You always used to preach it to us when we were beating ourselves up for not solving cases fast enough. The only one at fault here is the psychopath we're trying to catch."

Sighing heavily, she said, "When I heard she was going away for the weekend with a boy she'd just started dating, I was worried. I was going to say something to her, but...I decided it wasn't my place. I wanted her to have fun and be happy, and I didn't want to be a nag. What kind of dating advice would an old spinster like me have to give a young college girl?" She grunted bitterly. "Too late now."

I knew exactly where she was coming from. I'd had the same feelings toward many of Rachel's boyfriends. A couple of months ago when I voiced my displeasure about my sister dating an older man who was all wrong for her, she iced me out.

"If you'd said something, she wouldn't have listened. Rachel made a comment about it being too soon, and Jenna brushed it off. This guy is... persuasive and smart. I'm sure he had her head over heels for him in no time. I don't know if Baxter told you, but our killer came to my office Monday afternoon, posing as a student reporter. He certainly fooled me."

She nodded. "He told me, and I'm sick about that, too. I know you must hate it, but I agreed with him that you need police protection and signed off on it."

I smiled. "I could do without the shadow, but I know you guys are only looking out for me, which I appreciate."

Straightening in her chair, she said, "As much as I enjoy your company, your time is better spent working on this case instead of coddling me."

"Not true. But if it makes you feel any better, all that's left is the second examination of the evidence. And if Beck actually did his job today, he should have most of it done by now. There's nothing pressing to be done."

"Well, if nothing else, go home and console Rachel. I know she's hurting as much as I am."

I stood. "Okay, I'll go. But only because you kicked me out."

A ghost of a smile crossed Jayne's face. "Ellie, whatever you do, stay safe."

11

To say I wasn't looking forward to some time alone in the lab with Beck Durant was an understatement. When I got to the lab, he was, of all things, working. He had the clothing Amanda and I had processed during the night out on a worktable in front of him.

"Hey, Beck," I said. "I'm here to finish up on the Walsh murder case. Anything I can do?"

My attempt at civility only got me a sneer, which I'd expected. He replied, "I don't need your help."

"Okay, then do you mind telling me what's left to process just for my own information?"

He rolled his eyes at me. "The boots and the shirt. Happy now?"

Actually, I was elated. I'd processed the boots and the shirt, so that meant I couldn't do the second examination even if I wanted to. It had to be done by a different person to be legitimate.

"Very, because it means I'm done and out of here."

I sailed out of the lab and was almost to the front door when I realized two things: I'd forgotten my burly babysitter, and therefore had no way home, and I should probably at least tell Baxter goodbye, since it could be another three months before I saw him again.

I found him at his desk, flipping through an old case file. "Hey, making any headway?"

He rubbed his eyes and looked up at me. "Not as much as I'd like. You?"

I sat down in the chair next to him. "Well, it turns out I'm finished. Someone must have lit a fire under Beck, because he's processed nearly everything today, which means I have nothing left to do. I'll complete the finished sketch at school during some down time tomorrow."

Baxter's face fell. "Oh. I didn't realize."

An uncomfortable silence strained the air between us until I managed to think of something to say. "So the sketch artist you sent over was really great. She was easy to work with and incredibly talented. She captured the image I had in my head exactly. Did you get the local news to broadcast the pictures?"

"Yes. Most of the Indianapolis stations have been breaking in once an hour to run the shots of Parsons and the tip line number."

"Any luck on the tip line, or is it the usual bunch of nutjobs calling in?"

Baxter frowned. "The usuals so far. We normally start doing a little better after five. After the sane people get home from work and turn on the news."

"Right." I chuckled. "Well, um...I guess I should be going and let you get back to it."

When I got up to leave, he caught my arm. "Ellie, when we're both not exhausted, and I'm not under the gun...do you think we could get together to talk? I feel like there are still some things we need to work through."

I nodded. "I agree. I don't like the way we left things, either." Smiling, I added, "You know where to find me."

The corner of his mouth pulled up. "Especially since I have a tail on you. Let me find out who's got the next shift." He picked up his phone and made a call. After hanging up, he said, "Deputy Martinez will meet you out front."

My jaw dropped. "Martinez? Nick, come on. Please do not waste Martinez's time on babysitting me. He's one of the best deputies we have."

"When he heard it was you who needed babysitting, he volunteered. Besides, I don't think he likes his new partner much, so he's happy for a break."

I griped, "This is a monumental waste of department resources. As a taxpaying citizen, I want to lodge a formal complaint."

Baxter chuckled. "Duly noted. I'll put it in the circular file along with the tip line information."

Deputy Carlos Martinez was waiting for me in the parking lot in an unmarked car. I'd worked with him many times before. He was one tough cop when he needed to be, but personable and easygoing otherwise. He'd been with the department for a long time and had more commendations than practically anyone. I knew Jayne had offered to let him work his way up the ranks, but he loved being a deputy.

When I got in, he said, "Hey, Matthews. You drew the short straw today, getting stuck with me." I noticed he was in plain clothes. I hoped he wasn't offering to watch me on his day off.

I smiled. "Absolutely not. Don't tell anyone, but you're my favorite."

"I thought Sterling was your favorite." He tried to keep a straight face, but couldn't help bursting out laughing at his own joke.

"Keep talking, Martinez. I'll become a hostile prisoner, and then we'll see who's laughing."

He sobered. "I know it sucks to have someone looking over your shoulder, but with what I've heard about this killer, we don't want to take any chances." He put his vehicle in gear. "Where to? You gonna drag me to get matching mani-pedis or what? You know, my wife did that to me once, and it was a nightmare. I don't like people touching my feet."

I chuckled. "I would never make you do that. First I'd like to stop by my stepdad's house and see my nephew. Then it'll be straight home to sleep. I'm afraid I'm not going to be very interesting company, considering I haven't slept in nearly thirty-six hours."

"Fair enough. I'd say you've earned some rest."

I gave Martinez directions to David's house, and he sat outside in his vehicle while I went to the door.

When David answered, he took one look at me and pulled me into a hug. "I can't imagine what you've gone through in the past day, Ellie. Come on in. Marjorie's got supper almost ready."

"You know you don't have to feed me—"

"Auntie Ellie!" squealed Nate, rushing over to wrap himself around my legs.

I picked him up and held him tight. "Hi, baby boy. Did you have a good day with Grandpa and Nana?"

"I sure did. We made slime."

It floored me how Marjorie had had no problem welcoming Rachel and me into her family when she married David. It took a special kind of woman to take two girls she had absolutely no connection to (her husband's ex-wife's children, no less) and treat us like her own. She'd done the same thing for Nate when he came along.

I raised my eyebrows at David. "Sounds messy."

David smiled. "It was fun."

Nate wiggled out of my arms. "I'll go get it so I can show you."

When he raced off, I noticed David staring out the window at Martinez's car. "You have a police escort?" Turning to me with a worried expression, he said, "Ellie, is there more going on than you've told me?"

I sighed. "Yes, and that's partially why I came over here. I can't reveal case information, but it's possible that Jenna's killer may also be targeting me in order to get to Jayne. I'm under police protection until he's caught."

David's face became ashen. "I don't know if I can handle much more of you being in danger, Ellie. You don't know how happy I was when you decided to switch to teaching. And now with you working with the department again..."

I laid a hand on his arm. "I know you worry about me. And I appreciate it." I pointed toward Martinez. "But that guy out there is the best deputy in Hamilton County. No one can get to me with him around."

"What about Rachel?"

"I'm going to have Rachel continue to stay on campus. They've got that place locked down like Fort Knox after all that's gone on. She's much safer there, plus I think it'll help her to be with her friends right now."

He breathed a sigh of relief. "Okay. We'll keep Nate for as long as you need."

"Thank you. I hate to put you out like this, but—"

Holding a hand up, he said, "It's no trouble at all. We enjoy having him here. You know that."

Nate ran back to us, holding a large Ziploc bag full of green goo. "Feel the slime, Auntie Ellie!"

I dutifully opened the bag and squished the gooey mixture between my fingers. "Eww, gross."

Giggling, Nate snatched the bag from me and ran back to the kitchen with it.

I stayed for a while, after Marjorie wouldn't take no for an answer about eating dinner with them. After that, I had Martinez drive me home. To my dismay, Rachel's car was in the driveway.

I rushed into the house, Martinez on my heels. "Rachel? Rachel! Are you here?"

"In my room!" she yelled.

I hurried down the hall toward her open door. "Why in the hell did you leave campus?"

She appeared in her doorway just as I got there. "Would you relax? I'm going straight back. I needed some clean clothes, and I didn't feel like doing laundry at the dorm." She looked past me to Martinez. "Who's your friend?"

Rachel and I had a standing "no men in the house" rule, for our own safety as well as Nate's. Neither one of us had a great track record where dating was concerned, hence the rule.

"This is Deputy Carlos Martinez. He's going to be...watching out for me tonight."

She narrowed her eyes at me. "Why do you need watching?"

I frowned and flicked my eyes at Martinez. I pushed Rachel into her room and closed the door. "You remember when you came into my office yesterday?"

Her face fell. "Yes."

"You remember the guy who was in there?"

"Not really. I was kind of freaked out."

"Well...we believe he's...Jenna's killer."

Her jaw dropped as her eyes filled with tears. "You know who...who...?" She cleared her throat, unable to finish her sentence. "Is he the one whose photo is up all over campus? The guy who's 'potentially dangerous' but no one will come out and say why?"

"Yes."

"And he was in your office? Holy shit."

I nodded. "He said he wanted to write an article about me for the *Voice*. I thought he was a student."

She dropped down onto her bed, shock written all over her face. "What do you think he wanted with you?"

"One theory is that he wanted to use me to get to Jayne. I'm not supposed to tell you this, but he seems to have some kind of vendetta against county law enforcement. Please don't repeat that."

"You know I won't," she said quietly.

I sat down next to her and put my arm around her. "I know." After a moment, I asked tentatively, "Do you need to talk?"

She bowed her head. I knew she wanted to hide the tears that were no doubt flowing. "Probably, but I don't have time for a breakdown. I'm supposed to be at a study group in thirty minutes."

"Okay. I still feel bad about ditching you last night. I kind of shirked my big sister responsibilities."

Sniffling, she said, "It was more important that you did your job. It sounds like you did if you have a suspect already."

I hated to admit that was more luck than anything, or maybe even the killer purposely letting us see what he looked like, knowing we had no way of finding him.

"Um...right. Now we're to the point of looking for a needle in a haystack. It goes without saying that if you happen to see him, don't accost him. Run."

"Duh."

I gave her a squeeze. "I'll let you get back to packing. I want you to call me as soon as you get to study group."

"Yes, Mother." As I went to get up, she grabbed my hand. "Did you stop by David's to see Nate?"

"I did. He's having a ball there, as usual."

Her eyes filled with tears again. "Do you think I'm a bad mom because I haven't stopped by to see him yet?"

"No, you could never be a bad mom."

Rachel's face crumpled. "I don't think I can talk to him without breaking down, and I don't want him to see me like this. I don't want him to be scared. He senses when I'm upset, and it upsets him. I can't turn my feelings on and off like you can and pretend like nothing's wrong."

I smiled. That was where she was wrong. She could absolutely do that, just like I could, but she refused to be anything but truthful with her son. That was why, even at the young age of twenty-one, she was the best mom I knew.

"Rach, it's fine. He's fine. When you get yourself together, you can go see him. I'll go with you if you need the moral support."

She nodded. "Tomorrow. I'm too raw today."

"Okay. You know I'm here, whatever you need."

She threw her arms around me. "I know. Thanks, sis."

We clung to each other for a few moments, but not long enough to let ourselves get weepy. I left her to pack some clothes and met Martinez in my living room.

He cleared his throat. "I know it's maybe not my place, but I took the liberty of calling a deputy to escort your sister back to campus and get her settled."

I smiled. "Thanks, Martinez. I know I can always count on you to have my back."

12

Martinez and I watched the local evening news, and having seen the sketch of Hunter's haunting eyes one too many times, I'd had enough. After a much-needed nightcap, I put myself to bed at seven PM, leaving Martinez to keep himself entertained in my living room. My dog Trixie had taken a liking to him, and she'd hopped up on the couch next to him and laid her head on his lap.

I was awoken from a deep sleep by my phone ringing from the night-stand next to my bed. Worried that Rachel or Nate was in trouble, I answered on the first ring.

"Hello?" I croaked, my throat dry.

"Sorry to call so late, but I need you."

"Nick?" I asked.

"Yeah...you sound funny."

"I was *asleep*," I complained, trying to keep the slur out of my voice. Maybe I'd had more like two or three nightcaps before I'd decided to call it a night.

"A silver Corolla was found ditched in an empty parking lot over in Westfield. It's got the same plate number as the one from the mall surveillance photos. We need you to come out and process the vehicle."

Working Jenna's scene as a favor to Jayne was one thing. But coming in again, after only a little over five hours of sleep, to process this car—which in my opinion was going to yield a big fat nothing—was another.

"Don't you have two other criminalists on staff? Three people on a vehicle is overkill."

"Beck is off tonight."

"Call and wake *his* ass up, then."

He sighed. "The Fed asked for you."

"The Fed can go to hell."

"I told him you might say that. He said you're who he wants on the team. You're back on the task force."

"He is not the boss of me."

"I told him you'd say that, too. But he wants continuity on the case, and this is part of the case. He wants you and Amanda on whatever physical evidence we find from here on out. I assume his meeting with Beck went poorly."

Muttering curses under my breath, I got out of bed, swaying only a little as I stood. "I'm going to need some time to get dressed. I don't have clothes at the ready like I used to."

"Fair enough. I'll have coffee waiting for you when you get here."

I hung up with Baxter as Martinez started knocking on my bedroom door. "I know," I called. "We have to go to Westfield. Give me five minutes."

"Will do," Martinez replied.

After brushing my fuzzy teeth a few times and guzzling some mouth-wash, I felt sufficiently odor-free. Now to get something in my stomach to speed up the dissipation of the alcohol. Once I was dressed, I ran to the kitchen, pleased to find a remnant of the steak I'd grilled on Sunday night. That, along with some chocolate milk and a blueberry muffin, ought to do it.

Martinez gave my eclectic midnight snack an amused glance, but didn't say anything as we got in his vehicle and sped west to Westfield, with me chowing down the whole way. We ended up at an empty parking lot right on Main Street. A silver Corolla sat in the front of the parking lot, facing the road and under a streetlight, no less. The killer wanted the vehicle found, that much was clear, which meant there would be no useful evidence inside.

The parking lot was already crawling with law enforcement vehicles and personnel. As we parked and got out of Martinez's vehicle, I spotted Baxter, Sterling, and Amanda conferring near the Corolla. Agent Manetti was standing in front of a group of deputies, barking orders.

"This should be fun," I muttered under my breath, popping a couple of Altoids.

Martinez grinned. "I take it you've met our new fearless leader."

"Yeah. Not a fan. I guess this is your lucky night, though. You're rid of me now. I'm going to be working this scene and then spending the rest of my night in the lab, surrounded by cops."

He smiled. "I guess that's true. Sucks for me. Now I'll have to do some actual work. I was getting awfully comfy on your couch with your fluffy dog. Adult babysitting is a cushy job."

I gave him a punch on the arm.

Baxter saw us and came our way, coffee cup in hand. "As promised," he said, handing it to me.

I smiled. "Thanks, I guess. Not much compensation for missing my beauty sleep."

"Like I told you, take it up with the Fed." To Martinez, he said, "Thanks for covering the afternoon shift. I can take it from here. Hope she didn't give you any shit."

The two of them shook hands and chuckled, while I complained, "I'm standing right here."

Martinez said, "Nah. I only had to tase her once to keep her in line."

I growled to myself and drank my coffee while they had a laugh at my expense.

After Martinez left, Baxter beckoned me to follow him toward Sterling and Amanda. "The car is a mess, so good luck. It's registered to an elderly couple from Illinois, who reported it missing a month ago when they drove over to visit their daughter in Speedway. I'm thinking they're in no way related to our killer, but we're still going to check them out. And after ditching his car, Parsons is going to need some new wheels, so I'll also be running down every vehicle reported stolen in the area today."

"Ooh, sounds like a night full of fun for both of us, then."

"I say it's a ploy to keep us occupied and not out looking for our killer.

The good news is that we forced him to have to deviate from his plan. Once his vehicle's description and license number got plastered all over the news, it became a liability, so he had to spend time finding a new means of transportation. Maybe that'll buy Michaela Richards a few more hours."

When we walked up to Sterling and Amanda, Sterling turned to me and said, "You look thrilled to be here. What's the matter? You pissed about Special Agent Dick ordering you to get out of bed to come process a scene?"

Amanda wrinkled her nose. "Jason, I think his name is *Vic*."

Baxter rolled his eyes. "I think he was trying to be funny. The problem is that he's not funny."

As Sterling cuffed him on the arm, I said, "No, that one was pretty good. Give the man some credit."

"Thank you, Matthews," Sterling said, clearly shocked that I was the one out of the group agreeing with him.

Baxter looked unconvinced, so I explained, "It's actually quite clever. It's funny because—"

Sterling cut in, "If you have to explain a joke, it loses its appeal."

"Sterling, I'm helping you here. You see, Manetti is a detective of sorts, or a 'dick,' and his name rhymes with dick. See?"

Baxter glanced behind me. "I get it. It's funny. New subject, please."

I added, "Oh, and plus, Manetti is a total dick, so it also works on that level as well."

A voice behind me said, "Why is it that both times I've seen you today you're talking about male genitalia, Ms. Matthews?"

I shrugged and turned to face Agent Manetti, not bothered in the slightest that he'd overheard me calling him a dick. "It's as good a topic as any, I suppose."

Manetti glared at us. "If you'd all quit telling middle school jokes and get to work, I'd appreciate it."

I threw Sterling a smirk over my shoulder. "Ouch, Sterling. That was some of your best material, and he just called it 'middle school.' "

Sterling pinched the bridge of his nose and muttered, "Will you shut the hell up before you get us all fired?"

"I *wish* someone would fire me from this—"

Baxter interrupted me before I could finish. "Ellie, I have your jumpsuit and kit in my SUV. Let's go get you suited up."

I let Baxter usher me away from Manetti's steely glare.

"Are you trying to piss him off?" he asked.

"Not especially, but I'm not going to kiss his ass, either."

He shook his head. "You do not pull any punches, do you?"

"You should know this by now, Baxter."

I got suited up, and Baxter took the ball cap off his head and put it on mine.

He said, "I'm headed back to the station, but you're in good hands with the deputies securing the scene. If you find anything earthshattering, call me."

"You got it."

I took the field kit out of his SUV and headed over to where Amanda was taking photos of the exterior of the vehicle. While she did that, I made a rough sketch of the parking lot and the vehicle.

She said, "I hate processing car interiors. It's such cramped quarters."

"Agreed. Let's get this over with."

While Amanda began taking photos of the interior, I examined the exterior of the vehicle. The back right taillight had a hole in it. I was already cold from being outside in the frigid weather, but a new shiver ran through me at the thought of how that hole got there. An image of a young woman in that trunk, trying anything and everything to get out, flashed into my head, but I pushed it aside. I didn't even want to think about whether or not Jenna had been transported that way. The trunk would have to be processed, but I wasn't mentally ready for that yet. I got the camera from Amanda and took a few shots of the busted taillight.

As Amanda was dusting the steering wheel and lifting a few prints, I heard her groan. "There's mouse poop in the cup holders! This car is filthy. There's food and dirt everywhere, and...more mouse poop. Gross!"

I snickered, going over to examine the wheels on the driver's side. "I've seen you work death scenes that had much more disgusting substances than a little mouse poop going on. What's your problem?"

I shined the flashlight on the tires and wheel wells. I found mud with some straw in it clinging to the wheel well, so I took a photo of it.

She shuddered and hopped out of the car. As she was scribbling information on the back side of several fingerprint lifts, she explained, "When I was a kid, we lived on a farm in Ohio. There were field mice everywhere, and my stupid sister felt the need to keep food hidden under her bed. Once the mice found her stash, they set up shop and never left. My parents were always busy with farming, so they put us in charge of rodent extermination. Which meant *I* was in charge of rodent extermination, because my sister was too squeamish to do it. No matter how many mice I caught and killed, more came in. I lived with mouse poop in and on everything I owned for eighteen long years. Not doing it anymore."

I smiled ruefully. "I get it. My mom's old trailer was always full of roaches, because I don't think she ever washed a single dish in her entire life. I can't handle roaches. They would crawl on my sister and me at night while we were asleep. It would give Rachel night terrors, and she'd wake up to find actual roaches all over her and scream bloody murder all over again. I never knew what it was like to have a full night's sleep until I moved out."

She stared at me, eyes wide. "Okay, you win. None of the mice ever crawled on me, to my knowledge."

I smiled. "Well, the good news is mouse poop isn't evidence in this case, so you won't have to touch it." I thought for a moment. "However, it could be yet another indicator that the killer has been hanging out on a farm or in a barn. It's cold out. Maybe some field mice were looking for a warm place to sleep and found a way into the car while it was parked."

She turned and frowned at the car. "You may be on to something. Not that we didn't already have suspicions about a rural location, but this information could help solidify our theory."

I nodded. "I also found straw stuck in some mud in the wheel wells, so there's that, too. But back to the interior, if you take the passenger side, I'll take the back seat. Maybe I'll find something less disgusting, like a used condom or something."

"That would honestly be so much better."

I opened the driver's side rear door and looked in the back seat. It stunk of old food and mustiness. It was difficult to tell whether the food had been there for days or months. I could much more imagine a young man throwing half-eaten candy bars and boxes of fries in the back seat than an elderly couple, so I assumed that the killer had pretty well trashed the car in the time he'd been in possession of it. I sifted gingerly through the mess with gloved hands, careful not to dig down too far and touch something I couldn't see. I wouldn't put it past him to booby trap this thing, maybe with a few razor blades or shards of broken glass.

"Hey, Amanda, be extra careful in here. I'm thinking he could have left us a surprise just to twist the knife a little."

She had her head down in the floorboard, so her voice was muffled. "I know. I thought that, too. The guys looked for bombs under the car and under the hood, so we're good there at least."

I was finding a whole lot of nothing in the back seat. It was just someone's messy car. I got out of the back and changed my gloves. By that time, Amanda was finished with the front, so we both walked around to the trunk.

I said, "I've been putting this off."

"Me, too. Because of the, uh…" She pointed at the hole in the taillight.

"Yes."

"I guess we probably should get on with it."

She went to the driver's side and hit the trunk release, and the trunk lid popped up in front of me. Once she got back to my side, I slowly lifted the trunk lid all the way up. Surprisingly, the trunk was fairly clean. The interior was light gray, so blood would have shown up to the naked eye, unless it had been bleached out.

Amanda said, "I don't exactly know what I was expecting, but this is kind of a welcome surprise."

"Right. I had prepared for the worst."

She got out her flashlight and shined it on the trunk interior where the taillight had been busted out. "I think there may be some blood here around the hole. Like maybe someone got injured while trying to break the light."

I was busy looking at the emergency trunk latch, which was broken and mangled. The mix of food I'd thrown down on the way over here began to churn in my stomach. "Sick bastard. He disabled the safety feature that keeps people from getting trapped in the trunk."

Amanda grabbed the camera and took a couple of shots of the busted taillight and the latch. "He certainly thought of everything. Who is this guy? Is he an evil genius, or has he done this so many times before it's become second nature to him?"

"He's young, so unless he started early, he can't have much experience." I sighed. "I think he's just a sociopath."

When the camera's bright flash illuminated the trunk, I noticed a glint of something way in the back. Shining the flashlight in the area where the glint had come from, I saw that it was a piece of jewelry—a gold necklace. I had Amanda take some photos of it, then I retrieved it to get a closer look. A lump formed in my throat when I saw what it was. It was the beautiful gold scrollwork cross that Jayne had given Jenna for completing her confirmation class and joining the church when she was in high school. The necklace was something Jenna was rarely without. The chain was broken, as if it had been ripped from her neck.

"What's that?" Amanda asked, her expression guarded.

I cleared my throat and held up the necklace for her to see. "This was Jenna's." My voice broke as I said her name.

Amanda hurried to her case and brought back a small manila envelope, holding it out so I could drop the necklace into it. "Go take a break. I'll scour the rest of the trunk, and then we'll be done. Go."

I ripped my gloves off and threw them on the ground as I stalked toward the other end of the parking lot. I felt like something had snapped inside me.

Manetti, who was still hanging around with a few of the deputies, spotted me and came my way. He slowed as he got near me and asked, "What have you found so far? Anything we can use?"

I shook my head and brushed past him, not in the mood to stop and chat. He went on, thankfully, and I found a tree to kick at the other end of the parking lot.

Why did every bit of evidence in this case have to feel like such a sucker punch to the gut? Why couldn't I stay detached from my feelings like I used to be able to? I gave that huge speech yesterday about how my students should consider a new career if they couldn't hack the emotional pressure of forensic work, and here I was, wallowing in my own self-pity. Granted, I had realized a while back that there were some cases, like my mother's murder case, that were beyond my coping skills. That was why I quit. This one was too close again, and I had no business being a part of the investigation. At some point, my depressed mental state was going to cause me to make a mistake, and that wasn't fair to anyone involved. I had to pull back from this.

"What's your problem?" Manetti asked from behind me.

I wheeled around to face him. "What's my *problem*? This whole damn case is my problem."

His expression hard, he said, "First you're out here telling jokes with your pals, and now you're out here throwing a temper tantrum and taking it out on that tree. What's with the mood swings? Are you unstable or something?"

My jaw dropped. "Are you freaking kidding me right now? Jenna Walsh was a close family friend. Of course I'm having mood swings. I am *grieving*, here." At wit's end, I threw Baxter's ball cap on the ground and ran my hands through my hair. "And to add insult to injury, I have to have a round-the-clock bodyguard because I'm a potential victim for this psycho we're chasing. Because I have this giant target on my back, my family can't even stay with me at our home. I've had to farm out my sister and nephew so other people can watch out for them, because being around me is dangerous. I'm scared, and I'm lonely. Are you not aware of what I'm going through, or are you just too much of an asshole to be able to see it?"

He wiped a hand down his face. "I'm sorry. I guess I didn't realize all you had on your plate right now. Under normal circumstances, you'd be my top pick for the job. But...given that this situation is different..." He sighed. "I think you need a break. Go home and get some rest. Ms. Carmack has assured me that the two of you have found very little evidence, so there's not much to process back at the station. We don't need you any more tonight. And...I'm going to take you off the task force for the Eye for an Eye Killer. That doesn't mean if a question comes up that we won't call you, though. But I won't have you working any more new scenes or new evidence."

I blew out a pent-up breath. "Okay."

Manetti shook his head. "I know we got off on the wrong foot, but if you took the time to get to know me, I think you'd see that I'm not so bad."

Tears were threatening, so I only nodded in reply.

He gave me an awkward pat on the back. "I'll have Deputy Martinez take you home."

"I'll tell Amanda what's going on." I trudged back over to the vehicle, where Amanda was packing up her field kit.

When she saw me, she came over and took me by the shoulders, giving me a reassuring squeeze. "What happened over there?"

"Agent Manetti is taking me off the case. For good this time. I told him it's ended up to be more than I can handle."

She smiled. "I'll miss you, but at the same time, it's what's best for you that matters. I hope you can get some closure at the funeral. I'll be there as long as I can get away from the lab."

I tried to smile, but failed. "I'm sorry to ditch you, but I have to get out of here." I let out a mirthless laugh. "You wonder why I made the switch to teaching? Cases like this. I guess this proves I really can't hack it in the real world of criminalistics. I probably need to stick to teaching from now on."

"I hate to hear that, Ellie. But you have to take care of yourself first." She nodded behind me and took a step back. "I think Martinez is ready to take you home. At least you're in good hands."

I nodded. "I'll see you around." Turning my back on the scene for the last time, I followed Martinez to his vehicle and let him take me home.

13

My sleep was riddled with nightmares, most of them involving Hunter Parsons and Jenna. I woke up still tired, but that was no surprise. It would take a couple of good nights of sleep to make up for my all-nighter and then being dragged out late last night.

I headed to school, a fresh deputy in tow, and went about my normal routine. I wasn't in the mood to do anything to make my first class interesting, and as a result, it was boring as hell. I could tell from the looks on my students' faces, plus the fact that what I was saying could barely hold my own attention.

When I got to my office and pulled out my phone, I saw that I'd received a text from Baxter: *I heard you yelled at Manetti and called him an asshole and lived to tell about it.*

Cracking a smile for the first time today, I sat down at my desk and texted back, *Yes, I did. I guess you also heard I'm off the case. Sorry.*

Only a few moments went by until I had a response: *No need to apologize. I get it.*

It was only then that it hit me—I'd never work another case with Baxter. Last night had solidified my decision that I wasn't up for consulting with the department anymore. The hard part would be having to tell Baxter that this was it. That wasn't a discussion to have over text messaging. Our differences aside, I'd enjoyed working with him more than any other coworker I'd ever had.

When I offered no response to his last text, he wrote, *I'll see you at the funeral tomorrow.* Then he added, *If you need a friend, I'm here for you.*

For some odd reason, I got a warm feeling in the pit of my stomach after reading that last text. Typical Baxter, always the white knight.

I texted back, *Thanks.*

I did need a friend, but I wouldn't dream of clouding his mind with my problems. He had enough work to do to find this killer, especially with the clock ticking for Michaela Richards. If Hunter Parsons stuck to the same forty-eight-hour time period he had with Jenna, it stood to reason that if no one figured out where he was by midnight tonight, Michaela wouldn't live to see tomorrow. A cold chill ran up my spine as a morbid thought popped into my head. Jenna's funeral was tomorrow morning, and there would be scores of law enforcement and government officials in attendance. What if he decided to use it to make some sort of violent spectacle?

I called Baxter. "Hey, um...about the funeral tomorrow. Are you guys doing something to beef up security there?"

I could hear the smile in his voice. "Way ahead of you. We've got dozens of undercover officers that are going to be in the crowd, watching out for the funeral-goers. The Fed is even bringing in some fancy FBI badasses to oversee security. If the killer tries anything, we'll be ready."

Breathing out a sigh of relief, I replied, "Good. Even though I'm off the case, I can't turn off my brain."

"I figured as much. If you have any more ideas, don't hesitate to call me. Day or night. You know I'll be up."

Poor Baxter. And Sterling, too. Neither of those two would let themselves catch much more than a catnap until they had this case tied up.

"I know. Stay safe."

"That's my line. And don't try to ditch your deputy."

I smiled again. "Would I do that?"

"Yes. Talk to you later."

"Bye."

I managed to make a lunch date with Rachel, so after my next class I headed to the campus food court to meet her, my deputy shadow in tow. By the time I got my food, she was already seated at a table, waving me down. The deputy opted to keep watch near the wall.

Rachel said, "I see you have a new bodyguard today."

I blew out a breath. "Yeah. The guys have been nice and all, but I'm getting so tired of being watched all the time."

"And I'm getting tired of living out of a suitcase, away from my son. When can we come home?"

"Soon, I hope. The killer ditched his car last night, so there goes a big identifier for him."

"Anyone call in on the tip line?"

"No one who's mentally competent."

She nodded, focusing on her salad. After a moment, she looked up, and her eyes were misty. "So the funeral is tomorrow."

"Right. At ten. Want to ride with me and my deputy *du jour*?"

"Okay."

After a lengthy bit of dead air between us, I asked, "How is studying going for finals?"

Rachel shrugged. "Good, I guess. How are your classes?"

"Let's just say I've done better."

She nodded, and we slipped back into silence.

It felt like no subject was safe to discuss. Talking about Nate, which was what we usually did, would make both of us sad. The subject of school wasn't much better, because losing Jenna had put a massive hole in Rachel's campus life. I couldn't handle talking about Rachel's loser boyfriend, so that was out. Any mention of Christmas was off the table, considering we went to Jayne's every Christmas Eve for the get-together she always hosted for her family. I couldn't imagine that was going to happen this year.

Rachel put her fork down and looked at me with such haunted eyes my heart nearly broke. "Are you free tonight to go with me to David's to see Nate?"

I smiled. "I am. Why don't we meet after your last class, and we'll drive over together? Free ride in a sheriff's cruiser."

The corner of her mouth turned up barely. "Mmm. How enticing."

"You know it." I put my hand over hers. "We will get through this, Rach."

Her eyes filling with tears, she nodded. "I know. Someday."

———————

Rachel and I had a wonderful time with Nate, David, and Marjorie. I was proud of how composed my sister was around Nate after having been so worried about whether or not she could hold it together during the visit. The evening was over much too soon, and afterward my assigned deputy dropped Rachel at school and me at home. It was time for a shift change, and I got yet another deputy I didn't know. This guy wasn't chatty at all, and he didn't seem to like Trixie very much, so I didn't feel bad about holing up in my room with the dog for the rest of the evening while he sat alone in my living room. I watched the news, which probably wasn't a good idea, since it only made me sad. They'd interviewed Baxter tonight. He looked haggard and pale, and seemed downright depressed about how the case was progressing.

Worried, I called him.

When he answered, he said, "I hope you're calling with a brilliant thought that is going to crack this case wide open, because I'm officially out of ideas."

I winced at the despondent tone of his voice. "No, sorry. I called to ask if you were taking care of yourself. You looked pretty rough on the news."

His tone turned light, but I could still sense an undercurrent of dismay. "That cameraman promised me he got my good side."

"He lied."

Baxter chuckled. "I suppose I wasn't looking so good after our one and only lead turned out to be a total bust."

I sat up straighter. "You had a lead?"

"Yeah. We had a tip line call from up in Sheridan. An old farmer swears up and down he saw a silver Corolla parked at his neighbor's barn yesterday. This morning it was gone. That farm happened to be one of the ones we had on our list. It was owned by someone connected to one of the old cases we've been going over, and it went into foreclosure last month. It couldn't have fit the profile any better. Long story short, the Fed had us go in guns blazing, only to find nothing in the barn. Amanda and Beck combed the place, but it was clean. Not even any animal blood to be found. When we went next door to talk to the man, we found out that he's an Alzheimer's patient who is in and out of lucidity. His wife fell asleep while they were watching the noon news broadcast, and he called the tip line while she wasn't paying attention."

"Ugh. That sucks."

"Needless to say, we put a new person on the tip line—someone who'll vet the tippers a little better." He sighed. "I was really hoping this one would pan out. I'm afraid we're running out of time."

I knew everyone was on pins and needles, especially since the forty-eight-hour window closed tonight. Things did not look good for Michaela Richards.

"I'm sorry. I wish there was something I could do."

"You've done a lot. More than anyone could have or should have asked of you. Now you've got one job—to keep yourself safe."

"You sound like a broken record."

"I have to because you're so hard-headed."

I smiled. "Try to get some rest, Detective."

"I make no promises."

One of the reasons I hadn't wanted to cancel any of my classes earlier in the week was that I knew I had Jenna's funeral to attend on Thursday morning. I didn't want to miss any more work than I had to. I'd managed to wrangle Samantha's TA away for a couple of hours so my morning classes could go on as scheduled.

I took my time getting ready for the funeral, for the simple fact that I couldn't concentrate on the task at hand. My mind was on Jayne, on Rachel, on Nate, on Baxter, and ultimately always ended up on Michaela Richards and her dire situation. I kept going back to what Baxter had said—that it could easily have been me instead of her if Jayne hadn't asked me to help out when we realized Jenna was missing. I guessed in that sense it was something of a blessing. One of the most difficult nights of my life ended up being the one thing that saved me from kidnapping and certain death.

Today's assigned deputy was Chris Lester, who I'd met when I found Jenna's phone earlier in the week. It seemed like an age ago. Deputy Lester and I picked up a disturbingly somber Rachel and headed toward the funeral home. It was packed with people—a mix of law enforcement, students, friends, community members, and family. I spotted a few gawkers, which was standard for the funeral of a murder victim. I did, however, keep an eagle eye out for Hunter Parsons, in case he had the brass balls to show his face here.

I saw Baxter and Sterling, both dressed sharply in suits and ties. Both of them were carrying their service pistols in shoulder holsters under their coats, which made me feel at the same time safe and apprehensive. Baxter caught my eye and gave me a curt nod. It was clear to me that he was in cop mode rather than in funeral-goer mode. I returned a sad smile and guided Rachel to a seat behind Jayne.

When I reached forward and squeezed Jayne's shoulder, she put her hand over mine and drew in a shuddering breath. The family had opted for a closed casket rather than trying to hide the large gash on Jenna's neck, and I was happier for it. Even though my last glimpse of her was on the slab in the morgue, I couldn't bear to see sweet Jenna in a box.

The funeral was excruciatingly sad, with numerous friends and family telling stories about Jenna and her positive effect on their lives. Rachel and Jayne didn't get up to speak. I knew they couldn't. Miranda, Jenna's roommate, managed to get most of the way through her eulogy before breaking down. I dreaded the burial at the cemetery even more. For one thing, it had started snowing this morning, and it was bitterly cold. Even colder was the thought of leaving Jenna's body out there alone under the frozen earth.

I felt as if I were in a daze as we joined the funeral procession heading to the cemetery. There weren't nearly enough chairs for the attendees, so I had Rachel sit with Jayne while I stood off to the side. My sister looked downright frail, and I feared she didn't have the strength to stand through the short burial service.

Baxter came to stand beside me. He murmured, "Doing okay?"

"I'm holding it together," I lied. The only thing holding me together was that I didn't want to break down in front of Rachel.

It was snowing just enough to be annoying. I tucked the ends of my scarf into the neck of my coat and shoved my gloved hands in my pockets, hoping to better brace myself against the cold. Wordlessly, Baxter put his arm around my shoulders. The heat from his body warmed me considerably, but my head was fighting the sympathy radiating from him. I couldn't give in and cry on his shoulder, although that's what I wanted more than anything to be able to do.

The minister began giving the final burial rights, and I felt Baxter suddenly stiffen next to me and drop his arm. After looking at his phone, he turned and stared behind us, his face going white.

14

"What's wrong?" I whispered, turning to look out across the bleak, snow-covered cemetery, wondering what had him spooked.

"Sterling said he saw a man over there, crouched behind one of the headstones."

I squinted against the falling snow, but saw no people aside from the funeral-goers. But one by one, men and women who had the marked look of Feds began peeling away from the crowd and heading off across the cemetery in the direction we were looking.

After gesturing for Deputy Lester to come over to us, Baxter leaned toward me and grasped my arm. "Stay here."

My pulse quickening, I sucked in a breath. "You think it's him."

Nodding gravely, Baxter released me and strode toward the spot where the Feds and deputies were converging. I watched as they surrounded one of the larger monuments, one big enough for a grown man to hide behind. With a couple of swift movements, two of the Feds jumped behind the stone and wrestled a little. Then I saw three figures hit the ground. They had someone. My gut clenched, wondering if it could be Hunter Parsons, and this nightmare could finally come to an end.

Lester got a text, and after reading it said quietly to me, "Detective Baxter wants you over there."

"Me?" I whispered. I didn't want to get anywhere near Hunter Parsons.

"They're not sure it's him. You're the only one who's seen the guy in person."

"Oh," I breathed.

When I didn't make a move to go, he said, "Ms. Matthews, I think we need to be moving, here."

With my wobbly legs protesting every step, I followed Lester over to where Baxter and Sterling and a gaggle of other law enforcement officials were gathered around a man who was being held facedown on the snowy ground.

As we got closer, Baxter broke off from the group and came our way, taking me by the arm. "I can tell by the look on your face that this is freaking you out, but...I don't think it's our guy. He swears up and down someone paid him to put on a sock hat and glasses and creep around near the graveside service."

"What?" I cried. "That sadistic bastard."

"Yeah. The Feds don't believe a word of it, so we need some confirmation before they decide to book this idiot for murder."

I blew out a breath. "Okay. Just stay with me."

"I won't leave your side." He walked me up to the man on the ground. "Haul him up," he ordered the two Feds on either side of the suspect.

After the men wrestled their prisoner to a standing position, I could see immediately that this young man wasn't Hunter Parsons. He wasn't tall enough, for one. And he looked nothing like him. Big nose and ears, with sunken, flat eyes.

I shook my head. "It's not him."

"You're sure?" Sterling asked. "We can't screw this up."

"Positive."

"See? I told you pigs I'm not a killer," the suspect griped, which got him a rough shove from one of the Feds.

I lowered my voice and said to Baxter, "He's wearing the same glasses, jacket, and Ashmore hat that Hunter Parsons had on at my office, though. The jacket is frayed on one shoulder. I remember it."

Baxter said to the man, "Who put you up to this?"

"I already told you people. I answered an ad on Craigslist and got my instructions through there. Damn. Can somebody take some notes or something?"

"You still had to meet whoever gave you what you're wearing. Can you describe him?"

He shook his head. "I didn't meet nobody. A box with the jacket, hat, glasses, and money was left for me at Ritchey Woods. Hey, I didn't do anything wrong, here. I got my rights, and this is some straight-up bullshit going on."

I couldn't take another minute of his smug attitude. "At no point did you think maybe this wasn't a good idea? That what you were being asked to do wasn't on the up-and-up? Did you even give a thought to what this would do to the victim's family?"

"Shut up, bitch. You don't know me," he spat back at me.

Baxter started to lunge toward the guy, but I put my arm out to stop him. Glaring at the suspect, I fired back, "It takes a special kind of asshole to agree to terrorize someone's funeral. I hope you remember that the next time you look in the mirror or when your mother asks you what you did today, you piece of shit."

"Suck my dick."

Baxter was too fast for me this time. His fist shot out and clocked the guy square in the jaw.

The suspect wailed, "Police brutality! You all saw it!"

Sterling shook his head. "I didn't see anything." He turned to the Fed next to him. "You see anything?"

"Nope," the agent replied.

Baxter steered me away from the group as the suspect continued to spew curses and complaints until the two Feds holding him decided to put him facedown in the snow again. I noticed Baxter cradling his right hand.

I said, "You didn't need to defend my honor back there."

He grimaced and flexed his hand. "He had it coming."

"I can't disagree with you there." Across the cemetery, I could see that the graveside service had concluded and people were heading toward their vehicles. I sighed. "Well, so much for a quiet funeral so I could get some closure."

Baxter frowned and hung his head. "I'm sorry. That's my fault."

"Don't do that, Nick. It all goes back to the killer. This is him messing with us. Again."

He rubbed his forehead. "I know. It's starting to get to me."

"I can tell. You need some down time."

Regarding me for a moment, he said, "Hey, you want to grab dinner with me tonight? If I have to eat one more meal at my desk, I'm going to lose it. I promise not to talk about the case."

"I feel like you could find better company than me."

"Maybe our bad moods will cancel each other out."

I smiled. "Okay. See you tonight."

I wandered back over to Rachel, who demanded angrily, "Where did you go? Could you not take a break from work long enough to attend Jenna's whole funeral?"

"Rachel, I didn't have a choice. There was...a situation."

Her face was stuck in a tearful frown. "There's always a situation with you. If you love investigating so much, why don't you just go back to your old job? You have responsibilities, and you can't keep dropping everything when Jayne or Detective Baxter calls. You're letting things slide. Important things. Other people need you more than the department, you know."

Her words, although born out of grief, cut right through my heart. I reached out, not knowing if she was too angry to let me put my arms around her. She didn't resist, so I enveloped her in a hug.

"I'm sorry, Rach."

She put her arms around me and cried quietly against me. After she'd settled down, I managed to get her into Deputy Lester's vehicle so we could take her back to campus.

As we were walking Rachel back to the dorm where she was staying, I asked her, "What can I do for you? Are you taking a break this afternoon? Want to get something to eat? I can have Sam's TA cover another class for me."

She shook her head and sniffed. "Thanks, but no. A group of Jenna's friends is meeting in the food court for coffee in a few minutes, and then I have a...a study group at one."

"Later, then? Maybe we could go to David's after your study group. I'm having dinner with Baxter, but I can reschedule if you want."

Rachel eyed me skeptically. "I thought you said you were done with the department."

"This has nothing to do with the case. He needs some time away from the desk."

"Then it's a date."

"No, it's dinner."

"Whatever," she muttered. "I want to go see Nate as soon as study group is over at three."

"I'll meet you and we can drive to David's together."

"I'm getting a little tired of the police escorts, Ellie." She shot a look at Lester and added, "No offense."

He nodded. "None taken, ma'am."

I said to my sister, "You going off campus without a police escort is non-negotiable. I'll meet you here at three." We had arrived at the front door to the dorm, so I pulled her to me and gave her a hug. "If you need anything, you call me. I'll drop everything and be here for you. Okay?"

"Okay. I love you, sissy."

"I love you, too."

After reluctantly letting her go, I headed across campus toward the science building with Lester trailing only steps behind. My heart twisted in my chest. Poor Rachel was so distraught by Jenna's passing, it was playing havoc with her emotions. At only seventeen, she'd gotten pregnant and was a mom by eighteen. She didn't have a chance to live out the last of her teenage years like a normal teen, so sometimes when she got overwhelmed, she reverted back to a more child-like version of herself. I knew I couldn't have handled what she did at such a young age. Hell, I didn't think I could handle motherhood now. I wanted to be able to help her through her grief, but I had no idea where to start. It certainly wouldn't hurt to get her some professional help.

⸺

I taught my final two classes of the day, thinking it would have been better for everyone involved if I had just taken the whole day off and let someone else cover for me. I was scattered and kept losing my train of thought. Plus in my own emotional state, I was of no comfort to my students, many of whom were either upset or scared over the brutal murder of a fellow class-mate. The whole campus seemed to have a pall over it, today especially. There was no way of fixing it, either. The only bright spot was that the semester break was coming up soon. I hoped after a few weeks away the students would have a chance to heal and could come back and resume some semblance of normalcy.

When I went back to my office after my final class, I had a text message from Rachel: *Thinking about mom a lot today. Can you meet me at her grave? I'm there now.*

"What the hell?" I muttered to myself as I reread the text. It was only two-thirty, so Rachel should still have been in her study group. Why would she have ditched a much needed study session right before finals?

This made no sense. Our mother hadn't been a factor in our lives since I'd gone and taken a newly pregnant Rachel away from her so the poor girl could have a chance at a better life. The only time I'd ever thought about our mother since then was when I realized I'd been working on her murder case, unknowingly processing the garbage bags that had held pieces of her dismembered body. The case had caused me to quit my job, but not because I was distraught over her death. She'd had no use for Rachel and me in life, aside from the extra welfare money, so neither of us felt a reason to go out of our way to honor her in death. We didn't take flowers to her grave, and we sure as hell didn't go out there to weep over it.

This odd message—and the fact that Rachel had blatantly gone against my wishes and left campus alone—deserved more than a texted response. I called her cell, but it went to voicemail.

"Rachel, what in the hell are you doing leaving campus on your own? And why to go to mom's grave? I'm on my way out there, but...please stay in your car with the doors locked and call me when you get this."

I stalked out of my office. To Deputy Lester, who'd been standing guard outside my door, I said, "I need to get to Riverside Cemetery. Fast. I'll explain on the way."

After Lester heard that Rachel was out at the tiny, rather secluded cemetery all alone, he turned on his siren and lights and sped all the way to Noblesville, as fast as possible on the snowy streets. I continued to text and call Rachel on the drive there, but she wouldn't pick up. I didn't get how Jenna's funeral could make Rachel go off the deep end about our mother. Was it the fact that they'd both been murdered at the hands of a madman?

I couldn't stop the nagging feeling that Rachel's off-the-charts reaction was my fault for being gone and for breaking the family apart in an attempt to keep us all safe. But I didn't know what I could have done differently. Nate loved being with his grandparents, and Rachel needed the support of her friends who were all dealing with the same issue. Neither of them would have been happy being prisoners in their own home like I was. I'd thought I was doing the right thing, but maybe I'd only succeeded in making everyone miserable, including myself.

When we got to Riverside Cemetery, the small parking lot was empty. Rachel's car wasn't on any of the side streets.

"You're sure she's here?" Lester asked, his hand ready on his service pistol.

"She said she'd be here..." I replied uncertainly, peering out across the cemetery toward my mother's grave. I could barely see the top of someone's head peeking out above the back side of the headstone. "Wait, I think she's over there. Although why she's sitting in the snow, I don't have a clue."

I hurried toward the simple limestone grave marker that read "Patty Copland." I hadn't been out here since my mother's funeral, and I still couldn't wrap my mind around why after three years Rachel felt the burning need to make a visit.

As I neared the grave, I called, "Rach, what's going on? Why are you sitting out here in the freezing cold?"

When she didn't answer, I voiced an irritated grunt and walked around the grave to speak to her face-to-face. I let out a strangled scream when I laid eyes on the young woman sitting there. She wasn't my sister. She was Michaela Richards.

15

Deputy Lester sprinted over to me. "What's wrong? I heard you scream." When he looked down at Michaela's body, sitting there peacefully and heart-wrenchingly still, he said, "That's..."

I nodded, unable to speak, my eyes fastened on the body. Her torso was tied to the grave with fishing line, and her head was bowed, almost as if she were asleep. Her right hand was missing, and her left hand clutched a garden spade. I saw no note this time. Her clothing was similar to what the killer had dressed Jenna in when he'd posed her. Judging from the inch of snow covering some parts of her, I'd say she'd been out here since at least eleven, since it had stopped snowing around noon.

Lester snapped into action, using the radio clipped to his shoulder to call for any and all available emergency personnel to come here immediately. In one motion, he unholstered his gun, grabbed me, and threw me behind him. He then turned in a slow circle, scanning the area.

My mind was swimming with thoughts, the most frightening one being *where is my sister?* Did Rachel's weird text have anything to do with this scene, or was it more likely that her number had been spoofed in an attempt to get me out here alone? She regularly turned her phone off during class and during study groups, so it stood to reason that she hadn't returned any of my many texts and calls. That had to be it. Phone numbers were simple to spoof, so it wasn't a stretch that someone who could master-mind three murders without getting caught could have pulled it off.

Lester loosened his vise grip on me. "I think you should sit in my vehi-cle. It'll be safer than having you out in the open."

Trying to keep my composure, I nodded and replied, "Okay." I didn't like the thought of being a sitting duck out here, either.

By the time I got settled in Lester's vehicle, the first responders started pulling in. Two sheriff's department cruisers came screaming into the small parking lot as I tried to reach Rachel again by phone. It was past three PM, so I hoped she'd have turned her ringer back on by now. And knowing she was in a bad frame of mind already, I figured if she was stuck waiting for us for any amount of time, she'd be calling me, demanding to know why my police escort and I hadn't bothered to show up at the promised time.

Moments later, as I was keying in text message number ten, my door was wrenched open, and a hand grabbed my arm and dragged me out of the vehicle.

Baxter swept me into a crushing hug, asking in a tense voice, "Are you okay?"

"I'm fine. I'm just...confused."

When he let me go, he searched my face as he asked, "Did you see Parsons? Why are you even out here?"

I showed him my phone. "I got a text from Rachel asking me to meet her here. At our mother's grave."

His face became ashen, and he wiped a hand down his beard. "What? Why?"

"I don't know. When we got here, Rachel's car wasn't here, which I found odd. But then I saw someone's head over the top of the gravestone and thought for a moment it was Rachel. When I got a good look...it wasn't."

"So where's Rachel now?"

I hesitated. "I'm not sure. I guess on campus. She had a study group until three, and afterward we were supposed to meet and go to David's house to see Nate. But then she texted me early, saying she was out here. I've tried to reach her, but can't." When Baxter's eyes became strained with concern, I added, "But that's not out of the ordinary while she's in class or studying. I'm assuming the killer spoofed her number so I'd be the one to come out here and find Michaela."

The theory I'd formed made sense, but some variables bothered me. How did Hunter Parsons have my cell number and Rachel's? And how did he know that Patty Copland was Rachel's and my mother? That wasn't common knowledge. With Jayne's help we'd purposely kept our names out of any media coverage, had a quiet burial, and submitted no obituary in hopes of keeping Rachel and Nate out of the spotlight. It was our belief that Rachel's lunatic father, Marcus Copland, had killed our mother, and Rachel didn't want him trying to find her or contact her. Shortly after the funeral, Rachel changed her last name and Nate's to Miller in order to further hide from Marcus. On a selfish note, I wanted my name kept out of it because I was too ashamed to admit to my coworkers in the department that the known crack whore we'd finally identified was in fact my own mother. As of now my secret would no longer be a secret. That would be fun to explain.

Baxter got out his phone. "I'll have campus security find your sister. Where was her study group?"

I shrugged. "I think they normally meet in the library, but not always."

As if my day weren't going badly enough, Agent Manetti strode over to us, all business, and elbowed Baxter out of the way. Baxter threw a glare at the back of Manetti's head and walked a few paces away to make his phone call.

Manetti demanded, "What's going on out here? Last night all you wanted was to be far away from this case, and now you're right back in the middle of it."

I stared at him. "So now it's *my* fault that the killer is targeting me?"

"Why are you here?"

Frustrated, I handed him my phone showing the text from Rachel. "I got this text from my sister."

Manetti read it and frowned. "What does your sister have to do with this?"

"Nothing, I'm betting. I think this was all a ploy to get me out here."

"Does your sister know Hunter Parsons?"

"No."

"Are you sure? Would she hide something like that from you?"

I narrowed my eyes at him. "Are you asking me if my sister could be working with the killer?"

"I'm trying to get a frame of reference. Also, I need to take your phone."

My jaw dropped, and I snatched it back out of his hand. "Like hell you do. I have to keep trying to contact my sister. You don't need my phone to track this text. All you need is her phone number." I managed to refrain from adding, *idiot*.

He must have inferred my meaning, because he glared down at me. "What I don't need is you getting hostile, Ms. Matthews."

"Then go bother someone else," I fired back.

"Everything okay over here?" Baxter asked warily, having walked back over to us after finishing his phone call.

Ignoring him, Manetti demanded, "Did you touch anything at the scene?"

I rolled my eyes. "Of course not. How stupid do you think I am?" When he didn't reply, I added, "It bothers me that there's a brand-new active crime scene over there, and you're over here grilling me for no apparent reason."

"Don't judge my style of investigation, Ms. Matthews. Don't forget: you're a criminalist, not a detective."

As I took a breath to return a biting remark, Baxter cut me off. "Ellie, can I get your sister's number? I want to run a quick trace on her cell signal."

Manetti, evidently finished with me, stalked away.

I muttered, "Did you hear that? He actually insinuated that Rachel is somehow working with the killer."

Baxter shook his head. "I don't think he meant it that way."

"Why are you defending that...that uncaring cyborg?"

"I'm not. Hey, give me Rachel's number so we can try to pinpoint her location. I want to start figuring out where that bogus text came from."

I pulled up Rachel's contact info and let him take a photo of my screen. He typed a quick email and attached the photo.

"Someone will get working on it right away. I need to go take a look at the scene. Will you be okay here by yourself?"

"If Manetti keeps his distance."

He smiled. "I'll make sure he's otherwise occupied. You keep trying Rachel."

I got back in the cruiser and called Rachel, again getting her voicemail. I texted Miranda, but got back a message that she hadn't seen Rachel since they met for coffee at noon. Last she knew, Rachel was on her way to study group.

I called my friend Samantha. When she answered, I said, "Hi, Sam."

"Hey, how did the funeral go? You and Rachel doing okay?"

"Um...I guess. I'm looking for Rachel, and I think she turned her phone off when she went to her study group. Are you still on campus?"

"Yes."

"Would you have time to run over to the library right now and see if you can find her? I need to get in touch with her to...change the time I'm picking her up this afternoon."

"Sure. In fact, I'm in the courtyard right now. Hey, let's do lunch tomorrow, if you're free. Okay?"

"You bet. Thanks, Sam."

I knew Baxter already had campus security looking for Rachel, but sometimes they weren't as quick as they could be. Sam would have an answer for me within minutes. It was fifteen minutes past three, and I was growing anxious.

I hated to worry David, but no one had looked for Rachel there.

I called him, and when he answered, I said, "Hi, David. Is Rachel at your place?"

"No, should she be?"

I lied, "We were planning to come over this afternoon, but we got our wires crossed on who was picking up who to drive over. She's not answering her phone at the moment, but she might be driving or something. I'll keep trying her."

David's voice had grown concerned. "You're sure there's nothing wrong?"

I hated not being truthful with him. "We're just still emotional over the funeral this morning. Not thinking straight."

"Oh. Well, when you find her, please let me know."

"I will."

By now my stomach was churning. I looked through the windshield and saw Baxter coming toward me, a grim expression on his face. I got out of the cruiser to meet him.

He couldn't look me in the eyes. "Ellie, we can't locate the signal on your sister's phone. That text you got came from a tower in Fishers."

I stared at him in disbelief. "Fishers? I don't know why she'd drive all the way over there."

"She didn't. Her vehicle is still at Ashmore."

My body went numb. I whispered, "Maybe someone stole her phone." My phone rang in my hand, and it was Samantha. My heart pounding, I put the call on speaker and cried, "Sam, did you find her?"

Sam's voice was strained. "No, honey. Um...I did manage to find a couple of students from her study group, and they said...she never showed up today."

I looked up at Baxter, fighting tears. I could tell from the expression in his eyes that he thought the worst.

Sam said, "Ellie? Campus security is here with me. They've been looking for her all over campus. What's going on? Is she...is she missing?"

I choked out, "I don't know. I think...she could be..." As I broke down, Baxter took my phone and pulled me to him.

I heard him say, "Dr. Jordan, this is Detective Baxter. I need to speak to one of the security officers." After a pause, he continued, "This is Detective Nick Baxter. We need you to expand your search for Rachel Miller. I want an alert sent out to all students and faculty including Ms. Miller's photo, asking for information on when she was last seen on campus. I need you to contact the *Ashmore Voice* and have them run the same thing. I want a campus-wide search organized and up and running within the hour. This is your priority, and I want updates every fifteen minutes. Thank you. Goodbye."

"He has her," I rasped in between sobs.

Baxter held me tighter. "We don't know that for sure."

I pushed away from him and wiped my eyes. "Don't coddle me! I can tell by the look on your face you think the same damn thing."

There was a loud whistle from across the cemetery, and Sterling called, "Baxter, get over here. And bring Matthews."

"Why do they want me?" I asked warily.

"I'm not sure."

I swiped a hand across my face and pulled myself together. Baxter had me sign in on the scene entry log, and then we both approached my mother's gravesite. Sterling and Dr. Berg were deep in conversation, and Amanda was taking photos while Beck made some measurements and recorded them on a rough sketch he'd started. Manetti was standing a few feet away, phone glued to his ear.

When Sterling saw us, he ended his conversation with Dr. Berg. His voice off-puttingly gentle, he asked me, "Matthews, does this grave have some significance to you? Do you know a Patty Copland?"

I glanced at Baxter, who was watching me worriedly.

Before I could answer, Beck piped up, "Now I remember that name. From that case three years ago where the vic was chopped up and pieces of her were scattered all over the county. The one Ellie quit in the middle of."

Sterling barked, "Shut the hell up, Becky. Show a little respect."

I lowered my eyes and murmured, "Patty Copland was my mother."

Dead silence filled the air.

Finally, Sterling cleared his throat. "Well, that fits the pattern. I...I'm sorry to have called you back over, um...Ellie."

If Sterling was being this nice to me, something was wrong. I snapped my head up. "Wait. What's going on here? What pattern? What don't I know?"

They all turned to look at me with pity. Even Manetti.

"Someone tell me, damn it!"

Manetti held a plastic sleeve with a rumpled piece of paper in it. "We just found this in the victim's mouth. The poem this time... It references you. And your sister."

"No," Baxter breathed, staring at the poem in disbelief.

Manetti's words were like a kick to my gut. Amanda hurried over to me and put a hand on my shoulder. Baxter did the same on the other side of me. I struggled to focus, to not break down. Even though I didn't want to believe it, it was becoming clear to me that my sister was in grave danger.

I swallowed and whispered, "Read it."

Manetti read, "*You're still in the dark, so I'm going to be kind. I'm flattered how I'm on everyone's mind. A hand for a hand. Let me give you a clue. Now that I have your attention, I'll be the one telling you what to do."* Pausing for a moment, he flicked his eyes at me, and Amanda tightened her grip on my shoulder. He continued, *"If the professor plays nice, her sister lives. Stay tuned for the instructions I'll give."*

I felt like my whole world was shattering in slow motion, piece by piece. I couldn't breathe. My entire body was numb, and when my legs gave way, Amanda and Baxter were there to hold me up.

I choked out, "He has my sister."

Manetti nodded, his expression anguished. "Yes, we're afraid he does. But we're going to do everything within our power to—"

I cut him off, trembling. "The poem says if I play nice, she'll live. When he contacts you, don't do the standard police negotiation bullshit. You tell that son of a bitch I'll do anything he asks. Nothing is off the table. I will trade places with her. I will give him anything he wants. The only thing I care about is Rachel getting out of this alive."

Manetti said quietly, "Ms. Matthews, I think we need to talk about this and come up with a strategy—"

"I'm getting my sister out of this, and I don't care what it costs me." I shrugged out of Baxter and Amanda's grips. "I'm going home to wait for his instructions."

I turned and took off for Lester's cruiser, thinking I wasn't going to be able to hold it together much longer. I should have known after Baxter heard my little speech he wouldn't just let me go.

He fell in step with me as I hurried down the road toward the parking lot. "Ellie, I know your main focus is Rachel's safety, but you can't tell a sociopath you'll give him anything he wants. I'm not trying to tell you what to do, but—"

"Yes, you are. That's exactly what you're doing. You're going to say that trading my life for hers isn't going to solve anything. It's only going to fuel his ego, and it could totally blow up in my face. He might even decide to keep us both."

"You're right. That's everything I was going to say. You can't trust him, which is why it's a terrible idea to give in to his demands."

I stopped and looked up at him as tears started spilling down my cheeks. "I'm willing to take that risk, Nick. I can't stand by and not try to find a way around this. Even if there's a tiny chance he'll let Rachel go, I have to take it. I made a promise to always be there for her. I'm not breaking it now, even to save my own life."

I'd only seen Baxter look this frightened one other time before—when he thought I'd been shot a few months ago. "I can't let you do this, Ellie. We'll think of another way. We'll find this guy."

"You've said that all week, Nick. No offense, but you know you're not going to find him unless he wants you to. And the only way to do that may be to hand me over to him."

His eyes shone with tears. "I will not be a part of that."

"I'm not asking you to." I walked away, and this time he didn't follow.

16

Deputy Lester drove me to David's house in a deafening silence. Other than the short but heart-wrenching conversation I had with Samantha when she called to ask if the killer had Rachel, not a word was spoken in the ten-minute drive. Sam offered to come over and sit with me while I waited to hear the next set of instructions, but I turned her down. As soon as I could, I needed to be alone.

When we got to David's driveway and parked, I took a moment to compose myself. David didn't often get upset or emotional, but I had a feeling this was going to be more than he'd ever had to handle. I got out and walked to the door, dreading this conversation.

When he answered, he took one look at my face and said, "Where is your sister?"

I clenched my jaw hard. Then I managed to say, "The killer took her."

He staggered back, his mouth hanging agape. I followed him into the house and glanced around. No Nate.

I must have looked panicked, because David choked out, "Nate is napping."

"Good. David, I'm sorry. I don't know what the killer wants with Rachel or with me. The thing I'm clinging to is that we have a message from him saying if I cooperate, then he won't hurt Rachel. I'm assuming he's going to give us some kind of ultimatum or ask for a ransom or something. What-ever it is, I'll do it. This is a change to his normal routine, so I'm hoping that will work in our favor, at least. Unfortunately, now all we can do is wait to hear from him."

As I was speaking, David had collapsed onto the nearest chair and put his head in his hands. He said, "How could this have happened? I thought she would be safe on campus."

I'd been wondering the same thing in the back of my mind, but hadn't come up with a good answer yet. "I did, too. We all thought I was the target, and I thought she'd be safer away from me. I guess that wasn't the case." I put my hand on his shoulder. "David, I promise I will do everything in my power to get her back."

He looked up at me, his eyes filled with tears. "I don't want you doing anything dangerous, Ellie. I couldn't stand it for both of my girls to—" His voice broke, and he couldn't go on.

I squeezed my eyes shut, willing myself to keep it together. "Look, David, I hate to ask this of you, but...for Nate's safety...and so there's no chance of him happening to hear anything somewhere or see anything on TV about Rachel's disappearance...can you take him out of town for a few days? Just until we can get this sorted out?"

David seemed dazed. "I guess... Where?"

"Anywhere but here. In fact, don't even tell me where you're taking him. Just go. I'm going to have my assigned deputy drop me at home, and then I'll have him come back here to escort you out of town."

"But won't that leave you vulnerable?"

I shook my head. "I think the killer has what he wants right now." When David only cringed and wiped a fresh tear from his ashen face in response, I said, "Care if I look in on Nate for a moment?"

"Go ahead."

Heading down the hall to the bedroom David and Marjorie kept for their grandchildren, I got a hot, stabby feeling in my heart. I couldn't bear the thought of Nate growing up without his mother. I also couldn't shake the feeling that if things went badly and I did indeed have to trade my life for Rachel's that this could be the last time I saw my nephew. Sweeping aside a tear, I opened the door to find him sleeping peacefully in a bed filled with stuffed animals. I walked over and sat on the bed next to him, leaning down to give him a kiss on the forehead and breathe in his sweet little boy scent. His hair had been freshly washed and was still damp.

He stirred at my touch and opened one eye. "Auntie Ellie? Did you come to take me home?" he asked, yawning.

I swallowed around the lump in my throat. "No, sweetie. I came in here to tell you that Grandpa David is taking you on vacation."

Nate scrambled to a sitting position, now fully awake and alert. "Vacation? In the winter? Where are we going?"

"It's a surprise."

"Ooh, a *surprise* vacation!"

"Yes, sir."

"Is Mommy coming with us?"

I clenched my jaw so tightly I thought I might crack a tooth. "Not this time. She's still got another week of school."

His lower lip stuck out in a pout. "Okay. But I'll miss her."

Feeling like I'd had the wind knocked out of me, I murmured, "I know. But you'll have lots of fun. I'll see you when you get back, okay?" I gave him a hug, and he clung to me tightly.

"Okay. Bye, Auntie Ellie."

I stood, thankful the lights were off so he couldn't see me crying. "Goodbye, my sweet boy. I love you."

"You, too."

⸺⸺⸺⸺

Once I got home, I sent a protesting Deputy Lester away. My safety didn't matter now. Hunter Parsons—or whatever his real name was—had plans for me, and I was resigned to the fact that I had to go along with whatever they were. If that meant him coming for me at my home, then so be it. A deputy would only get in the way and complicate things, plus it would put yet another person in danger, which was the last thing I wanted.

After I shut the door behind Lester, I sagged against it, allowing the all-consuming guilt and horror I'd held at bay to come crashing over me. My knees buckled and I landed on the floor, not even feeling the hard fall. I wept, heaving out racking sobs. Sensing something was wrong, Trixie came over to nuzzle me, but I couldn't handle it.

"Get away from me!" I roared, making her whine and run for the safety of her dog bed in the corner of the room.

Clawing my way up the door to a standing position, I could think of only one thing that could numb the pain. I stumbled to the kitchen and found a new fifth of vodka. I opened it and drank deeply straight from the bottle. My throat was on fire, but that momentarily took my mind from everything else. I dropped my coat on the floor and kicked off my boots, heading back to the living room to find my phone.

As I exited the kitchen, my eyes landed on our Christmas tree. Our tradition was to put it up the day after Thanksgiving, which we'd done again this year, oblivious to the unthinkable happenings that would transpire during the holiday season. A fresh wave of tears falling, I took another swig and turned the tree's lights on. While I watched the twinkling lights illuminating Nate's homemade "ornaments"—badly cut out shapes with chicken scratches and glitter on them—a blinding rage tore through me. I grabbed the closest branches and slammed the tree to the floor. In my blind fury, I stomped on the tree and the ornaments, only to get tangled up in the strings of lights and fall down. Sprawled out next to the disheveled tree, I howled and moaned, my heart feeling like it was tearing into two pieces.

I must have either passed out or fallen asleep, because I awoke to a pounding on my front door and someone yelling my name. Before I could get up off the floor, Baxter had opened the door and barged into my house, his face creased with worry as he took in the pathetic and deranged holiday tableau in my living room.

Wordlessly, he scooped me off the floor and settled me onto my couch. After flicking his eyes toward the fallen Christmas tree again, he asked, "You're not hurt, are you?"

I ached all over after falling down twice, but I didn't want to admit it. "Only on the inside."

"Where's Deputy Lester?"

"I sent him away."

"That wasn't your call."

I shrugged. "My body, my choice."

Running his hands through his hair, he sat down next to me and gestured toward the bottle I'd set on the coffee table. "Was that full when you started?"

"No," I lied, eyeing the missing third of the bottle of vodka I only vaguely recalled drinking. I squinted at him. "Why are you here?" Remembering why I'd got drunk in the first place, my fuzzy mind snapped into action. "Did you hear from—"

Baxter nodded. "We received a message."

"What was it?" I demanded.

"Are you sure you're in the right frame of mind to—"

"Damn it, Baxter! Tell me what he said!"

Frowning, he got out his phone. "He emailed us a video."

I grabbed his arm. "Is Rachel in it?"

He hesitated. "Yes."

"Play it!"

Bringing up the video, he warned me, "There's a lot to take in, so if you need me to stop, tell me."

I'd had enough of his stalling. I reached across him and hit play on the video myself. Sighing, he handed me his phone.

A young man's face filled the screen. With his clean-shaven skin and spiky, bleached-blond hair, I didn't recognize him at first. But once he started speaking, I recognized Hunter Parsons's voice.

"Well, hello there, Detective Baxter and Professor Matthews, you two rock stars, you. I've heard so much the past few weeks on the news about your bravery and your excellent investigational skills that I couldn't resist trying them out for myself." He made a pouty face, and I heard some bumping and other noises in the background. "But this time, you haven't been such smarty-pantses, have you? I've killed what...three women? And you still don't have a clue as to who I am?" Shaking his head, he made a "tsk-tsk-tsk" noise. "Maybe I'm being too evasive. Now that I have your attention, and the professor's sister...." He grinned evilly at us. "I thought you'd be more open to helping me out with something. Oh, and if you're wondering if I'm bluffing about the lovely Rachel Copland Miller, here's your proof."

The camera swung around to an animal stall filled with hay, a small figure huddled in the corner. It was my sister, hands and feet bound and her mouth gagged. My stomach plummeted and began rolling. I dropped the phone and stumbled across Baxter, scrambling for the nearest bathroom. I barely made it to the toilet in time to vomit. Collapsing on the cold tile floor, I looked up to see Baxter standing over me, looking as sick as I felt.

He said quietly, "I know it's one thing to know that he's holding your sister, but it's quite another to see it. I understand if you need a minute."

My eyes filled with tears as I whispered, "How could he keep her there like an animal? She doesn't deserve that."

"I know." He reached out his hand. "Can you watch some more? We're kind of on a timetable now."

I nodded, letting him help me up and back to the couch. Once I was seated, he handed his phone to me, and I hit play. Thankfully, the camera was back on Hunter's face.

"So, here's the deal. There's a case from thirteen years ago I want reopened and solved correctly. And I want you two geniuses to do it all by yourselves. Your mentor, the Sheriff, and her fat-ass partner weren't nearly bright enough to solve it properly in the first place, so I thought your two brilliant minds should take a crack at it." He frowned. "I'd hoped my choice of victims, my crafty little poems, and my carefully placed props would point the department in the right direction sooner, but maybe those involved all those years ago were simply too emotional this week to be able to recall the details of my mother's case."

"His *mother's* case?" I repeated. "Shit."

Baxter murmured, "Yeah."

Hunter Parsons continued, "My real name is Justin Fox. My mother's name was Leann Fox. My father's name was Samuel Fox, and he was wrongly charged with my mother's murder and incarcerated for it. He died in a prison riot, when he should never have been there in the first place. I want you to find the real killer and bring him—or her—to justice. I'm going to give you seventy-two hours, starting now, five PM on Thursday evening.

If you manage to crack this case, sweet Rachel here goes free." He turned the camera toward Rachel again. I didn't want to see her like this, but I couldn't look away. Panning back to himself, he said, "If not...she'll join the ranks of my three other innocent angels with incompetent family members. Get to work, and we'll talk soon. Bye, now."

The screen went black. I sank back on my couch, unable to move. We had to come up with a brand-new suspect from an already solved murder case from over a decade ago, and we only had seventy-two hours to do it? That was impossible. He was asking the impossible of us and using Rachel's life as a bargaining chip. This was never going to work. There wasn't time to get through the red tape to exhume the body for a new autopsy. There wasn't time for DNA analysis of evidence, if there was even any evidence left, viable or otherwise. Jayne was an excellent investigator and always had been, and Frank was no slouch. If she had arrested this Samuel Fox person and testified in court, then he was the killer. Was Hunter...or Justin, if that was his real name, doing this for a good laugh—watching us race against the clock, killing ourselves to somehow pluck a new murderer out of thin air? Maybe this was another wild goose chase to keep us off his scent.

Rage started bubbling up inside me, replacing my despair. I hopped up off the couch, swaying a little as I did so. I began pacing the room, broken twinkle light bulbs and glass ornaments crunching under my feet. "That bastard. If he thinks for a minute that he can get away with this, he's wrong. Dead wrong. I will kill him myself if I ever get my hands on—"

Baxter came over and put his hands on my shoulders to stop my pacing. "Hold up. Channel that. We need your head in the game now more than ever. We've already got people working on reopening the old case and getting the evidence from storage."

"Meanwhile, that nutjob has my sister!"

"Ellie, we'll find her. I promise."

I wrenched away from him. "Did you make that promise to Jayne when we were looking for Jenna? Did you make that promise to the Richards family, too?"

He looked at me like I'd slapped him. "Ellie, that's not fair. I'm sick over Rachel's disappearance."

"*You're* sick over it? Oh, how awful for you, Baxter. Tell me—did you raise her? When you were ten years old, did you get up in the middle of the night every night to give her a bottle and change her diaper because her father was off on a bender and her mother had abandoned the two of you to go screw some random guy? Did you have to walk an extra mile on your way home from school to go to the supermarket to steal the expensive formula because she couldn't tolerate the shitty welfare formula our mother insisted on giving her? Did you help her with her homework every night after finishing your own or take her to buy her first bra? If we can't find her or solve this stupid case in time, are you going to be the one who has to tell her precious baby boy that his mommy is never coming home again?"

I lashed out, striking at his chest with both fists. Baxter didn't flinch, and in response pulled me close to him. I cried against him, unable to find a glimmer of hope in this utterly hopeless situation.

After I'd quieted down enough to hear him, Baxter said, "Let's get you sobered up. I think our best shot is looking into this case. If nothing else, maybe it'll give us some clue as to how to find this guy." When I pulled away from him, he gave me a hard stare. "Ellie, are you up for this? If not, we can get someone else—"

"No, this is my fight." I willed myself to get my act together. Using every last bit of strength I could find, I locked down my emotions. Steadying my voice, I said, "You know I can't sit idly by if there's something I can do to save my sister."

His expression softened. "I figured as much. Come on. I think all you need is a couple of cups of coffee and a greasy cheeseburger and you'll be good to go."

17

I rode with Baxter to the station feeling like I'd been run over by a truck. The coffee and cheeseburger had hit my empty stomach like a ton of acidic bricks, making me feel worse, not better. The only positive side was that I had managed to channel my rage, frustration, and terror over Rachel's abduction into working on the case Hunter/Justin wanted us to re-solve. With Jenna's case, I'd never been able to fully flip that switch and become a dispassionate investigator, and as a result, I'd gotten way too emotional too many times. This time, everything was on the line, and I wasn't letting anything get in the way of what I needed to do.

Baxter worked the whole drive to the station to convince me that the best way to get inside the killer's head was to understand what he'd gone through as a child and how it had affected him. There was also a strong possibility that in studying the old police files from his mother's murder case, we could find names of relatives, friends, or neighbors who might still have ties to him. Baxter believed that was the key to finding where he was hiding Rachel.

The physical evidence from the Fox murder case was being located and transferred to the sheriff's station, and the incident files were being pulled and copied for our use, so there was no investigating that could be done yet. Our first task was to attend a meeting headed, of course, by Agent Manetti.

The moment Baxter and I entered the conference room, it became deadly silent. Sterling, Amanda, Beck, Chief Esparza, and Manetti all stared at me, radiating pity, just like they had at the cemetery earlier today. Everyone seemed to be afraid to speak.

I cleared my throat. "I appreciate your concern for me and for my sister's safety. But I can't handle you all treating me like some victim's distraught family member. Even though I am." I rubbed my forehead. "Look, just bust my balls like usual and don't try to sugarcoat anything for my benefit. I need to be aware of all the gory details, or I'm going to miss something. I'm a liability as it is, and I'm trying so hard to be dispassionate and professional. No pity, okay?"

Sterling grinned. "You all heard it. Matthews just gave me a free pass to say whatever I want to her. Someone write that shit down."

I gave him a half-hearted smile. "Yep. Bring it."

Amanda pulled out the seat next to her and gestured for me to sit. "You realize you've just undone all the progress I've made with his attitude in the last couple of months."

"I know. And he was so close to becoming somewhat human."

Sterling snorted. "Oh, it's on, Matthews."

Manetti, the human buzzkill, said, "Clock's ticking, people. Detective Sterling, can you quickly bring everyone up to speed on the Richards case from this afternoon?"

Sterling nodded. "According to Dr. Berg, Michaela Richards died sometime this morning, roughly six to eight hours before she was found. COD was exsanguination again, same MO as Jenna Walsh. Hand missing, following the pattern as expected. This time the victim was holding a garden spade. We found a note in her mouth like in the Donovan case. The victim was again redressed in dated clothing like we saw in the Walsh case."

Manetti said, "Ms. Carmack and Mr. Durant, a forensic report?"

Beck whined, "We've hardly had time to do a thorough analysis of the evidence."

I saw the other four men in the room simultaneously clench their jaws.

Amanda chimed in, "But of the evidence we did process, which included the poem and the spade, we found the same fingerprints as we had on evidence from the Walsh case and on the award from Ellie's office.

It's the same suspect as before, as we all thought. I don't expect the victim's clothing to be of too much use, but we'll be processing that as soon as we're done here."

Manetti glared at Beck as he said, "Thank you, Ms. Carmack." To the rest of us, he said, "I take it you've all watched the video that Justin Fox sent. He seems to have changed his appearance since Ms. Matthews saw him on Monday. We took new images of him from the video and cleaned them up and distributed them to the news outlets, hoping someone will recognize him that way. We've also distributed photos of Rachel Miller in hopes that we can trace the last place she was seen, or find out if she was ever seen with Fox. I've sent the video to some of my guys to analyze and hopefully find some kind of clue as to where he's holed up. Cyber said the email itself was sent from a Hotmail account on a free Wi-Fi network at a Starbucks in Carmel. That could have been done in the parking lot from the comfort of his vehicle, but we've sent deputies out to interview the employees just in case. Detective Baxter, do you have anything to add?"

Baxter shook his head. "Not much. Now that we know his real name, we found Justin Fox's driver's license number and ran it. We checked out his current listed address and his last known address, but both are in apartment complexes that have no record of him living there. Deputies canvassed both complexes, and no one recognized him from any of the photos we have. So that's a dead end, but no surprise there. We've got people digging through his financials, but in the last six months, he's become a ghost. We've got a work history for him, but again, nothing in the last six months. It feels like he's been planning this for a while. I guess all I have to say is that once we have the incident files and the evidence, we can use all the help we can get."

Esparza said, "You've got the full resources of the department at your disposal. Everyone who isn't scheduled to be out on patrol is available to help. Also, there have been multiple offers from deputies who'd be happy to come in and work on their days off. Don't hesitate to ask for anything you need."

Manetti nodded. "The same goes for my field office. I'm calling a meeting with the key players from the original case, which I hope will give us some insight into the bigger picture. We'll have Sheriff Walsh, Frank

Donovan, and DA McAlister put their heads together and reconstruct the case for us, and we'll Skype in the former coroner, Dr. Franklin. You're all welcome to attend that meeting later, if you like. I'll have a firm time once I speak to the four of them."

I didn't particularly want to be stuck in a room with two people who'd lost loved ones to this psycho while Rachel was in her current situation. It could prove to be too much for me. Besides, I thought it would be better for me to work the evidence from a fresh perspective with no preconceived opinions or theories.

Manetti said, "I think that's everything from my end. Work fast and work smart. Thank you all." When we all got up from our seats to go get to work, he added, "Ms. Matthews, I'd like to speak to you for a moment."

Fighting the urge to utter a heavy sigh, I stayed put. I wondered what kind of reprimand he'd have for me this time.

Baxter said to me, "I'll be at my desk. Come find me when you're done."

Once everyone was out of the conference room and the door was shut, Manetti came over and stood in front of me. His expression and tone softer than I thought possible, he said, "Ms. Matthews, please know that this department and the bureau are committed to bringing your sister home safely. This case is priority number one, and I will personally see to it that anything within our power will be done. You have my word on that. I know you don't want my pity, but I want you to know you have my sympathy." His eyes held mine. "And you have me, anytime—day or night. If you need something analyzed in a hurry or a favor called in for anything, I want you to come to me. If you need to blow off some steam and yell at someone, you come to me." His mouth pulled up in the corner. "Not that you don't do that already."

I was floored by his kind words. I didn't think he had it in him. Maybe I was wrong about him, like he'd said. "Thank you, Agent Manetti. I appreciate it."

"No thanks needed. We're going to continue to work the current cases as well, hoping something will give us a clue as to where the killer might be hiding. If we can get to him before the seventy-two hours is up, I think we'll have a much better chance of freeing your sister. I don't want to hang all our hopes on being able to re-solve a thirteen-year-old murder case in three days, or, for that matter, on a sociopath's promise that he won't hurt your sister. I like to have a backup plan."

I nodded, trying not to think about the fact that my sister's life and safety rested on the whim of a serial killer. What if she were to say or do something that made him angry and he lashed out?

I must have seemed uneasy, because Manetti laid a hand on my shoulder. "We'll bring her home. You focus on staying positive, because that's the only thing that's in your control."

Frowning at him, I said, "I thought we weren't going to treat me like some victim's distraught family member."

He smiled and lifted his hand away. "Right, sorry." His tone turning gruff, he said, "Get to work, Ms. Matthews."

"Much better."

I found Baxter at his desk, perusing a scanned autopsy report on his computer screen.

"You look like you feel better. I can't imagine Manetti gave you a pep talk."

I dropped down into the chair next to his desk. "Surprisingly enough, that's exactly what he did."

"So he's not in fact a cyborg like you previously thought?"

"Possibly not."

He gestured to his screen. "I've got a copy of the autopsy here, which I've sent to Dr. Berg to have him look over. The previous coroner conducted this autopsy. The victim, Leann Fox, suffered blunt force trauma to the head before being strangled to death."

"That's how Amy Donovan was killed." I rubbed my aching forehead. "He was killing mommy all over again."

"Exactly." His desk phone rang, and he answered it. After a few moments, he said, "Excellent. Thanks," and hopped out of his chair. "There are boxes waiting for us in evidence."

My body tensed. I was raring to dive into this case so we could get it solved and get my sister back. But at the same time, I had a gnawing apprehension that the evidence would be unusable and of no help.

Baxter and I walked to the evidence room in tense silence. As outwardly positive as he always tried to stay, he had to have some of the same fears as I did. Baxter signed the two boxes out of evidence, and we took them to the lab. Amanda was in there, processing some clothing, but Beck was not around.

"Hey, is that the evidence from the old case?" she asked, stripping off her gloves and coming over to the workstation where Baxter had set the boxes.

I blew out a breath. "That's it."

Baxter removed a knife from his pocket, put on a pair of gloves, and sliced open the tape holding the smaller box shut. He opened the lid, and to my delight, the box was fairly full. He took out paper bag after paper bag of what I assumed to be clothing, and then got down to several other items, all hidden from view in paper bags and manila envelopes.

Unable to wait any longer, I snapped on a pair of gloves and started pawing through the parcels, scanning the evidence tags to note the contents. I set aside the clothing, which wouldn't be likely to yield much information, and went for the possibly more interesting items. Unfortunately, aside from the victim's clothes, the other bags and envelopes only contained accessories such as shoes, a belt, and jewelry.

I slammed the bag of shoes down on the worktable. "This whole box is full of the clothes the victim died in? Big freaking deal. Where's the good stuff?"

Baxter pulled a longer box over in front of him. "This is the murder weapon... Well, maybe not exactly."

"How is it not exactly the murder weapon?" Amanda asked.

"The autopsy report said the victim sustained a blow to the head before she was manually strangled. Now, I haven't read through the entire report yet, but I assume she was stunned by whatever's in here and then finished off by the killer's own hands."

She shuddered. "Just like Amy Donovan."

Baxter slipped his knife through the red evidence tape and opened the box. He lifted out a four-foot long garden spade that had seen better days.

The metal blade had a dent it and was covered by dirt, rust, and a substance that could be dried blood. I set out a sheet of clean butcher paper on the table, and Baxter set the spade down carefully on it.

"Ouch. It would hurt like a mother to get clocked in the head with this thing," he said.

"Mmm-hmm. I guess this is a good place to start," I murmured, already zeroing in on the smudges of fingerprint powder that were visible on the spade's wooden handle.

He nodded and backed away from the table. "If you guys want to run with this, I'll keep going on the autopsy and then get cracking on the case notes once I get them."

I barely heard him, already whizzing around the lab, donning a clean lab coat and gathering a camera and fingerprinting and blood collection supplies. I heard Amanda say something to him, but didn't register it. I had my job now, and nothing was going to take away my blind concentration.

Moving the bench magnifier over to the work surface with the spade, I turned on the magnifier's light and brought the arm down to get a good look at the handle. There was residue from fingerprint powder over most of the handle, but I was hoping whoever had originally processed this item had missed a print that I could pull myself.

I changed my gloves and put on a mask, then took a deep breath. This was it. I had to find something on one of these items that had been over-looked thirteen years ago. The spade's handle was made of a light-colored wood that had been sanded smooth and varnished, and the D-shaped grip was made of red-painted metal and wood. Good old-fashioned black fingerprint powder was the perfect choice. I took several photos first, before I disturbed any potential evidence.

Before I applied any more fingerprint dust, I looked for smudged finger-prints I might use to be able to get some DNA. Not that we could get a DNA match returned from our lab in seventy-two hours, but if we really were chasing a new killer, it could come in handy if there were a court case in the future. I saw a blurry partial print that seemed to have escaped the first round of dusting, so I took a photo, then swabbed what I could of it.

After I'd packaged the swab, I dipped my fingerprint brush in the powder and gently swiped it on the grip and the top few inches of the handle. When I set my tools down to inspect the handle, I was disappointed to find no evidence of fingerprints. Not to be deterred, I went on swiping fingerprint dust in six-inch sections down the handle. Finally, near the socket that attaches the spade's blade to the handle, I found one lone fingerprint. My heart hammered in my chest. On a small curved surface like the handle, it would be best to use Mikrosil, like Amanda and I had used on the boots Jenna had been wearing the night she was killed. Fighting to steady my shaking hands, I took several photos of the print, then mixed the Mikrosil base and hardener and dabbed a small amount over the fingerprint. The twenty-minute wait was going to kill me this time if I didn't move on to something else. I decided to concentrate on the blade end of the spade.

I moved the arm of the magnifier down to the other end of the spade, taking in the mess on the back. If this dark substance was in fact blood, that meant the killer had to have hit Leann Fox at least twice with this thing. Like Baxter had said, that would have been extremely painful. Two blows from the heavy spade could have disoriented her enough for her attacker to easily overpower and strangle her. She may have been knocked out and unable to fight back at all. I wondered briefly whether or not there were any scrapings taken from underneath her fingernails during the autopsy— not that there was anything we could do about it now.

Ripping off my gloves, I texted Baxter: *Fingernail scrapings done at autopsy?*

His quick response was: *Yes, but no DNA was found.*

Damn. Regardless of the fact that she'd raised a serial killer, this poor woman had met a violent death. Granted, Justin Fox had to have been young when his mother was killed. It was possible he'd developed his sociopathic tendencies after she was gone. Maybe it wasn't her fault, but I still couldn't bring myself to feel a normal amount of empathy for her because of what her son was currently doing to my sister. In some ways, it almost made it easier to focus since I wasn't spending any time feeling sorry for my victim.

I put on new gloves and took several photos of the bloodlike substance on the blade of the spade. I then moistened two swabs and went over a couple of areas where the substance was more concentrated. After setting those swabs aside to dry, I staked out another worktable and started on the clothing. Amanda had taken the boots, jewelry, and belt to her workstation and was working quietly, not being her usual conversational self. I knew she understood the stakes here and was pleased to see she wasn't wasting any time. Beck, on the other hand, had just returned from one of his breaks. I took the victim's shirt and began examining it, thinking if I stopped to berate Beck about wasting time, I might lose my cool and not be able to get it back.

Amanda, however, jumped on him the moment he walked in the door. "Beck, where have you been? We have evidence to process."

Beck replied, "I—"

"Save it," she snarled. "Grab an item and start working. No more breaks."

"I'm *your* boss, not the other way—"

"I don't care. If I see you slacking again, I'll have Manetti in here, and he will crawl up your ass."

I smiled to myself as I turned out the light over my new workstation and began shining a UV light on the blouse I'd chosen. I heard Beck stomping and banging things around, so I assumed he had at least obeyed her command to get to work. Evidently, for as much as Amanda had rubbed off on Sterling, it had gone the other way as well. Sterling would have been proud of the way she shut down Beck, who was his least favorite person in this department, if not the entire county.

The shirt I was examining was intact, with no clippings having been taken from it. Aside from a few grass and dirt smudges, the thing was pristine, with no stains illuminating under the UV light. The white fabric had yellowed a bit over time, but not nearly as much as the copycat blouses Justin had bought to dress his victims in.

The door to the lab swung open, and Jayne entered, making a beeline for me. She looked even more frail and drawn than when I'd seen her at the funeral this morning. I removed my mask and gloves as she approached.

Enveloping me in her arms, she said, "I've had my phone off all afternoon and just got Agent Manetti's message about Rachel. Ellie, I'm so sorry. What can I do for you? I am one hundred percent at your disposal."

I hugged her back hard, hoping to stave off any cracks in my emotional armor. "Just think back and remember anything you can about the Leann Fox murder, and about her son. We need all the information we can get." I let go and took a step back. "Agent Manetti said those of you on the original case are going to meet soon and put your heads together. I know it's going to be tough on you and Frank, but—"

"But we're doing this for Rachel. Don't you worry about us old-timers. We're tough."

"I know."

She sighed and ran her fingers through her hair. "Leann Fox. I don't know why we didn't have her case pulled for the detectives to look into. I guess since it seemed to be such a slam dunk all those years ago, we didn't spend a lot of time investigating. It was a no-brainer. Frank and I had been out to that house on several other occasions for domestic disturbance calls, so no one was surprised when drunk, abusive Samuel Fox finally killed his pretty wife. Even though it was a murder, I don't remember it being one of my more remarkable cases. I'm sorry we didn't realize it sooner."

I shrugged. "Even if you had, I don't know that it would have helped. We were looking for Hunter Parsons, not Justin Fox."

Jayne took me by the shoulders. "I am throwing every available resource at this case and calling in every favor I have coming. Ellie, we're going to find Rachel, and we're going to nail this son of a bitch to the wall. I promise you that."

I smiled. I'd balked at Baxter's promises only an hour ago, but somehow these words from Jayne felt like something I could hold onto. She'd never disappointed me once in all the time I'd known her, and I knew for a fact that she would move heaven and earth if Rachel and I needed it.

She released me. "I'm going to prepare for my meeting. You keep doing what you're doing. We *will* figure this out. Meanwhile, if there's anything you need, you find me. Got it?"

I nodded, feeling better than I had in a while. There was nothing like a pep talk from Jayne Walsh.

18

I put on new gloves and a mask, and once the Mikrosil on my fingerprint from the spade handle was ready, I peeled it off. It revealed a perfect print, this one in a nondescript loop pattern. I took it to the computer and scanned it, and once I'd plotted the individual characteristics of the print, I ran it through AFIS. After a few minutes, I had a list of possible matches, with Samuel Fox, Leann Fox's husband/convicted killer, at the top.

Deep in thought, I drummed my fingers on the desk. It stood to reason that a garden tool found at the Fox home would have Samuel Fox's fingerprints on it. It was also quite possible that he was indeed guilty of murdering his wife, and their son simply couldn't come to terms with daddy being a killer. Maybe Justin Fox's insistence in us reopening his mother's murder was less about finding the "correct" killer and had more to do with him wishing that his father was innocent and that things had turned out differently for everyone involved.

Delving into a sociopath's motivations and feelings only made my head hurt, so I gathered the fingerprint evidence, boxed it up to take to the clerk, and logged my information. I then went to process the victim's skirt. I ran the same procedure as I had on the blouse. The skirt was clean as well. Beck had taken the bra, so the only thing left was the underwear. I got it out, fearing the worst, but it was surprisingly clean for underwear from a death scene. When I shined the UV light on the fabric, however, the crotch illuminated all over. Leann Fox had had sex before her death.

Taking a step back, I thought for a moment. If things were so bad with her husband that he was the cops' one and only suspect, it stood to reason that their marriage was degraded enough that sex wouldn't factor in. Unless they had one of those overly passionate, volatile relationships where the line between love and hate was so blurred that sex was still a major component. Or unless he raped her before he killed her.

I stripped my gloves off and texted Baxter: *Rape kit done or evidence of rape found during autopsy?*

After a few moments, he texted back: *No, why? Did you find some kind of evidence of rape?*

Evidence of sex. Forming a theory. I'll get back with you after more tests.

I put on a clean pair of gloves and marked the area around the stain with a Sharpie. There had been no cutting made from the underwear, so the previous examiner had not sent a sample in for DNA testing in the original case. Before I did any tests to check for semen, I carefully snipped a small area from the center of the stain, placed it in a tiny manila envelope, and labeled it as a possible DNA test. The only problem with that was I had three days to get a DNA test back—not thirty, which was the standard. It could be done, but a few dozen other cases would have to be pushed aside and this one put at the top. I wasn't sure Jayne had that many favors at her disposal.

Heading to the chemical cabinet, I found containers of sodium alpha naphthyl phosphate and Fast Blue B dye. After making a small amount of solution with the two substances, I got out a piece of filter paper and sprayed it with water. I blotted the crotch area of the underwear in hopes of transferring the potential semen to the paper. I then laid out the paper on a sterile tray and dripped a couple of drops of my solution onto it. After about ten seconds, the area on the paper where I'd added the solution began turning purple. This presumptive test for the presence of acid phosphatase, a concentrated enzyme in seminal fluid, indicated the presence of semen. In any other case, there would have to be confirmatory tests done. But for my tight time frame, it was good enough for me.

"Yes!" I exclaimed, stripping off my mask and wiping the sweat from my forehead with the sleeve of my lab coat.

From right next to me, a deep voice asked, "Did you find something?"

I jumped, placing a hand on my thudding heart. "Agent Manetti, didn't anyone ever tell you it's rude to sneak up on people?"

He rolled his eyes. "I've been here in the lab for several minutes, talking to your fellow criminalists. I'd hardly call that sneaking."

I had a thought and turned to face him. "You said if I needed something analyzed fast that you could hook me up."

Nodding, he said, "I can. What do you need? Name it."

I handed him the small manila envelope with the underwear clipping in it. "I'm not sure on this, but..."

"But what? Any theory is a valid one at this point," he said, his eyes kind.

"Okay, so I found evidence—presumptive evidence, which is all I've got time for right now—of semen in the underwear Leann Fox was wearing when she died. According to the autopsy, she hadn't been raped. Here's my problem with the situation, though—is it the most likely assumption that a married couple with a history of domestic disturbance incidences has consensual sex shortly before the husband kills the wife in such a violent way? Of course it could happen, but I think there's a strong possibility that this semen does not belong to the husband."

His eyebrows shot up. "You make an excellent point, Ms. Matthews. I'll get this sample sent off right away. It might take a couple of days, but I'll personally make sure you have it back before Sunday evening."

I smiled. "Thank you, Agent. It means more than you know."

He grinned down at me. "See? Told you I wasn't so bad."

After cleaning up my workstations and making copious notes about my findings, I set the evidence I'd processed aside for Amanda or Beck to make a second examination. I stripped off my gloves, mask, and lab coat and headed for the break room. My head was pounding, probably from the combination of focused concentration and impending hangover, so I stuffed my face with a chocolate bar. Halfway through, I began wondering whether or not Rachel's captor was feeding her and instantly became ill. I trashed the rest of the candy bar and headed to Baxter's desk.

Partway there, I happened to glance through the window of the smaller conference room and noticed that Sterling and Baxter were inside. After knocking, I entered and saw that they'd set up a command center. There were notes scrawled all over a dry erase board that took up most of one wall, and another wall was plastered with crime scene photos. The conference table was littered with files, court notes, police reports, phone records, and handwritten case notes.

"Wow. Looks like there's plenty of documentation on this case. That's good," I said, walking over to stand in front of the wall of photos.

Sterling kept working, shuffling papers around and making notes on the dry erase board, but Baxter came over and stood beside me. "We were able to get the public defender's files as well, so that will give us some extra insight on Samuel Fox's side of things."

In glancing over some of the photos, something popped out at me. "Based on the clothes, the garden spade, and Amy Donovan's manner of death, I get that Justin Fox's victims are meant to be his mom." I pointed to one of the photos where Leann Fox's entire body was shown lying on her back on the grass. Her head had ended up in a flowerbed, with white daisies surrounding it almost like a halo. "Now I get the daisies."

Sterling said from behind us, "Our killer came home and found mommy dearest dead, if you're wondering why he's so screwed up. He was ten years old at the time."

Feeling a fleeting moment of empathy for Justin Fox, I said quietly, "It'll screw you up to see your mom meet a violent end."

Baxter cast a worried glance at me.

Sterling went on, "I'm sure that scene was seared into his mind. Once he went full-on psycho, there was probably some part of his brain that wouldn't rest until he recreated the scene himself in one way or another."

I turned to Sterling. "What happened to Justin once his dad got arrested? Did he get put in the system, or was there a relative who took him in?"

"The system."

"No wonder he's nuts," I muttered, thinking back to the time Rachel and I were put in foster care.

Our stint in the system only lasted for six months, but foster care was even worse than living with my horrible mother, which I hadn't believed was possible. That difficult time period was the catalyst for my downward spiral into teenage delinquency. If Jayne hadn't come into my life and scared me straight, I could have ended up like Justin Fox.

Baxter said to me, "I have an appointment tomorrow to meet with his former social worker. I assume you'll want to come along."

"Absolutely. I hope she'll be forthcoming. Sometimes social workers get all high and mighty about sharing information on minors."

Sterling snorted. "The Sheriff has already taken care of that. I don't know who she threatened, but we were told Social Services would hold nothing back."

It was no surprise to me that Jayne was already working to hold up her promise. "Does he have a juvie record?"

Baxter said, "Surprisingly, no. The guy's a clean slate as far as we can tell. This killing spree is his first offense."

I wrinkled my nose. "Don't you think that's weird? No gateway crimes—just zero to serial killer?"

Sterling shook his head. "Oh, I guarantee he's committed other crimes. He's slick and simply hasn't gotten caught. Yet."

Baxter said to me, "What about the theory you said you were forming earlier? Anything pop?"

Deciding it was time to sit down and delve into the case with the detectives, I took a seat and rested my aching feet. "I found seminal fluid in Leann Fox's underwear. You said according to the autopsy there was no evidence of rape. I find it hard to believe that the man she had consensual sex with was her drunk, abusive husband shortly before he snapped and killed her."

"I think you could be onto something there." Sterling tapped the white board with the end of a dry erase marker. "We've listed out the *seven times* the cops went out over domestic disturbances at the Fox house in the five months leading up to the murder. The last time was two weeks prior.

Normally when a relationship gets abusive, so does the sex. But then again, these are not normal people we're dealing with."

Baxter stroked his beard. "So let's say Leann Fox was cheating on her husband. That gives him an even better motive to kill her."

Sterling said, "True, but it also gives us another angle to consider, and another suspect. Two if her side piece was married. The problem is, if a semen stain is the only evidence we find of an affair, it won't help us. DNA won't come back soon enough to fit into our seventy-two-hour window, especially since we're running up against a weekend."

I replied, "According to Manetti, it will. He took the sample and promised he'd have the results back to me in time."

"I'll believe it when I see it. Feds. Always trying to throw their weight around," Sterling grumbled.

"In this case, it's a good thing. I'm not looking a gift horse in the mouth."

Baxter asked, "Did you not get anything else from that whole box of evidence?"

"I didn't process all of it myself, but I did look at what I assumed was the most pertinent evidence. I managed to find a fingerprint on the spade handle. It was Samuel Fox's, so that's not news. And of course I found the blood on the business end of the spade. Also not a surprise."

Baxter nodded, deep in thought. "Aside from the Hail Mary of the seminal fluid, I'm afraid this case is not going to be cracked by the physical evidence. We need to spend tonight going over these reports and looking for something that could have been missed. I also want to come up with a list of people to speak to and then hit the pavement bright and early tomorrow."

The three of us descended into silence as we started pouring over the documentation from the case. I began with the autopsy report, which didn't have much more information than what Baxter and I had texted about earlier. The victim's hyoid bone had been broken, which was a hallmark of manual strangulation. The autopsy showed that, other than being dead, Leann Fox was an otherwise healthy thirty-two-year-old woman. I shivered, noting that she'd been barely older than I was now. Amanda came in after a few minutes and informed us that she and Beck had finished the first examination of the evidence from the Leann Fox case, but they had found nothing of consequence. As I was setting the autopsy report aside, my phone rang. It was Samantha.

Surprised that she'd be calling so late, I hurried out of the room to take the call. "Hello?"

Sam's voice was strained. I could tell she was trying not to show her own devastation over the situation as she spoke. "Hey, Ellie. Rich and I have been going around campus tonight, trying to figure out where Rachel was last seen before..."

I felt a glimmer of happiness in spite of the dire situation. Samantha and Professor Rich Porter were my closest colleagues in the forensic science department, and some of the most brilliant minds I'd ever come in contact with. It meant the world to me that they were doing what they could to help, and giving up their evening to do it.

Sam cleared her throat. "Anyway, we think we have something."

My heart rate quickened. "You do? What is it?"

"You know the coffeehouse about a block away from the admin building?"

"Sure. Java Roasters. Rachel loves that place."

"We found a student who saw her walking that way just before one today, so we decided to check it out. Then we talked to one of the baristas there, who said Rachel came in and ordered two coffees...one for herself and one for her 'date.' Anyway, she ended up changing her order and getting the coffees to go before anyone joined her. Did you think to check with Tony?"

I blew out a breath. "Honestly, I hadn't given him a thought. Rachel hadn't said a word about him lately, so I was hoping maybe things had cooled between them. You know I don't discuss him with her if I can help it."

"I know. Want me to find him and grill him for you?"

I smiled. Good old Sam. Always willing to go to bat for me, or at least get in the middle of some juicy relationship gossip. "Nah, this is one conversation that probably needs to be more official." I hesitated for a moment. "Thanks, Sam. For everything you're doing. And Rich, too. We can use all the help we can get right now."

"We're more than happy to. By the way, don't worry about classes or finals or anything. Rich and I have it managed for you, so don't give it a second thought. He already hacked into your computer and found your tests for next week. And I spoke to Rachel's professors, who all said she's exempt from finals this semester."

I was floored. "Thank you. I don't know what to say."

"I'd do anything for you two. You know that, right?" Her voice broke, and I had to fight to keep my emotions in check.

"I know. I'll talk to you soon."

After hanging up, I went back to the conference room. "That was my friend Samantha. She and another Ashmore professor have been canvassing and found that Rachel made an appearance around one PM at Java Roasters, which is just off campus. She mentioned to the barista that she was getting coffee for herself and a date."

Baxter looked up. "Is she still dating that pervert dorm director?"

"As far as I know. In all the confusion, I didn't even think to check with him to find out if he'd seen Rachel today."

Baxter stood. "I want to talk to him, as well as the staff at that coffeehouse. Do you know if they're still open? It's past ten."

"They cater to college kids. They're open until midnight every day."

He stuffed some loose papers into a file, which he handed to me. "Here. You can read some incident reports to me on the way so we don't waste any time. Sterling, you got this?"

Not looking up from the file he was perusing, Sterling gave Baxter the finger.

"I'll take that as a yes."

19

"I guess I'll start with the first domestic disturbance call from the Fox household, which was placed five months before the murder occurred. Looks like Leann Fox made this call." From the passenger seat of Baxter's fast-moving SUV, I used my phone's flashlight to skim the police report and relay the highlights aloud. "She stated that her husband was drunk and smashing items in the house and that she was afraid for her and her son's safety. Once the police got there, though, the two of them were talking calmly and nothing seemed amiss aside from some broken dishes and a busted dining room chair."

"Any mention of signs of the wife or child sustaining any physical abuse?"

I speed-read the rest of the report. "No, nothing."

"On to the next one, then."

I flipped to the next report. "This one is from February of that year, a month later. This report shows that the hospital initiated the call to the police when Leann's neighbor brought her to the ER for a broken wrist. The neighbor stated that he heard yelling coming from the Foxes' back-yard. When he went outside and peeked over the fence, he found Leann Fox on the ground, holding her wrist. She told him she slipped on some ice, but he didn't believe her. He insisted on taking her to the ER. The hospital staff noticed that her wrist had a handprint around it, which made them suspect abuse even though she told them repeatedly that she'd fallen."

"Great. Another instance of a victim covering for her abuser," Baxter griped, turning a corner so sharply I almost dumped the file sitting on my lap.

"Speaking of covering things up, do you think that the abuse had gone on prior to this slew of calls?"

"I would assume it probably had, unless there was some kind of catalyst that caused a sudden and major breakdown in their relationship."

"It would have to be monumental to kick-start this list of atrocities. Moving on, the third call came from the same neighbor, only two weeks later. And since the last incident had had some question of assault, they sent out detectives—Jayne and Frank—to check it out. Evidently the neighbor heard yelling again and wasn't taking any chances. The fight was still going strong when Jayne and Frank got there, so they got to hear some of it. The Foxes were arguing about how the husband hadn't made any effort to find a new job after losing his old one, and how he spent his days at the local bar instead of doing anything productive."

"Sounds like a great guy. Tell me again why we're busting our asses to exonerate this shitshow, when it doesn't even matter anymore because he's dead?"

"Whoa, there. Have you forgotten how our partnership works, Nick? *I'm* the one who gets to throw around the pissy remarks while *you* talk me down off the ledge."

He grinned. "I'm sorry. I'll keep my pissy remarks to myself from now on."

"See that you do. Looks like no evidence of any physical abuse this time, although after only two weeks, Leann's wrist would still have been hurting."

"Right. A broken bone—the gift that keeps on giving."

"What did I just say about the pissy remarks?"

"That was some of my terrible gallows humor."

"Oh, yeah. I nearly forgot about your bad jokes. I haven't heard as many of them this time."

Shrugging, he said, "Well, there's a time and place for everything. But I'm flattered that you seem to have missed my wittiness."

I shook my head and turned to the next report. "Domestic disturbance number four." I read the beginning of the report and chuckled. "You're gonna love this one. Mr. Shitshow called the cops on Mrs. Shitshow. Said she hit him in the head with a frying pan."

"Now you're just making stuff up. That's so cliché."

"It's true. It says so right here. Martinez handled that one."

"I bet he laughed his ass off."

"Yes, but more importantly, that gives us another person with some insight into the Fox family. We need to have a sit-down with him at some point."

"We do. Next."

I perused the next report, my fleeting bit of good humor fading back into the depression I'd been stuck in all week. "Number five was no laughing matter. Leann Fox didn't show up for work one day, so her boss, aware of the history of abuse, immediately called the police. The first responder who went out for this one found Leann naked, gagged, and tied to the bed. Husband and son were not in the house."

I happened to glance over at Baxter at that point, and even in the meager light of my phone's flashlight, I could see his cheeks getting red. The man could not talk about sex with me.

Continuing to give him the highlights of the report, I said, "Because of the sexual nature of the incident, Jayne and Frank took over the investigation, but Leann refused to be examined by a sexual assault nurse, even though there was some irritation around the ligature marks on her wrists and ankles. She insisted that she'd asked to be tied up tight and that bondage was a normal part of their sex life. When they asked her why she'd been left like that, she said she and her husband had lost track of time and he'd had to run to take their son to school. She refused to press any charges against her husband and even tried to laugh it off as a big misunderstanding. Frank found the husband at a bar a few hours later, dead drunk, with no recollection of tying Leann up." I sighed. "Again with the bullshit. I guarantee she didn't ask to be tied up, because she didn't have time for it. She had a kid to get ready for school. Let me tell you, when I'm scrambling in the morning to get myself to work and help Rachel get Nate ready to go to daycare, the last thing on my mind is sex." I shook my head.

"When kids are involved, your morning routine is set in stone. No deviations. You don't 'lose track of time.' "

"It's no wonder this guy went down for the murder. The signs are all here—verbal, emotional, sexual, and physical abuse. And every time, it gets covered up and she refuses to press charges. He knew he could do damn near anything to her and get away with it."

Worry taking over my thoughts, I said, "What if the guy really is guilty and we have to go back and tell Justin Fox that he was wrong about his dad? What will happen to Rachel then?"

Baxter had just pulled into the parking lot by Harris Hall. He placed his hand over mine. "The plan is to use this case to figure out all we can about Justin Fox and find him first. There has to be someone from his past who knows where he's been all these years."

"But if that doesn't work—"

"If it doesn't work, then..." He shrugged. "We'll throw some random low-life under the bus. Say he did it."

My jaw dropped. "Nick Baxter! You cannot do that."

He squeezed my hand. "You're not the only one who's willing to do something crazy to save your sister."

Baxter released my hand and got out of his vehicle, leaving me in shock. I didn't think a straight shooter like him would resort to such questionable tactics, but then again, this wasn't just any case. Justin Fox had declared war on Hamilton County law enforcement. They were clearly prepared to take him down by any means necessary.

I stepped down from the SUV and fell into step with Baxter on the sidewalk leading to Fenton Hall, where Rachel's boyfriend, Tony Dante, was the dorm director. We headed for his office. After a minute's worth of knocking at his door, a group of boys walked by and huffily informed us that Tony had been holed up in his room most of the week and was not making himself available to help with student issues.

Once Baxter flashed his badge, they let us into the locked dormitory floors and gave us directions to Tony's room.

Baxter pounded on Tony's door and called, "Tony Dante, this is Detective Baxter with the Hamilton County Sheriff's Office. Open up."

After a few moments, a disheveled and distraught Tony answered the door. When he saw us, he immediately shrunk back from Baxter and turned his frightened eyes at me. "Is it true about Rachel? Is she—" He bit back a sob.

I had to admit I didn't take the time to think about how Rachel's disappearance would affect her boyfriend, such as he was. For one thing, I didn't believe that he had it in him to be particularly faithful to her, so I couldn't imagine he cared too much about her. Plus, he was a total sleaze, never passing up the opportunity to hit on any female he came in contact with.

Baxter said, "She's missing, yes. And we believe that the Eye for an Eye killer may have something to do with her disappearance."

Tears welled up in Tony's eyes. He muttered to himself, "I wish she wouldn't have... If I'd only been there..."

"What do you mean *if you'd been there*? Were you supposed to meet her today? Did you flake out on her and leave her vulnerable?" I demanded. "When was the last time you saw her?"

He hung his head. "I haven't seen her since she dumped me on Tuesday."

I stared at him. "She *dumped* you? I mean, not that I'm not happy to hear it, but why?"

Shrugging, Tony looked from me to Baxter with sad eyes. "She said that I didn't challenge her and make her feel alive."

Baxter asked, "Did she say if there was someone else who did?"

"She didn't come out and say that she was interested in someone else, but I had the feeling she was. Rachel isn't the type of person who'd cheat, so I was kind of assuming she'd met someone she wanted to get to know better and decided to cut me loose so she could do that."

It was true—Rachel was no cheater. She'd watched our mother manipulate men and be manipulated by men all her life and vowed never to be like that. She might have made bad choices about which men to date, but she was never cruel to them, even when they'd been cruel to her.

Baxter said, "Just to be clear, you did not have plans to meet her this afternoon at one PM at Java Roasters, correct?"

Tony sighed. "That's correct."

Baxter shot me a worried glance. In that moment, I stopped thinking about the demise of Rachel and Tony's relationship and realized exactly what he was thinking—this new guy Rachel was interested in could very well be Justin Fox.

My hand flew to my open mouth, and Baxter grabbed my arm, throwing a "Thanks, Mr. Dante," over his shoulder and steering me toward the stairwell.

Questions started pouring out of my mouth as we thundered down the stairs. "Why didn't Rachel tell me she'd broken up with Tony? Why didn't she tell me about the new guy? Why didn't she realize that she was dating a sociopath?"

Baxter said, "We don't know for sure that she was dating our killer."

"Don't blow smoke up my ass, Baxter. I can see it all over your face."

"Okay, so maybe she was dating him. But didn't you say how personable the guy was when you talked to him? Maybe he's charming like Ted Bundy."

"Ted Bundy? You're making me feel worse, not better."

We exited Fenton Hall and hurried back to the SUV.

Baxter said, "I'm sorry. I didn't mean to make a frightening analogy. I only meant that he's exceptionally good at getting young women to believe he's the perfect guy. It's one of a sociopath's best skills. And as for telling you about dumping that idiot we just talked to—why do you think Rachel kept that to herself?"

I frowned as we got in Baxter's vehicle and he pulled out of the parking lot. "What? Are you saying that she didn't want to tell me because I'd gloat and say 'I told you so'?"

"No offense, but that's exactly what I'm saying. Don't forget I was with you when you found out the two of them were dating. I had to physically restrain you from beating the shit out of him."

I groaned. "When did I become *that* sister—the one Rachel can't come to for advice and understanding?"

"From what I gather, it was Tony Dante that was the problem, not your sisterly bond. If she mentioned a new guy she was interested in, you'd put it together that she was dumping Dante."

I griped, "Freaking Tony Dante strikes again. If she'd been dating anyone but him, she would have gladly told me about moving on with someone else. But no. This is the one time that it matters, and I'm in the dark. Damn it!" I hit the dashboard. "And more important than any of this, how in the hell did she not recognize Justin Fox from his photo and sketch that's been plastered everywhere since Tuesday morning?"

Baxter pulled into the parking lot behind Java Roasters. "You saw the video he sent. He transformed his appearance entirely. I didn't recognize him at all. Maybe he didn't seek out Rachel until after he'd made the change. Or maybe he was wearing a disguise in your office."

I shook my head. "No, the hair and beard weren't fake. I sat across from him for thirty minutes. I would have noticed."

We got out of the vehicle and went inside. The place was warm and inviting, adorned with rustic Christmas decorations in keeping with the shabby chic coffeehouse vibe. How many times I'd met Rachel or Sam here for coffee—we'd relax in the overstuffed chairs by the window without a care in the world. Now I felt like I shouldn't be here. It felt wrong to be in such a comforting place when I knew where Rachel would be spending tonight.

While I was lagging behind, Baxter had already gone up to the counter and flashed his badge. One of the baristas left her post behind the counter and came around to meet him at a table. I walked over and took a seat with them.

"This is my partner, Ellie Matthews," he said to her. To me, he said, "This is Sophie King. She served Rachel her coffee this afternoon."

Sophie's lower lip trembled. "I didn't know she was missing until about thirty minutes ago. I'm so sorry. There aren't any TVs in here, and we're not allowed to be on our phones during our shifts. I had no idea anything was wrong until those two professors came in and—" Her eyes widening, she stopped abruptly and stared at me. "Wait, I recognize you. You're in here a lot with...her."

I cleared my throat. "Rachel is my sister."

She covered her mouth with a trembling hand. "Oh, I'm so sorry. I can't imagine—"

I interrupted her. "I appreciate your concern, Sophie. Thank you. Can you tell us everything about Rachel's visit here today? Start from when she walked in the door to when she left—as much as you can remember. No detail is too insignificant, even if it's a feeling you had about her demeanor."

Sophie nodded. "She came in and...well, I remember thinking to myself that she seemed kind of sad. But once she placed her order and said that the second coffee was for her date, her face lit up." She sniffed. "She has such a pretty smile. Anyway, I took the next customer's order, and then she was back at the counter, saying she'd had a change of plans and that she was going to need her two coffees to go. I happened to glance up and see her walk out the front door a few minutes later."

"Was she alone the whole time she was in here?" Baxter asked.

"Yes."

"What made her change her mind about the coffee? Did she get a call or a text?"

"I'm sorry, but I don't know. I was busy taking the next customer's order."

He glanced around the room. "Do you have any surveillance cameras in here or outside?"

"We have a camera outside, but it's not really for surveillance, I don't think. We use it to see how backed up the drive-thru line is."

Baxter glanced at me. "We need to see that."

Sophie rose from the table. "I'll get the manager."

Baxter keyed in a quick text and turned to me. "I'm going to have Sterling find out if Rachel got a call or text around one and where it came from." When I didn't respond, he said, "I know what we learned here maybe isn't a lot, but at least now we have a timeframe nailed down. I have to say, this guy is smart. With the exception of Michaela Richards, he hasn't abducted his other marks outright, which could cause a scene and make him memorable to bystanders. With Jenna and Rachel, he took his time and got to know them. He pretended to take them out on a date, and then I assume he instead drove them to wherever he ended up holding them."

I nodded, wishing now that I hadn't asked him to be so blunt and forthcoming about information with me. Changing the focus from Rachel, I asked, "Why do you think he abducted Michaela in a different way? I mean, he clearly didn't cause a scene, because he didn't get caught. You said it only took him seconds to subdue her and get her into his car, but it was still a gamble. If someone happened to have been watching, they could have thought something was off and tried to stop him."

He looked away. "I don't know why he decided to take more of a risk with that one."

I said quietly, "I think you do know. You think he was going to abduct me and had to go another direction when he couldn't get to me. He had to improvise."

Baxter conceded, "Since you brought it up...yes, I'll agree that's a theory. Or, you know, maybe it was simply because he wasn't able to charm Michaela like the others and had to resort to more forceful tactics. Michaela was in a relationship, so maybe she didn't fall for his act. As for Amy Donovan, she was my age, so it's possible he assumed she wasn't going to be easily infatuated by a young man and coerced into getting into his car. That could be why he chose her as his first victim and used her to mirror his mother's murder, rather than going to the trouble of abducting her and using her as one of his freaky tableaus." He sighed. "I think that's why I'm having such a hard time getting a handle on how he thinks. He adapts to his situation. Serial killers are generally going to choose potential victims who fit their needs and their skill set. This guy is a vendetta killer with a serial flair. You don't often find a killer who checks more than one box."

"And that makes him more dangerous," I murmured, worrying over what Baxter had said.

A middle-aged woman came to our table. "I'm Cynthia Marsh, the manager. Sophie said you wanted to speak to me about the camera outside?"

Baxter stood. "Yes. Do you keep any recordings for surveillance purposes? And if so, could we see them?"

"Yes, absolutely. Please come with me."

The manager led us behind the counter to a tiny office. Going over to a computer on a messy desk, she opened an application that showed a black and white video of the coffeehouse's drive-thru lane, which also offered a view of the building's back door and a partial view of the parking lot.

"I told my staff that the owner and I had this installed to keep tabs on the length of the drive-thru line, but it's mainly to watch the back door. We've had two after-hours break-ins in the past six months, which I didn't tell the staff. Of course since we put in the camera, there've been no more break-ins, but if it can help find the girl you're looking for, I'd say it's more than done its job."

She quickly showed Baxter how to reverse and fast forward the video, then left us alone. Baxter ran the video back to just before one o'clock. We watched a few vehicles come and go, and then a familiar figure appeared at the edge of the screen and walked toward the parking lot.

I drew in a breath. "That's Rachel."

Rachel continued walking to the back of the parking lot. She then disappeared between two tall vehicles, both of which were partially hidden behind other vehicles due to the angle of the camera. After a moment, one of the tall vehicles, an old truck from the look of the top of the cab, pulled backward out of its parking space and disappeared out the back entrance of the parking lot.

Baxter said, "That was it. She got in that truck and left. It's got to be him."

Swallowing, I realized I'd just witnessed the last time Rachel was safe before relinquishing herself into the custody of a psychotic killer. The image of her tied and gagged in that barn stall hit me, and I fought hard to keep my composure.

Shaking his head, Baxter said, "Shit. I'm sorry, Ellie. I should have thought how watching this might affect you."

I clenched my jaw. "No, I told you before, I need to be aware of every last detail about this case, no matter what it is. I'm fine."

He stared at me with troubled eyes for a moment. "I need to get a copy of this video from the manager. Why don't you go get a coffee or something and take a break? I saw some chocolate muffins in the case—"

"I'm not going to go lounge around and have a latte and a muffin while my sister is tied up God knows where," I snapped.

"I'm only saying that we have a long night ahead of us, and we have to keep up our energy so we can think straight. I'm sure anything we can get here would be preferable to the station's stale coffee and questionable vending machine cuisine."

I could see his point, and my stomach would probably thank me for it later. Rubbing my aching forehead, I said, "Okay. Tell me what you want, and I'll get it."

20

I had to admit that the mind-numbing task of placing our order and waiting for it to be prepared was preferable to being cooped up in that suffocating office any longer. I got a text as the barista handed me our food and drinks, so I hurried to set them down on a nearby table. The text was from Rachel's number: *I hear you haven't been doing what I asked tonight. We need to have a chat. Check your partner's email.*

Going numb all over, I snapped my head up to glance around the room. How did Justin Fox know we had pushed aside his dad's case to track down Rachel's last known whereabouts? Was he watching us?

Baxter approached me, his expression guarded. "What's wrong? You're white as a sheet."

Wordlessly, I turned my phone's screen so he could read the text.

The color drained out of his face, too, as he made a visual sweep of the room. One hand at the ready on his gun, he put his other hand on the small of my back and ushered me into the office again. Once we were inside, he commandeered the landline phone on the desk to call dispatch for backup, at the same time taking out his phone and opening up his email folder.

My head spun as he spoke, only catching bits and pieces of him calling for officers to secure the coffeehouse and scour the parking lot for Justin

Fox, then calling for a trace on the last text that came into my phone as well as for information on the email that had just come to him.

When he was finished, he held his phone out between us so I could see the email he'd been sent. It was like the last one, only containing a video attachment. He hit the play button, and Justin Fox's face filled the screen, like the other video.

Justin said, "I see that the Hamilton County Sheriff's Department has been busy this evening—and you've even invited the FBI to the party. On the news, some cocky special agent said the whole department and the local FBI field office were working tirelessly to bring me to justice, plus they were pooling their resources and bringing in former specialists to work on another angle that could get your sweet Rachel released from my clutches."

Justin frowned, and his eyes took on an evil glint. My mouth went dry.

He continued, "Tell me, Detective Baxter and Professor Matthews, did I stutter when I told you that I wanted you two specifically to solve my mother's case all by yourselves? Did you not understand that I meant for you to do it on your own? You know as well as I do that some of your friends at the department do nothing but stand in your way and screw things up, and I didn't want you to waste any of your precious time dealing with their incompetence. Plus, having those useless old people helping out on my mother's case is asinine. No cop is going to admit they made a mistake, even all those years ago. They are a liability to you. They made up lies about my dad then, and they'll do it again to save face."

Baxter paused the video. "So the Fed went on TV and spilled our entire plan? What the hell was he thinking?"

I wiped both hands down my face. "I don't know, but Justin Fox is pissed now. He didn't take the risk to send us a video only to give us a talking-to. He's changing the game. Go."

Baxter pressed play, and the video started again.

Justin said, "I figure you've ruined around five hours of your investigation by working with those other schmucks. So, to show you how serious I am that I want this done right, I'm going to take five hours away from you. Your seventy-two-hour window just became sixty-seven hours. Disobey me again..."

He panned the camera over to Rachel, who was in the same position as before in the same cattle stall. As the camera came near her, her eyes widened. She began to shake her head furiously and make strangled noises, an expression of sheer terror on her face.

I tensed, and Baxter laid a hand on my shoulder.

A red-hot fire poker appeared on the screen. The poker and the camera moved closer to Rachel. Tears began pouring down her cheeks as Justin's voice continued, "And your sister will pay for it. I was going to go with 'a foot for a foot' with this one, so as not to break the sequence, but I might consider skipping the foot and going straight for 'a burn for a burn' if you two don't do what I ask. Remember, you only have until noon on Sunday. If I were you, I'd get to work."

Right as the poker was about to touch the bare skin of Rachel's arm, the video cut off.

I let out an anguished cry. "If he so much as harms on hair on her head, I will kill him with my bare hands." Turning to Baxter, I asked, "You don't think he hurt her, do you?"

He squeezed my shoulder. "No, I don't. He's all about spectacle and getting in your head. If he were going to hurt your sister, he'd make you watch. I'm sure of it."

Letting out a pent up breath, I croaked out, "What are we going to do now? Without help, we're never going to have time to get through all the case information and interviews and—"

Baxter shook his head. "We're not going to do this without help."

"But he said—"

"I know what he said. But the only reason he knew we had help was because of the press conference Agent Manetti called. We muzzle Manetti and pare our team down to a handful of people who can keep a lid on this. There's no way Justin Fox is going to find out about it. I know it's not in keeping with his rules, but I think it's important that we don't go this alone. Do you trust me?"

That was a loaded question where the two of us were concerned. But in this situation, I knew that Baxter would do anything and everything in his power to make sure Rachel got out of this alive. I had no doubt that Rachel's safety was his number one concern.

"Yes."

After several deputies arrived, Baxter gave them directions to secure the coffeehouse and surrounding area. Then he and I headed back to the station.

"Do you feel like picking up where we left off on those old domestic disturbance files?" he asked as we sped back to Noblesville. The snow that had fallen this morning was already beginning to melt, which enabled us to move more quickly.

"Sure," I said, happy to have something to distract myself from my anxiety over our new deadline. I got out the files and flipped to the sixth police report filed on the Fox family. "A week after the bondage incident, it looks like Jayne and Frank made an unannounced welfare check to follow up. Leann was home, but no sign of her husband. The son was there, but once Jayne and Frank started interviewing Leann, he holed up in his room." I read, " 'Female subject seemed nervous and was perspiring during the interview. Even though outside temperatures were unseasonably high and there was no air conditioning in the home, the subject was wearing a thick turtleneck and long pants. When asked about her attire, subject ignored the question and gave no answer. When asked to push up her sleeves so detectives could note whether her prior injuries had healed, she refused.' "

"Dressed for winter, sweating like a whore in church, and refusing to roll up her sleeves? I bet you fifty bucks that woman was black and blue underneath her clothes."

"That's what Jayne and Frank thought, too, according to the notes. But you can't force a wife to rat out her husband." I turned to the next report. "Seventh and final incident report before the murder. This one occurred at the beginning of June, about a month after the welfare check. Leann's friend, Mariella Vasquez, made the call. She said Samuel wouldn't let Leann leave the house with her. Jayne and Frank went out, but like so many of the other domestic disturbance calls from that house, by the time they got there, all was well. Mariella Vasquez recanted her statement and said it was a big misunderstanding."

Baxter shook his head. "Did they check the friend for injuries?"

"It says in Jayne's notes that the friend seemed scared and looked like she'd been crying, but no amount of coercing could get her to say anything against Samuel."

Sighing, he said, "I don't get why Justin Fox is so convinced of his father's innocence. If your dad is a worthless excuse for a human being, don't you know it? Even if you're only ten years old...you know, right?"

"From my experience, yes. It doesn't take long to figure that kind of thing out."

He glanced over at me uncomfortably. "When did you know?"

"I was three, I think. I have two memories of my father. One of him slapping the crap out of me for no apparent reason and another of him driving away and never looking back." I looked at him. "Judging from the way you turned out, I bet your dad was father of the year."

Smiling to himself, he replied, "Yeah. I have to admit, my dad is the best." He cleared his throat and changed the subject. "Have you taken a look at the report from the murder yet? I want to know if anything stands out to you now that you've processed most of the evidence."

"Not yet. I read the autopsy all the way through, but that's as far as I got."

"Speaking of the autopsy, I got an email from Dr. Berg saying everything seems to be in order with it. No oversights as far as he can tell."

"Good." I took out the file from the murder investigation and found the police report, which I began reading to myself. "The murder occurred only a couple of weeks after that last incident. Wow. If Leann Fox had only said something against her husband one time... Who knows? She could still be alive today." I kept reading on down the page. "It says the neighbor who took Leann to the ER for the broken wrist heard arguing in the backyard but for some reason didn't feel the need to call it in. A while later, the kid came knocking on his door, begging for help. When the neighbor went over and found Leann dead, he called nine-one-one." I skimmed over the description of the scene, which I was already familiar with thanks to the graphic photos posted in the conference room at the station. "There was no forced entry and there were no suspicious vehicles reported in the area."

"And Mr. Shitshow had no better alibi than he was passed out drunk inside the house during the whole thing. I'm telling you—he did it," Baxter said, frowning again.

I shook my head. "Don't you think someone who'd made sure to cover his ass for several instances of assault would have come up with an iron-clad alibi if he had in fact killed his wife? Probably one of the major reasons he got arrested is that he couldn't prove he was unconscious at her time of death. He'd coerced people before to lie to the cops for him. What's one more time, especially when it really mattered? I say Leann Fox knew her killer, but it wasn't her husband."

I continued to peruse the police report the rest of the way to the station, but nothing else jumped out at me as out of the ordinary. Baxter seemed to be deep in thought.

Once we were heading into the station, I said, "Something's bothering you. What is it?"

He stopped in the hallway and faced me. "That last video from Justin Fox. All this time, I've thought his 'eye for an eye' bullshit was referring to a passage from Deuteronomy about the type of punishment that should be dealt to someone who gives false testimony, which is what I assumed he was alluding to in all of his weird poems. The FBI crypto guys thought that as well. But the Deuteronomy passage stops with 'foot for foot.' No mention of 'burn for burn,' which he referenced tonight. There's another passage, though, that's similar...found in Exodus, I think. After 'foot for foot,' it keeps going with burn for burn, bruise for bruise, and wound for wound."

My eyebrows shot up. "Someone's been to Sunday school."

"Worse. Nine years of Catholic school."

I nodded. "Ah. Now I get the whole straight-shooter thing. It was beat into you at a young age."

He held out his hands toward me. "Many nuns have broken many rulers over these knuckles."

Chuckling, I asked, "So why does it matter which Bible passage he's using?"

"It's about the context. The Deuteronomy passage, like I said, is about punishment for lying at a trial. The Exodus passage, however, is about punishing someone who causes a pregnant woman to miscarry."

I shrugged. "I wouldn't know the difference. Maybe Justin Fox doesn't either."

"Or maybe his mother was pregnant when she was killed and the Bible passage is right on the nose."

My jaw dropped. "Holy shit, Baxter. That's an excellent theory. What better way to get rid of an unwanted baby than to pop its mom?"

He made a face. "I think there are better ways than that."

"I'm saying that men have been known to freak out over impending fatherhood and literally shoot the messenger. For women in rocky relationships, announcing a pregnancy can be a dangerous event. So are we thinking that Samuel Fox didn't want another kid?"

"My money's on that it wasn't *his* kid."

"Ouch. That's definitely possible. But if she'd had sex with her lover and then blindsided the guy with a surprise pregnancy, that might have caused him to get violent with her."

"Even worse, let's say she'd had sex with her lover, told him she was pregnant, and he was happy about the news. What if he wanted her to leave her husband for him? If Leann Fox told her husband she was pregnant by another man and that she was leaving him, I'd say that's an even more violent scenario."

I blew out a breath. "True. The problem is, I don't recall the autopsy report saying she was pregnant, so we may not have a leg to stand on."

"You're right—it didn't. But unless the coroner knew she was pregnant or that the detectives thought a pregnancy factored into the murder, she wouldn't have been tested. If it was early on in the pregnancy, the baby wouldn't have been noticeable during a physical exam. In that situation, presence of a baby would have to be determined by a blood test."

"How do you know so much about babies?"

His cheeks flushed. "I don't. I've been to way too many autopsies."

I thought for a moment. "If Samuel Fox had known that his wife was pregnant by another man, wouldn't his lawyer have tried to use that at trial to introduce the possibility of another killer? That fact alone could have bought him a heap of reasonable doubt."

"I don't know. I haven't read all the way through the court transcripts yet."

"I think that's our next step. If Leann Fox was in fact pregnant, my money is squarely on her baby daddy."

"I have something I need to do first."

"What's that?"

"Ream Manetti's ass for showing our hand."

My eyebrows shot up. "Oh, this I've got to see."

21

We found Manetti in the conference room with Sterling, both of them staring bleary-eyed at the stacks of files in front of them.

Baxter walked in and stood over Manetti. "What the hell were you thinking going on the news and blabbing about the specifics of our investigation?"

Sterling had to hide a smirk, but he wisely kept his mouth shut.

Manetti glared up at Baxter, his jaw set. "I was letting the citizens of this area know that there's no cause for panic. That we're throwing every available resource into catching this guy."

"Did you see the new video he sent?" Baxter demanded.

"Yes, I did, and I—"

"Your damn press conference cost us five hours. *Five hours*. How do you think Rachel Miller feels about that, huh? Do you think it matters to her that her fellow citizens aren't in a panic?"

Manetti stood so he could look Baxter in the eye. He seemed ready to puff his chest out if needed. "Detective Baxter, I understand your frustration, but keep in mind, I'm still the lead on this case."

Baxter didn't back down. "Then act like it. Think before you tip our hand to a deranged serial killer."

Manetti turned to me, ignoring Baxter. "Ellie, please know that it wasn't my intention to anger Justin Fox with what I said at the press conference. It would kill me to think that my actions put your sister's life in jeopardy."

Baxter was about to continue with his rant, but I spoke first. "It's over and done, and it's only wasting time to argue about it. Baxter and I discussed it, and from now on, we need to be careful about what information we broadcast and also about who we choose to help us with the investigation."

Baxter said, "Ellie and I will put together a list of who we want on this."

Manetti nodded. "Do that, and I'll make it happen."

"And no more press conferences without our okay," Baxter added.

Flicking his eyes at me, Manetti replied, "Done."

Baxter and I put our heads together and decided that we'd keep the key investigators who had been working on the recent murder cases—Baxter, Sterling, Manetti, Esparza, Amanda, and myself. We also added Jayne and Martinez, but Beck didn't make the list. Manetti left to pull everyone else off the case and impress on the department how important discretion was in light of the killer's new demands.

Feeling like I'd wasted precious time that I could have spent researching the case, I said, "I need the court transcript for Samuel Fox's trial."

Sterling shuffled some files and came up with it, tossing it down the table in my direction. "Here you go. Have fun with that."

I sat down and dove into the court transcripts, focusing mainly on Samuel Fox's attorney's defense strategy. There wasn't much to it, which wasn't terribly surprising out of a public defender and given the fact that Samuel's actions screamed "guilty." I assumed since Samuel didn't get himself a real attorney that money was tight, which made sense considering one of the Foxes' knock-down-drag-out fights had been over him losing his job and wasting their money on booze. The public defender put Samuel Fox on the stand, which I thought was a horrible idea given his history of violence toward his wife. No surprise, DA McAlister crucified him for it. But Samuel did manage to get across the idea that his wife had at one point had a problem with a stalker. He called him by name—Richard

Kendrick—and went into great detail about how he'd stalked Leann for several months during the year before she died. Richard Kendrick was evidently a coworker of hers, and he'd been fired once Samuel went to Leann's workplace and made a stink about it.

Rubbing my eyes, I asked, "Has anyone run into any information on a Richard Kendrick?"

Sterling reached behind him and tapped the dry erase board with the pen he had in his hand. "He's up here somewhere—Leann Fox's alleged stalker."

"Why alleged? Was he never charged or never investigated?"

He grunted at me. "Why don't you look for yourself?"

Manetti had walked in the door in time to hear his gruff comment. "Detective Sterling—" he began, frowning as he sat down and pulled another file from the stack.

I held up a hand. "No, it's okay. This is Sterling not giving me special treatment, and I'm fine with it." I looked at the messy table. "At least point me in the general direction of where you saw the information."

Baxter wordlessly pawed through a stack of files to his right and handed me a thin file marked "Richard Kendrick."

"Thank you."

On paper at least, Richard Kendrick seemed like a stand-up guy. No priors; the only thing marring his pristine record was a couple of old speeding tickets. He'd been with the company for five years—a supervisor at the plastics manufacturing plant where Leann Fox worked—until he was fired for supposedly stalking her. At the time, he'd been married for ten years and had two small children. He was on the governing board of the local youth baseball league. Unless he had some kind of alter ego, this guy didn't seem a likely candidate for Leann Fox's killer. However, looks could be deceiving.

I murmured to Baxter, "Do you have Richard Kendrick on your list of people to speak to?"

"I would if he were still alive."

Mouth open, I turned to him. "What?" I flipped a couple more pages in the file and came up with a police report detailing a fire in which Richard Kendrick and his young son perished. "A house fire? What are the odds?"

Manetti blew out a disgusted breath. "Pretty good, actually. The Foxes' neighbors, Earl and Judy Shively, also died in a house fire. Both occurred shortly after Samuel Fox's death, and arson was suspected in both instances."

My eyes widened. "You think Justin Fox was lashing out?"

"We do."

I frowned at Sterling. "You could have just told me that."

Sterling rolled his eyes. "The fact that Kendrick is dead doesn't mean he's not a good suspect. You needed to be objective and make up your own damn mind about him."

"Fair point," I conceded.

There was a knock at the door, and Esparza stuck his head inside. "We're ready if you are."

Manetti closed the file he was reading and stood. "Give us a few minutes." Esparza left, and Manetti said to us, "The leads on the original case are ready to give their rundown. Get some coffee or whatever you need and meet in the conference room in five."

What I needed was a drink, because I had felt a hangover-style headache coming on all evening. The drink wasn't going to happen, so some Advil would have to suffice. I went to the break room to grab some water and found Jayne staring at one of the vending machines.

"Tough choice?" I asked.

She turned and gave me a tired smile. "Trying to decide what I can stomach. My ulcer decided to flare up this week."

I wasn't surprised, given the week she'd had to endure, and was still enduring. My stomach was a wreck, and I didn't have an ulcer to contend with on top of it. "I hear that."

She put her arm around me. "I know you don't want to be coddled, but tell me—how are you really doing? Do I need to worry about you, too?"

"No, you focus your worry solely on Rachel." My voice broke as I said her name, and Jayne tightened her grip around my shoulders. I heaved out a sigh. "Speaking of worrying...do you think there's any kind of heat in that barn? Rachel gets so cold. She sleeps under an electric blanket in the winter, even when the house is plenty warm. I bet she's freezing. She wasn't even wearing a jacket in the video."

Jayne shook her head. "You can drive yourself crazy worrying over the little things. What's important is that she's alive, and Justin Fox seems to be serious about wanting you to complete this investigation. I don't think he's planning to do her any harm."

"Until Sunday at noon, you mean."

"We will not miss that deadline, Ellie. I won't let it happen."

Our handpicked team had assembled in the larger conference room. At the front of the room stood Manetti, Jayne, Frank, and DA McAlister, all of whom looked more haggard than I'd ever seen them.

Manetti said, "Since Justin Fox has made it clear that he doesn't want the entire department working on his mother's case, we're paring down our task force to the people seated at this table plus myself and Sheriff Walsh. Again, I want to ask all of you to not disclose anything you hear tonight or anything you discover through your investigation to anyone outside these walls. We want to keep up the appearance that Detective Baxter and Ms. Matthews are working this case on their own, but at the same time continue to work as a team to bring this son of a bitch down. I'll turn the floor over to the principals from Leann Fox's murder case so they can give us an overview."

He sat, and Jayne took charge of the meeting. "As you know, Frank and I investigated Leann Fox's murder thirteen years ago. After seven instances of domestic assault issues over the course of the five months leading up to the murder, Frank and I were called out to attend Leann Fox's death scene." She pointed to some photos they'd tacked to the white board, copies of the ones lining the walls in the adjacent conference room. "As most of you know, the victim was initially struck with a spade, which was found near her body. Samuel Fox's prints were found on the handle of the spade, and the victim's blood was found on the blade end. Ellie, is this in keeping with what you found upon your examination of the evidence?"

"Yes. I found a print on the handle, and it was a match to Samuel Fox. I also found a substance I assume is blood on the blade, but I've yet to send it off for testing since there didn't seem to be an issue with the original test."

Jayne nodded. "The cause of death was asphyxiation, and the coroner's report confirmed that the victim's hyoid bone had been broken due to manual strangulation. Samuel Fox claimed to have been in the house while the murder occurred, but insisted he was unconscious at that time. Neighbors confirm his vehicle was in the driveway during the time of death window. The victim was found by her son, Justin Fox, and he ran to a neighbor, Earl Shively, for help. When questioned, Mr. Shively stated that he'd heard raised voices outside. But having been threatened by Samuel Fox a few months earlier about staying out of his family's business, Mr. Shively made the decision not to call the police this particular time. As I recall, he was quite distraught over the incident, blaming himself for not having put a stop to the argument before it turned violent."

DA McAlister said, "Shively was a key witness in Samuel Fox's trial. His testimony about the abusive nature of the couple's relationship was the final nail in Fox's coffin."

Sterling added, "Which is why we believe Justin Fox may have had something to do with the Shivelys' untimely deaths."

Jayne pointed to a photo of a young boy that had been tacked to the white board. "Justin Fox was only ten when his mother's murder occurred. His father was taken immediately into custody and bail was denied. Since Justin had no relatives in the area, he was taken by CPS that night and placed in foster care. Detective Baxter, I believe you and Ellie have a meeting scheduled tomorrow with the social worker who was put on his case."

"Yes, Sheriff," Baxter replied. "We're hoping she can point us to some foster families who might have kept in touch with our suspect and be able to give us some insight into his current whereabouts."

"Good. As for our investigation at the time, it seemed to be an open-and-shut case. Samuel Fox had repeatedly abused Leann Fox, and he'd finally gone too far. We questioned her friends, neighbors, and coworkers, and they all had the same thing to say—her husband finally finished the job. There didn't seem to be any other people in her life who wished her harm." She turned to Frank. "Frank, do you have anything to add on the investigation side?"

Barrel-chested and permanently flushed, Frank Donovan always looked to be one cheeseburger away from a heart attack on a good day. This evening, his skin had a gray cast and he seemed almost frail. Amy had been the light of his life, and it was as if her death had taken the fight out of him.

He shook his head. "No. I think you've covered everything, Jayne." Mopping his forehead with a handkerchief, he dropped down into the nearest chair.

"DA McAlister?" she asked.

The DA said, "In my mind, the only other possible suspect who made sense was Richard Kendrick, the alleged stalker. He had an alibi, though. He was at a little league board meeting that night with three other parents." He let out a disgusted breath. "I don't know how you all are going to manage to find anyone else who looks as guilty as Samuel Fox."

Baxter glanced at me. "I guess now is as good a time as any to tell everyone your theory."

Clearing my throat, I said, "*Our* theory is that Leann Fox had a lover." I explained my thoughts on finding the semen stain in her underwear. "In fact, it's a possibility that she was pregnant at the time of her murder. Again, just a theory, but we thought maybe the news of the pregnancy caused either the boyfriend or the husband to become enraged."

The three old-timers stared at me, their expressions blank.

Jayne finally found her voice. "There was no mention of a pregnancy by anyone we spoke to..."

Baxter said, "We're wondering if only Leann and her lover knew about it. And her son." He quickly explained his reasoning, based on the context of the Bible verses he and I had discussed earlier. He ended with, "Whether Leann Fox was pregnant or not isn't going to make or break our investigation. But if she was, it could point to one hell of a motive, either for a boyfriend or her husband."

Manetti said, "I think it's a good theory, and may be one we can work with. I've already sent off the cutting of the semen stain, and we should have the DNA results by Sunday."

Amanda's eyebrows shot up, and she glanced over at me and mouthed, "What the hell?"

I shrugged. All I had to cling to right now was hope, and if Manetti could deliver, all the better.

He continued, "Looking forward, what's on everyone's agenda?"

Baxter said, "Tomorrow morning, Ellie and I will begin our interviews of people associated with the case. As soon as this meeting is over, we'll be compiling that list."

Looking at his watch, Manetti shook his head. "It's past two. The only thing you two will be doing right now is going home and getting some sleep. We need you sharp."

Sterling said to Baxter, "I've already started a list from the research I've been doing. I'll finish it and have it waiting for you when you get here tomorrow."

"Whoa, wait," I said. "You people actually think I'm going to go home and waste time sleeping while my sister's being held captive?"

To my surprise, I received stern looks from all around the table.

Jayne said, "Yes, you are. There are plenty of capable people in this room who will be working on the case while you're gone."

"But—"

"Keep talking and I'll cuff you to the couch in my office. Don't think I'm above any tactic that will force you to get some rest."

I sighed, realizing I was bested. "Okay."

While the rest of the team was watching our exchange, no one noticed that Frank had begun to shake. But when he uttered a strangled noise, everyone whipped their heads in his direction. Frank's eyes fluttered shut, and he slumped over in his chair. If it hadn't been for Manetti jumping out of his seat and catching him, Frank would have keeled over headfirst onto the floor.

As Jayne and Baxter hurried over to Frank and loosened the buttons of his collar, Martinez shot out the door, yelling for medical help. DA McAlister had his phone out calling 911. Shocked by Frank's sudden collapse, the rest of us quickly vacated the room to give medical responders some space.

Within seconds, the staff medic arrived. We watched through the window as he cleared Jayne and Baxter away from Frank to kneel over him. Only minutes later, two EMTs came rushing down the hallway with a gurney and barreled into the conference room. At that point, Jayne and Baxter joined us in the hallway. Jayne beckoned us down a couple of doors to the break room.

She said, "Frank is conscious, barely. He mumbled something about low blood sugar, so I'm hoping that's all this is. He's diabetic, and I'm pretty sure he hasn't had a proper meal since Amy passed. Looks like they're going to take him to the hospital for some tests and will probably keep him for observation."

Manetti's face was pained, and he trained a worried gaze on me as he addressed the group. "Please let this be a reminder to all of you to take care of yourselves. Rest, hydration, and food are a must. Do not run yourselves into the ground, and if you see someone else doing it, put a stop to it. Now go do what you need to do."

22

Although I didn't expect to, I was able to sleep for short periods. The downside of falling asleep was waking in a sweat from nightmares of Rachel being tortured at the hands of Justin Fox. It would have been preferable to stay up all night. Every time I woke up screaming, the jumpy young deputy who'd been assigned to sit in my living room would burst into my bedroom, demanding to know if I was all right. Of course that would wake up my dog, and she would start barking. Between that and the news vans that had begun to line the street in front of my house around sunup, I decided not to come home again until I could bring Rachel and Nate with me. I made arrangements for my neighbor to take care of Trixie until this nightmare was over.

To my surprise, when I came out of my bedroom and headed to my living room to find my coat, Agent Manetti was there and the deputy was gone, as were the news vans. Manetti was petting Trixie's head as she gazed up at him adoringly. Traitor.

I blurted, "Why are you here?"

"Good morning to you, too. I thought I'd come get you and bring you up to speed on our progress with the case on the way to the station."

My heart clenched. "Any leads on finding Rachel?"

"Not anything solid."

"Oh." I had a headache, and being forced to have a conversation with Manetti first thing in the morning wasn't helping. "You know, people usually don't like it when a Fed shows up at their house unannounced."

Manetti grinned at me. "Well, if that's how you feel, then I'll take the coffee and muffins I brought and leave." He gestured to my coffee table, where sat two steaming cups and a bulging bakery sack.

"Fine. Let's go."

As we headed for the door, my eyes landed on my Christmas tree, which was standing again. It had still been in a mess on the floor when I'd gotten up to let Trixie out thirty minutes ago.

On our way to Manetti's vehicle, he said quietly, "I had the deputy help me set your tree upright. Trust me, if I'd been in your shoes yesterday, I would have done far worse than that."

I nodded and got into his car.

He put the coffee and muffins on the console between us. "Eat. I wasn't joking about what I said last night."

I took a muffin and broke off a piece. It was delicious, but I had to choke it down. All I could think about was how selfish I was being, sleeping in my own bed, taking a hot shower, and having a nice breakfast while Rachel had probably frozen to the core overnight in a drafty barn, sore and stiff from being tied up.

"Well, what are the developments?" I asked, ready to get to work.

"We managed to track down most of Leann Fox's coworkers, some of Samuel Fox's old coworkers, a few of the Foxes' neighbors, and a couple of family members and friends. You should have an email with a detailed list including current addresses and contact information that you and Detective Baxter can work off today. Later this morning, Detective Sterling and I are meeting with Samuel Fox's public defender and driving down to speak with the warden at his prison, because we figure they'll be the least likely to have any ties to Justin Fox and won't tip him off to our involvement."

I took out my phone and pulled up my email, opening an attachment from Sterling. Scrolling through several pages of names and information, I was impressed by their work. Maybe it hadn't slowed the overall investigation for me to take a few hours away from the station.

Manetti continued, "Now that we have a solid list to work from, I'm having Deputy Martinez and Chief Esparza run those names against county records of properties with barns. Justin Fox doesn't own property in the county unless he has a damn good alias that can fool a bank, a title company, and the county assessor. Therefore, he's not going to have access to a barn unless he's either taking a big risk by squatting in an abandoned property or he knows someone who owns one. I'm thinking it's more likely the latter. Once we have a few matches—which I'm confident we will— Deputy Martinez and Chief Esparza are going to make some house calls."

I looked over at him. "Won't that run the risk of tipping him off?"

"Not when the property owners are told that the reason for the visit is because we got an anonymous complaint about the smell of meth coming from the direction of their barn. When people aren't cooking meth, they tend to be pretty forthcoming about proving it. We shouldn't even need warrants for those."

"Oh." Not above board at all, but I liked it. "Are you normally this much of a rogue agent?"

He smiled. "I can be when it counts. If someone gets adamant about not showing us what's going on in their barn, then we'll know to dig deeper and let you and Detective Baxter take a crack at them. On the forensic side, the second examinations of the evidence from the Leann Fox case have been completed. No new findings there. Oh, and Frank Donovan is going to be fine. Like the Sheriff said, his fainting spell was brought on by his diabetes coupled with missing a few meals, and of course stress. He's being released later today."

"That's at least some good news," I murmured, watching as the sunrise started to light up the bleakness of the town, the remnants of yesterday's snow reduced to ugly gray piles on the side of the road.

Manetti put his hand on my arm. "We're going to find your sister."

At the station, Manetti and I met a weary-looking Amanda in the hallway. But when she saw the two of us together, her eyes began sparkling. She waylaid me as he continued on down the hall.

"You doing okay this morning?" she asked, eyeing the coffee and half-eaten muffin in my hands.

I sighed. "You want the stock answer or the honest answer?"

"Actually, your face says it all," she replied, giving me a sympathetic smile.

"Great."

"Since you said we shouldn't coddle you, I'm going to bypass the pleasantries and get to what I really want to know."

"Okay, shoot."

"First there was the hate flirting between you and the G-man, and now you two are all buddy-buddy. What's up with that?"

I let out a snort of laughter in spite of myself. "First, there was never any —what did you call it? Hate flirting? And now, Agent Manetti is actually being nice. He's bending over backward to help, especially with getting that DNA test done for me in record time. I'm sure that was a lot of strings for him to pull."

"This morning I hear he picked you up at home and drove you to the station."

"Yeah, so he could bring me up to speed on everything you guys worked on last night."

"And he brought you breakfast. He likes you."

"Amanda, he feels sorry for me. There's a difference."

"I don't think so." She gave me a wicked smile. "I'm only saying that when this is over and life goes back to normal for you, the handsome Special Agent wouldn't be the worst person to curl up with in front of the fire."

"Have you been sniffing chemicals in the lab? How did it go from me not completely despising the guy anymore to us dating?"

"A lot of times that's how it happens."

"Well, not this time."

Baxter yelled from down the hall, "Hey, Ellie. You ready to head out?"

I gave him a thumbs-up and said to Amanda, "Anything to get out of this awkward conversation."

As I turned to head Baxter's way, she stopped me. "All joking aside, if you need me, I'm only a phone call away. I'm going home to rest, but if you need some new evidence processed or if you just need a friend, don't hesitate to call."

I smiled. "Thank you."

Our first meeting was with the social worker who'd overseen Justin Fox's time in the foster system. In her late forties and the victim of a bad dye job, Desiree Gray had the look of a woman who'd witnessed too much pain. I couldn't imagine working in social services and having to deal day in and day out with the atrocities unfit parents inflicted upon their poor children. Deviant crime was something I could stomach for the most part, but ongoing abuse of kids was quite another.

Desiree ushered Baxter and me into her cramped office and had us take the two seats facing her desk. Her desk was littered with files and papers, but she managed to pluck Justin Fox's file out of the mess.

She said, "I took a look at his file before you got here, and I'm sorry to say that Justin was one of those kids who slipped through the system."

Baxter's face fell. "What are you saying?"

Desiree replied, "Well, it seems that at age sixteen he ran away from his foster family. I'm embarrassed to admit that we lost him at such a critical age. He didn't resurface again until after he was eighteen, when he got his driver's license. Once he became an adult, he was no longer under our care, so no follow-up contact was made."

"So you have no record of him since seven years ago?" Baxter said.

"I'm afraid that's right."

I grunted. When I was a teen, my social worker hadn't been any more of a go-getter than this lady.

Baxter was clearly as impressed as I was. "What *can* you tell us?"

She pulled a single sheet of paper out of the file and handed it to him. "This is a list of names and the most up-to-date contact information we have on the foster families Justin Fox lived with during the six years he was in our care."

Baxter held out the paper so I could read it. There were four households listed. While I couldn't find it in me to feel sympathy for the sociopath holding my sister, my heart did ache for ten-year-old Justin Fox. After losing his mother and being taken from his father, he bounced around in the system way too much to have any kind of healthy family life. No wonder he ran away and went insane. His situation didn't excuse his behavior, but it certainly helped explain it.

I asked, "Why four homes in six years? Was he a problem child?"

Desiree frowned and flipped through her file. "Yes and no. In the first home, the foster dad lost his job, and the new employment he got was in Colorado, so they had to give Justin up when they moved. In the second home, we suspected abuse, so we pulled the children living there. He and another boy seemed to have bonded in that household, so we managed to find a family who would take them both. By that point, the boys had just entered high school and were becoming quite a handful. One night, a fire occurred in the home, and the family barely got out in time."

Baxter and I exchanged a glance.

"The fire started in the boys' bedroom. Justin and the other boy blamed each other, so we never knew who was at fault. The foster parents had already given them several second chances, but when their house burned down, that was the last straw. We split the boys up after that. Justin was only with the last family a few months before he ran away."

"Do you have contact information on the other boy?" Baxter asked.

"Yes, his name is Wyatt Churchill, and he's currently a guest of the Hamilton County jail."

"Of course he is," I muttered under my breath.

Desiree focused her dead eyes on me. "What was that?"

I cleared my throat. "For how long?"

"The past seven months. Serving an eighteen-month sentence."

Baxter said, "Anything else you can think of that might help us, Ms. Gray?"

She shrugged as if the weight of the world were on her shoulders. "No, I don't think so."

Baxter grumbled all the way back to his vehicle.

"We got the names. It's not like she was going to provide us with some magical clue that solved the whole thing," I pointed out.

He shook his head. "I know, but it's frustrating to deal with another typical government agency refusing to go the extra mile."

Sure, Baxter worked for a government agency, but he was one of the ones who went above and beyond to make sure justice was served. He sure as hell would never have lost a kid, then thrown his hands up and said, "Oh, well." If nothing else, he would have used his personal time to investigate, like he had with my mother's case. We needed more Nick Baxters in the world.

"What's next?" I asked as he started his SUV and let it warm up for a moment.

He took a photo of the list Desiree had given us. "Once I email this to Sterling and let the team get to tearing these people's lives apart, we're headed to Leann Fox's work, PXT Corporation. Many of her former coworkers are still employed there."

As he started driving north out of town, I asked, "Are you thinking Wyatt Churchill could be of any help?"

Baxter shrugged. "Possibly. Depends on if they kept in touch over the years. Clearly he's not an accomplice, but any connection is worth checking out."

"If they're still tight, what makes you think he's going to rat out his friend?"

Grinning, he said, "Oh, I can be persuasive."

PXT Corporation was an aging plastics manufacturing plant north of Noblesville. Manetti had called ahead and briefed the plant manager, which saved us a lot of time and allowed us to jump right into our interviews. I had to admit that Manetti was one Fed who seemed to be working to make things easier on us instead of the other way around.

We headed first to speak to Lamar Sanders, PXT's plant manager, who met us in the receiving office and began taking us on a quick tour of the facility.

"Leann worked in quality control, which meant she split her time between her cubicle in the office wing and the floor down there," Sanders explained as we walked past a picture window overlooking the manufacturing area. "She knew the whole staff by name, and despite her being one of the QC specialists, everyone liked her."

Baxter nodded. "Mr. Sanders, you're sure that everyone liked her? There was no animosity toward her of any kind by anyone? Surely working in QC she'd ruffle some feathers once in a while."

Sanders shrugged. "Not that I knew of. If she saw a problem, she'd go to the line supervisor and help find a way to solve the issue before filing her reports. She was always fair and helpful, which not all the QC specialists were. I was one of the line supervisors at the time, so I worked with her quite a bit."

I asked, "What about her fellow QC workers? If she was so well-liked, did that create jealousy within her own team?"

"There was one woman who was catty as hell, but she was that way with everyone, not just Leann."

"What's her name?" Baxter asked.

"Linda Beasley."

"Does she still work here?"

Sanders shook his head. "No, I fired her a couple of years ago. I can give you the contact info I have for her, though."

"Good. Now, about Mrs. Fox's alleged stalker—"

Rolling his eyes, Sanders said, "Richard Kendrick? That was a bunch of horseshit. He never stalked Leann. They'd worked in the same department for years and were friends, and her husband didn't like it. Some of us would go out as a group and grab a drink after work. Leann and Richard were always part of that group, but there was nothing more to it than that. I think he might have given her a ride home one time when her car wouldn't start, and her husband hit the ceiling. She came to work the next Monday with a broken wrist."

Baxter and I shared a glance. Now we knew what the catalyst for another of their fights had been.

Sanders continued, frowning. "Then one day Samuel Fox comes barging in here, screaming about how Richard was stalking his wife and trying to take advantage of her at work. Richard had just been promoted to QC supervisor, so he'd recently become her boss. About a month prior to that, PXT had gotten slapped with a sexual harassment lawsuit, and the plant manager at the time was taking no chances on this one. He didn't wait for a second lawsuit to be filed—he fired poor Richard on the spot. Leann was in his office all afternoon trying to talk him out of it and explaining that her husband was overreacting, but the firing stood."

"Thank you for the information," Baxter said, making a few notes in a small notebook. "I guess now we should speak with any of your employees who worked closely with Mrs. Fox."

Sanders nodded and motioned for us to follow him down the hall. "We've got you set up in an empty office. My secretary will see to it that you have a steady stream of people to interview." He hesitated. "Just my two cents, but Samuel Fox was as guilty as sin, and he got what he deserved. I knew something was wrong at home—we all knew it—but what could anyone do when Leann wouldn't admit there was a problem and accept our offers for help? We were all devastated when we heard she'd been killed. But not one of us was surprised."

"Mr. Sanders, did Leann ever mention leaving her husband or wanting another child? Anything like that?" I asked.

"Not to me."

"What was her demeanor like in the weeks leading up to her death?"

He showed us into an office containing a desk and several chairs. After thinking for a moment, he replied, "Happy, for the most part, as I recall. She'd have bad days every once in a while—which I assumed were the times her husband was abusing her. But right before she died, she had a spring in her step that hadn't been there in a while. I hoped things were turning around for her...but I was wrong." He gave us a sad smile. "If there's nothing else, I'll leave you to it."

Baxter said, "Thank you, Mr. Sanders."

After Sanders left, I turned to Baxter. "Spring in her step and semen in her panties? Leann Fox was definitely having an affair. We need to figure out who this guy is. Now."

23

We interviewed seven of Leann Fox's fellow coworkers, and they all said the same thing Lamar Sanders had said: Leann was great, everyone liked her, and her husband had no doubt killed her.

It wasn't until the eighth and final coworker came through the door that we caught a break. Jessie Metz was a fellow quality control specialist and seemed to have been closer to Leann than anyone else we'd talked to.

"We hung out fairly often after work, but not as much the few months before she died. We'd have plans, but more times than not she'd send me a garbled text at the last minute and make up some lame excuse why she couldn't go. She didn't fool me. I knew it was because her jackass husband wouldn't allow her to leave the house."

Baxter nudged my leg under the desk while Jessie was talking, but I didn't know why. Then he asked her, "Leann texted you? So she had a cellphone?"

Jessie nodded. "She had a cell, but she didn't advertise it. I don't think her husband knew about it—in fact, I know he didn't. It was one of those pre-paids. She wanted to be able to keep in touch with her friends without him hovering over her shoulder. He was such a control freak when it came to who she hung out with. He'd sometimes find out what bar we were going to—I think he followed her—and then come in and make her go home.

Give her some sob story about how their kid was sick or something like that. It worked every time, because Leann loved that kid more than anything. The only reason she stayed with her stupid husband was to keep the family together."

Baxter said, "Not that it would do us any good, but you don't still happen to have her cell number, do you?"

Laughing mirthlessly, she said, "That was a half-dozen phones ago, before it was easy to transfer your contacts."

"I figured as much. How did Leann seem right before her death? Was there any kind of change in personality or anything you noticed that was different about her?"

"She maybe wasn't as closed off as she had been. She smiled more. I remember her saying that she thought everything was going to work out." Her shoulders slumped. "Then she died."

I asked, "Do you know if she was in any kind of extra-marital relationship? Did she ever confide anything like that in you?"

Jessie gave me a puzzled look. "Leann? I don't see her as the cheating type. I mean, I would have in her situation. But she always stood by her husband, even when..." She sighed.

"Even when he beat her up?" Baxter supplied.

"Yeah. A bunch of us wanted to do an intervention with her, but...one time at a meeting Richard brought up the fact that we were all worried about her, and she lost it. She got pretty fierce about defending her husband and wouldn't hear another word about it. We got the message."

I felt another nudge from Baxter.

His tone softened. "Ms. Metz, we're sorry for making you relive this after so long. If there's anything else you can remember, please give us a call." He handed Jessie his card. Once the door had closed behind her, he turned to me. "There was no cellphone found at the scene. I remember reading it in the case notes. The Foxes' only registered phone was a landline, but the Sheriff noted that there was a thorough search of the home for cells and for computers. They found a computer, but all they got off it was Samuel's porn."

"Lovely. But if Leann was hiding her phone from her husband, maybe she kept it somewhere else, like in her car or at work."

"Her vehicle was also searched, as was her desk at work."

"Hmm. Well, it didn't just disappear."

"Or maybe it did if the killer took it so no one would find his number on it."

I nodded slowly. "I could get behind that."

"Besides, if Samuel Fox somehow knew about his wife's secret cell, he might have automatically assumed she'd been using it to contact other men. He would have tried to use that in his defense at trial."

"Right. Even if he'd found it and smashed it or threw it away, he would have at least had his lawyer bring it up and subpoena the phone records. He didn't know about it."

"But the killer did. Also, I'm starting to understand why Samuel Fox set his sights on Richard Kendrick. Say Leann came home, angry with the guy for what he'd said in that meeting. She'd made it abundantly clear to anyone who'd listen that her marriage was fine. Maybe she lets it slip about what Kendrick had said, knowing that her husband would go postal and shut him up like he did their neighbor. Only she doesn't expect Kendrick to lose his job over it, which is why she freaked out and begged the boss not to go through with the firing."

I sighed. "This is a sick, sick relationship we've got going on here. I say Justin Fox got screwed up long before the foster system got hold of him."

Our next stop was at Russell and Cynthia Hawker's house. They had been the Foxes' neighbors opposite the Shivelys, but they'd since moved to a nicer neighborhood. The Foxes' old neighborhood hadn't been in the best part of town. I'd read in one of the files that the family had been forced to sell their former home when Samuel lost his job and move into a less expensive place.

Russell and Cynthia Hawker were a newly retired couple. Cynthia warmly invited us in and insisted on serving us coffee, which I didn't mind. Hers was much better than anything I'd get at the station, and I was growing tired of fast-food coffee as well.

Once we were settled in the Hawkers' homey living room, Baxter said,

"Thank you for meeting with us today. We're investigating an old case, the murder of Leann Fox, your former neighbor."

I saw Cynthia's hands begin trembling and Russell's face twist into a frown. The murder that had occurred next door was probably not their favorite thing to discuss.

Russell said, "We were out of town, thank goodness, when it happened." He glanced over at his wife. "We heard some of the things that went on over there. But after talking to Earl...well, we decided to look the other way. At that time, I was traveling quite often for work, and Cynthia would be at the house alone. I didn't want that crazy man to have a reason to come after my wife, so we let him be."

Unable to meet our eyes, Cynthia looked down and admitted, "It may not have been the right thing to do, but we were scared of retaliation. The neighborhood was starting to go downhill so fast at that time, and..." She shrugged tearfully. "We just didn't want to get involved."

"It's understandable," Baxter said, his tone kind. His disappointed eyes told a different story. "Did you ever notice anyone lurking around the Foxes' home? Or anyone coming and going at odd hours? Anything out of the ordinary aside from the domestic disturbances when the police got involved?"

The Hawkers glanced at each other, then shook their heads.

Russell said, "Like I mentioned, we stayed out of their business. We kept the blinds down on that side of the house and tried not to even look that direction if we could help it."

I frowned. "So there's nothing you can tell us about the Fox family? What about the boy? Did you ever speak to him or see him out playing? Anything?"

Sighing, Russell replied, "He was a quiet kid. Seemed like he kept to himself and didn't have a lot of friends."

Baxter stroked his beard to hide a grin. Russell Hawker was *that* neighbor, who if interviewed on the news would give the stereotypical "he was quiet, kept to himself" answer when asked if he was aware he was living next door to a crazy person.

Cynthia held up one finger hesitantly. "I think... I think I might have seen the boy around the neighborhood a few times after the murder, if that's of any interest to you."

All business now, Baxter asked, "When was this? What was he doing?"

"Um...I don't recall exactly. It was maybe a couple of times the year or so after. He was just hanging around, staring at the house. He seemed...sad."

No shit.

Baxter said, "What about around the time of the Shivelys' house fire? Did you see anyone lurking around then?"

Russell shook his head. "We'd already moved by then."

Feeling like this trip was a giant waste of time, I stood. "Thank you for the coffee and for your candor. If you think of anything else, please don't hesitate to contact us."

Barely containing my disgust as I hurried out the door, I got into Baxter's SUV and waited until the doors were closed before beginning my tirade. "Could they be any less helpful? I mean, come on. They closed their blinds on the side facing the Foxes' house and hid, hoping Samuel Fox would forget that they were there? How could you listen to a screaming match next door and do nothing? Especially after the cops started making a couple of visits a month. There was a *child* in that house."

Baxter nodded. "I'm right there with you. Then again, Earl Shively did the right thing, and it probably got him and his wife killed. What's a neighbor to do?"

"Um, not piss me off when I'm one more dumb comment away from kicking their asses?"

"At least the coffee was good."

We returned to the station at lunchtime to regroup and share what we'd learned this morning. Jayne had sent out for lunch for the team, and for once I was in the mood to eat. Delving into the leads we'd spent last night gathering had helped my emotional state considerably, knowing I was doing something to get to the bottom of the case.

Manetti had efficiently divided up our down time. Jayne and Amanda had gone home to rest this morning after Baxter and I had gotten back, and after lunch it was Sterling and Martinez's turn. Esparza and Manetti would be off in the early evening. With our time off spaced out like that, I felt better about the progress being made. There would be six of us working at all times.

We got our sandwiches and congregated around the conference room table. The four guys who had yet to get some sleep looked pretty rough, but none of them complained.

Manetti said, "I'll start. This morning Detective Sterling and I visited Samuel Fox's public defender as well as the warden at Fox's prison. The public defender didn't have a lot to say about the viability of her client's defense. She believed he was guilty and had a hard time finding any shred of evidence to suggest otherwise. They tried to bring up the angle of Leann Fox having a stalker, Richard Kendrick, but there was no evidence to support Samuel Fox's accusation that Kendrick had killed her."

Baxter added, "In our interviews with their fellow PXT Corporation employees, we found that Richard Kendrick was fired practically without cause in the wake of an unrelated sexual harassment charge already facing the company. Kendrick was collateral damage because of it. No one thought he was actually stalking Leann Fox or had any kind of relationship with her aside from that of being friendly work colleagues."

Manetti nodded. "Barring any other information that might come to light about Richard Kendrick, I think we can cross him off our suspect list. On to the warden—I think you all know that Samuel Fox died in a prison riot two years ago. The warden said Fox was an exemplary inmate during his eleven-year stint. He made no trouble, but unfortunately got caught in the crossfire when two rival gangs went at it one day. The warden was able to provide us access to the visitor logs that showed Justin Fox made regular trips to see his father in prison, starting when he was eighteen. Detective Sterling, do you have anything to add?"

"I have one more lead to run down before I cross Richard Kendrick off the suspect list. Other than that, I'm good," Sterling replied.

Manetti said, "Detective Baxter, what else did you and Ms. Matthews uncover this morning?"

Baxter recounted our interviews with Desiree Gray and with the employees at PXT while I sat and wondered why Sterling was so interested in Richard Kendrick. From everything we'd heard today, he didn't seem to be the type to snap and kill a coworker, nor did anyone suggest he'd been sleeping around. Something was stuck in Sterling's craw, and I wanted to know what it was.

Thinking about Richard Kendrick made me wonder more about Leann Fox's missing cellphone. When Baxter was finished, I said, "Jayne, one of Leann's coworkers mentioned she had a cellphone that she kept a secret from her husband. Your report shows that no cells were found belonging to either of the Foxes. Are you sure every avenue was explored in the search?"

She replied, "Yes, I remember doing the requisite cellphone search myself..." Frowning, she flipped through her file, lost in thought.

Baxter murmured to me, "We already talked about what the report said."

I murmured back, "But I want to hear it from her."

Jayne tapped her pen on the table as she scanned the file. "I checked the house. The crime scene techs checked the house. We all checked her car. I even drove over to her work and went through her desk, hoping to find something. At home, they had a landline and a computer, which seemed to be Mr. Fox's, judging from the amount and type of pornography on it. The only email account we could find for Leann was her work account. That was before the days of widespread use of social media, so there was really nothing else to check, communication-wise. There was no phone to be found." She regarded us for a moment. "What do you think happened to it?"

Baxter replied, "We think the killer took it because it would tie her to him."

Sterling snorted. "This case just keeps getting better and better."

Frowning, Manetti said, "Chief Esparza and Deputy Martinez, an update?"

Martinez said, "We made calls to two residences this morning and checked out the barns on the properties. No dice."

"Where are we on the background checks on the foster families?"

Esparza slid a file down the table toward Baxter and me. "Done and done, plus we pulled property records including parcels with barns owned by anyone related to them. We also had an expert determine that the truck our boy was driving was Ford F-series from the eighties, so we got county BMV records of those, too. Deputies are out canvassing as we speak, and I'll join them after this meeting."

"Excellent," Manetti said, his mouth pulling into a tired smile. "Detective Baxter and Ms. Matthews, is there anything else you need us to work on while you're out this afternoon?"

Baxter thought for a moment. "How about home arsons in the last seven years? Can you check those against our master list of Fox family connections? Maybe something will pop there."

Jayne scribbled something in her notebook. "Amanda and I will research those this afternoon."

"I think we all have our marching orders, then. Thanks, guys," said Manetti.

We all picked up our files and the remains of our lunches and began going our separate ways.

Baxter said to me, "Ready to head out again?"

"Almost."

"I'll be at my desk when you're ready," he said, heading out the door.

I hung back for a moment and stopped Sterling in the hallway. "Hey, what's your theory on Richard Kendrick? You've been saying from the beginning that he's a good lead. What are you thinking?"

"Don't micromanage me, Matthews. I said I'd handle it."

"Don't you think I deserve to know?"

He pinched the bridge of his nose in frustration. "It's a long shot, and I don't want you to get your hopes up. Now get off my ass about it."

I was speechless. He might have talked tough, but Sterling was trying to spare my feelings. Who'd have thought?

"Um...okay. Consider me off your ass, then."

"Keep it that way."

24

Since we were near the county jail, we decided to pay Wyatt Churchill a visit. He was nothing like I'd pictured. I'd assumed he was some scrawny, punk-ass kid like Justin Fox. Instead Wyatt Churchill looked like a giant teddy bear. He acted like one, too.

When Baxter and I entered the tiny room where he was shackled to a metal table, Wyatt gave us a genuine smile. "It's not everyday I get a visitor, let alone two."

Baxter and I sat down across from him. Baxter said, "I guess it's your lucky day. I'm Detective Baxter and this is Ms. Matthews. We'd like to speak to you about a former foster brother of yours—Justin Fox."

Wyatt's smile faded. "I've been seeing on the news about what he's done to those girls. He was always doing crazy stuff that would get me in trouble, but I never thought he'd turn out to be a psycho. We were pretty close for a while."

"Tell us about the night seven years ago when the fire started in your bedroom."

Slumping in his chair, Wyatt said, "Justin was in a weird mood that night. He'd turned mean for some reason. I think something had happened at school with a girl, and he was upset. He had this fancy lighter he'd stolen, and he was dying to use it. He kept threatening to light my stuff on fire with it. Finally he calmed down, and I thought he went to sleep, so I figured it was safe to doze off. But then all of a sudden the whole room was on fire, and I could barely breathe."

"And he blamed you for it," I said.

"Yeah. I really liked living there, too. Our foster mom reminded me of my real mom."

Baxter asked, "Have you had any contact with Justin Fox since the incident?"

Wyatt shook his head. "I was happy to be rid of him after that."

"Did he ever talk about anyone he was close to—a family member or family friend, another foster family or foster kid...or maybe a friend at school?"

"Justin didn't have a lot of friends at school. But he did talk about his real dad a lot. About how he wasn't allowed to see him until he got older."

"Did he talk about his mother at all?"

"No, just his dad. He also used to go on and on about his first foster family who'd moved. He got letters from them sometimes. I think he had a crush on the daughter from that family or something. He kept her picture under his pillow and talked about her in his sleep—Alyssa something."

While Baxter noted that, I said gently, "I know there was abuse in the first foster home you were in together and that the two of you bonded. Were there any other kids there who either of you were close to?"

Wyatt thought for a moment. "Justin was pretty close to Courtney. Courtney Kapinski. She wasn't there as long as we were, though. We ended up going to the same high school as another foster kid from that house, Tyrone Leonard, but not for long. And the Greens—the ones whose house Justin burned down—wanted nothing to do with either of us afterward. They kicked us out that night, and I never saw or heard from them again."

I shook my head. "Wyatt, you seem like a nice guy. What in the world did you do to get eighteen months in here?"

He bowed his head. "I broke into the video game store I used to work at and stole some money and some merch. See, I got my girlfriend pregnant, and...she kept needing all this stuff to get ready for the baby. She wasn't working, and I couldn't afford all the extra stuff, so...I took the easy way out." Sighing, he muttered, "I'll never make that mistake again. I didn't get to be there when my little boy was born."

I made a mental note to track down Wyatt's girlfriend and send some of Nate's outgrown clothes and toys her way. Rachel could easily have found herself in a similar situation, but at least her loser baby daddy had done her the favor of dumping her at the first mention of the word "pregnancy." Thinking about my sister took my head out of the game momentarily, but I managed to pull my focus back to our interview.

"I'm sorry to hear that, Wyatt. One more thing: can you think of anyone Justin would turn to for help? If he needed a place to live or something like that?"

"I don't know. I guess either that first family or Courtney. Maybe Tyrone, but probably not. He was older, so he didn't pay much attention to us. But that was years ago, and I'm sure there were other foster families after that, right?"

"Not exactly. Justin ran away from the family he was placed with after the Greens. We assume he was on his own after that."

"Whoa. I would not have survived all by myself as a teenager."

"Justin Fox is proving to be rather resourceful," Baxter griped.

⸻

I was off in my own little world on the drive to Linda Beasley's home. I'd let that errant thought about Rachel get in while we were at the jail, and I couldn't seem to shake the worry I had in my gut. If Justin Fox had lashed out so horribly toward Wyatt—a guy who was practically a brother to him, and one of his only friends in the world—what might he do to Rachel in the time he was holding her? He seemed to be obsessed with fire. Would he go through with his threat to burn her? Or would he abuse her in other ways?

"Where's your head right now?"

I turned to Baxter. "Nowhere it should be."

"I have to hand it to you, Ellie. All I've seen out of you today has been game face. Last night, too, once we started the investigation. I don't know how you're doing it, but keep it up."

"Let's talk about something else, okay?"

He smiled sheepishly. "Sorry. New topic. You want to be the bad cop at our next interview?"

I chuckled. "No, thank you." I looked at the info sheet we had on Linda Beasley. "Why would you assume that a fifty-seven-year-old grandmother would need someone to go bad cop on her ass?"

"You heard what Lamar Sanders said this morning. She's mean, and he had to fire her. What if I'm too much of a gentleman to go up against her? You might need to save me with some of your trailer park sass."

My jaw dropped. "Hey! It's okay for me to make fun of my white trash roots, but it's not cool when you do it."

He was fighting a grin. "Pretend she's a reporter trying to get a story out of you. That ought to get your more colorful vocabulary flowing. You know, like that video of you on the *Ashmore Voice* video blog."

"Tell me you did not watch that video."

"Only a couple dozen times. I didn't know you could string that many cuss words together and still form a coherent sentence."

I shook my head, not really minding the needling. I knew exactly what he was doing, and I appreciated it. "What can I say? I have a gift."

We pulled up to Linda Beasley's residence, which was a condo in one of those fifty-five and older complexes. I took her a moment to answer the door after I knocked. When she opened the door and saw me, her mouth twisted into an instant frown. But when she looked past me and laid eyes on Baxter, her demeanor changed instantly.

"Well, hello there," she drawled, smiling wide.

I thought I saw her actually bat her eyes at him. I had to bite the inside of my cheek to keep a straight face.

"Hello, Mrs. Beasley. I'm Detective Baxter and this is Ms. Matthews. We're with the Hamilton County Sheriff's office, and we'd like to ask you a few questions about a former coworker of yours, Leann Fox."

"It's *Ms.* Beasley, Detective. I'm not married," she replied, giving him a wink. "Please come in."

"I could wait in the car if you want to run point on this one," I murmured to Baxter as we followed her inside.

"Oh, hell no. You are *not* leaving me alone with this horny cougar," he hissed back.

In her defense, Linda Beasley looked good for fifty-seven. She was in great shape and could easily have passed for late forties. But the fact remained that she was old enough to be Baxter's mom.

She sat on her sofa and patted the seat next to her for Baxter sit down. I snagged a nearby chair before he could get to it, so he had no choice but to sit with her. He shot me some daggers, but sat where he was instructed.

"Ms. Beasley, you worked with Leann Fox at PXT Corporation for a few years, correct?" Baxter asked.

She shrugged. "Sure. Until she died." Linda Beasley didn't seem terribly sorry about Leann's passing.

"Did you know her well outside of work?"

"No. Didn't care to." She leaned toward him. "Detective, can I get you some coffee?"

He scooted a few inches away from her. "Oh, no thanks. I'm good."

She leaned closer. "A soft drink, maybe?"

"No, thank you. Back to Mrs. Fox—do you remember if anyone at work had any disagreements with her before she died?"

Linda rolled her eyes. "No, of course not. She was the Golden Girl. Everyone loved Leann."

"You say that like it's a bad thing. Was there something not to like about her?"

"She was cheating on her husband, for one."

I sat forward in my chair. "You know that for a fact? Did you see something?"

Frowning at me, she said, "Why are you coming around asking about Leann all of a sudden? Does this have to do with her weird kid killing those women? Following in his father's footsteps, that one."

Ignoring her question, I replied, "Could you tell me about why you think she was cheating on her husband?"

She crossed her arms. "Are you a detective? He didn't introduce you as a detective."

I had best leave the questioning to Baxter, because it was fast becoming apparent I was going to get nowhere with her.

Baxter said, "My partner is a criminalist working with me on the case."

Linda's frown turned into a beady glare as she kept me in her sights. "Your *partner*. Professional or otherwise?"

"Strictly professional," I said.

She relaxed and pasted on a smile, leaning again toward Baxter. "You want to know if goody-two-shoes Leann had a lover?"

"Yes. A name, too, if you have one," he said. I could tell he was tiring of her games.

Putting her lips near his ear, she whispered, "Richard Kendrick."

He jerked back from her. "Do you have proof of that?"

"Not concrete proof. But the two of them were always deep in conversation and going to lunch alone together. He gave her special treatment once he was our supervisor. You could tell they were doing it by the way they looked at each other." She gave Baxter a smoldering glance. "You know how it is, Detective."

"So you're saying you have no actual proof of their affair," he said, his disgust barely veiled.

"No, but...it was pretty clear when her crazy husband came barreling into the office and started going off about Richard coming onto Leann at work and stalking her." She let out a mirthless laugh. "Leann threw herself at Richard, so if it was anyone's fault, it was hers."

Baxter stood, and I could tell he was ready to get out of here.

I regarded Linda Beasley for a moment. "Did you ever see Leann use a cellphone?"

"Yes, and on company time, too. A couple of times I overheard her making plans to meet someone, and it wasn't one of her girlfriends, if you know what I mean."

"So she was making plans to meet a man on her personal cell. You said there was no question in your mind that she was having an affair with Richard Kendrick. Why use a phone to talk to the guy instead of walking a few feet to his cubicle to speak to him face-to-face? That doesn't track."

Linda's face fell, and she started backpedalling. "Oh, well...well, maybe the little hussy was juggling more than one boyfriend."

Baxter said between gritted teeth, "I think we're done here."

He took off for the door, Linda trailing behind him. "Detective, are you sure you don't have any more questions for me? We could meet again at another time—"

"I don't think that'll be necessary."

Fighting to keep a straight face, I followed him out the door, throwing a "thanks for your time" at Linda over my shoulder.

Once we got in his SUV, he shuddered. "I feel dirty now."

I burst out laughing. "Yeah, but it was priceless watching it."

His only response was to glare at me.

I sobered up and said, "It was also helpful in a roundabout way. If what Linda was saying about Leann's phone conversations was accurate, it means that she was not in fact having an affair with Richard Kendrick. Or at least not only with him. There's another guy out there somewhere."

"Let's hope Leann's best friend has some idea of who he is."

25

Mariella Vasquez was another one of the character witnesses who spoke against Samuel Fox at the trial. She'd also called in one of the Foxes' domestic disturbance incidents when Samuel had refused to let Leann leave the house. We had to meet Mariella at her work, and she only had a few minutes to speak to us on her break. We met her at the back door of the local Dollar General store.

After we introduced ourselves, Baxter asked, "How long had you been friends with Leann Fox?"

"I knew Leann from way back in high school. Back before she met that dick Samuel," Mariella said, sneering.

"Was their relationship always like it was near the end?" Baxter asked.

"No, not at all. If you can believe it, he was a real catch back in the day. College grad, good job, handsome. He was even nice to me and her other friends, which is usually a sure sign a guy's a keeper. They made the cutest couple, and then when Justin came along, they were the perfect little family." She wiped a tear from her eye. "That was, until she lost the baby."

I tensed. "Baby? You knew she was pregnant?" I shot a look at Baxter, who seemed equally surprised by this news.

She smiled slightly. "Well, sure, she told her closest friends, but she hadn't broadcast it or told her work yet. She was like three months along."

At three months, Leann Fox's belly would have begun to swell. And while it would have been easy enough to hide under baggy clothes, there was no way a coroner would have missed it—unless it was a pregnancy prior to the possible one at the time of her death. Mariella had said they were the perfect family *until* Leann lost the baby.

"When was this?" I asked.

"Um...a year, maybe two before she died. They were both in a dark place afterward. Samuel never recovered from it. Then when he lost his job and started drinking..." She shook her head. "That was it. Their marriage was over, but Leann refused to give up on it. She wanted things to go back to how they were before, and she wouldn't listen to reason. I begged her to leave him, but she wouldn't. She said the old Samuel was still in there somewhere, and if she stayed with him, he'd eventually come around." Mariella lit a cigarette and took a long drag from it.

It was sad to hear that the heartbreaking loss of a baby was what had paved the path for their marriage to implode and the abuse to start. "Is that why you changed your story after placing a domestic disturbance call to the police two weeks before Leann died? Did she put you up to it to keep the peace?"

Frowning, she replied, "Leann asked me nicely to say I blew things out of proportion. Samuel, not so much. He said if I didn't tell the police it was all a misunderstanding, he'd beat up Leann and then come after me."

Baxter shook his head. "So you think he was the one who killed her?"

"I do. He'd turned into a monster."

"Near the end, when things were so bad between them, did Leann ever tell you that she'd turned to someone else for comfort?" I asked.

"Like another man?"

"Yes. We're thinking she was seeing someone else."

She let out a sigh. "She was, but...I don't think she would have told me about it if I hadn't guessed. She was suddenly happy again, and I knew it had nothing to do with Samuel. When I called her on it, she was horrified that I'd figured out her secret. She said she felt so guilty about cheating, but that she needed it. It had been over a year since she and Samuel had sex." Mariella shrugged. "I told her to go for it and not be ashamed, but she said she still loved her husband and wanted their marriage to work. She made me promise not to tell a soul. I haven't until now. Her secret can't hurt anyone at this point, right?"

I had begun trembling inside while she spoke. This could be exactly what we needed. "What was his name?"

"She wouldn't tell because he was married, too. And don't think I didn't try to get it out of her."

I felt myself deflating. I didn't know how much closer we could get to Leann Fox than her best friend. If she didn't know, then the secret had died with Leann.

Baxter asked, "Did it not occur to you to tell the police she had a secret lover? He might have been the one who killed her. Maybe she told him she was going back to her husband and he got violent."

Shaking her head, Mariella said, "No way. She said this guy was a prince. They both knew their relationship wasn't supposed to last forever, which was why I think she even agreed to it in the first place. It was just a fling, and they both knew it."

Baxter shot a glance at me. "Do you know if she was pregnant at the time of her death?"

"Pregnant? That would be news to me." Mariella thought for a moment as she puffed out a plume of smoke. "Although...she did mention the day before she died that she thought she had something that would fix their relationship for sure this time. I was hoping it was a divorce, or at the very least some anger management for Samuel. She said she wanted to tell him before she told me, but then..." She wiped away another tear.

I asked, "How close were you with Justin? Have you had any contact with him since Leann died?"

She shook her head. "I tried to get social services to let me look in on him now and again, but I was told the foster families wouldn't allow it. I don't know if that was a line to make me quit harassing them or what. I haven't seen hide nor hair of the kid until I saw his picture on TV this week. Wouldn't have known him if they hadn't given his name. But when I took a closer look, I noticed he has those same big eyes he always had." She chuckled. "One look from him, and Leann was putty in his hands. She loved that kid." Pausing for another drag, her face twisted into a frown. "It's a shame he's so screwed up now. Leann would roll over in her grave."

Baxter nodded. "I know you have to get back to work, so we'll wrap this up. What do you know about Leann having a cellphone?"

Mariella smiled and flicked her cigarette butt onto the ground. "Her boyfriend gave it to her so they could plan their little romantic trysts. I know you have your suspicions about him, but trust me, he was good for her."

I stood there, speechless.

Luckily, Baxter kept his head. "You've given us a lot to think about, Mrs. Vasquez. We appreciate you meeting with us."

Once she'd gone back inside, Baxter said, "Holy shit. The boyfriend gave her the phone? No wonder they never found it. *Because he took it after he killed her.*"

"Yes, absolutely. Also, if Leann and Samuel supposedly had zero sex in the year before she died, who tied her up buck naked the day her boss alerted the police after she was late to work?"

"Are you thinking it was the boyfriend instead, so she lied to the cops?"

"It kind of had to be if what Mariella said is true. Leann could have made up the whole story. Maybe her husband left for the day and she dropped her kid at school. Then her boyfriend booty calls her, she blows off work, he comes over, and *they* lose track of time. If they got interrupted by the cops knocking on the door, maybe he ran for it so no one would find out about their affair."

"Unless her husband was enough of an asshole to tie her up for no apparent reason."

"That's still a valid point." I ran my hands through my hair. "I can't believe we're so close, but we have no name. Anyone who could have told us definitively who the boyfriend was is dead. This *sucks*." I kicked a plastic bottle that had been tossed on the ground.

Baxter placed a hand on my shoulder. "We'll find him. Maybe Manetti's DNA results will be all we need."

"If and only if the guy is in CODIS, which is a serious long shot." I heaved out a sigh. "I think at this point our best option is to forget this case and work on finding Justin Fox before the deadline."

"Okay. If you want to switch our focus to trying to find someone who knows his whereabouts, I'm all in. We can start on that list of foster families and go ask around at the businesses listed in his employment record. I want to end this son of a bitch as much as you do, and it makes no difference to me how we do it."

We drove over to meet Courtney Kapinski at her workplace in Carmel. She was a server at one of the nicer restaurants in the Carmel City Center. The restaurant was all but deserted in the mid-afternoon, so she was able to show us to a table in the posh bar and sit down with us.

Although normally it would have been a chill place to be, I was anything but calm. I'd become increasingly anxious and shaky on the drive over, and I was afraid I knew the cause. It had been nearly twenty-four hours since I'd had my last drink, and as much as I hated to admit it to myself, I'd been drinking daily for the better part of three months. I'd not taken even a sip since last night, wanting to stay clear-headed for this case, but I was becoming more frightened of what might happen if I didn't keep at least a little alcohol in my system. I couldn't go into full withdrawal and do what I needed to do in the next forty-eight hours.

I struggled to keep my mind off the rows and rows of glittering bottles behind the bar and on the conversation as Baxter began asking Courtney about the time she spent living in the foster home with Justin Fox. As he built a rapport with her, he very carefully avoided the direct question of whether or not she'd had any contact with Justin lately. With people who were acquaintances of Justin's, it was imperative that we didn't tip our hand, keeping the guise of working his mother's case as he'd asked. If one of them figured out we were trying to find Justin and told him, chances were he'd get pissed off and send us another angry video. Then at least we'd know we were close. At the same time, I hoped that didn't happen, because I didn't want to risk Rachel's safety by enraging him.

Baxter asked her, "Did he speak about any people who might have had a grudge against his mother?"

Courtney shook her head sadly. "He never talked about her. He couldn't. We all knew he'd lost his mom. The one kind thing the Reubens—our foster parents—ever did for him was warning the rest of us never to bring up the subject of his mother."

"We met with Wyatt Churchill earlier. It seemed that the abusive nature of that household helped him and Justin form a quick bond. Was that true for you as well?"

"It was. I was a little older than them, and it bothered me to watch them get slapped around. I tried to intervene a few times, but I only ended up making our foster dad angrier and making it worse. I felt terrible sitting back and watching them suffer, but it was over faster if I did."

Baxter got at call, and he excused himself to take it, leaving me alone with Courtney.

She regarded me for a moment. "You look unwell, Ms. Matthews. Can I get you some water?"

I swiped the back of my hand over the sweat beaded on my upper lip. "No, thank you. I'm fine. It's...all the running around in the cold...in and out of heated buildings with this big coat on..." I wrestled to remove my coat, only succeeding in making myself sweat more.

Baxter rushed back over and said, "Ellie, we need to go. Ms. Kapinski, we'll have to continue our discussion some other time. Thank you for meeting with us."

I grabbed my coat and followed Baxter out the door. I had to practically run to keep up with his long strides. He didn't say a word until we were in his vehicle and speeding north, lights and siren on.

"Look, Ellie, I don't want to get your hopes up...but the Chief said he found a farm property in Jolietville that belongs to a brother of Tim Flynn, Justin Fox's first foster dad. The guy also owns a 1985 Ford F-150. They thought it could be a strong lead, so they didn't do the initial canvas—they went straight for a warrant to search the property."

My breath caught in my throat. "This could be it," I whispered.

"Let's not get ahead of ourselves. In fact, the Chief didn't want me to tell you about it."

"Why?" I demanded.

His only answer was to cast a worried glance at me.

I muttered, "I wish people would stop trying to protect me."

"I gathered that. And that's why I told you. I thought you had a right to know."

The drive to Jolietville was the longest ten minutes of my life, with me waffling between the excitement of possibly having found Rachel to the sheer panic of not finding her, or worse, happening upon something horrific that I would never get over.

When we arrived at the Flynn farm, the area in front of a ramshackle barn was packed with police vehicles, lights flashing. I hopped out of Baxter's vehicle before it even came to a stop and raced toward the barn, disregarding shouts from various officers to stay back. Martinez grabbed me before I reached the barn doors. I struggled against him, but he had me in some kind of hold I couldn't get out of.

Just then, Esparza and Manetti, wearing Kevlar vests and deep frowns, exited the barn.

When their eyes landed on me, I demanded, "Well? What did you find?"

While Esparza threw a disgusted glare in Baxter's direction, Manetti came my way. Martinez released me to Manetti, who took my arm and guided me away from the circus in front of the barn.

His voice rough, he said, "I'm sorry, Ellie, but we didn't find Rachel here. The interior of the barn looks nothing like the one in the video. This isn't it. Again, I'm sorry. I was hoping to have it checked out before you were made aware of the situation, but I guess that didn't happen."

Tears sprang to my eyes, and I snapped, "I am so done with everyone else making decisions on my behalf. Baxter is the only one around here who treats me like an adult."

Manetti's jaw clenched. "Chief Esparza and I discussed it, and we thought it would be best not to take your focus off your investigation. It wasn't as personal as you're assuming. We need you not to get bogged down with the things that you can't be a part of, anyway. Even if you'd gotten here sooner, you couldn't have gone in there with us. You know that. And now you've wasted time running all the way out here."

Incensed, I sputtered, "You... You don't need to tell me... Damn it! I... Shut up, Manetti."

I brushed past him and stalked back toward Baxter's vehicle. Not having found a better outlet for my rage, I slammed my fists down on the hood.

Baxter appeared next to me and said quietly, "Come on. Let's get out of here."

26

We rode in silence toward downtown Indianapolis for our next interview, which was with Tyrone Leonard. Baxter had rescheduled with Courtney Kapinski for tomorrow to pick up where we left off. After the disappointment of not having found Rachel, I barely had the energy to hold my head up on the long drive.

Tyrone Leonard worked in one of the big bank buildings downtown as an asset manager. His assistant showed us to his office, which had a stunning view of the Indianapolis skyline. Certificates of his accomplishments, a diploma for graduating with honors from Indiana University, and photos of him with his well-to-do friends lined the walls. His expensive suit still sharp after a day's work, Tyrone carried himself in a manner that suggested pride and confidence.

After our introductions, he smiled and shook our hands, saying smoothly, "What can I do for you today?"

Baxter said, "We're investigating a murder case involving a former foster brother of yours. Justin Fox. Remember him?"

"Vaguely." Tyrone thought for a moment, and his eyes widened. "Wait, a murder case? Are you saying my old foster brother is the same Justin Fox who's all over the news? Wow. I hadn't thought about him in years. Didn't even make the connection."

"We're actually investigating his mother's murder case from years ago. Did he ever talk about her or make mention of her death?"

"No, and we were told not to bring it up. He was a bit of an odd bird— not at all surprising given the fact that Steve Reuben beat the hell out of us on a nearly daily basis. After we were removed from the Reuben house, we went our separate ways, but we did happen to end up at the same high school. I heard he burned down his next foster family's house. I can't say I was too surprised when the news came out."

"Why were you not surprised?"

He frowned. "Mainly the way he would react to Steve hitting him. He got a wild look in his eye, like he was some kind of animal. He'd lash out at us other kids. Then he'd steal our belongings and burn them in the backyard."

"Did your foster parents know this?"

"No. For as much as I didn't like the kid, I didn't narc on him. Mainly because once Steve started dishing out punishment, we all got some. So I took care of it myself." He smiled slightly. "I wasn't always as mild-mannered as I may seem now."

Baxter said, "You said you hadn't thought about him in years. Was there no contact between the two of you after high school?"

"For the most part, there was no contact after we were taken from the Reubens. Justin was still in middle school at the time. When he got to my high school, I was a senior, so I rarely crossed paths with the guy."

"Would he know how to contact you if he needed to?"

Tyrone shrugged. "I have no idea. I mean, I guess he could find me online easily enough."

"What about the others who lived in the Reuben house with you? Was he closer to them?"

"He and Wyatt were joined at the hip. Little freaks, both of them, and together they always managed to make trouble for the rest of us. For whatever reason, Courtney took a liking to them and felt the need to protect them. All it got her was beat up."

Baxter asked, "Do you know if he kept in contact with either of them?"

"No idea, besides the fact that he and Wyatt were a package deal going to the next foster home."

"Do you keep in contact with Courtney Kapinski?"

"No." Tyrone frowned. "What does all this have to do with Justin's mother's murder case? It happened before he was in the system. It was the *reason* he was in the system."

"That's correct. But we've found in reopening her case that many of the people involved have passed away. It would be helpful to speak with Justin Fox, but of course he's hiding out at the moment. We were hoping to find a friend or two he'd confided in all those years ago, thinking maybe they'd have information we need."

I could see the wheels turning in Tyrone's head. He was a bright guy, there was no doubt.

He finally asked, "Why? Do you think he killed his mom, too?"

Feeling a cold shiver run up my spine, I glanced at Baxter. That thought had never crossed my mind. I couldn't imagine a ten-year-old boy killing his own mother. But if anyone was that deranged, it was Justin Fox.

Baxter didn't miss a beat. "No, we think maybe he has some insight into the events leading up to the murder that would be helpful to us."

Tyrone shook his head. "Sorry I couldn't be of more help, but I've done my best to leave my past behind me."

Handing him a card, Baxter said, "Thanks for your time, Mr. Leonard. If you think of anything, or if Justin Fox or any mutual acquaintance of yours tries to contact you, please give me a call."

"Sure thing."

As Baxter and I walked down Meridian Street toward the parking garage where we'd left his vehicle, I said, "What do you think about Tyrone's question of whether or not Justin killed his mom?"

"Ah, I don't think it's possible. I don't think any ten-year-old would have the strength to crush an adult's hyoid, even if said adult was incapacitated. Besides, why would he want us to figure out that he was to blame?"

"Because he's freaking nuts, and one more murder charge won't make a damn bit of difference to the life sentence he'll be facing."

"Someone's awfully cynical." When we got to Maryland Street, Baxter gestured to a restaurant across the street called Nada. "While we're here, you want to grab some dinner? I think we both could use some downtime."

"It probably wouldn't hurt."

Once inside the chic, vibrant restaurant, we were shown to a semi-secluded booth in the bustling dining room. We were lucky to not have to wait for a table on a Friday night in December. It was only five PM, and while most restaurants downtown normally didn't get packed until much later, the closer it got to Christmas, the more difficult it was to get a table at any time. I ordered a stiff drink, and aside from flicking a glance at me, Baxter didn't object.

But when my drink came and I guzzled it in under a minute, he couldn't keep quiet any longer. "I don't want to start anything, Ellie, but I've been wondering lately if maybe you're not working through your problems in the healthiest way." He eyed my empty glass.

"I'm having one drink with dinner, Nick."

"We're in the middle of an investigation."

It seemed to me he *did* in fact want to start something, and I wasn't having it. "Yes, but I'm a civilian, I don't carry a gun, and I'm not a county employee, so that rule doesn't really apply to me."

"I need you sober if we're working a case together."

"I *am* sober."

"At the moment. How many drinks do you have a week?"

I sat back and crossed my arms. "I see what you're doing, and you can cut that shit out right now. You're trying to fix me again, and I don't need it."

He blew out a breath. "Ellie, I care about...your wellbeing. I've seen enough people battle addiction, and...I want to make sure you get help before it gets too far out of hand."

I could feel heat rising on my cheeks. "Are you calling me an alcoholic?"

"If the shoe fits. You've had alcohol on your breath nearly every day for the past week."

"I have not," I fired back, my heart hammering in my chest.

Narrowing his eyes, he said, "Do you think I'm stupid? All the cough drops and mints in the world can't cover up the smell of alcohol, Ellie. I don't know who you thought you were fooling."

I began to have that feeling again, like my world was crumbling before my eyes and I couldn't do a damn thing to stop it. I couldn't respond. I thought I *was* fooling everyone. Evidently I was only fooling myself.

Baxter's expression softened. "Quitting is not going to be easy, but you're not in this alone."

I took a deep breath to settle my nerves. "You don't need to supervise me. I'll handle this."

"You're not handling it. You're brushing it under the rug, like you do with everything else you don't want to deal with."

"What do you want me to do, Nick?" I snapped. "I can't go cold turkey right now. It would wreak havoc on my system and on my head."

"You do realize that what you're doing could kill you. You have to quit."

"I'm doing what I can. Don't judge me."

"I'm not judging—I'm trying to help." He added under his breath, "And trying not to enable you in the process."

I hung my head, knowing he was right but at the same time not wanting to give up the one thing that was keeping me sane right now. "I'll admit I'm not in the best place at the moment."

"No shit."

"But I can't deal with what's happening to Rachel, work this case, and go through withdrawal all at the same time." I looked up at him pleadingly. "I won't survive it, Nick. Please don't try to make me. I've been a wreck this afternoon, all shaky and unfocused."

He wiped a hand down his face. "Okay. But let's taper you off now, and then when this is over you have to get help. No excuses."

Mortified that Baxter of all people had guessed my so carefully controlled secret, I looked down again so I didn't have to see the disappointment on his face. "I will. I promise."

Dinner after that discussion was a real downer. We wolfed down our food, barely saying two words to each other, and the deafening silence continued until we were in his vehicle and heading back north toward Noblesville.

"I want to start hitting up Justin Fox's old places of employment tonight after the meeting. The list is mostly restaurants, stores, and gas stations, so they should all be open late. Maybe tomorrow we can start running down more foster families like the Reubens and the Greens. I'd also like to track down Alyssa Flynn from Justin Fox's first foster family if we can. She probably doesn't live around here, but I think it's worth contacting her."

"What meeting?"

"The one with the Fed that we're going to be late for if this traffic doesn't ease up," he said, frowning at the line of slow moving vehicles in front of him.

I checked my phone. I'd gotten a text from Manetti, but I'd ignored it after our heated exchange earlier. Had I bothered to read it, I would have known about the meeting. "I hope the others have more to report than we do."

Baxter and I got to the conference room fifteen minutes late, but the rest of the team had waited for us.

Manetti should have taken his break at six, but he was still here after seven. The man was dedicated, I had to give him that.

He said, "Let's make this quick. Sheriff Walsh and Ms. Carmack, you're up first."

Jayne passed each of us a printed sheet. "We've researched every unsolved auto and home arson in the county in the past seven years, large and small. We also cross-referenced commercial arsons against our list of Justin Fox's former places of employment. Aside from the fires that killed the Kendricks and the Shivelys, three stand out to us as being particularly interesting. The first was at a convenience store that Justin had been fired from a week prior. It's the first job we have on record for him. The second was Mariella Vasquez's vehicle. Someone threw a Molotov cocktail through the window of her car one night while it was sitting on the street in front of her house. The third was a fire that destroyed the home of Rajit Prasad, Leann Fox's former boyfriend, who she was living with shortly before she met Samuel. No injuries on that one. The family was out of town."

Shaking his head, Baxter said, "I can imagine the kind of screwed-up history the Foxes had with Leann's ex. I guess we'll put Prasad on our list. Can someone run background on him?"

Martinez made a note on the legal pad in front of him. "Will do."

Manetti said, "Speaking of those arsons, I managed to find Samuel Fox's former cellmate and spoke to him over Skype. He had a lot to say about his old friend. The way this guy tells it, Fox thought of nothing else while he was in the joint besides making everyone who had wronged him pay. It infuriated him that his kid was forced into the system, but when he found out his baby boy had been living on the streets for years, he lost it. He made a list of everyone who'd screwed him over, and when the kid would come to visit, they would decide who they wanted to target next. Then the kid would go out and deliver the punishment."

Amanda sighed and rubbed her eyes. "There could have been dozens of incidents over all those years. And maybe his retaliations didn't all involve arson."

Who knew what kinds of "punishment" the Fox men had decided to mete out? There could have been even more murders, for all we knew. The sooner my sister was away from that maniac, the better.

Manetti replied, "Could be. At the same time, Justin Fox was taking the occasional community college course in criminology, with the intent of becoming some kind of investigator who could reopen his dad's case and get him exonerated."

Sterling pulled a face. "Wouldn't it have been faster to appeal?"

Shrugging, Manetti said, "With what money? Samuel Fox was dead broke, and his kid had been living on the streets."

Baxter asked, "Did the cellmate ever hear Samuel Fox talk about his wife? Did he ever brag about killing her?"

"I asked him that, and he said Fox never uttered a word about her. The one time the cellmate brought it up, Fox beat the hell out of him."

His anger barely contained, Sterling griped, "Exemplary inmate, my ass. Samuel Fox turns his pyromaniac kid into his errand boy, causing all kinds of death and destruction out in the world, all the while sitting pretty in his cell pretending to be wrongly accused. If he was blabbing to his cellmate, then it was common knowledge in the joint. Was the warden lying to us or does he just have his head up his ass?"

Manetti said, "Neither of those choices are favorable. But considering the cellmate's story verifies our theory, I'm inclined to believe him. Deputy Martinez, will you give us an update on what you, your fellow deputies, and Chief Esparza found in regard to the agricultural properties?"

Martinez said, "As many of you know, we thought we'd found a lead, but it turned out to be nothing." Glancing my way, he said, "I'm sorry for that. The rest of the properties we visited checked out. There was no evidence of anyone holding hostages in those barns, nor did any of the barns' interiors match the one in the video. We'll expand our search and head out again first thing tomorrow morning."

"Thank you, Deputy," Manetti replied. "Detective Sterling."

Sterling said, "I had a hunch about Richard Kendrick, and I found out that his alibi wasn't so solid after all. When I re-interviewed two of the parents who'd said they were at a little league board meeting with him that night, I found out they were Kendrick's bros from way back. Now that Kendrick is dead..." He grimaced. "*And* I promised not to bust their asses for lying to the authorities all those years ago, they decided it was time to come clean. Kendrick asked them to vouch for him during the time of the murder because he said he was 'out driving around' and didn't have an alibi."

Baxter sat forward in his seat. "That puts a different spin on things."

"I agree, but the problem is going to be proving he did it. Without being able to interrogate him, we have no way of gauging whether or not his story is legit." He turned to Jayne. "Sheriff, did you question him?"

She nodded. "Yes, Frank, Wade, and I met with him once Samuel Fox started accusing him of killing Leann. I don't recall having any reason to believe that he wasn't telling the truth at the time. We questioned him thoroughly because we didn't want any surprises at the trial."

Glancing at me, Baxter said, "I guess we can try to talk to Kendrick's widow and see if she knows anything. My guess is that whatever he was doing that night, he was hiding from his wife, too. Otherwise he would have had her vouch for him."

Manetti said, "I think it's worth a shot to speak with her. What else did you learn today?"

"Multiple people verified that Leann Fox had a cellphone, and her best friend, Mariella Vasquez, said that her 'boyfriend' had given it to her to plan their hookups. Now I'm more convinced than ever that the boyfriend killed her and took the cell so it couldn't be traced back to him. But then again, that proves nothing if we can't figure out who the boyfriend is."

"And her best friend had no idea who her boyfriend was?" Amanda asked, her brow furrowed.

"No. Leann wouldn't tell her his name because he was married at the time, too. She didn't want either of their lives ruined by their affair."

Jayne said, "I'd like some follow-up done with Mariella Vasquez about Leann's relationships with the mystery boyfriend as well as the former boyfriend, Rajit Prasad. I'd also like to speak with her about the vehicle arson. Do you think she would be one I could contact without running the risk of it getting back to Justin Fox?"

Nodding, Baxter said, "I think so. Thanks, Sheriff." He cleared his throat and addressed the others. "And not for nothing, but one of Justin Fox's foster brothers we visited suggested that Justin himself could have killed his mom. So there's that to chew on."

Everyone in the room took a pause to think that one over.

Jayne finally said, "In my mind that's a stretch. His prints weren't on the spade. Leann's cell was never found. And the neighbor heard adult voices arguing in the backyard. Justin Fox was a scrawny little kid. I don't think he would have had the physical strength."

Manetti's gaze was on me. "Ms. Matthews, you've been quiet. What do you think of all this?"

I'd been digesting everything that was said, and the more I heard, the more convinced I became that there was only one person who could put all the pieces together for us. "I think I want to talk to Justin Fox. Face-to-face."

27

Everyone decided to barrage me at once, except for Jayne, who put her head in her hands.

Next to me, Baxter hissed, "You want to what? We did not discuss this."

Manetti said firmly, "No way."

Amanda wore a terrified expression. "It's too dangerous."

"Bad idea," Martinez said.

Sterling's eyebrows shot up. "How in the hell do you think you're going to make that happen without getting yourself killed?"

I put my hands out. "I didn't mean to make you all nuts. I'm only saying that if he and his dad spent all those years brooding over Leann's murder and planning their retaliation, they had to have some idea of who could have killed her. And the fact that we felt forced to go to him for help will make him think he has the upper hand."

Manetti's face seemed even more drawn than before, if that was possible. "I would consider a phone call or a text or email conversation...maybe even Skype. But I can't in good conscience let you or anyone else on this team near him."

Sterling added, "And what makes you think he'd even want to meet you? The situation has 'it's a trap' written all over it. He's too smart to agree to that."

I replied, "He's also cocky and demented. He'd love to rub what he's done in my face and watch my reaction. Besides, he'd make sure he has some kind of failsafe. Like...I don't know...if we try to capture him, then we'll never find Rachel or some shit like that. You know how he is."

Sterling's words were sharp, but his eyes were troubled. "Yeah, we all know how he is. He's an unstable serial killer who might just snap your neck for the hell of it. It's a stupid idea."

"Normally I would take offense, but I know your words are coming from a place of love," I replied, giving him a fake smile.

Baxter had been deep in thought while we'd been talking. He said quietly, "I think it could work."

Frowning at him, Jayne said, "I thought you of all people would be against it."

"Look, we're getting nowhere fast on who killed Leann Fox. We've got a few leads, but they're crap and we all know it. Aside from trying to find Rachel before our window is up or pinning the murder on a dead guy, we don't have a lot of options. We need to change the game."

"What if something goes wrong? What if *he* decides to change the game?" Jayne demanded.

I said, "Then so be it. None of you know what it's like for me to keep running into these roadblocks and dead ends while knowing my only sister is waiting for us to figure this out so she can live to see another day. I'm willing to do anything to get her out of this nightmare. *Anything.* Think if Justin Fox were holding the person you love most in this world. What would you all do?"

Tears glazing her eyes, Amanda said, "I'd do whatever needed to be done if it were my sister."

Manetti rubbed his forehead. "You're not going to back down from this, are you Ms. Matthews?"

"No."

Baxter said, "I'm not either. And I'm going to be there with Ellie to meet with Justin Fox. I'm part of this package, too."

Since we knew Justin had been monitoring our progress on the case through local newscasts, Manetti made a special statement to the press including a direct message to Justin that he should contact us at once. Of course that brought out all the crazies, and the tip line got jammed. But I knew that the only legit call would come to my phone from Rachel's number.

While all that was being set in motion, Baxter and I wasted no time, heading first to a mom and pop electronics shop in Noblesville that was Justin's last known place of employment. They were getting ready to close for the evening, but we managed to get in before they locked the doors. Manetti's face was on the big screen TVs lining the walls, as local stations pre-empted their evening programming to run his statement.

Baxter showed the owner, Marshall Babcock, his badge and made our introductions. "We'd like to ask you a few questions about a former employee of yours, Justin Fox."

Babcock's face turned grey. "That boy. He was a whiz at tech, but his people skills..." He shuddered. "He frightened the customers, and he frightened me. He stole things and intimidated his fellow employees. I was scared to fire him, worried I'd anger him and he'd come back and shoot up the place. But by some miracle, he came in and quit one day, out of the blue. I wrote out his last paycheck on the spot and never heard from him again, thank goodness. Now he's moved on to terrorizing law enforcement. None of us are safe."

I saw Baxter's jaw clench. He said, "We want to know if he had any friends who he worked with that he might turn to if he needed something."

Babcock didn't answer his question, too busy peering at me over his glasses. "Aren't you the woman whose sister he took? I've been seeing your face on TV all day."

I bit back a groan. I hated to think I was in the limelight yet again. The only saving grace this time was that the media hadn't been able to get hold of my phone number since I'd changed it. I'd made it a point to only give it out to a handful of people, so I hadn't had hundreds of calls from reporters begging for interviews like I'd had during the last case. I was sure that my home was surrounded by reporters since no one had been there all day to shoo them away.

I cleared my throat. "Yes. Please answer the question."

"Sorry. Um...I don't remember him being chummy with anyone here. Like I said, he intimidated the rest of my staff. No one wanted to be on shift with him, so I would schedule myself at those times as often as I could. He didn't talk to me aside from the occasional work-related question."

"Did anyone ever come in to see him?" Baxter asked.

After thinking for a moment, Babcock said, "I think a girl came in once."

"What do you remember about her?"

"She had blue hair."

"Anything else you can tell us?"

Babcock shrugged. "Not really. I couldn't get past the hair. Oh, and the dark makeup. It wasn't Halloween, but she sure was a fright."

"If we showed you a photograph, would you be able to ID her?"

"Maybe."

I turned to Baxter and murmured, "Who do you think it could be?"

"Courtney Kapinski is the only 'girl' who lives in the area that we know he's been close to at some point." He sent a text to Sterling, and after a few seconds got back a BMV photo of Courtney Kapinski, a bottle blonde wearing a normal amount of makeup. Showing the photo to Babcock, he asked, "Could this be her?"

Babcock peered at the photo. "I don't know. It's hard to tell. This girl isn't all made up, so I don't think so. I don't remember any facial features or anything like that. Sorry."

My phone beeped and displayed a text from Rachel's number. I grabbed Baxter's arm and showed him the screen. Without so much as a goodbye to Marshall Babcock, we raced out of the store and to Baxter's vehicle. On the way, he made a call to Sterling to have him trace Rachel's cell signal. Once inside, I pulled up the text and held out my phone so Baxter could read it.

It said, *Your Federal mouthpiece got on TV and ordered me to get in touch with you. That's not how our arrangement works.*

My stomach clenched, dread filling me that we had made the wrong move.

Another text came in. *But I have to say I'm intrigued. Have some information for me about my mother's killer?*

With trembling fingers, I texted back, *Not yet. We contacted you because I wanted to ask if you'd be willing to meet in person.*

A tense few seconds went by until he replied, *You're joking, right?*

Baxter shook his head. "I was afraid he'd balk at this. He's been smart so far about staying in the shadows."

Justin had said he was intrigued, though. He seemed to like playing games. I could work with that.

I texted back, *No, but I think you want this case solved as much as I do. And considering you've killed some key players and possible suspects, you owe me.*

After only a moment, he replied, *Fair enough. I'll think about it.*

I let out a pent-up breath. It wasn't a yes, but it was something.

Baxter started his vehicle and called Sterling. "Did you get anything?"

Sterling's voice came over the car's audio system. "Not anything helpful. There's no GPS signal coming from Rachel's phone, which I assume is because he disabled it. We managed to determine that the tower used to send the texts is near Castleton Square. Finding him in a big shopping area like that two weekends before Christmas would be like trying to find a needle in a haystack. Did he agree to meet you guys?"

"He said he'd think about it," Baxter replied.

"Well, if you do get a meeting with him, you want me to come along with my sniper rifle and pop him in the head? He'll never know what hit him."

"One thing at a time." Baxter ended the call and turned to me. "Do you want to go to the station and wait for his reply or would you rather continue our interviews?"

"I can't just sit. Let's keep going."

―――――――――――

Our next stop was at a convenience store in Noblesville—one Justin Fox did not burn down. Judging from the glassiness of their eyes, the two employees working tonight were on something. I hoped they'd be able to give us a straight answer.

When we asked them about Justin, only one of them had been working there long enough to know him. It had been a year since Justin had left this place, and I was worried it might be a long shot to find a coworker in a job that had such high turnover.

"Do you keep in touch with him?" Baxter asked the twenty-something guy whose name tag read "Nolan."

Nolan shrugged. "I've seen him around since then."

"Where?"

"He still comes in here sometimes."

"When was the last time you saw him?"

Staring off into space, Nolan was quiet for a minute.

Assuming he was zoning instead of thinking, I snapped my fingers. "Nolan. Answer the question."

He shook his head, seeming dazed. "Um...the last time I saw him was...today."

Baxter and I both tensed.

Nolan shook his head again. "No, wait. That was on TV. He was here at the store a couple weeks ago, I think."

Baxter rolled his eyes at me.

Nolan lowered his voice to a whisper. "Sometimes I look the other way so Justin can shoplift. He's one scary dude, so, you know, I don't narc on him or anything."

"What does he steal?" Baxter asked.

Shrugging again, he replied, "Food, mostly. I think he's, like, poor now or something."

"Why do you say that?"

"Because he told me he doesn't have a job and he lives in a barn."

I took in a sharp breath. "Did he tell you where this barn is?"

"Um..." Nolan began staring off into space again.

Slamming my hands down on the counter between us, I cried, "Where's the barn, Nolan?"

"Um...I don't remember."

Fuming, I grabbed the nearest thing, a candy bar from a rack on the counter, and chucked it across the store. I walked several steps away, worried I'd grab Nolan next.

Shooting me a frown, Baxter asked him, "You're sure you don't remember what he said?"

Nolan shook his head. "Sorry, man. My memory is for shit sometimes."

"I wonder why," Baxter muttered. He handed Nolan his card. "If you manage to come down off your high and think of anything you forgot, please call me. And call me if you happen to see Justin Fox again. A young woman's life depends on whether or not we can find this barn."

Once we were outside, Baxter said, "You need to calm the hell down."

I stopped in the middle of the parking lot. "And you need to back the hell off me. That numbnuts could be one of the only people on the planet who knows where my sister is, and he's too high to be able to tell us!"

Baxter stared stonily at me. "Substance abuse sucks when you're on the other side of it, doesn't it?"

"Oh, don't get back on your high horse, Baxter. You've already done your intervention. Haven't you nagged me about my problems enough for one day?"

"So I'm a nag because I care about whether you live or die?"

His comment took me aback. I had no response for it, so I wordlessly went to his vehicle and got in. We drove to our next destination without speaking.

The aging chain restaurant we visited was a place Justin had worked at as a busboy nearly two years ago. No one currently employed had been there that long, and the shifty manager was either unwilling or unable to find any of the old employee records to give us contact information of people who had worked with Justin.

Baxter finally broke the tense silence between us as we exited the restaurant. "I'm afraid these other places are going to be more of the same. Turnover is rampant in the service industry, so I think we'd be wasting our time if we dug much further. It's coming up break time for us, so why don't we go back to the station and tie up any loose ends from today, okay?"

"Okay."

―――――――

Jayne found us when we got to the station and brought us into her office to brief us on her conversation with Mariella Vasquez.

She said, "She didn't have much to say about the vehicle arson—just that her neighborhood wasn't terribly safe, so she didn't think much of it until now. But she did have some insight for me about Rajit Prasad. I held off on contacting him about the home arson because I thought it might be better for you two to take a crack at him regarding Leann Fox's case."

"You think he's a good lead?" I asked.

"I do. Mariella said she and Leann ran into Prasad while they were out having dinner one night about five or six months before Leann died. Mariella said he'd always been nice looking and fun to be around, but after over a decade, he was even more handsome and charming. He sat down with them and had a drink, and then he and Leann exchanged info. A week later, Leann told Mariella the two of them went out for coffee and caught up even more. He was married with a couple of kids; had a good job. That was right around the time Leann and Samuel started having marital problems, which Mariella did not put together at the time. Looking back, she's wondering if maybe the boyfriend was Prasad. It all fits."

Baxter nodded. "We'll find him first thing in the morning."

Jayne slid a file across her desk toward us. "Here's the information Deputy Martinez pulled on him. He's clean as a whistle on paper, but as you well know, that doesn't make a difference in a crime of passion."

"Thanks, Sheriff." Baxter and I got up to leave.

She said, "Ellie, a moment?"

After Baxter left and closed the door, I asked, "What is it?"

Smiling, she replied, "I'm checking up on you, that's what. It's almost time for you to head home. Are you going to be able to turn your mind off and sleep?"

I sighed. "Honestly, it's too hard to be at home without Rachel and Nate. I may crash somewhere here instead."

She gave me an admonishing frown. "It's too loud here for you to get the rest you need. Why don't you go to my house?"

"Really, I'm fine. I'll make it work."

"Okay. But know that I'm going to check to make sure you're actually sleeping and not up pawing through files and driving yourself crazy."

I smiled. "I'd be disappointed if you didn't."

On my way down the hall I received a text from Rachel's number: *I'll meet with you, but only if you come alone right now. I'll pick you up a block east of the station. You've got sixty seconds. Tell no one.*

My heart beat wildly in my chest. This was my chance. Without another thought, I hurried out the front door and into the frigid night without even stopping to grab my coat or purse.

28

I ran full speed down the sidewalk, cutting it almost too close in front of a couple of cars at the cross street. Panting, I made it to the end of the next block, and a sleek sports car pulled up beside me. When the passenger window buzzed down, I saw Justin Fox leaning over from the driver's seat, grinning at me.

"Need a ride?" he joked.

I hadn't had time to think about how dangerous (not to mention stupid) it would be to get into a vehicle and drive off with a killer. But I had to. Anything to save Rachel.

Puffing up my courage, I opened the door and slid into the passenger seat.

He said, "Throw out your phone."

"Seriously?" I griped.

"Do it."

The door was still open, so I placed my phone carefully on the sidewalk, hoping no one would come by and take it or destroy it. I closed my door and asked, "Where'd a guy like you get a car like this?"

He peeled away from the curb. "The Fashion Mall parking lot. Dozens of sweet rides for the taking. Did you do what I asked and tell no one what you were doing?"

"Yeah. You only gave me a minute to meet you. I didn't have time to stop and talk to anyone."

"Good. You know I'm not planning to kill you, but I wouldn't want to have to hurt you." He flicked open a switchblade he'd been hiding in his left hand, out of my view.

My stomach clenched. If he wanted to, he could do a lot of damage to me with that knife without killing me.

"So, what did you want to talk to me about?"

My voice faltered as I said, "I want to pick your brain. You've made it difficult for us to find the person who murdered your mom, since you've made it your life's work to kill practically everyone involved in the case."

Justin laughed. "Oh, I guess I did, didn't I? I hadn't realized that would make it so hard for you, but I see what you mean. I guess I owe you a couple of clues, then, right?"

"Yes."

I noticed he was weaving around town fairly aimlessly. We didn't seem to be going anywhere in particular, and I was almost relieved that he wasn't whisking me away to his torture barn. It wouldn't help Rachel to get myself stuck out there with her.

"Okay. Who are you looking at?"

"Rajit Prasad, your mom's old boyfriend, and Richard Kendrick, the man your dad thought was stalking your mom. They're really the extent of our solid leads at this point."

"Right," he said thoughtfully. "My dad was convinced that Kendrick asshole did it."

"So I've heard."

"But to get my dad's name cleared, you're going to need proof."

I could tell he was playing with me, and between my irritation about that and my nerves, I found it difficult to hold my tongue. "No shit."

I noticed a slight smirk form on his lips in the intermittent lights of passing cars. He said, "Okay. Dad said some coworker of Mom's called him up one day and told him Kendrick and my mom were doing it at work. He went in there and threw a fit and got Kendrick fired."

"Wait. I thought he accused Kendrick of stalking your mom, not sleeping with her."

Justin shrugged. "You've got to know my dad to understand. He wasn't going to admit that someone had moved in on his territory. So he made up the thing about the stalking. It sounded better, and all he really wanted was the guy away from Mom."

"Who was the coworker who called him?"

"Linda—"

"Beasley," I finished for him, groaning. That bitch. She lied to us, or at least omitted a lot. But why? "How did she know your dad?"

"Only through Mom."

I wasn't sure I believed that. "So his only proof of an affair between your mom and Richard Kendrick was Linda Beasley's word for it?"

"That and Kendrick brought Mom home from work a couple of times when her car wouldn't start."

Rolling my eyes, I said, "Oh, clearly they were doing it, then."

He screeched to a halt in the middle of the street. I hadn't put my seatbelt on, fearing I might need to make a quick exit. I managed to throw my arms out in time to ensure my face didn't slam into the dashboard.

He turned a murderous gaze toward me. "Are you calling my father a liar?"

I kept my voice even. "I have several terms I like to call your father. But in this case, I'm calling him gullible. If you want my opinion, Linda Beasley was trying to start shit. She's a real piece of work."

"My dad was not gullible," he spat.

"From what I hear, he was drunk most of the six months before your mom died. Alcohol is known for messing with your head. It stands to reason it would make him easily swayed by things he heard from other people."

Justin had calmed down somewhat and had started driving again.

I continued, "What about Rajit Prasad? You didn't manage to kill him in his house fire since he was out of town. Did you make a mistake or were you only trying to send him a warning?"

His knuckles turned white as his grip on the steering wheel tightened. He was still pissed. "I...didn't check that they were home before I started the fire. Dumb luck."

"Why kill the ex? Did your dad think he was sniffing around your mom again or something?"

"He *was* sniffing around her again. Dad saw them having coffee together."

"That's it?"

Frowning, he said, "What do you mean, 'that's it'? They were out on a date."

"They were two old friends catching up. Damn. Your dad had some serious jealousy issues."

"If you knew how many times Prasad had tried to get my mom back when my parents were first together, you'd understand."

"Okay, tell me."

"I even remember as a little kid when that guy would come pulling up in his douchey sports car and parade it around in front of us. Finally, one day when my mom wasn't home, my dad decked the guy and told him to never come around again."

"Did he stay away then?"

"Yeah."

"Does this mean that your dad had a longer history of being violent? It didn't just start after he and your mom lost the baby and he lost his job?"

He flicked a glance at me. "You really have done a lot of research on my parents."

"Yeah. I'm kind of busting my ass since you have my sister and all." I swallowed. "How...um...how is she?"

"She's pissed at me, that's for sure. She did not appreciate being lied to."

"That's not what I meant. Are you feeding her and keeping her warm enough?" After a pause, I choked out, "And not hurting her?"

He ignored my questions. "This discussion is about the case, not your sister. What else have you got?"

I willed my tears to stay put. The last thing I wanted was to appear weak in front of Justin Fox. He'd crucify me for it. "Tell me about the night you found your mom. Did you see anyone fleeing the house or anything like that?"

He sobered. "No, the cops said she'd been dead an hour or so before I got there. The kid down the street invited me to his birthday party, so I went. When I came home to tell my mom all about the party, I found her dead. I ran for help, and then the cops came." His eyes registering hurt, he turned to me. "Do you know what I went through that night? Oh, right. I think you sort of do. I hear your mom got chopped up and put in a bunch of garbage bags, which you had to examine."

I breathed, "Where did you hear that?"

Again ignoring my question, he said, "Your mom's death was really hard on your sister, and you acted like you didn't care. She resents that about you. Did you know that?"

I clenched my jaw. He'd heard it from Rachel. I didn't know if she'd told him voluntarily before he turned psycho on her or if he'd forced it out of her under duress. Either way, he was a bastard for coercing her to bare her soul for him to exploit.

I fired back at him, "I thought this discussion is about the case, not my sister."

The corner of his mouth pulled up in an evil grin. "Touché."

"How did you know your mom was pregnant when she died?"

Justin again crammed on the breaks in the middle of the street, and I slammed into the dashboard once more. "Get out," he growled, his voice taking on a dangerous edge.

He clearly didn't like my question, which gave me all the more reason to dig deeper. "No. We're not done yet. Your dad obviously didn't know about the baby, and it's pretty safe to say it wasn't his. Otherwise he would have brought it up at the trial and tried to use it somehow for his defense. Did you tell him later? Did he know before he died?"

Justin's expression was a mix of anguish and pure hatred.

I pressed on. "I thought maybe your mom was going to try to pass the baby off as his to save the marriage. But I don't get why she told you about her pregnancy and not your dad. Was she considering taking you and the baby and leaving him instead? What did she tell you?"

"Shut up, you *bitch*!"

I tried a different tactic. "Did you *not* want Baxter and me to know about the pregnancy, even though you very cleverly left us a clue through your stupid Bible quotes?"

He suddenly let out a guttural roar and lunged at me. I managed to get my hands out in time to shield my face and upper body, but his razor-sharp blade made contact with my left forearm. As it sliced through the soft skin and left behind a searing pain, I cried out and clamped my wounded arm against my torso. With my other hand, I fumbled for the door handle. Before he could come at me again, I was out the door and had slammed it in his face. We were in a quiet neighborhood, so I took off in between two houses and didn't look back. When I heard the sports car roar away, I slowed my pace, deciding it was best to weave my way through people's backyards rather than risk going near the street, lest he decide to come back and finish the job.

My arm was on fire. When I lifted it up, I noticed a good-sized stain where I'd had it pressed against the fabric of my sweater. The gash continued to ooze blood, so I had no choice but to try to control the bleeding by holding it tight against my abdomen again. I needed to figure out where in the hell I was and go somewhere to get patched up. I shivered as a gust of wind whistled past, wishing I'd kept my head. I only hoped Justin had managed to take enough of his rage out on me and wouldn't feel the need to turn it on Rachel.

I trudged on and finally came to a cross street. I had paid little attention to where he'd driven us, but surprisingly enough, I was only about six blocks from my house. Feeling better instantly, I jogged the rest of the way. There were still a couple of news vans hanging out on my street, so I ducked behind my house and used the spare key I kept hidden in the back-yard to unlock my back door.

Once inside, I breathed a sigh of relief, only to nearly be scared out of my wits when Trixie galloped into the kitchen to greet me. My neighbor had been coming over to feed her and let her out, but the poor dog hadn't had any other human interaction. After taking time to pet her and scratch her ears, I went to my cupboard and took out a fifth of vodka and a glass. An image of Baxter's face flashed through my head. Grudgingly setting the bottle aside, I reached instead for a bag of chocolate chips and downed a handful of them. I had to 'fess up to Baxter about going off on my own with Justin Fox, and I had to be clear-headed when I did it. He was going to lose his shit over this, but there was no way I was keeping it from him. Not having a landline or my cell, I got out my laptop and sent him a text message with it.

I need to talk to you. Can you stop by my house on your way home?

I got a text back from him instantly. *I've been looking everywhere for you. Where in the hell have you been? The deputy at the front desk said he saw you run out of the station. And how the hell did you get to your house?* He was angry with me all right. I was surprised he wasn't using all caps.

I promise I'll tell you everything when you get here. And can you pick my cell-phone up on the way? It's on the sidewalk a block east of the station.

It's in my hand.

Wondering how and why he'd tracked down my phone already, I headed for the first aid kit in my bathroom, Trixie dutifully at my side. I hadn't much more than glanced at my arm before now. It was a giant mess, and it had begun to throb. Not a terribly deep cut, but it ran the whole length of my forearm. I probably could have used some stitches, but I couldn't stomach them right now, or the thought of wasting hours in the ER. I found a box of butterfly wound closures that would have to do and began to rinse the blood off my arm and cleanse the wound. No sooner than I was soaking wet up to my elbows, my doorbell rang. Trixie started barking and bumped me out of the way to make it to the door first.

When I opened the door, Baxter barged in and gripped me by the shoulders. "You were gone for over thirty minutes, without your phone, purse, or coat. You didn't tell anyone where you were going—you just disappeared. I thought—" He stopped short and then choked out, "I thought he had you."

I could hardly bear to look up into his troubled blue eyes. "He did. I agreed to meet him, but—"

His face dark with fury, he gave me a shake. "You went by yourself to meet with him? The only reason I agreed to go along with your ridiculous plan is because I thought I would be there with you. Did you even think about the consequences before you acted? He could have..." With great effort, he lowered his voice and said, "You're lucky you lived to tell about it."

A wave of horror coursed through me as I realized how right he was. "I know, and I'm sorry. But I had no other choice. He texted me and gave me one minute to meet him. If I hadn't come alone, the deal would have been off."

Baxter let me go and stood there for a moment, finally taking in my bloodied shirt and the towel I had pressed against my forearm. "Did he hurt you? Do I need to take you to a hospital?"

"I'm okay. He had a knife, and...he cut me with it. But it's not deep."

His face draining of color, he didn't respond.

I took a step back. "Does blood on living people trigger your gag reflex?"

He scowled at me. "No." He bent down to pet Trixie, who'd been trying to get his attention all during his tirade. "And stop deflecting." After straightening up, he said, "Let me take a look at your arm."

I peeled back the towel to show him the gash. He clenched his jaw.

"I was starting to patch myself up when you got here. Give me a second and I'll finish the job so you won't have to look at it anymore. I'll be right back." I headed toward my bedroom.

"You'll need two hands for that one. I'll do it," he grumbled, stripping off his coat as he followed me down the hall. When we got to my bathroom, he ordered, "Sit down," and began washing his hands.

I sat on the edge of my tub, hoping he wouldn't insist I go to the hospital once he examined my wound up close. He kneeled down in front of me and gently took my arm, removing the towel. The bleeding hadn't stopped yet.

Furrowing his brow, he said, "This isn't just a scratch, Ellie. I'll do what I can." As he began cleaning my wound again, he said, "Tell me everything."

29

While Baxter worked on my arm, I launched into my story about Justin and our joyride around town. I had to pause a few times, twice for him to let out a string of curses—like when I told him that Linda Beasley had been the one to tell Samuel Fox about Leann's alleged affair with Richard Kendrick, and also when I recounted Justin trying to stab me. I halted my story a third time so he could make a call to Sterling to have someone look into the stolen sports car and do a background check on Linda Beasley.

After Baxter had put a dozen or so butterfly closures in place, he covered my wound with gauze and wrapped my entire forearm in a protective bandage. Once he finished, he grasped my hand and turned my arm over to inspect his handiwork.

His grip tightened on my hand as he said, "You know, you're really lucky this is all he did to you."

"I know," I replied, relaxing for the first time since he'd started tending to my wound. Even with his gentle touch, the experience had been excruciating. I wiped the cold sweat from my face with my free hand. "So why had you already tracked down my phone by the time I contacted you? I wasn't gone that long."

"It was long enough that I started to worry. You vanished into thin air, and we were supposed to work on a couple of things before we left for the night. I called your phone, but it went to voicemail. I looked all over the station for you. At one point, I thought maybe you'd gone home, but then I found your coat and purse on the chair by my desk. When I heard you'd run out the front door, I knew something was up and GPS tracked your phone. I found it tossed on the sidewalk, and that's when I really got worried."

I hung my head. "I'm sorry. I didn't have time to stop and think."

Baxter squeezed my hand again, and I looked up to meet his eyes. He didn't seem as angry anymore. "Would your decision have been different if you'd had the time to stop and think?"

Smiling slightly, I said, "Probably not."

"Come on. Let's get you somewhere more comfortable."

He helped me up, but as soon as I was in a standing position, my head got woozy.

"Ooh, going down," I murmured as my knees gave out.

Baxter caught me around the waist, and in one swift motion scooped me up into his arms. He carried me toward my bed, but I said, "No, please take me to the living room."

"You need to sleep."

"We need to talk more than I need sleep."

"Okay," he conceded, heading toward the living room. As he leaned down to deposit me onto my couch, our faces were only an inch apart. My pulse quickened, and our eyes locked for a moment. After he straightened up, I felt an odd twinge of disappointment that he no longer held me in his arms.

What was wrong with me? I shouldn't be having that kind of reaction to Baxter of all people. It had to be the exhaustion and stress playing games with my mind.

I cleared my throat. "Thanks."

"Let me get you some water. You're still pale." He disappeared into the kitchen. When he returned and handed me a glass of water, he said quietly, "I, um...noticed you were ready to pour a drink in there. But the glass was unused."

"Excellent attention to detail, Detective."

A smile played at his lips. "It looks like you raided a bag of chocolate chips instead. Good for you."

Shrugging, I said, "Trading one vice for another isn't the best kind of progress."

He sat down next to me. "Considering the vice in question is chocolate, I'm okay with it."

"You won't be saying that when you have to rent a crane to get my fat ass out of this house."

Chuckling, he said, "I think we have a little time before we have to worry about that."

I faced him. "Nick, all joking aside, I want you to know that it wasn't my intention to go behind your back tonight. I feel like I broke your trust." I paused, trying to find the words to convey something I'd been wrestling with all week. "And speaking of trust, I wanted to tell you... I've let go of my issue about you looking into my mother's murder case. I get it that you were only trying to help me get some closure." I took a deep breath. Apologizing didn't come too naturally to me. "I'm sorry I was such a shit about it."

"Don't sweat it. I should have listened to what you said and left it alone."

He still hadn't addressed the situation tonight. I couldn't bear not knowing where he stood. "But about me agreeing to meet Justin alone...I hope you understand that I did it because I thought it was my only chance. You know that, right?"

Nodding, he replied, "Even though I wish you'd come to me, I know it had nothing to do with me. The guy is a master at manipulation, and he's going to do things his way. I fully believe that you would've lost your chance to talk to him if you hadn't agreed to his demands." His eyes came to rest on my bandaged arm. "I just hate that you had to pay the price."

The pain in my arm had descended into a dull, burning ache. "Me, too."

"But I'm happy to hear you've finally forgiven me. You can hold a grudge like nobody's business." He nudged my leg with his.

Smiling, I patted his knee. "Bad habit. Truth be told...I don't mind so much when you look out for me. I even kind of like it." His eyes flicked down, and I realized I'd left my hand on his leg. Mortified, I snatched my hand away and cleared my throat again. "I mean, it's nice to know my partner has my back."

His brow furrowed, and he leaned closer to me. "Do you think I go out of my way to protect you because you're my partner? I'd never do this kind of stuff for Sterling."

My cold sweat came back. I made a point to steady my voice before I replied, "Right, because Sterling is a cop who can take care of himself. I'm an unarmed civilian."

"No, it's not that. It's because..." He stared at me for a moment, then placed his hand on my cheek. "I care about you, Ellie."

A surge of heat shot through me at his touch. Blown away by his admission, I didn't know how to respond. I'd been starting to feel the same way about him, but I didn't want to ruin what we had by crossing a line. I managed to wreck every romantic relationship I had, and Baxter was way too good a guy to become another casualty of my love life. He was a man who deserved a happily ever after, not a hot mess like me. Before I had a chance to figure out what I was going to say to him, he came closer and brushed my lips with his. With the exception of my inner struggle, everything else about this moment felt right. Too raw to employ what little self-control I possessed, I leaned into him and kissed him back, good intentions be damned.

His lips were warm on mine, soft but urgent. But pure, unadulterated bliss only lasted for a moment until he pulled back and sighed. "I'm sorry. My timing sucks. We're in the middle of a case. You're emotionally drained. I don't want to make things weird between us."

With him being the one who pulled away, I didn't want to come across as overeager. I took a deep breath and let it out before saying, "No, Nick. It's fine." I knew I had to put a stop to this, but all I could manage was trying to table discussing our feelings until later. "But you're right. Your timing does suck."

He smiled.

I added, "And we both need to rest. You should go."

His face fell. "You think I'm leaving you alone after you pissed off a serial killer enough to cut you? No way. I'm sleeping right here."

If he didn't leave, then how could I hope to keep my mind off him? I let out a nervous laugh. "Well, the joke's on you, because if last night was any indication, I'm probably going to wake up screaming several times. I think you should run for it while you have the chance."

He scooted away from me and stretched out on the other end of the couch. "Not happening, especially if you're having nightmares. If you get scared, I'll be here for you."

"Not that I don't appreciate it, but...you know you don't have to."

"Haven't you listened to a word I said? I want to."

I leaned back against the fluffy cushions behind me, thinking I hadn't felt this safe in a long time.

I was in the barn with Rachel, standing over her tiny frame huddled in the dirty straw of the cattle stall. It was so frigid I could see my breath, and I was chilled to the bone. Rachel was shivering, wearing the clothes Jenna had been wearing when we found her at the park. Out of the corner of my eye, I saw Justin Fox approaching us, a red-hot cattle brand in hand. I tried to position myself in front of Rachel to stop him, but he walked through me like I was a ghost. My sister was tied up, helpless to get away. I tried to grab him from behind, but my hands went through his torso. As he thrust the brand against her bare leg, I screamed, "No!"

"Ellie."

Something had hold of my shoulders, but I couldn't pull away or see what it was. All I could see was the frightening scene in the barn. I flailed my arms, trying to get free from whatever was holding me, intent on finding a way to pry that psychopath away from my sister. I screamed again as Rachel cried out in pain.

"Ellie, wake up."

My eyelids fluttered open. Baxter's face was directly over mine.

"I was... Rachel..." Tears streamed down my cheeks. "He was hurting her, and all I could do was watch."

Baxter's expression softened. He sat back and pulled me toward him so my head rested against his chest. "It wasn't real. It was just a dream."

"He was...branding her," I choked out. "And it was so cold in that barn. She was so cold."

He tightened his arm around me. "Look, you can't go there. You have to assume she's okay or you'll go crazy."

I sat up straight and demanded, "What do you know about how to behave in a situation like this?"

Letting out a heavy sigh, he said, "It's time I told you." After a long pause, he said, "My brother was kidnapped when he was a kid."

I stared at him, shell-shocked. "What?"

"It's not something I tell many people. Of course everyone from my hometown knows about it, because they remember when it happened. But here, only the Sheriff knows. And now you. It was a dark time in my life and my family's life, and I don't like to talk about it."

"Kind of like me with my mom's case."

"Exactly."

"I'm sorry I snapped at you. I won't ask you to talk about it."

"I want to tell you. I want you to know why I'm like I am."

I smiled, touched that he wanted to open up to me. "Okay."

His gaze trained on what was left of my Christmas tree, he began his story. "My dad was the high school football coach in our small town. Everyone knew him. And most people liked him, at least when the team was having a winning season. My brothers and I grew up at the football field. When I was sixteen, on the night of our homecoming game, my brother Tom and I were out on the field when the referees called a halt to the game. My dad rushed out and told us our little brother Shawn had gone missing. He was only four at the time. Mom was running the concession stand, like she always did, and she'd paid a neighbor girl to watch Shawn at the game. The girl got to talking with some of her friends, and she lost track of Shawn. She looked all over for him, but couldn't find him anywhere. I remember hearing the announcer at the game calling his name over and over again." He shook his head. "He was a good kid. He would have come running if he'd been there."

I reached over and squeezed Baxter's hand, my heart aching for him.

He stared at our hands as he continued, "The whole stadium went nuts. Everyone who knew Shawn started looking for him. The police got there within minutes. We went over every inch of the place. The police checked every vehicle before they let people leave the parking lot, but he was already gone. No one had seen anyone take a kid out of the stadium kicking and screaming. It was as if he'd vanished." He sighed. "The detective that got assigned to the case was very much by the book. He called in a ransom negotiator, although she did nothing because there was never a ransom demand. He compiled a list of everyone with a vendetta against my dad or mom and investigated them. He worked with some civilian agencies to conduct several widespread physical searches of the town. He got news coverage for us, and the story even got picked up nationally. He did everything right except care about what he was doing. And after four months, he still hadn't found my brother."

"Four months? Did you...start to give up hope?"

Nodding, he said, "Tom and I did. Mom did. But my dad never did. Tom and I started acting out at school, and our grades dropped. Mom got so depressed she couldn't get out of bed most days. My dad held us together."

He dropped my hand and hoisted himself up off the couch. I could tell it was a difficult topic for him to talk about from the deflated way he carried himself.

Pacing back and forth in front of the Christmas tree, he continued, "Then the detective came to us one day and told us he was transferring to a different department. He was going to work narcotics instead of missing persons. So we assumed that was basically the end of Shawn's case. We figured no one was going to swoop in and take over an investigation that had gone so cold. But then along came Detective Joe Finnegan. The first few weeks he was assigned to the case, he simply got to know us. He took my dad out for coffee. He and his wife brought dinner over and ate with our family. He shot hoops with Tom and me after school. He talked with us for hours on end and made us feel better. He treated us like human beings rather than a victim's family. What we didn't realize was that he was also finding out who really knew us and who knew Shawn well enough to kidnap him in a crowd without being noticed. I showed an interest in what he was doing on the investigative side, so he would take me to the station with him sometimes and let me look over his shoulder while he ran background checks and wrote reports."

I smiled. "Sounds like something you would do."

Shrugging, he said, "I try every day to live up to the standard he set."

"I'm pretty sure you've exceeded it, especially this past week."

Blushing, he said, "So, after a couple of months, he shows up one day out of the blue at our house, and he has Shawn. After we'd all but given up on ever finding my brother, there he was, not a scratch on him. One of my mom's friends had moved away a couple of weeks before my brother was abducted, so she wasn't originally on anyone's radar. But Joe managed to glean from my mother that the woman had lost a child. He checked her out and found that she'd taken all of her savings out in cash and was living in a remote cabin. On a hunch, he made the two-hour drive and found her outside playing with Shawn."

"Wow. Amazing hunch."

"If it weren't for him, we never would have seen my brother again. That's when I decided I wanted to be a cop. And not just any cop—a cop like Joe Finnegan. I wanted to be able to do for other families what he'd done for mine."

I shook my head. "I had no idea...all this time you knew exactly what I was going through. I guess that's why you always knew what to say."

"I probably should have told you sooner. I wanted to a few months ago. Remember when I said I'd tell you my life story someday?"

"I remember."

He grinned at me. "Well, before I got the chance, you quit talking to me."

"Right. Stupid mistake."

Baxter came my way and picked up a throw blanket from a nearby chair. He spread it over me. "Tough situations can have happy endings. Try to think about that instead of focusing on the bad stuff. Get some sleep."

30

As soon as Baxter and I got to the station in the morning, our team was raring to brief us on what they'd worked on the previous night. I appreciated their dedication, especially since the clock continued to tick, with time seeming to slip by faster and faster as we approached the deadline. By noon today, we'd have only twenty-four hours left.

But before the team meeting, Jayne called me into her office. Manetti was already inside. I'd known at some point I'd have to face the music for going off alone with Justin. I was a coward and had let Baxter pass the news to them through Sterling last night, so at least they'd had a few hours to digest it.

"How could you have taken such a stupid risk?" Manetti demanded the moment the door was closed. His face was twisted into a furious frown. "You could have been killed."

I lowered my eyes and tugged at the sleeve covering my bandage. When he'd talked to Sterling, Baxter hadn't mentioned my injury and had promised—against his better judgment—to keep it between us. In my mind, there was no real harm done, and it would only worry everyone for nothing.

Jayne took a different approach. Coming over to sit in the chair next to me, she took my hand. "This isn't like you, Ellie. I think your judgment is clouded because of Rachel, otherwise you would never have taken a chance like this."

Manetti said, "Anytime you're not out on an interview with Detective Baxter, you're going to have a permanent deputy shadow. Even inside this building. If you decide to shake him and go off on your own again, I'll take you off this case, sister or not."

As angry and mortified as I was about having my babysitter back, as well as about Manetti's ultimatum, I knew I couldn't possibly do anything so crazy again. I didn't feel like my luck would hold out for a second time.

"I understand."

Manetti stared at me for a beat, probably expecting a fight, given our tendency to butt heads over much less. "Okay."

Jayne asked me, "Did he say anything about Rachel?"

I shook my head. "Not really. I asked him how she was, but he wouldn't answer me."

She squeezed my hand and gave me a sympathetic smile. "At least you got some information out of him that should help the investigation."

Manetti glanced at his watch. "Speaking of which, we have a meeting to attend."

We exited her office and went down the hall to the conference room, where the rest of the team was assembled. I took a seat next to Amanda, who gave me a quick one-armed hug.

Manetti threw down the file he'd brought on the conference table and ran a hand through his already disheveled dark hair. "As expected, the tip line went nuts last night. And when I say nuts, I mean every mentally unstable person in this part of the state decided to call in either pretending to be Justin Fox or swearing up and down they'd seen him or Rachel Miller. Sheriff Walsh, Ms. Carmack, and I, along with several deputies, spent the night running down the more credible tips. Deputy Martinez, we have a list of farm properties we'd like you to add to the list you worked last night to compile for your investigation today." He slid a stack of papers toward Martinez. "Detective Sterling, can you tell us about the research you did with Dr. Berg last night?"

Sterling said, "Dr. Berg and I compared the autopsies of Amy Donovan and Leann Fox. The manner of death was the same—blunt force trauma to the back of the head followed by manual strangulation. In going over the photos of Leann's injuries, we determined that the two blows she suffered to her head came straight at her. If done by a ten-year-old boy, they would have been upswings, which her injuries did not indicate. Also, Dr. Berg is convinced that according to how the bones in her neck were broken, it would have taken hands larger than a ten-year-old's. So we can cross Justin Fox himself off the suspect list for his mother's murder. For my money, it's Richard Kendrick. According to Matthews's conversation with the serial killer last night, Samuel Fox was convinced Kendrick was to blame for his wife's death. In my mind, there's got to be some merit to that."

Baxter said, "We're planning to speak to Kendrick's widow this morning."

Manetti nodded. "Good. Chief Esparza, your report?"

Esparza said, "I was able to track down the stolen sports car that Justin Fox took last night from the Fashion Mall. It was ditched here in town. A vehicle that was reported stolen last night in Westfield ended up at the Fashion Mall near where the sports car had been parked, so I assume that in order to cover his tracks, Fox stole more than one vehicle to get from place to place. Smart, although it was a risk to steal one car, let alone two." He handed Baxter a file. "I also ran a full background on Linda Beasley. She's a real piece of work. Have fun with that."

Anger still evident in his tone, Manetti said to me, "Ms. Matthews, would you like to share with everyone what you learned from your one-on-one conversation with Justin Fox last night?"

All eyes swiveled toward me.

I cleared my throat. "As Sterling said, Justin told me his father truly believed Richard Kendrick killed Leann. He'd heard about the affair from Linda Beasley, a catty coworker of Leann's."

Baxter said, "I don't get why she didn't tell us that she'd been the one to tip off Samuel Fox about their supposed affair. She seemed to be forthcoming about everything else. The only havoc she caused by her actions was angering Fox, which resulted in getting Kendrick fired."

Esparza shrugged. "If she called Fox to tell him his wife was cheating, she had to have known him. Would she have called a coworker's husband out of the blue only to narc on his wife? Why would it have mattered to her that he knew? If her intent was to get Leann into trouble or to embarrass her, it would have caused a bigger splash to tell the boss or to spread the rumor around the office."

Jayne said, "You're right. It would have. If Linda hated Leann enough to ruin her marriage, why not get her fired and be rid of her?"

Amanda said quietly, "Unless Linda knew about the abuse and was so sadistic that she wanted to see Leann suffer physically."

Sterling's eyebrows shot up. "That's pretty dark."

I thought back to the visit Baxter and I paid Linda yesterday. "I think it's a possibility she had eyes for Samuel Fox and wanted to break up Leann's marriage. When we met with her, Linda came off as..."

"A nympho?" Baxter supplied for me.

I shrugged. "For lack of a better word, yes. Maybe she decided she wanted him and lied about Leann having an affair. Or told the truth about it. Nobody but Linda can seem to confirm or deny a relationship between Leann and Richard."

Manetti asked, "Do you have a reason to believe that Linda Beasley could have been the one to kill Leann?"

The room got quiet. I'd always imagined it was a man who'd killed Leann over an affair or over her unborn baby. It hadn't occurred to me that it could be a woman, which would make the motive a different kind of jealousy.

Baxter nodded slowly. "Honestly, I could see it."

Esparza gestured toward the file he'd given Baxter. "She has a history of assault, mostly against other women. Now, they could all have been harmless catfights, but history is history. She has no problem getting violent."

Baxter said, "We're planning to have a follow-up visit with her this morning, also."

Manetti said, "Ms. Matthews, I think we derailed your report. Please continue."

I said, "Right. Um...Justin also verified what Mariella Vasquez had said about Leann and Prasad having coffee together before her death. His dad followed them and saw them together. And oddly enough, Justin got really angry when I brought up the subject of his mom's pregnancy at the time of her death, but his reaction verified it was true. We thought since he'd alluded to it through his use of the other 'eye for an eye' Bible passage that he wanted us to know, but after talking to him I'm not convinced. Which I think is a good thing—he's been pulling all the strings so far, and the more we can force him to deviate from his script the better the chances are that he'll make a mistake."

Manetti asked, "How did you leave things with him?"

I glanced at Baxter, whose expression was grim. "Not good."

Manetti's jaw clenched. "Did he threaten you? Did he threaten to do something to your sister?"

My wound throbbed under its bandage. "No, but he kicked me out of his car in the middle of the street. He was done with me."

Manetti grimaced, but didn't pry any more. "Well, we all have a lot to do today. Get to work."

Our first order of business was to find Rajit Prasad, so Baxter and I took off for Carmel in his SUV.

On the way, I said, "I've been thinking about Leann's pregnancy and why it was such a sore subject with her son. What if she got pregnant by another man and decided to pass the baby off as her husband's in order to save her marriage? Mariella Vasquez told us that the Foxes hadn't had sex in a year. What if Leann had just found out she was pregnant and died before she had the chance to seal the deal with her husband to fool him into thinking the baby was his?"

Baxter's jaw dropped. "Do women actually do that?"

"It happens. It would only be the difference of a couple of weeks in her pregnancy, so Samuel would probably have been none the wiser."

"That's sick."

"Agreed, but these are not exactly healthy, well-adjusted people. Let's focus on the case, here."

He frowned. "Okay, fine. So somehow the son knew about the pregnancy. Maybe he found out by accident and Leann talked him into keeping it a secret from his dad. He didn't see his dad again until eight years later. Maybe he told him about it then and Samuel went ballistic. If the baby didn't belong to his dad, then his image of his mother could have been tarnished."

"That's a good thought. Wish I'd had it last night so I could have asked him."

Throwing me a dubious glance, he said, "Why? So he could have flown into a bigger rage and gutted your other arm, too?"

"Not funny."

"It wasn't supposed to be. I hear you have your shadow back when you're not with me."

I sighed. "Yes, lucky me. I'm basically on supervised house arrest except when I'm with you. They might as well get me an ankle bracelet and be done with it. Then Manetti can track my every step."

He smiled. "You know it's for your own good."

"I feel like no one trusts me."

"Kinda brought that one on yourself."

I grumbled under my breath, but otherwise didn't defend myself. He was right.

We pulled up in front of Prasad's McMansion and went to the door. After a few minutes of knocking, there was no answer. Baxter tried both contact numbers we had for Prasad, but both went straight to voicemail. His office was in a complex on North Meridian, so we decided to try there. When we arrived, the lights were off and the door was locked.

Richard Kendrick's widow didn't live far away, so we headed to her house. Same story—no one was home, and no one answered the phone.

Baxter frowned. "Where the hell is everyone this morning?"

"Christmas shopping, probably. I would have been, if..."

An image flashed into my head of Christmas morning last year—Rachel, Nate, and me in our pajamas opening presents. It was the first year Nate had really understood what was going on, and I had never seen the kid so excited. I struggled to put it out of my mind and focus back on the present.

Laying a hand on my shoulder, he said, "Come on, none of that. You've been doing great. Don't get discouraged. We've got plenty more people to talk to, and we can come back to these two later."

As much as I tried to bottle that memory back up, being apart from my nephew suddenly hit me like a ton of bricks. "I'm sorry. It's just... I miss Nate," I whispered, brushing away a tear that escaped my eye.

Baxter gripped my other shoulder and turned me to face him. "I promise this will be over soon and you'll have Rachel and Nate back safe and sound. We have plenty of time—"

"Nick, we have twenty-eight hours and still no suspect."

"No, we have twenty-eight hours and three excellent suspects. While I'm not convinced about Prasad's guilt, I wouldn't feel at all bad about pinning it on our dead guy or our nympho. Either way, no harm, no foul."

I scrunched up my nose. "No harm, no foul? What about tarnishing Richard Kendrick's memory? And last I checked, a rabid sex drive is no crime."

He released me. "She's guilty of something. Let's go rattle her cage."

Big, wet flakes of snow had just begun to fall when we pulled into Linda Beasley's condo complex. As we were walking up the sidewalk toward her door, Baxter got a call. He kept walking and answered it, but when he heard the person on the other end of the line, he immediately stopped and put the call on speaker.

He elbowed me and said, "Hi, Nolan. Nice to hear from you."

My jaw dropped. I whispered, "The stoner from the gas station?"

Baxter nodded.

Nolan's voice was rough and scratchy, like he'd stayed up all night partying. "Yeah, so I remembered something."

Baxter asked, "What is it?"

"The town Justin said he lived in. Sister...wait. Yeah. Sister something."

Baxter and I shared a confused glance.

"Cicero?" Baxter suggested.

"Aw, man. Yeah. That's the one."

"You're sure?"

"Positive."

My heart clenched. Rachel was somewhere in the small community of Cicero, just north of Noblesville. This was the break we'd been waiting for.

"Thanks, Nolan." As soon as he disconnected with Nolan, he was on another call to Sterling. "Hey, we talked to a former coworker of Justin Fox's. He said Justin had told him he was living in a barn in Cicero. I want every farm property in that zip code researched and cross-referenced against every person even remotely connected to this case." After a pause, he said, "Thanks," and hung up. Turning to me with a huge grin on his face, he said, "We're close now. I have no doubt in my mind that we can find Rachel before tomorrow at noon."

Even with the biting wind that had kicked up and the snow swirling around me, I felt a newfound energy coursing through my veins. I could sense the tide turning in this investigation, enough that I could find it in my skeptical self to be optimistic. We were going to find my sister. I knew it.

31

"Let's get this done so we can join in the search for Rachel. I'll be the bad cop this time," I said, marching straight for Linda Beasley's condo. Baxter followed, shaking his head and chuckling as I beat my fist against the door.

Linda answered the door, huffy about the insistent pounding. "One knock would have sufficed." When she realized who was standing there, she changed her tune. Ignoring me, she said, "Oh, why hello, Detective. Back to see me so soon?"

I barged in and said, "Cut the shit, Linda. We know you were the one who tipped off Samuel Fox that Richard Kendrick and Leann Fox were having an affair. You neglected to tell us that when we talked to you yesterday. Why?"

Her eyes got wide as saucers. "I didn't... I don't know what you're—"

"I talked to Justin Fox last night."

"The serial killer? And you're taking his word over mine?"

"Oh, let's not pretend you're some innocent schoolgirl, Linda. You've got a rap sheet a mile long of bar fights and catfights and bitchery of all kinds. You want to know what I think? I think you despised Leann Fox because everyone liked her and they all hated you. She was prettier than you, better at her job than you, and she was married. Plus she may have even had something on the side. She had it all, and you were jealous. So you figured you'd ruin her marriage to knock her down a peg."

Linda's whole head turned beet red, and she began sputtering. Baxter had his head bowed and the brim of his hat pulled low over his brow to hide what he could of his amusement.

I wasn't finished. "Or maybe you decided it wasn't enough to ruin her marriage. Maybe you wanted her out of the way so you could replace her. It was no secret that she and her husband were having trouble. You could solve his problem and walk into a ready-made family. All you had to do was kill her."

Linda collapsed onto the sofa and put her head in her hands. She wailed, "I didn't kill her! I swear!"

"Then who did?"

"I don't *know*!" Sniffling, she added, "But...I do know it wasn't Richard."

Baxter asked, "How do you know that?"

She looked up at him, tears and mascara running in rivers down her cheeks. "He and I were together that night."

Floored, I dropped down next to her on her sofa. "What? I thought you said he and Leann were having an affair."

She wiped her nose on her sleeve. "I made that up. Richard and I were the ones having the affair. One day he told me he wanted to end our relationship; that he wanted to try to reconcile with his wife. I got angry, and the way I lashed out at him was to call Leann's crazy husband and tell him the lie about the affair. I figured he'd kick Richard's ass and be done with it."

I glared at her. "You could have gotten Leann beat up in the process. Did you not consider that?"

"I didn't care. I hated Leann." She grumbled under her breath, "Stuck-up bitch."

Baxter didn't think this was funny anymore. He walked closer so he could tower over Linda. "You ended up getting Kendrick fired. How then were you back together shortly afterward? He had to know it was you who called Samuel Fox and started the whole mess."

Sitting up straighter, she said, "Richard was mad at me, but not for long. He never could resist me."

"So this is the actual truth now? You lied to us yesterday, which obstructed justice. If I feel like you're leaving anything out this time or not being honest again, I will arrest you, and you'll spend Christmas in jail. Do you understand that, Ms. Beasley?"

Her face went white. "I understand. I'm telling the truth, and I didn't leave anything out. I swear on my life...on my grandkids' lives."

Seeming satisfied, Baxter nodded at me. I got up from the couch and followed him out the door.

"Decent bombshell, that one," I said, pulling my coat's collar tight around my neck to keep warm. "But we lost two suspects—the ones who you wanted to be guilty."

"True, but now we have one suspect to focus on—Prasad."

"But you don't think he did it. Why?"

As we got back into his vehicle, he said, "I guess it's because there isn't enough information about him to make him seem like a major player. The only thing we know is that he and Leann ran into each other by chance one day, exchanged contact information, and then later met for coffee. That's not an affair."

"I agree. Justin did mention, though, that he has early memories of Prasad coming around their house and trying to chat up his mom. Samuel put a stop to it one day, and supposedly Prasad never came back."

"Right, and that was ancient history. The part I can't see is the timing for Prasad. Why after over a decade come back and kill an ex-girlfriend? If he was going to kill her, why not do it when she broke up with him all those years ago? He didn't have much of a motive at the time of her death."

I shrugged. "I guess it could all still go back to her pregnancy. Prasad is Middle Eastern, and the Foxes were both fair-skinned blondes. If the baby was Prasad's, it would have been obvious, and therefore important for him to get rid of in order to keep his affair a secret from his wife."

"But that also means Leann couldn't have tried to pass the baby off as her husband's in an attempt to keep her own family intact."

"Ooh, good point. Well, I guess there could have been something else she mentioned to Mariella that she thought might fix their marriage. Maybe she'd just won the lottery or found her husband a job or something."

"Or something. We need to make it a priority to find Prasad, but in the interest of time and safety, I'll have a deputy work on finding him and bringing him to the station for us. If he's our guy, the two of us don't need to be alone with him at his house."

"And yet we just barged into Linda Beasley's home after you said you thought she could be the killer."

He grinned. "I figured either one of us could have taken her in a fair fight."

Since we now had a much narrower search area for Rachel's location, we decided to knock out all of our interviews as quickly as possible so we could join in the rescue effort. Even though the appointment we'd made with Courtney Kapinski wasn't until noon at a coffeeshop in downtown Noblesville, we figured it couldn't hurt to try to find her earlier at home.

Baxter drove us to Courtney's apartment in Noblesville. After he parked, he got out his phone and read a text he'd received on the way over. I could tell by the look on his face that it was something monumental.

Turning to me, he said, "Sterling gave me a heads-up that they're mobilizing Noblesville ESU to go out to a property north of Cicero." He was referring to Noblesville PD's Emergency Services Unit, which was their SWAT rescue team.

I sucked in a breath. "They think it could be the one?"

"Maybe. If you want to head up there, I'm fine with it. But he did mention that they just got the word, so if we left now, we'd probably beat them there. I feel like we have time to do this interview and still arrive in plenty of time. But again, it's up to you."

My nerves were jangling, but thinking back to yesterday, I said, "We're here. Let's talk to Courtney and then decide if we even want to drive up. Although I want to be there when we find Rachel, I also don't want to waste time like we did yesterday. We're getting too close to spare even a few minutes on a wild goose chase."

He smiled. "I know that was a tough decision, but I think it's the right one. Come on. This should be quick."

Courtney answered the door in her pajamas and a fuzzy robe, her face marred with confusion. "Detective Baxter. I thought we were meeting later and...not here."

"Sorry, Ms. Kapinski. Our schedule for the day changed at the last minute. Hope you don't mind if we go ahead with the interview now."

She pasted on a smile. "Not at all."

We entered her apartment, which was homey and warm, decorated with dozens upon dozens of framed photos. I found it difficult to concentrate on interviewing her with the imminent prospect of finding the barn where Rachel was being held, so I hung back while Baxter took the lead.

While he made some small talk and put Courtney at ease, I perused her living room. Several of her knickknacks and wall hangings said "family" and had various syrupy sentiments on them. Her photos were all of smiling people with their arms around each other. It struck me that she was so family-oriented after having grown up in the system, and in at least one abusive household. Many foster kids became resistant to the idea of a close family, thinking if they didn't get attached to anyone that they couldn't be hurt if everything got ripped away again. But then again, Wyatt and Tyrone had both said that Courtney took on the role of protector in their home. She might have been the other extreme, whose sole desire was to obtain a tight-knit family bond like she'd once lost.

Mulling that over, I began looking more carefully at the people in the photos.

I tuned back into what Baxter was saying in time to hear him ask, "Have you had any contact with Justin since you were both taken from the Reuben household?"

"A little when he and Wyatt were at their next home. Our social worker was kind enough to try to bring our families together so we could see each other. But once he ran away, I never saw him again."

My gaze came to rest on two photos of Courtney, taken not terribly long ago. Her hair was bright blue, and her makeup was hideous.

I turned to them. "You sure about that? You didn't maybe go visit him at Babcock Electronics about a year ago?"

Baxter gave me a curious glance but said nothing.

Courtney's eyes widened a fraction. "No, sorry. I know where that place is, but I've never been in there."

"Oh, okay," I said, not believing a word of it. I kept on with inspecting the photos.

Baxter said to her, "Do you know of anyone else he might have confided in about his mother's death? We'd like to be able to find the real killer and exonerate his father."

"Oh, right. So he'll let that girl go. I don't know of anyone he would have kept in touch with besides Wyatt."

I moved to look at the photos on a bookcase in the corner of the room, hoping to find one of her with Justin so I could bust her lying ass. Instead, I found something much more earth-shattering. With shaking hands, I picked up a framed photo of Courtney and a guy her age. It was a professional shot, artsy and rustic, with the two of them sitting on the hood of an old Ford pickup truck. There was a ramshackle barn in the background.

Working to keep my voice steady, I said, "This is a great photo. Where was it taken?"

She froze. "Oh...some random farm the photographer uses for photo shoots..."

I walked toward her. "You're lying. Try again." I handed the photo to Baxter, whose eyes bugged out when he took a look.

"I'm not lying. It was over in Westfield, I think."

Baxter's voice was sharp. "You sure it's not in Cicero? Who does the farm belong to?"

Shaking her head, she said, "I...I don't know what you're talking about."

"Who's in the photo with you? A boyfriend? Is it his farm?" I demanded. She didn't reply.

I took a step toward her, fists clenched. "What's his name?"

Her jaw set defiantly, she raised her voice and said, "My personal life has *nothing* to do with your investigation."

"The hell it doesn't. You're harboring Justin Fox. Tell me where he is!" I cried.

"Oh, I get it. Now I know who you are. The girl he's holding is your sister. In your situation, do you really think you're stable enough to be investigating this case?"

I ignored her. "You protected him when he was a kid, and you're protecting him now! Where is he?"

When Courtney had started resisting my questions, Baxter slipped away to make a quiet phone call. I heard enough bits and pieces to know that he was calling for backup to haul her in to the station.

Her face turned red with rage. "I know my rights! This isn't a formal questioning, and I don't have to talk to you if I don't want to. In fact, you need to leave my home. Right now."

A young man hurried out from the hallway behind Courtney, rubbing the sleep from his eyes. It was the same guy from the photo Baxter held. "Babe? I heard yelling. You okay?" When he saw Baxter and me, he tensed. "What are you two doing here?" He moved to stand between Courtney and us.

Baxter showed him his badge. "I'm Detective Baxter, and this is Ms. Matthews. We're with the Hamilton County Sheriff's Department. We're here asking Ms. Kapinski a few questions about her relationship with Justin Fox. And you are?"

"Kyle Clark."

Courtney clutched at the back of her boyfriend's T-shirt. "I told them they needed to leave, and they won't. Make them leave, Kyle."

Kyle's face registered confusion as he turned to her. "What's the big deal with answering their questions? You haven't seen that psycho since you were kids."

Baxter held the photo out so Kyle could see it. "We'd like to know where this photo was taken."

Kyle's expression registered confusion. "What does that have to do with Justin Fox?"

"We have reason to believe that Ms. Kapinski might know of Justin Fox's whereabouts and is concealing that information in order to protect him. We think he could be using this property and that he may even be holding a hostage there."

"What?" he breathed, seeming dazed. He turned to Courtney. "Grandpa Harold's farm? I don't understand."

From the wild look in her eyes, I could tell Courtney knew she was cornered. "They're making it up, Kyle. Why would I do that?"

Baxter shrugged. "Prove us wrong. Give us the address and we'll check it out."

Courtney looked up at Kyle pleadingly. "Don't do it. We don't have to tell them anything."

"That's true," Baxter agreed, his tone subdued and reasonable. His gaze was fixed on Kyle now, who seemed the far likelier of the two to break down and give us the information. "You don't have to tell me anything. But given the severity of this case and the fact that a young woman's life is in danger, if you refuse to cooperate, I can bring you up on obstruction of justice." Knowing he had the upper hand, Baxter crossed his arms, a smirk playing at his lips. "I'll let you mull that one over. Take your time."

"Don't say a word, Kyle. We'll fight this," Courtney murmured to him.

"What's to fight? What the hell's wrong with you? You're acting crazy," he hissed back.

There was a knock at the door. "Hamilton County Sheriff's Department," called a voice from outside.

Within seconds, Kyle had given Baxter the address and two deputies had come in to haul Courtney and Kyle to the station. After Baxter gave the deputies strict instructions not to let Courtney anywhere near a phone so she couldn't warn Justin, he whisked me out of the apartment.

As we hopped into his vehicle, Baxter said, "Amazing catch, Ellie." Before I could reply, he was already on the phone to Manetti to let him know we had a hot lead on finding Rachel. A couple of inches of snow had accumulated in the short time we'd been inside. Visibility was bad, and the streets were slick. Baxter had to go slowly, even in his four-wheel-drive SUV.

I was beside myself knowing that we were headed to find Rachel. I knew this was the one. It had to be. My entire body shook uncontrollably.

After hanging up, Baxter sighed. "They're a ways out. They just arrived at the property they were heading to earlier, so it's going to take them some time to regroup and get to where we're going. I know you're not going to like this, but I think we should wait for them."

I clenched my jaw. "I know you and I can't go in there by ourselves. We can't afford any mistakes. We have to do this right, otherwise..." Shaking my head to clear out the negative thoughts, I said, "I'm okay with waiting."

He reached over and gave my hand a squeeze.

32

We drove past the front of Harold Clark's property. There was an old farmhouse near the road. With the snow falling hard, we couldn't see a barn anywhere in the distance, but noticed a dirt lane leading toward a grove of trees.

"Pull up a satellite map of the area," Baxter said as he drove past the farmhouse. He parked far enough down the road that we wouldn't be seen by any inhabitants of the house.

I did as instructed and noticed the roof of a barn behind the trees we'd seen. I pointed to my phone's screen. "There. That could be it."

"Good. Those trees will give the team some cover as they approach."

I turned to him, worry gnawing in my gut. "What's to say that when they go in guns blazing that Justin won't freak and try to hurt Rachel?"

He smiled. "I've seen them work, and they know what they're doing. Trust me, Justin Fox will never know what hit him. If he even makes a move, they'll pop him."

I nodded and ran my nervous hands through my hair.

After several minutes that seemed like an eternity, we noticed a caravan of police vehicles coming our way. They blocked the road and began gearing up. Baxter and I exited his vehicle and headed to meet Manetti and Sterling.

Manetti regarded me for a moment as he finished strapping on his bulletproof vest. "We're not going to have a repeat of yesterday, are we Ms. Matthews?"

"I want to be there when you bring Rachel out, but I promise I won't get in your way."

Manetti said to Sterling and Baxter, "You two, see that she doesn't."

As Manetti walked away to confer with the Noblesville ESU officers, Sterling griped, "I've been on this case since day one, and the Fed has reduced me to a damn babysitter. I want to go in and kick some serial killer ass."

Baxter said, "You know ESU has their thing that they do. They don't need us. I'm surprised they're letting Manetti in."

"Only because he pulled rank on them. That guy is one pompous asshole."

When Sterling stalked off, Baxter rolled his eyes. "It takes one to know one, right?"

I smiled slightly, my mind on the barn in the distance.

Giving me a pat on the back, he said, "Cheer up. I have a good feeling about this."

We followed the Emergency Services Unit at a safe distance as they made their approach toward the grove of trees. Once we got there, we could see the barn in the distance. My heart clenched. On the ESU team leader's mark, the unit fanned out, their footsteps quiet on the blanket of new-fallen snow. Baxter, Sterling, and I waited at the edge of the trees as the team surrounded the barn.

I drew in a shaky breath, and Baxter put his hand on my shoulder.

Three of the officers had flash grenades in hand. At their designated spots near the main door of the barn and two of the windows, they simultaneously busted in the openings and threw in the grenades.

The team leader yelled, "Go, go, go!" and the members of the unit poured into the barn. A single gunshot rang out. As I let out a strangled cry, Baxter tightened his grip on me. A moment later, Manetti appeared in the doorway to the barn and waved us over.

I took off at full speed, slipping and stumbling in the snow.

When I reached Manetti, he smiled. "It's over. Justin Fox is dead, and your sister is alive and well."

Overcome with emotion, I threw my arms around him.

He hugged me tightly and added, "If you think you can handle going in there, you can go get your sister."

"Thank you," I breathed. "For everything."

I broke away from him and hurried into the barn. One of the ESU officers pointed me toward the third stall on the right. On my way there, I caught a glimpse of Justin Fox sprawled out on the ground, a small hole in the center of his forehead. It took some restraint not to go spit on his corpse, but I had more important things to do. As I came up on the stall, I saw two ESU officers kneeling over a figure in the corner.

"Rachel," I choked out.

"Ellie?" she breathed, her voice barely above a whisper.

I ran to her, and the ESU officers cleared out of my way. I dove onto the ground in front of her and took her into my arms. She was trembling and freezing cold to the touch. She began whimpering as I held her. Tears rolled from my eyes uncontrollably.

I said, "Shh, Rach. Everything's going to be okay now. You're safe."

Between sobs, she said, "I kept dreaming you'd come and get me. Tell me this isn't another dream."

"It's not. I'm here. I love you, sis."

"I love you, too."

Baxter's voice was rough as he said from behind us, "I can't tell you how happy I am to see you, Rachel."

"Thanks for finding me," she whispered.

"You can thank your sister for that. She's the one who figured it out."

I turned to look up at him.

He had tears shining in his eyes as he smiled at me. "See? I told you there were happy endings."

While the EMTs treated Rachel for mild hypothermia in the waiting ambulance, I watched as the stealth rescue op morphed into a bustling active crime scene. Emergency response vehicles of all kinds began converging on the property, and soon the area was teeming with personnel from several different agencies.

Jayne arrived first and made a beeline toward me, sweeping me up into a crushing hug. "I'm so thrilled that you found her. And that that son of a bitch can't hurt anyone anymore."

"I know. I don't think I've ever felt so many emotions in one day. Rachel's in the ambulance if you want to say hi. They're making her drink some kind of warm herbal tea, and I think she's hating it. She's a coffee and hot chocolate girl."

She let me go and smiled, tears streaking her face. "I'll go see what my clout can do for her."

Amanda came up next, throwing her case down in the snow so she could tackle me in a bear hug. "I'm so relieved that your sister is okay!" Stepping back, she held me at arms length to watch my reaction as she asked, "Did you really figure out where Rachel was from a random photo and nearly throttle Courtney Kapinski to get the address out of her, or is Nick exaggerating?"

I chuckled. "He is not in fact exaggerating. If he hadn't played the obstruction of justice card on her boyfriend to make him talk, it could have gotten real ugly in there."

Winking at me, she said, "I don't know if the department is going to let you walk away after you found a serial killer, Ellie. They may strong-arm you into coming back, at least part-time."

"I think I'll worry about that later." I head-nodded toward the ambulance. "I'm taking a break for a while."

"Right. Which means I'm back with Beck." She made a face at Beck's back as he stumbled in the snow toward the barn.

"You have fun with that."

After the EMTs were satisfied that Rachel's body temperature had returned to normal, Baxter drove the two of us home. It wasn't time to relax yet, though. Rachel would still have to go through some extensive questioning about her time in the barn with Justin Fox, but Jayne had insisted it be done in the comfort of our living room instead of at the scene or the station.

I worried over my sister on the drive home. I'd sat in the back seat with her, holding her hand, but she wouldn't utter a word. She sat with her head bowed, her tangled hair covering most of her face. Once we got home, the first thing she wanted to do was take a hot bath. After I drew it for her and got her some fresh towels and clothes, I left her in private and wandered back to the living room where Baxter was staring at my Christmas tree.

"Is Nate coming home today?" he asked.

I smiled. "He is. I called David, and they're on their way back from Cincinnati. Should be here in a couple of hours."

"Then you need to do something about this tree." He gestured to it. "This is the stuff of nightmares for a kid."

My smile fading, I said, "You have a point. I think I have some extra decorations I can use to fill in what I broke."

"I'll help."

As we cleaned up the mess underfoot, strung new lights, and replaced the shattered ornaments, I noticed Baxter watching me.

"What?" I asked.

"I want to offer some unsolicited advice."

"Go for it."

He scratched his beard. "Well, I noticed on the drive over that Rachel wasn't incredibly talkative. That's completely normal. Don't push her."

"I think Sterling and Manetti are planning to come over soon and do just that. Is that going to be a problem?"

"Yes and no. We need to get her statement, and I promise I'll do everything I can to rein those guys in. But for a while, she's probably going to be kind of closed off. I feel like she's going to think it's somehow her fault because she let Justin Fox in. There'll be a lot of guilt that goes with that."

I sighed, angered that my baby sister had to endure the pain of working through this. "I didn't think of it that way, but I see your point."

"If it would help, I can meet with her sometime. Be a sympathetic sounding board for her frustrations."

"I'll let her know that. Thanks."

We continued to work on the tree for a while longer until he said, "You know, I meant what I said back there in the barn, Ellie. If you hadn't noticed that photo, we'd still be looking for Rachel. Her rescue was all you."

I smiled. "I feel like you're downplaying your role a little, but thanks for saying that."

"It's the truth. You did an amazing job on this investigation, and that's besides the fact that you were stressed out of your mind. I know you've said in the past that you're not cut out for this job, but I think you just proved that you are. I don't know of anyone who could have done what you did."

Feeling heat creeping up my cheeks, I said, "Aw, stop. You're making me blush."

He took my hand. "Ellie, don't make light of this. I hope you'll think about coming back to help the department on more of a regular basis. And maybe when things slow down for you, we can finish the conversation we started last night."

Looking away, I pulled my hand away from his. "Actually, I've been thinking about all of that. I feel like maybe I'm ready now to come back and consult."

"That's great news."

"Right, but the problem is we can't have both. We can't work together and be in a relationship."

"Sterling and Amanda seem to be doing just fine."

"Yeah, but this is me we're talking about. Trust me, Nick. I'd find a way to screw it up, which would ruin our partnership. We work too well together to let that happen."

He frowned. "I'm a part of this, too. It takes two people to ruin a relationship."

Shaking my head, I said, "You had a front row seat to watch the last relationship I was in implode because of my bad judgment. Surely you don't want to get yourself mixed up with me after witnessing that."

"So you're not even going to give it a try because you've already decided it's going to fail?"

"No, I'm saying that you deserve better than what I can give you."

Baxter's eyes registered pain. "You think you're not good enough for me? That's not true."

My doorbell rang, and I breathed a sigh of relief to be able to put an end to this conversation. Manetti and Sterling walked in, and it was time to lock down my emotions one more time.

I sat on the couch with my arm around my sister while Manetti, Sterling, and Baxter did their best to coax information out of her. They started with her initial relationship with Justin Fox and her abduction. I could tell from the color on her cheeks that Baxter had been right about the guilt and embarrassment she felt over having been played. At first, Rachel would only give non-verbal answers—shrugging, nodding, and shaking her head. The three men adapted their questioning to what she could manage, but there finally came a time when they needed to know more.

Baxter sat down on the coffee table across from her so he could look her in the eye. "Rachel, I'm sure the last thing you want to do is relive any of this experience, but we need to know a few things to be able to close this case once and for all. Did Justin Fox ever mention to you that he had abducted or hurt any other people besides Amy Donovan, Jenna Walsh, Michaela Richards, and yourself?"

Rachel shook her head.

"Did he talk to you much while you were in the barn with him?"

She lowered her head. After a long pause, she whispered, "Yes."

"What kinds of things did he talk about?"

She turned anguished eyes on me.

I placed my hand on her head and pulled it down to rest on my shoulder. Stroking her hair, I said, "It's okay, Rach. Tell us what you can."

She turned so her face was hidden against my neck. I felt her hot tears on my skin. It broke my heart to see her like this, but I knew the sooner she got this out, the sooner she could put it behind her.

I tried a different tactic. "Rachel, honey, I know it's hard. But these guys aren't going to leave us alone until you talk. Personally, I want them the hell out of our house. Don't you?"

After a moment, Rachel raised herself up and wiped her face on her sleeves. She stared at her hands as she began to speak so quietly we had to strain to hear her. "He told me every last detail of what he did to Jenna. He knew she was my friend, so he tortured me with it. He talked about shoving a knife into her neck and letting her blood drain out. He showed me the table where he did it." She shuddered. "He told me about pulling her tooth and dressing her up like his mom. And how he strung her up with fishing line in the park." Tears spilled down her cheeks. "But what he wouldn't shut up about the most was telling me how gullible and stupid she and I were to have let him into our lives."

Baxter reached out and covered her hands with his. "That is not true. Justin Fox was a sociopath. People like him are masters of manipulation and have the ability to talk people into nearly anything. It wasn't your fault—it was his. He targeted you and used everything you ever told him against you. There's no way a normal person can compete with that."

I said, "He manipulated all of us, Rachel. I fell for his bullshit, too. More than once."

Looking over at me, she choked out, "He told me." Before I realized what she was doing, she pulled my sleeve back to reveal my bandage. "So it's true. He said he cut you because I was an uncooperative bitch. I'm sorry, sissy. I'm so sorry." She put her head in her hands and sobbed.

Manetti's jaw clenched as he stared at my bandage. "He *cut* you? Why is this the first I'm hearing of it?"

I ignored him and pulled Rachel to me. "That was a lie. He cut me because I pissed him off talking about his mother. It had nothing to do with you. Please don't blame yourself."

Sterling stood. "I think between Rachel's statement, Justin Fox's boasting on the videos he sent, and what evidence they've already begun collecting at the barn, we'll have enough to wrap this thing up. Rachel, thank you for speaking with us. We're glad you're home safe. We'll get out of your hair now."

Baxter hung back as Manetti and Sterling headed for the door. He said quietly, "If either of you need anything—day or night—you call me. We've stationed a deputy outside so you won't have to worry about reporters knocking on your door."

I smiled. "Thanks, Nick. I'll see you later."

33

Once I had my family back under one roof, I slept like the dead. Rachel hadn't let Nate out of her sight since their reunion, even insisting on staying in his room all night. In the morning, her eyes were sunken and ringed with dark circles, a sure sign she hadn't gotten much sleep, not that I was terribly surprised. I had David come back and keep them company while I returned to the station for the requisite debriefing now that the Justin Fox murder cases had been put to bed.

I had a some notes to make about the investigation Baxter and I had conducted over the past couple of days, so I headed in early to finish them up before the meeting. While I was typing my report in the lab office, I got a text from Manetti.

Where are you right now?

Lab office, I replied.

Within a minute, Manetti burst through the door with a big grin on his face. He was so handsome when he smiled. It was probably partially my fault that he didn't do that a lot around me.

He said, "I have a present for you."

I sat back in my chair. "I like presents."

"Oh, but first before I forget, I'm taking the team out for drinks tonight at O'Loughlin's. I figure you'd rather be with your family, especially since I pulled you away from them this morning, but with you having been the one to crack this case wide open, I'd feel bad if I neglected to invite you."

I smiled. "Thanks for the offer, but yes, I'd rather hang at home tonight."

Manetti's expression grew serious. "Then maybe you'd consider letting me take you out for a drink another time."

I hesitated. "You mean...just the two of us?"

The corner of his mouth curved up. "Yeah."

While I wouldn't dream of ruining my work relationship with Baxter, I had no problem taking that chance with Manetti. We didn't work well together in the first place, and we'd likely never have a reason to work together again, anyway. Plus, he was more my type—a pompous asshole, as Sterling had so succinctly put it.

"Okay."

"Don't act so excited." Getting out his phone, he said, "As promised, and within our allotted time frame, I have the DNA results you wanted."

My jaw dropped. I hadn't thought there was any way he'd be able to make good on his promise. "Okay, now I'm excited."

Grinning again, he said, "I have to admit it takes some of the wind out of my sails that my little favor isn't going to be the thing that saves the day."

"Wow. Way to make it about you, Manetti," I said, smiling.

He chuckled and handed me his phone. "I thought you should have the honors, since you were the one who found our killer. I showed great restraint in not looking at the attachment with the CODIS hit."

I took his phone and opened the attachment on the email he'd pulled up. When I read the name on the form, I felt like the bottom dropped out of me.

"What is it?" he asked, his voice concerned.

I looked up at him. "Are you sure this is right? There was no mix-up of samples?"

"Not possible. What's wrong?"

"It says the DNA from the semen I found in Leann Fox's underwear belongs to Frank Donovan."

Manetti's face went ashen as he took his phone back from me. He stared at the screen in disbelief. "Wait. So Frank Donovan is the mystery boyfriend we've been looking for?"

I didn't want to believe it, but DNA results were unquestionable. "I guess it fits, sort of. Frank and Jayne made multiple calls to the Foxes' home after Samuel roughed Leann up. Maybe...Leann thought of him as her knight in shining armor. But I don't see Frank as a killer."

"Frank was married at the time, right?"

"Yes. He's been married for thirty-some years."

"And it would have been a big conflict of interest to have a relationship —extra-marital or otherwise—with a victim whose case he'd worked."

I nodded. "Right. That could explain why it was such a carefully guarded secret."

Manetti sighed. "A pregnancy would bring that secret to light, though. Frank could easily have lost his job and his marriage. You back someone into a corner, and you never know what he'll do. You said yourself that if we find the lover, we find the killer. I'm bringing him in."

I put my head in my hands. If this was true, it was going to kill Jayne. Frank had been her partner and friend for years, and she didn't even know him at all.

"If you don't mind, can I be the one to break the news to Jayne?"

"Sure, but make it quick. The meeting's in five minutes. We've got a lot of brass coming in for it, so don't be late."

I had him send the email to me, and then I printed out the CODIS results and called Jayne to ask her to meet me in the lab office, where we would have more privacy to talk. Manetti headed off to dispatch some deputies to pick up Frank.

Jayne smiled me as she came in the door. "I hope you slept well. Rachel doing okay today?"

"She's quiet, but of course happy to be home." I cleared my throat. "Um...I have something I need to tell you, and you're going to need to sit down."

Eyeing me warily, she sat down on the couch. "Tell me."

I sat down next to her. "You know I found semen in Leann Fox's under-wear, and we all agreed that it would have to belong to her boyfriend, who was most likely her baby daddy...and her killer?"

"Yes."

"Well, Manetti got me the results, and it pulled a name from CODIS."

"Who?"

I swallowed. "Frank."

She stared at me, stunned.

I handed her the paper I'd printed. "I didn't believe it either, but here are the results. We can have them run again if you want. There's enough fabric to make another sample for testing."

A tear escaped her eye as she read the information on the sheet. "How is this possible? He and I investigated the murder together. How could he have been as dispassionate as he was if he were the killer? How could he have let an innocent man go down for murder?"

"I don't know." I let out a sigh. "Maybe we've got it all wrong. Maybe—"

The door opened a crack. "Jayne? You in there?" Frank Donovan entered the office. "Oh, there you are. I wondered if I could talk to you—"

Jayne was up off the couch and in Frank's face in an instant. "You son of a bitch. What in the hell were you thinking sleeping with Leann Fox? We have your DNA—"

"Whoa," I said, getting in between them and pushing Jayne back by her shoulders. "We don't need to get into that right now."

If Frank was indeed guilty, what we needed was him under arrest and in custody before we had this conversation. Jayne was not thinking straight.

Her steely glare landed on me. "This is between me and Frank."

Frank said from behind me, "Jayne, no. I didn't sleep with Leann. I barely knew her. The only contact I had with her was when we kept getting called out to her house all those times."

She replied, "You're lying. What else are you lying about?"

I heard Frank begin to breathe heavily. I would have liked to distance myself from him, but I had to stand my ground and keep my hands on Jayne's shoulders to keep her from lunging at him.

He said, "Are you trying to insinuate I had something to do with Leann's death? That's crazy. We worked the case together, remember? Her husband did it. There was a ton of evidence stacked against him."

"Evidence that could easily have been planted by someone who knew what he was doing. When we reexamined the evidence, we got back a hit on your DNA, Frank."

"I worked the scene! Of course my DNA would be there."

"Was the scene in Leann's panties?" she snapped.

"Okay," I said. "We need some kind of mediator here that isn't me."

I hated seeing Jayne and Frank at odds. They made a great team back in the day, reminding me a lot of the way Baxter and I worked together. It would be like a knife to my heart to fight with him this bitterly.

Jayne stepped back and held up her hands, conceding, "You're right. We need to do this the proper way." She got out her phone. "I'm going to have to turn this over to Agent Manetti. Sorry, Frank."

Before she had time to make the call, I heard the cock of a revolver. At the same time, one of Frank's meaty hands closed around my throat. He jabbed something hard into my side, which I assumed was the .38 Special he always carried with him. Jayne froze, gaping at us in horror.

Jerking me backward, Frank growled, "I can see that you all have decided I'm guilty already. It doesn't matter what I say. Some law enforcement family you've got here, Jayne—turning on your own kind. I gave this place half my life, and I'm not going to let you screw me out of the rest of it. I'm getting the hell out of town, and your little friend here is going to be my insurance policy."

Damn it. "Frank, please," I choked out. "Don't you think we've all been through enough this week?"

He tightened his fingers around my neck, making it difficult for me to breathe. I couldn't get free from his grip, so I had no choice but to stumble along with him as he retreated backward into the lab.

Jayne followed us. "Frank, don't do this. Take me instead."

Frank snapped, "Shut up. Your days of telling me what to do are over. But don't worry. Once I get out of town, I'll turn your girl here loose."

Manetti's voice barked from behind us, "Frank Donovan, put down your weapon and release Ms. Matthews."

Frank spun both of us around to face Manetti. Manetti was pointing a gun in our direction. I was beginning to get lightheaded from the shallow breaths I could get, and having two guns pointing at me was not helping matters.

"No, I'm getting out of here," Frank said.

I could feel him shaking against me, which was both a good and a bad sign. He was beginning to crack, but that meant he was also becoming increasingly erratic. I hoped he could keep control of his trigger finger.

"You're not going anywhere. It's over, Frank. You're under arrest for the murder of Leann Fox," Manetti replied, flicking a glance at me. I couldn't be sure in the state I was in, but I thought I actually saw fear in his eyes. That was a first.

Frank roared, "I've worked too damn hard and put in too many hours in this department to go out like this! So I killed one slut—so what? She had the nerve to dump me so she could go back to her good-for-nothing bastard of a husband. *And* hand my baby over to him. No way I was letting that happen. And no way I was going down for it, either." I felt his hot breath wheezing out fast on the side of my face.

Edging around us toward Manetti, Jayne said, "You did plant that evidence, didn't you?"

Frank let out a sharp laugh. "You mean when I wiped down the spade I hit her with and put it in passed-out Samuel's hands so his fingerprints would be all over it?"

"And when you took the cellphone you gave her?"

"That, too. I had a good laugh watching you run around like a monkey looking for it. I bet the brilliant Jayne Walsh never thought old Frank would have the smarts to pull the wool over her eyes like that." Although his words were hateful and indifferent, he was shaking even worse now. He'd even loosened his grip on my neck enough that I could breathe almost normally.

"Enough!" Manetti shouted. "This ends now. Frank, *put down your weapon.*"

"Screw you! I'm getting the hell out of here," he rasped.

"Wrong. You have two options—surrender now or I shoot you."

Frank let out a strangled cry. "You're not in charge! I say when this ends! *I* say how I go out!"

Flinging me aside, he put the muzzle of his gun under his chin and pulled the trigger. Jayne screamed, "No!" as Frank dropped to the ground. She rushed to kneel beside him as Manetti ran over to kick Frank's gun away. Manetti then pressed his fingertips to Frank's neck and shook his head. Jayne wept over Frank's body as I stood rooted to the spot, watching the pool of blood under Frank's head spread out across the tile floor. Manetti came my way and wordlessly pulled me into a tight embrace. I clung to him, unable to do anything else.

EPILOGUE

Rachel wasn't herself. It was to be expected, of course, after what she'd been through, that she be withdrawn and introverted. But it still made my heart ache to have to watch her go through this and be powerless to do anything to make it stop. It didn't help that suddenly every student at Ashmore wanted to be her best friend and that every news outlet in the country wanted her story. The poor thing just wanted to be left alone.

It helped somewhat when I changed our phone numbers and personal email addresses. But then Rachel got to the point where she wouldn't leave the house, even to go get coffee or to take Nate outside to play. Nate noticed she was acting strangely and asked me what was wrong with his mommy. She lashed out at me when I offered to get her an appointment for counseling with a psychologist. I didn't know what else to do, so I called Baxter.

He came over and brought pizza for dinner, which made him Nate's new best buddy. I could see Rachel warming to Baxter as he played on the floor with Nate, and I had to fight to not warm to him, myself. We hadn't revisited our relationship conversation, which was fine with me. But I couldn't help thinking it was inevitable that it would come back up.

I put Nate in the bathtub in order for Baxter and Rachel to have some time alone to talk. From the hallway, I could hear them speaking quietly as they sat in the living room, but I couldn't hear what they were saying. It was really none of my business, and as long as Rachel was opening up, it was a step in the right direction. I was happy she was talking to someone who would understand what she'd gone through, and more importantly, who cared enough about us to want to help.

Once Baxter got up to leave, Rachel was in good enough spirits to take over wrestling Nate into bed. I got my coat and walked out the front door with Baxter.

"I don't know what you said to her, but it helped. Thank you, Nick."

"No problem. I hate that she's got all this stuff to process. Unfortunately, it's a long road. You have to be patient with her."

I smiled. "You say that like you think I'm impatient."

"You are."

"Guilty."

"What about you? Are you still going to your meetings?"

Nodding, I replied, "Yes. One week sober today."

"I'm proud of you. That's a big step." He looked away. "Speaking of drinks, I heard you went out with Manetti a few days ago."

I felt a chill, and it wasn't from the cold night air. "I did."

"And?"

I sighed. "And what? What do you want me to say?"

His face was stony. "I want you to tell me why you'll date him, but not me."

"It was one date, Nick. We're not *dating*."

He continued to stare at me.

Finally, I said, "Look, I don't have to work with Manetti anymore. And I don't even know if I like him...at all. It doesn't matter if we crash and burn."

His brow furrowed. "Are you saying you'll only go out with men you don't care about?"

"Well...it sounds bad when you put it like that, but...isn't it easier that way? Then nobody gets hurt."

"And you end up alone."

"I'm not alone. I have my family."

"What happens when Rachel finds a guy and goes off and gets married?"

I laughed. "Like that'll last. She's worse than I am at choosing men. Case in point, our dearly departed serial killer."

He frowned and shook his head. "You refuse to let yourself be happy."

"I refuse to get my heart broken. Big difference."

"But the outcome is the same." After regarding me for a moment, he backed away, saying, "I guess I'll see you at work sometime."

I felt a stab to my heart as I realized I was letting a good man get away. I couldn't see it working out any other way, though. I knew his anger would fade, and he wouldn't let it get in the way of our partnership. I could have chosen to stay away from the department and focus on my teaching career. Then I might have been able to bring myself to give it a shot with Baxter. But after having conquered my fears of not being strong enough to handle the tough cases, something inside me compelled me to dive back into law enforcement. I was no longer content to sit on the sidelines.

DEAD SPRINT
Book #3 of the Ellie Matthews Novels

Criminalist Ellie Matthews' latest case pushes her to the brink, both personally and professionally, as she throws herself into the hunt for a twisted killer.

Determined to leave her traumatic past behind and turn over a new leaf, former criminalist Ellie Matthews is taking some time for herself. Competitive running and a budding relationship with FBI Agent Vic Manetti are working wonders. But after she stumbles upon a woman brutally murdered on a local running trail, Ellie dives head first back into a dangerous world.

A photo of the victim's gruesome killing explodes online, and a string of chilling threats quickly thrusts Ellie into a desperate race to unmask the culprit before any more innocents die. But to solve the case, she'll need to salvage her strained relationship with her old partner, Detective Nick Baxter.

With tensions threatening to boil over and loyalties pushed to the breaking point, Ellie, Nick and Agent Manetti must delve into the twisted mind of an elusive murderer. But what they discover will shock them all, and it might be too much for Ellie to bear...

Get your copy today at
severnriverbooks.com/series/ellie-matthews

ACKNOWLEDGMENTS

I could not do what I do without my fabulous editing team, Julia Maguire and Deborah Nam-Krane. Big thanks to Mitzi Templeton, my forensics professor, and her coworkers at the ISP lab—Kim Early, Susan Laine, and Mallory Johnson for their continued help and willingness to answer my many questions.

ABOUT THE AUTHOR

Caroline Fardig is the *USA Today* bestselling author of over a dozen mystery novels. She worked as a schoolteacher, church organist, insurance agent, banking trust specialist, funeral parlor associate, stay-at-home mom, and coffeehouse owner before she realized that she wanted to be a writer when she grew up. When she's not writing, she likes to travel, lift weights, play pickleball, and join in on vocals, piano, or guitar with any band who'll have her. She's also the host of a lively podcast for Gen Xers called *Wrong Side of 40*. Born and raised in a small town in Indiana, Fardig still lives in that same town with an understanding husband, two sweet kids, and three exhaustingly energetic dogs.

Sign up for Caroline Fardig's reader list at
severnriverbooks.com/authors/caroline-fardig

Printed in the United States
by Baker & Taylor Publisher Services